THE BONE THIEF

THE BONE THIEF

JEFFERSON BASS

Quercus

First published in Great Britain in 2010 by

Quercus
21 Bloomsbury Square
London
WC1A 2NS

A CIP catalogue reference for this book is available
from the British Library.

ISBN (HB) 978 1 84916 056 8
ISBN (TPB) 978 184916 057 5

10 9 8 7 6 5 4 3 2 1

Printed and bound in Great Britain by Clays Ltd, St Ives Plc.

*To Jane Elizabeth McPherson and Carol Lee Bass,
our beloved wives and also our best friends*

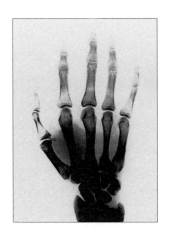

CHAPTER 1

THE WOMAN'S FACE BLURRED AND SMEARED AS I pivoted the camera on the tripod. Then her familiar, photogenic features—features I'd seen a thousand times on my television screen—whirred into autofocused perfection: wavy honey-blond hair, indigo eyes, a model's cheekbones, polar-white teeth outlined by Angelina Jolie lips. Knoxville news anchor Maureen Gershwin was forty-two—middle-aged, technically speaking—but she was a low-mileage, high-dollar version of forty-two. She was beautiful and vibrant and healthy-looking, except for one minor detail: Maureen Gershwin was dead.

"Pardon my cynicism," said Miranda, "but I can't help noticing that out of dozens of corpses to choose from, you've picked one worthy of Victoria's Secret for your little photo shoot."

Miranda Lovelady was both my graduate assistant and my self-appointed social conscience. A smart, seasoned Ph.D. candidate in forensic anthropology, Miranda was a young woman of liberal opinions, liberally dispensed. We didn't always see eye to eye, but five years of collegiality and camaraderie tempered our occasional personal differences. One of Miranda's duties was running the Anthropology Department's osteology laboratory, the bone lab tucked deep beneath the grandstands of the University of Tennessee's football stadium. Miranda also helped coordinate the body-donation program at the Anthropology Research Facility—"the Body Farm," UT's three-acre plot devoted to the study of human decomposition. By studying bodies as they decayed in various settings and conditions, we'd gained tremendous insights into postmortem changes—insights that allowed forensic scientists all over the world to give police more accurate time-since-death estimates in cases where days or weeks or even years elapsed between the time someone was killed and the time the body was discovered.

Despite the rural-sounding name, the Body Farm was beginning to resemble a city of the dead, at least in population density. The number of bodies donated to our research program had grown steadily—from a handful a year in our early years to well over a hundred a year now. Scientifically, the population boom was a bonanza, but it was also an embarrassment of riches: The facility was rapidly running out of elbow room—and rib-cage room, and skull room; lately Miranda had taken to mapping the location of each body with GPS coordinates with just a few keystrokes, she could print out an up-to-the-minute map of our postmortem subdivision. The technology helped us keep track of where we'd already put people, and it also helped us pinpoint patches of unclaimed ground on which to house new residents. Unfortunately, the patches of unclaimed ground were becoming scarce and small.

We'd tucked Maureen Gershwin—known to television viewers throughout East Tennessee as Maurie, or sometimes by her nickname, "The Face"—in the most distant corner of the fenced-in area, to minimize the gawking. Gershwin had risen through the television ranks, from weathergirl to reporter to anchorwoman, and recently she'd added occasional commentaries she called "Maurie's Minutes," which took a more personal, reflective tone. Those had made her more popular than ever, so I wanted to give her some measure of privacy at the Body Farm, even though I was photographically invading that privacy. The facility was off-limits to the general public, of course, but a surprising number of living, breathing people passed through its gates: anthropology grad students, the UT police force, the instructors and students of the National Forensic Academy, FBI trainees, even the occasional strong-stomached VIP visitor from the university's board of trustees. Like all our donated corpses, Maurie Gershwin was identified not by name but by a number—her metal armband and legband identified her only as "21-09," the twenty-first donated body of the year 2009—but she was so well known to Knoxville television viewers that there was no hope of keeping her anonymous, at least not until the bacteria and bugs had rendered her famous face unrecognizable.

As I tinkered with the camera's zoom control, Miranda took the opportunity to chide me further. "The T-shirt and sweatpants she's wearing—you sure you don't want to swap those out for something flashier? Maybe a little black dress that shows some thigh and some cleavage?"

"Come on, Miranda," I snapped, "you saw the letter she sent with her donor form. She *asked* to have her decomposition documented. Why is that worse than honoring other donor requests, like being put in the shade of a maple tree?" She frowned, unwilling to concede. "Besides, I'm only photographing her face, not the rest of her."

"But you can see my point," she persisted, "can't you? Don't you think it's a tad creepy that you're aiming this camera at this particular corpse, the most beautiful corpse in the history of the Body Farm? Crap, Dr. B., she looks better dead than I do alive."

I glanced from the newswoman's face to Miranda's: peaches-and-cream skin and green eyes, framed by a cascade of chestnut hair. I actually preferred Miranda's looks, but I knew she wouldn't believe me if I told her so. "Not for long," I said. "Day by day—hell, hour by hour—she'll get a lot less gorgeous. We'll end up with one glamour shot and hundreds of pictures where she goes from bad to worse and from worse to worser."

"I don't understand why she asked for this."

"Doesn't matter," I said. "*I* understand, and, more to the point, *she* understood. She talked to me about it a year or so ago, back when she produced that three-part series about the Body Farm for Channel 10. You remember the end of the series, when she added a 'Maurie's Minute' about the importance of body donations? I thought that was a great touch, signing the consent form at the very end of the newscast."

"I hated it," Miranda said. "She was playing to the camera. Or maybe just to Dr. Bill Brockton."

I stepped away from my own camera and caught Miranda's eye. "Excuse me," I said, pointing to the corpse, "but I refute you thus. Looks to me like she said what she meant and meant what she said. Remember what the letter said? 'I wish I could watch what happens to me'? Her coanchor, Randall Gibbons, said she'd told him she wouldn't mind being the subject of a science documentary. Postmortem participatory journalism, I guess—one last story, filed from beyond the grave."

"Swell. Film at eleven, smell at twelve," Miranda joked mirthlessly. "*Deathstyles of the Rich and Famous*. We do bow before beauty, don't we?"

I snapped a picture, then checked the display on the back of the camera. The framing was slightly off and the screen was washed out by the daylight, but I had to agree that Miranda had a point: Even dead, Maurie Gershwin was a beauty, at least for a few more hours. "Her looks did have a lot to do with her success," I conceded, "but I don't think they defined her, at least not to herself. In fact, I think she had a healthy sense of irony about the fleeting nature of physical beauty."

"Yeah, well. Too bad her cardiovascular system wasn't as strong as her sense of irony," said Miranda. "Stroking out at forty-two, and right there on camera no less."

"Aneurysm," I said. "Not stroke." Gershwin had died of an aortic aneurysm that ruptured catastrophically—and in the middle of a newscast. In hindsight, a diagnostic clue had gone undetected. "Did you see the news any of the last few nights before she died?"

Miranda nodded.

"Did you notice that her voice was a little hoarse?"

She looked at me sharply, her eyebrows shooting up in a question.

"One of the laryngeal nerves—the recurrent vagus nerve, which controls the voice box—wraps around the aortic arch. A fast-growing aneurysm on the aorta can stretch that nerve, causing hoarseness. Maurie thought she'd just strained her voice last week during a charity telethon—that's what she said on the air two nights ago, right before she died—when in fact her body was trying to warn her."

Miranda shook her head. "Sad. Ironic. Here's another irony

for you: Her death made her a lot more famous than all those years of reporting the news. Somebody posted an Internet video of that clip from the newscast where she collapses in midsentence. They called it 'Film at Eleven: Hot News Babe Dies on Camera.' As of this morning, thirty million people had watched her die."

"Thirteen million people have seen that footage?"

"*Thirty* million."

The figure stunned me. "That's probably twenty-nine and a half million more than ever watched her live."

"Web fame's an odd, viral thing." She shrugged. "You remember Susan Boyle?"

I shook my head.

"Sure you do; you just don't realize you do. That dumpy, middle-aged Brit who belted out a song on the limey version of *American Idol*?"

That did ring a bell, I realized.

"Her YouTube clip's been watched fifty or sixty million times. She became this overnight megacelebrity. Of course, that was a year or so ago. She's old news by now." Miranda studied the newswoman's face, reaching down to shoo away a cloud of blowflies. It was absurd, of course, since the whole point of putting Gershwin out here was to allow nature to have its way with her, but the fly shooing was a reflexive gesture of respect, so I kept my mouth shut. "What do you plan to do with all these pictures of The Face of Channel 10?"

"Couple things, probably," I said. "I need to do a funding proposal for the dean's office—apparently they've got some deep-pocket donor they think might be interested in adopting us—and I could see using a few of these photos to illustrate our decomposition research. I'll probably also do a slide presentation at the national forensic-science conference next February. 'Decomposition Day by Day' or some such. Thirty slides, thirty days, talk for a minute about each slide."

Miranda closed her eyes and let her head slump forward, then feigned a loud snore. "A slide presentation? That's lame, totally twentieth century," she said. "How about a podcast—a real-time video camera, streaming continuous images to the Web? That would actually fit the spirit of our gal's life and work and last request."

"Broadcast this on the Web?" I shook my head. "No way. I don't have nearly enough fingers and toes to count the ways that could get us in hot water."

"Well, at least make a movie instead of slides for your presentation," she said.

"But this is a still camera," I pointed out. "Besides, neither one of us has the time to hang around and film a documentary."

"Neither one of us needs to," she said. "You're setting the timer to take a picture, what, every few minutes or every few hours?"

I nodded.

"So once she's through skeletonizing, in a month or two, string all the pictures together into a video and it'll fast-forward through the entire decomp sequence in a couple of minutes. That would be cool."

"You think that would work for the funding proposal, too?"

She cringed. "Why would seeing this woman's face decay inspire some rich alumnus to fork over big bucks for body bags and bone boxes and the like?"

"Actually, I'm hoping to raise money for your assistantship," I said. Miranda's head whipped around, and I wished I hadn't said it, even though there was some truth to it. "Sorry. Bad joke.

You're covered." She shot me a piercing look, hard enough to make me flinch. Miranda would make a terrific prosecutor or detective, I thought, if she ever got tired of forensic anthropology. "At least I *think* you're covered."

"You're the chairman of the Anthropology Department," she responded. "If anybody should know, it's you."

"I do know you're not affected by the cuts I proposed," I said. "But the dean has to approve the budget before it goes to the chancellor and the president. The football scholarships are safe and the coaching salaries are safe, but nothing else is guaranteed." She didn't say anything, but the worry in her eyes pained me. "By the way," I added, "I'm giving a lecture at the Smithsonian on Saturday afternoon, and I'm having lunch with Ed Ulrich beforehand." Ulrich had been one of my earliest and brightest Ph.D. students at UT; now he was head of the Smithsonian's Division of Physical Anthropology. "I'm going to see if I can twist his arm for some research funding. Enough to support two graduate assistantships."

"Tell Ed I said hi." She was too young to have been a classmate of Ulrich's, but she'd talked with him at conferences many times, and he'd made two or three trips to UT during the time she'd been my assistant. "Tell Ed I said help!"

I zoomed in a bit more, filling the viewfinder with The Face, then snapped another test picture. Taking care not to jostle the tripod, I removed the camera from the mount and huddled under my jacket to block out the daylight. The photo showed a lovely woman, but her face had gone slack, and the light and life had faded from her eyes. I used the cursor to enlarge the center of the image and saw that the camera had caught one blowfly in mid-air, just above her face; another was already emerging from the slightly opened mouth. Looking from the camera's display to the body on the ground, I saw that those two flies had been joined already by dozens of others, swiftly drawn to the odor of death, even though I could detect no trace of it yet. Within minutes small smears of grainy white paste—clumps of blowfly eggs—would begin to fill her mouth and nose and eyes and ears, and by this time tomorrow her face would be covered with blowfly larvae, a writhing mass of newly hatched maggots.

I fiddled with the camera's digital menu, calling up the control screen for the built-in timer. Initially I'd planned to set it to take a photo every twelve hours, but as I glanced down at the swarming flies, I realized that twelve-hour intervals would miss many details of her decomposition. The funding people might not be interested in the subtle shifts of her decay, but I certainly was. What about a photo every half hour, or even every ten minutes? For that matter, why not just camp out here in person and watch it all in real time? Finally I compromised: one picture every fifty minutes, the length of a typical classroom lecture. I did the math: A picture every fifty minutes would yield thirty pictures a day. At the end of two months, I'd have eighteen hundred images. At thirty images a second—the speed of television images, I'd heard—eighteen hundred images would make a video sixty seconds long: exactly the running time of "Maurie's Minutes."

Swapping out the camera's small digital memory card for a larger one—a two-gigabyte chip, large enough to hold hundreds of images—I latched the camera back onto the tripod, and Miranda and I left the Body Farm, chaining the wooden gate shut and fastening the metal fence behind us. As I snapped the outer padlock shut on the Body Farm's newest and most famous resident, I found myself thinking of the words she'd used at the end of every newscast for years. "Good night," I murmured. "See you tomorrow."

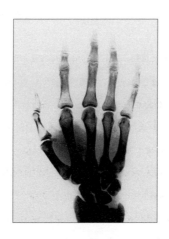

CHAPTER 2

THE MAN'S FACE STARED BACK AT ME, HIS EXPRESSION hovering somewhere in a zone bordered by detachment, curiosity, weariness, and disappointment. I wished I could discern more kindness and compassion in his eyes, because his eyes were my own: I was scrutinizing Bill Brockton's face in my bathroom mirror, much as I'd scrutinized Maureen Gershwin's features through a camera lens six hours before.

I glanced down to the counter, at the photo of Gershwin I'd taken at the Body Farm and printed before leaving campus for the day. Seeing it gave me a pang of guilt—partly because Miranda had seemed uncomfortable about the photo shoot and partly because, anthropologically speaking, Miranda had a lot of opinion on her side. People in a number of cultures—Native Americans and Chinese, for instance—traditionally believed that taking people's pictures could steal their souls. By that reasoning, Maureen Gershwin's soul had been stolen on a nightly basis for years, sucked into television cameras and dispersed like dust—puffs of electrons or photons or whatever television sets generated—throughout East Tennessee. Was I now stealing whatever scraps had remained? On the other hand, since Gershwin was already dead, might the camera somehow be restoring a bit of soul to an empty husk of a body? Studying her image, I revised the assessment I'd made earlier in the day. There certainly wasn't light or life in Gershwin's eyes, but there was something eerie, a haunting quality, in the photo. It was elusive, but it was there all the same: almost as if the eyes were challenging me, challenging the world, by their very vacancy. *I'm not who you think I am,* they seemed to say. Or maybe just, *Nobody's home. Leave a message.*

I raised my hands, stretching my thumbs and forefingers into L-shaped brackets, and framed my face in the handmade viewfinder. Leaning closer to the mirror, I turned my head slightly to the right and widened the space between my hands. There: That was how I'd framed the shot of Gershwin's face, almost face-on but favoring the left side just a bit. Glancing down at Gershwin's photo again, I realized that I'd photographed her at exactly the same angle as the television camera had, night after night. *Interesting,* I thought. *Even though she's dead, I still wanted her to look the same; I still wanted her to be the same.*

But even before death, who had she been? For that matter, who was I? A professor, a scientist, a student of death, a consultant to the state's medical examiners and the Tennessee Bureau of Investigation. I was also a father, a grandfather, and a widower; since losing my wife to cancer several years earlier, I'd had two brief romances. A year or so back, I'd fallen for a smart, sassy medical examiner from Chattanooga; then, just months ago, I'd gotten involved with a beautiful, baffling librarian. To say that both romances had ended badly would be a huge understatement: the M.E. had been murdered, and—by a twist of fate whose bizarre mirror-image symmetry I only now recognized—the librarian had turned out to be a murderer.

I caught myself frowning in the mirror. Those episodes, those details of my life, seemed oddly unrelated to the face of the middle-aged man staring out at me from the wall of glass. His face seemed almost to belong to someone else, not me. I glanced to my left, where a side mirror caught the same half-stranger's face in three-quarter profile. In the corner, where the two mirrors met, was a third take on the same face, this one bisected by the vertical seam in the glass. Thus reflected and bisected, I stood transfixed by these partial, unrevealing stand-ins for myself, whoever "me" really was.

The jangle of the telephone interrupted my reverie. The lateness of the call surprised me; as I answered the bedroom extension, I noticed that Randall Gibbons—formerly Maureen Gershwin's coanchor and now the solo anchor—was wrapping up the eleven o'clock newscast. Usually the only calls that came this late were from police, so I suspected I was being called to a death scene, and as I hurried to the phone on the nightstand, I found myself hoping for the distraction and the mission of a case. Perhaps that was who I really was, I thought, perhaps that was what really defined me: Maybe I was merely a reflection of the call, the case, the crime scene, the forensic puzzle.

The phone's caller ID display told me it wasn't the police contacting me. But it also told me that the caller—"Burton DeVriess LLC"—might have something almost as interesting to offer.

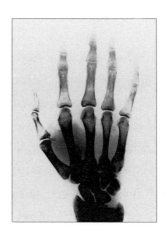

CHAPTER 3

THE BACKHOE LURCHED AND BUCKED AS ITS CLAW
tore into the wet, rocky clay of Old Gray Cemetery, one of Knoxville's oldest and loveliest burial grounds. The name felt apt; the
day was dreary, and the air was as cold as the mound of chilly
soil piling up beside the monument. Officially, spring was only a
few days away, but the earth itself still felt as devoid of warmth
and life as a corpse.

The diesel engine labored against some sudden resistance, and
as the machine strained, it wheezed out a cloud of black smoke.
The soot drifted on a whisper of breeze for ten feet or so—just
far enough to engulf Miranda and me—and then hovered.

Miranda fanned a hand dramatically across her face. "Remind
me why we're courting lung cancer and pneumonia here?" She
punctuated the question with a delicate little stage cough.

I was still a bit vague on our mission as well—not the task itself but the late-night, last-minute nature of the phone call I'd re-

ceived barely ten hours before, asking for my help. "We're here to help figure out if Trey Willoughby fathered a child by Sherry Burchfield," I said.

Miranda nodded toward the inscription chiseled into the grave marker, a towering obelisk of polished pink granite. " 'Trey Willoughby, beloved and faithful husband'?"

"Trey Willoughby, at least," I said. "Not sure about the 'beloved' and 'faithful' bits. 'Beloved' is in the eye of the beholder, I suppose, but the bone sample we're about to take could cast a serious shadow on the 'faithful' part."

"Or the unfaithful part," she said. "So to speak."

"So to speak."

"What if the DNA's too degraded for a paternity test?" I shrugged in response. "And what's the story on Sherry Burchfield, who might be the mama? I take it she's not Trey's loving wife and grieving widow?"

I shook my head. "Sherry might have been someone's loving wife and grieving widow," I said, "once upon a time, but she wasn't Willoughby's. When I moved to Knoxville twenty years ago, Sherry Burchfield was Knoxville's most famous madam."

Miranda laughed. "She was definitely well named, I'll give her that. Isn't 'Sherry' taken from the French word for 'dear' or 'darling'?"

"French is Greek to me," I said, "but that sounds right. And it's certainly consistent with her history. Sherry was arrested a bunch of times for prostitution-related crimes—pandering, soliciting, I don't know what all—but she never actually came to trial. Perhaps the pen really is mightier than the sword."

"The pen?"

"The pen that wrote in Sherry's little black book," I said. "Apparently she was a meticulous record keeper, and rumor had it that her client list included half the judges, prosecutors, and defense attorneys in Knoxville. Funny thing: When she died, which was maybe ten years ago, her little black book was never found. I wouldn't be surprised if some enterprising associate of hers got hold of it and has been collecting hush money for a decade now."

The backhoe's bucket screeched—a harsh, grating sound, like immense steel fingernails on a monumental blackboard—as the claw raked mud from the top of Trey Willoughby's metal burial vault.

Miranda grimaced, then shook violently, like a wet dog flinging water from its fur. "Argh." She shuddered. "Glad I don't have any fillings—my head would be exploding right about now. So what's the scoop on this love child Sherry might or might not have had with our man Willoughby? You say she died ten years ago; unless she died in childbirth, I assume the child is older than that."

"Considerably," I said. "Somewhere in his thirties. I'm not sure why he's just now getting around to tracking down his paternity."

Miranda shrugged. "Maybe he just found Sherry's black book in a shoe box of memorabilia—with the words 'Big Daddy' down in the W section, beside Willoughby's name."

"Maybe," I said. "All I know is that Judge Wilcox signed the exhumation order last night, and here we are this morning, at the request of the man behind the wheel of that car." I pointed to the cemetery's entrance, where a gleaming black sedan was gliding through the wrought-iron gates.

Miranda groaned. "Oh, God, you didn't tell me we'd be working for Satan on this case."

"Now, now," I soothed. "Grease isn't really the Prince of Darkness; he just puts on the horns and the hooves when he goes to court."

"Grease" was Burton DeVriess, Esq., Knoxville's most color-ful and aggressive attorney. Over the years DeVriess and I had sparred repeatedly and roughly, in murder cases where I'd tes-tified for the prosecution and he'd defended accused killers. A masterfully manipulative cross-examiner, Grease had always managed to get my goat, or at least infuriate my goat, on the wit-ness stand—not by successfully refuting my forensic findings but by baiting me into losing my temper. After years of antagonism, though, Grease and I had turned an unexpected corner a couple of years back: Confronted with an unusual situation—namely, a client who was actually innocent—Grease had hired me to help clear the man's name. The so-called murder victim had not, I was able to show, been stabbed to death but had died of injuries sustained in a bar brawl. During that case I'd grown to respect DeVriess's intelligence and commitment to his client. My respect had later turned to deep gratitude when DeVriess helped me clear my own name. Framed for the murder of a woman with whom I'd just begun a love affair—Chattanooga medical examiner Jess Carter—I'd swallowed my pride and turned to DeVriess for legal help. He'd responded by saving my reputation, my career, and my skin. In the process he lightened my bank account by fifty thou-sand dollars, but he'd earned every penny of it and more. He'd also revealed more human decency than I'd suspected he pos-sessed. Grease wasn't a saint—not unless the ranks of the saints included materialistic, cutthroat lawyers—but he was a far better guy than most of Knoxville gave him credit for being.

Miranda's eyes tracked the sedan—it was a Bentley, one of several thoroughbreds in DeVriess's automotive stable—as it eased toward us, curve by curve. She frowned, probably out of habit, then laughed at herself. "Much as it pains me to admit it, he does seem to have a warm-blooded mammalian heart beating somewhere in that chest, beneath the reptilian scales," she said. "But I think maybe I see a pitchfork in the backseat of the car." She paused. "And get a load of that tag." A vanity plate on the front bumper read $2BURN. I assumed it was a reference to a multimillion-dollar settlement Burt had won recently, in a class-action suit against a crematorium that was caught dumping bodies in the Georgia woods rather than incinerating them. The tag's combination of cleverness and boastfulness was classic DeVriess. But as I read the plate again, I realized it also sounded like an offer: a taunting Faustian bargain, rendered in stamped metal on a luxury sedan bumper. And that, too—the in-your-face frankness of the crass equation—also smacked of pure Grease.

The sedan eased off the pavement and hushed to a stop on the brown grass, its mirror finish reflecting the leaden sky and my bronze pickup truck. The driver's door swung open, and DeVriess slid off the glove-leather seat. His car was worth more than my house; his outfit—a suit of pale gray wool, probably handmade in Italy, the trousers draping onto lustrous black shoes—was probably worth more than my car. Walking toward us, he stepped into a stray clod of clay, which oozed up the side of the shoe and clung to the cuffs of the trousers. He stopped, glanced down, and then laughed. "Morning, Doc," he called over the din of the backhoe. "And the Amazing Miranda," he added, bowing slightly and smiling broadly. Miranda—possibly in spite of herself—gave a tiny mock curtsy and smiled back.

DeVriess walked to the edge of the grave, where more mud coated his shoes and oozed up his cuffs, and he peered in. The backhoe was now chewing through waterlogged clay at the base of the vault, and water seeped from the surrounding walls and poured back into the grave each time the operator lifted another bucketful of soil from the opening. The man had evidently foreseen this complication, for he paused, easing the machine's giant mechanical arm toward the ground, resting its weight on the curved underside of the bucket. It put me in mind of a human wrist, flexed into an acute, bone-breaking angle, and I flashed back briefly to my son's tumble from his bicycle twenty years before, and the way his hand had hit the driveway at just that angle.

Clambering down from the backhoe, the operator lifted a torpedo-shaped pump from the ground and lowered it into the watery grave. A muddy, flattened fire hose, connected to one end of the pump, slithered down the slight slope behind the backhoe and into a swale at the edge of the cemetery. The man clambered up onto the machine again and flipped a switch, and the rumble of the diesel engine was joined by a higher-pitched whine as the impeller of the pump spun up and began sucking water from the grave. The hose swelled slightly, pulsing occasionally as the pump's intake slurped and gasped. Judging by the granite obelisk that towered above the grave and above our heads, Trey Willoughby's burial had been quite an affair. His unburial, though less posh, was something of a production as well.

Thirty minutes later—a half hour marked by three repositionings of the sump pump and two wrestling bouts with a sling of steel cable and a bracelet of heavy chain rattling from the wrist of the backhoe—the steel vault emerged from the grave, trailing muddy water and watery mud. The operator swung it expertly to one side and set it gently on the ground. Then, after opening a pair of latches at the base of the vault, he hoisted the domed top off the vault, exposing the coffin underneath.

"Kinda like Chinese boxes," said DeVriess, "one inside the other."

"Or Russian *matryoshkas*," added Miranda. DeVriess looked puzzled, so she added, "Those nesting wooden dolls."

"Oh, right," he said. "I was thinking that, too. Russian *matry-whatevers*."

"Or Egyptian burials," I said. "Be interesting if the vault and the coffin were painted with Willoughby's image, like King Tut's sarcophagus."

The coffin was gunmetal blue, its glossy finish dulled by years of dampness and postmortem vapors. A few patches of superficial rust marred the lid, but considering that it had been in the ground for years—eight, according to Willoughby's death date—its condition was superb. Miranda glanced from the coffin to my truck. "You should park in the underground garage on campus instead of the outdoor lot," she said. "That coffin's paint job is holding up a lot better than your truck's."

"Yeah, but I bet the interior of my truck smells sweeter."

"We'll see," she said. "Like beauty, sweetness is in the nose of the beholder, and on the way over here this morning I think my nose was beholding some not-so-sweet aroma from that body we hauled back from Nashville in your truck last week." She was probably right; Miranda had a keener nose than I did, and the Nashville body—a floater fished from the Cumberland River—had been particularly ripe.

"Speaking of the truck," I said, "would you go get the Stryker saw, the scissors, and the pliers while I open up the coffin?"

"I live to serve," she said, and although it was a joke—one of her favorite ways of simultaneously acknowledging and mocking the professor-assistant disparity—she said it with genuine goodwill.

"So, the pliers," DeVriess said. "I'm thinking those aren't for opening the coffin."

"Right," I said. "I'm an anthropologist, but what I really want to do is postmortem dentistry. Enamel's the hardest substance in the body, so the DNA in the pulp of the teeth has a decent chance of being undamaged. I'll pull a couple of molars, but I'll also cut cross sections from the long bones of the upper arm and the thigh."

Burt nodded, and I thought I saw a flicker of impatience in his eyes. Was I droning on in too much detail? Had I already explained, in last night's phone call, why I needed to go to such lengths to get samples for a simple paternity test? Or had he done enough research on his own, before calling me, to know that DNA could be destroyed by the formalin in embalming fluid and that the teeth and long bones were the body's most protective vaults for archiving genetic material?

"It looks like there's not a lot of research data out there yet on DNA degradation," he said, as if reading the question in my mind. "Nobody seems to have a good handle on how long our nuclear DNA hangs around after death and what factors affect the rate of decay."

"Not much," I agreed. "Forensic DNA analysis is still a brave new world. Remember, it wasn't until the early 1990s that DNA testing became readily available."

"I remember," he said. "I was at the beach when the O. J. Simpson case began. I vividly recall sitting in the living room of that beach house watching him inch along the freeway in that white Ford Bronco, with dozens of cop cars trailing him like some huge police funeral procession. That, and the World Trade Center collapse, and the first moon landing, back when I was a ten-year-old kid—those are the three most powerful television events I can remember, the only three where I can tell you exactly where I was and what I was doing when the story unfolded on the screen."

"The moon landing, the O. J. circus, and 9/11," said Miranda, back with us, tools in hand. "From the sublime to the ridiculous to the truly tragic."

I knelt at the head of the coffin and groped the underside until I found what I was looking for, a hinged metal crank that I unfolded and began turning counterclockwise. Slowly, almost as if it were levitating of its own accord, the upper one-third of the lid swung upward, revealing the face of Trey Willoughby. The skin was ashen, with a slight mottling of dark gray mold—just as the coffin was tinged with rust—but otherwise the face in the coffin was a good likeness of the face I'd seen in an old photo I'd found on the Internet a few hours before. In life he'd been a handsome man—not the looker Maureen Gershwin had been, but attractive—and even now, even eight years postmortem, he was still looking pretty good.

"You don't always get what you pay for," I said, "but in this case the funeral home did a good job. Which one was it?"

"Ivy Mortuary," said DeVriess. "Not in business anymore. The owner—Mr. Ivy—died in a car accident a few years back. No heirs."

I nodded; the name was familiar, but only vaguely. Over the years many of Knoxville's funeral homes had sent corpses to the Body Farm, but Ivy never had, to the best of my recollection.

I shifted to the foot of the coffin and cranked up the lower portion of the lid to expose the arms, torso, and legs. Willoughby had obviously been dressed for an open-casket viewing. His suit, I noticed, rivaled DeVriess's in elegance, though it was silk rather than wool. That made sense: According to the obelisk and the newspaper archives, he'd died in August; heaven forbid that the corpse should swelter in wool in the heat of summer. The thin, finely woven fabric clung damply to the arms and legs and to the laces of the black wing-tip shoes.

I reached out behind me, and Miranda wordlessly placed a pair of scissors in my palm. Reluctantly—for this was a far better suit than any I'd ever owned, or ever would—I grasped the cuffs of the left sleeves of the jacket and shirt and stretched them taut, so the V of the scissor blades would slice through more easily. Just as I began to cut, the corpse's hand shifted and slid from the end of the sleeve. It fell, landing with a dull thud on the corpse's stomach.

"Crap," I said. "Maybe the embalming job wasn't so good after all."

I'd already begun to cut, so I kept going. The scissors easily parted the thin, rotting fabric, sliding swiftly up toward the shoulder. Too smoothly, in fact. Normally when I cut shirts or pants from a body, the tip of the lower blade tended to snag in the soft flesh of an arm or a leg. But this time it moved in a smooth, slick glide. As the fabric parted, the reason became clear. I stared briefly, then reached across the body and lifted the corpse's right hand, grasping the gray, clammy fingers cupped around the end of the sleeve. The hand slid from the sleeve, and I found myself in a bizarre, armless handshake. Both hands, I saw when I looked at the wrists, had been severed at the wrists.

"Holy handoff," squawked Miranda.

"I'll be damned," said Grease.

Both of Trey Willoughby's arms had been neatly amputated at the shoulders. The sleeves of his silk jacket—like the legs of his silk trousers—were filled with white PVC pipe: plastic plumbing in place of human flesh and bone.

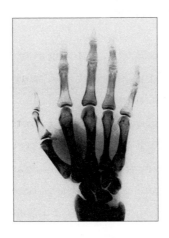

CHAPTER 4

THE NEXT CAR THAT ENTERED THE CEMETERY'S GATES
was the polar opposite of DeVriess's lustrous Bentley. As it
swayed and chugged around the curves of the cemetery's road,
this new arrival—a filthy, dented Crown Victoria that had been
white once upon a time—seemed to be nearing the end of a long
and brutal life, and I wondered how much time it might take the
backhoe to carve out a grave for the vehicle.

The car planted its flat-black wheels and bucked to a stop behind the Bentley, coming close enough to make Grease flinch. A
plainclothes investigator, mid-thirties, levered his lanky frame
out of the sagging driver's seat and slouched toward us. His
shambling walk and tousled hair made him appear laid back,
but he was chewing a piece of gum with swift ferocity. As did
most detectives, he dressed more like a businessman than a cop,
or at least my idea of a cop: He wore a starched white dress shirt,
a maroon silk tie, dark gray pants, and shiny black wing tips.

He glanced at the three of us standing graveside—DeVriess, Miranda, and me—and then bent down to peer into the coffin at Willoughby's limbless torso.

"Huh," he said, then turned to me. "Never a dull moment, eh, Dr. Brockton?" He held out his hand for me to shake. "Gary Culpepper," he said. "We met twelve years ago. You lectured to our class when I was a new recruit in the police academy. You probably don't remember me—actually, I hope you don't. I was the one who dropped the skull that you passed around."

"I thought you looked familiar," I fibbed. "This is my graduate assistant, Miranda Lovelady, and Burt DeVriess, the attorney who needs a DNA sample from Mr. Willoughby here."

Culpepper nodded curtly at Burt, saying, "I'm familiar with Mr. DeVriess. Very nice to meet you, Ms. Lovelady." He shook Miranda's hand but not Burt's, a snub that didn't come as much of a surprise to me, and surely not to the attorney. During his reign as Knoxville's toughest defense lawyer, Grease had earned the loathing of most of the city's police and prosecutors. "So what've we got here, Doc?"

It was an irresistible opening. "Well, just offhand I'd say we've got a head and a torso."

He redoubled his assault on the gum and took another look at the body. "Tell me what I missed before I got here."

I described the sequence of events that culminated in the discovery that Willoughby's limbs were missing.

"Before you cut into the clothing, did you notice anything that made you think the body or the grave had been disturbed?"

I shook my head.

"And the clothing was undamaged?"

"Well, the fabric was beginning to rot in places, but otherwise yes, it was intact."

"That means whoever took his arms and legs did it before he was buried," he mused. "Not exactly a case of grave robbing. Mutilating a corpse, I guess, unless the limbs were amputated while he was still alive."

I shook my head again. "There's no sign of bleeding or healing to the tissue at the shoulders and hips," I explained. "That means he was already dead when he was cut."

"Hmm . . . theft of property? I don't know—who owns the bodies in a cemetery?"

I shrugged.

"Fraud or breach of contract, maybe," he mused, "if the funeral home didn't provide the services it got paid for." He massaged the back and sides of his neck, just below the base of his skull, even as his jaw muscles continued to knot rhythmically. "We need to get the evidence techs out here to go over the coffin and the body, see if they find anything that sheds light on this. After that I guess we need to send the body to the forensic center for a more detailed examination."

DeVriess took a step toward the coffin. "Detective," he oozed in his smooth, courtroom voice, the one that sounded like old money, cigars, and fine whiskey, "surely I don't need to remind you that I have a court order authorizing the exhumation of this body and the collection of DNA samples."

"Of course," replied Culpepper, and DeVriess smiled warmly. The smile froze, though, when Culpepper added, "You surely don't need to remind me. But this is now a crime scene, and the samples for your civil suit will have to wait until we've finished our search for evidence in the criminal case."

I could see DeVriess drawing himself up to bluster, so I reached out and touched his shoulder briefly. There was nothing to be gained—and certainly no fun to be had—in a graveside pissing match over a dismembered corpse. "Burt, your client's gotten by without this paternity test for a lot of years already. You reckon maybe he could get by without it for maybe one or two more days?"

DeVriess stared at me. I'd seen that stare a few times before, in court, just before Grease ripped into me on the witness stand. He looked from me to Miranda, as if to say, *Did you see what he just did?* Miranda simply shrugged and smiled, as if to say, *He's crazy, but he's harmless.*

She held his gaze, and as swiftly as he'd puffed up, DeVriess suddenly deflated, and then he laughed. "Damned if I'm not going soft in my old age."

Culpepper was as startled by Burt's acquiescence as Burt himself was. "Well, then. Great. I'll call out the evidence techs. Dr. Brockton, I suspect we'd like you or the medical examiner to examine the body, so I'd like to arrange to have it transported to the forensic center once we clear the scene here."

I nodded. "Dr. Garcia's still on medical leave, but he's getting better. I imagine he'd be interested in taking a look at a case this unusual." I pulled out my pocket calendar. "I'm flying to Washington tomorrow to give a talk at the Smithsonian. Could we stick this guy in the cooler until first thing Monday morning?"

Remarkably, Culpepper and DeVriess both agreed that Monday morning was soon enough. I still had some work to do on the next day's talk in Washington, so after packing the slightly soiled scissors and the unused Stryker saw and pliers in the back of my truck, Miranda and I departed for campus. DeVriess followed us down the driveway, leaving the body of Trey Willoughby—what was left of it—in the keeping of detective Culpepper and the forensic technicians who would comb the coffin for clues to the postmortem butchery.

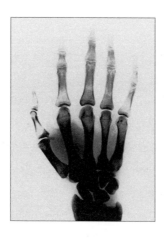

CHAPTER 5

THE DOT OF THE LASER POINTER DANCED ACROSS THE rib that was projected, ten times larger than life, on a screen deep beneath the Mall in Washington, D.C. I was lecturing, as part of a series called Smithsonian Saturdays, to three hundred people who'd given up a weekend afternoon—and given up fifty bucks apiece—to sit in a windowless underground auditorium and view slides of decaying corpses, bullet-riddled skulls, and incinerated skeletons.

I'd had a disappointing lunch meeting with Ed Ulrich, my former student. Actually, the lunch was great—we sampled a tasty variety of Native American dishes at the Museum of the American Indian—but the meeting was discouraging. Ed had sympathized with my funding plight, but his own program at the Smithsonian was confronting painful budget cuts, too, so he had no research money to funnel to his alma mater.

Deflated by the bad news, I'd gotten off to a slow start in my talk, but by the time I reached the slide of the rib, my energy was as focused as the laser pointer. "That little notch in the rib is a cut mark made by a knife," I told the audience. Clicking the projector's remote, I advanced to the next slide, a close-up of the notch. At this magnification the rib looked the size of a tree trunk, and the cut might have been inflicted by a dull chain saw. "See how the outer layer of bone, the cortical bone, looks torn? You can tell by the way the fibers angle that the knife thrust was going from front to back." I tapped my chest, just below my right collarbone. "This is the first right rib, by the way, so as the knife penetrated beyond the rib, it punctured the upper lobe of the lung."

"Excuse me?" A woman's voice floated up to me from the darkness at the rear of the auditorium.

"Did you have a question?"

"Yes. You said a medical examiner did an autopsy on this girl's body?"

"Yes. The state medical examiner in Kentucky. The body of the girl—Leatha Rutherford was her name—was found hidden in a trash pile outside Lexington."

"Why didn't the medical examiner see the stab wound?"

"Good question. By the time she was found, she'd been dead nearly six months, so there just wasn't enough soft tissue left to show the traces of a stab wound. The M.E. also took X-rays, but because the first rib runs underneath the clavicle"—I tapped my chest again—"the knife mark was masked on the X-rays."

"And how did you happen to find it?"

"Dumb luck," I said, earning a few laughs. "Actually, I have to give maternal doggedness the credit for this. Leatha was eighteen when she disappeared. The M.E. ruled her death a homicide, but he listed the actual cause of death as 'unknown.' She was buried, and the case more or less came to a dead end, but her mother wouldn't give up. She kept nagging the detectives, and then she contacted me. She'd seen me on a television show—*60 Minutes?* no, wait, it was *48 Hours,* I think—and she sent me a letter. 'If anyone can figure out how Leatha died, it's you,' she wrote. 'Please help me.' How do you say no to something like that? So I took a graduate student up to Kentucky, and we exhumed the bones. We brought them back to the morgue in Lexington, cleaned off the remaining tissue, and we got lucky. If dogs had gotten to the bones or if the knife had passed cleanly between the ribs instead of nicking this one, we would never have known what killed her."

The red laser dot twitched and skittered along the cut mark again. *No wonder cats love these things,* I thought. "That nick in the bone is about half an inch long, an eighth inch wide, and a quarter inch deep," I said, "but here's how it looks up really, really close." I flicked to the next slide. "We wondered if we could learn anything more about the murder by examining the cut mark more closely, so we took the rib back to UT and looked at it under a scanning electron microscope." At this scale, magnified hundreds of times, the edges of the rib could not be seen; instead an area measuring less than one inch square filled the Smithsonian's twenty-foot screen. The surface of the outer, cortical bone—ivory smooth to the naked eye and to probing fingertips—appeared ragged and spongy, like bread dough allowed to rise for too long. The small notch was now an immense fissure, wider than the span of my arms. I outlined it with the pointer. "Look carefully at the cut mark," I said. "What do you see?"

"There's a chunk of something down in the cut," a man near the front called out quickly. This fifty-dollar-a-head crowd was quick and competitive, like a bunch of straight-A students competing in Brain Bowl.

"Very good," I said. Lodged deep in the fissure was what appeared to be a boulder, several times the size of my head. "That looks pretty big under the electron microscope, but it's actually a tiny speck, about a thousandth of an inch in diameter. About the thickness of the down on a newborn baby's head. We analyzed that speck with an attachment to the microscope, something called an atom probe. Anybody want to guess what that speck is?"

Comments popped like kernels of corn. "Blood." "DNA." "Semen?" "Ooh, gross." "Blood." "Steel."

"Steel's close," I said, "but not quite right. That's a particle of cerium oxide. Cerium oxide is a ceramic that's used to make knife sharpeners. The man who stabbed this girl had just sharpened his knife."

A woman exclaimed, "Oh, dear God."

The man near the front said, "So they did catch the killer?"

I always hated answering this question. "Unfortunately, no. If this were an episode of *CSI*, they would have arrested him after fifty-nine minutes. But in real life, people get away with murder. The police thought she'd been killed by one of her relatives, an uncle; the rumor was, he had a big pot patch and Leatha had threatened to tell the police about it. Her body was found in the woods near his house, hidden in a trash heap." I always had trouble telling the next part. "The police actually found a cerium knife sharpener in his kitchen drawer." I heard murmurs of distress and indignation from the audience. "But there was no direct evidence tying him to the crime. 'A lot of people have cerium knife sharpeners,' the prosecutor told me. 'Hell, *I* have a cerium knife sharpener, but that doesn't make me a killer.' They never made an arrest, and that's one of the sad parts of this job: Sometimes your best just isn't quite good enough. I think we let Leatha down."

I ended my lecture with a case that was gruesome but not so sad: the case of a woman who died at home and whose body was eventually eaten by her three hungry dogs. By the time I recounted the search for the woman's missing diamond ring—a search that required a hapless sheriff's deputy to collect a bushel of dog crap, which I X-rayed in a fruitless search for the ring— the audience was shrieking in horrified amusement. *Leave them laughing if you can,* I thought. *They'll get sad again soon enough.*

After the lights came up and the screen came down, I packed up my slides and answered a few individual questions, things people hadn't felt comfortable asking in a crowd—one woman wondered whether I would be able to tell, twenty years postmortem, if a sister's fatal gunshot wound was a case of murder or suicide. "I don't know," I said honestly. "Women don't tend to commit suicide by gunshot, but if the M.E. who did the autopsy was competent, I doubt that I'd see it any differently."

As the crowd gradually trickled out, I noticed a man lingering near the back of the auditorium. Unlike most of the jeans-and-sweater crowd, he wore a wool suit, an oxford-cloth shirt, and a silk tie. The clothes looked expensive but subdued, as if the man wore them because he liked them, not because he wanted to impress others. He made his way forward as I finished packing my slides and projector. "Fascinating talk, Dr. Brockton," he said. "Especially the SEM case—great use of heavy research artillery on a forensic case. Cutting-edge work, if you'll pardon an inappropriate pun."

"I'm the world's worst punner, I'm told. No pardon necessary. You must have a science background if you're on a first-name basis with a scanning electron microscope."

"I do. I'm in research and development at a company called OrthoMedica." He said it offhandedly, as if he doubted I'd ever heard of it, but the truth was, OrthoMedica was one of the nation's biggest and best-known biomedical companies. An international conglomerate, it sold billions of dollars' worth of medical supplies, artificial joints, and consumer health-care products every year. He fished a business card out of his shirt pocket and handed it to me. *"Dr. Glen Faust, M.D., Ph.D.,"* it read. *"Vice President, R&D."* The OrthoMedica logo intrigued me: It took Leonardo da Vinci's classic drawing of the proportions of the human figure, *Vitruvian Man,* and gave it a high-tech, Bionic Man twist, superimposing X-rays and robotic prostheses and scans on various parts of the body.

I glanced at the address. "I didn't realize OrthoMedica was based in Bethesda."

"Spitting distance from here," he said. "We collaborate closely with the National Institutes of Health. Our campus is less than a mile from theirs. We also work with Johns Hopkins, just up the road in Baltimore. And with Walter Reed Army Hospital and the Pentagon."

"The Pentagon?"

He nodded. "Sure. The military drives a lot of health-care R&D, especially in areas like wound care and trauma surgery and prostheses." It made sense: Tens of thousands of U.S. soldiers had been wounded in the Iraq war, many of them by improvised explosive devices that blew off arms or legs.

He reached into his pocket again, removing a printout that he unfolded and handed to me. "Did you happen to see this story in the *New York Times* a while back? I thought of it when I saw the announcement about your talk."

I glanced at the story, which described how the U.S. military was now doing "virtual autopsies"—CT scans—on the bodies of all soldiers killed in Iraq. "Yes, I remember reading this," I said. "Fascinating. They're using scanners to examine lethal wounds so they can develop better body armor and helmets and armored vehicles, right?"

"Exactly. CT scans are such a rich vein of biomedical data. As you might imagine, OrthoMedica has quite an interest in mining that vein. Which brings me to you."

"Me? How so?"

"During your presentation today, I was struck by what a unique resource your Body Farm is. A thousand modern skeletons—specimens whose age and race and sex and stature you know—plus, what, a hundred donated bodies every year?"

"Actually, we're getting closer to one-fifty now."

"And do you scan those bodies as they come in, before they go out to the Farm?"

"I wish," I said. "We've scanned most of the skeletons in the collection—we got a grant to do that—but we don't have a way to scan the bodies. The hospital's Radiology Department isn't too keen on having dead bodies hauled up there and run through the same machines they use for live patients."

He chuckled. "What would you think of having a dedicated scanner at the Body Farm?"

"I'd think it was swell. But those things cost serious money—hundreds of thousands of dollars, even used ones. Our entire annual budget for the Body Farm is less than ten thousand, and we're looking at budget cuts that might whittle it down even be-low that."

"Terrible. A one-of-a-kind, world-renowned research facil-ity, and you're running it on a financial shoestring. Would you be interested in some research funding? A collaborative project involving the Body Farm, the university's Biomedical Engineering Department, and OrthoMedica?"

I felt the beginnings of a smile tugging at my face. "Sounds like you have an idea. Tell me more."

"I need data," he said. "I need to know more about the hu-man body, and I think you can help me learn. OrthoMedica will manufacture and sell sixty thousand hip implants and two hun-dred thousand knee replacements this year. We're the nation's second-largest source of artificial joints and orthopedic prosthet-ics. We want to be the biggest, and we want to be the best—the gold standard. To achieve that, we're targeting breakthroughs in two critical areas. One is materials research. Artificial joints have to be incredibly tough and durable, and they have to survive in a surprisingly corrosive environment. We're conducting or spon-soring dozens of projects geared toward creating better alloys, plastics, and ceramics for joint replacements and prosthetics."

"What's the other area?"

"Biomechanical engineering. Developing ways to customize every patient's new hip or knee or shoulder implant for a perfect fit. Engineering computer-controlled surgical systems that can in-stall those implants with absolute precision, within a tolerance of a ten-thousandth of an inch. Human surgeons can be remarkably gifted, but there's simply too much slop, not enough precision, in orthopedic surgery today. Hell, if we put together airplanes with as much variation as we put in artificial joints, the planes would fall out of the sky." He chuckled—a practiced chuckle, it sounded like, the sort you'd script into a briefing for investors or the board of directors. "What I'm trying to say, not very eloquently, is that if we had more data on the muscular and skeletal systems—if we had access to a shared database of cadaver scans, for instance—we could design better artificial joints, better surgical tools, and a host of other products. We could help a million patients a year achieve better surgical outcomes and better quality of life."

"Sounds great," I said. "How do you envision this collaboration with UT?"

"I'm just thinking out loud here, but my thought is that Ortho-Medica could provide a scanner and a technician to run it. We might even be able to underwrite some research projects in anthropology and in biomedical engineering."

I thought of our shoestring budget and of the administrative scissors poised to cut it. I thought of Miranda and the possibility of her losing her assistantship. "Where do I sign," I said, "and when do the scanner and the check arrive?"

He laughed. "How about we start with a memorandum of understanding next week—a draft, mind you, for the university's lawyers to look over. I'd be glad to hand-deliver it, if you've got the time and the willingness to show me around the Body Farm."

A week seemed head-spinningly fast; the wheels of progress evidently spun far more swiftly in the world of multibillion-dollar biomedical conglomerates than in the dusty corridors of the ivory tower. I extended my hand. "As we say in the South, y'all come see us."

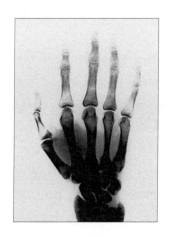

CHAPTER 6

THE NAKED AND DISMEMBERED CORPSE OF TREY Willoughby lay faceup on an autopsy table in the Regional Forensic Center, a warren of offices and labs in the basement of UT Hospital. The forensic center and the hospital morgue shared space, including the autopsy suite into which Miranda and I had wheeled Willoughby bright and early on this Monday morning. He'd been chilling out in the cooler since Friday afternoon, when KPD's evidence techs had finished checking the coffin at the cemetery and sent it to UT.

The table—a rectangular stainless-steel counter on wheels, essentially, with a flange around its edge to collect body fluids and a drain to funnel them out—was latched to a large sink along one wall. The drain was set into the foot of the table; it hung over the sink, so any liquid from the body would flow directly into the hospital's waste system. In Willoughby's case the drain would be carrying away not blood or other body fluids but vestiges of embalming chemicals. During the seven years since Willoughby's burial, most of the preservatives had leached out of the body, but enough remained to sting my eyes and nose.

Detective Gary Culpepper had arrived a few minutes earlier, accompanied by KPD's resident fingerprint guru, Art Bohanan. One of Art's claims to fame was the invention of the "Bohanan apparatus," for which he was awarded U.S. patent 5395445. The Bohanan apparatus was a boxy, portable superglue-fuming system for detecting latent fingerprints. A heated tray in one chamber of the unit was loaded with a small amount of superglue; when the tray reached a temperature of a hundred degrees Celsius—equal to the boiling point of water—the glue vaporized. A small blower wafted the glue fumes into a second chamber, which contained an object to be checked for prints, such as a murder weapon. As anyone who's ever superglued his fingers together can attest, superglue bonds strongly with chemicals in human fingerprints. Art was a pioneer in harnessing this particular chemical reaction to reveal latent prints—not just on objects but on human skin, too.

Art hoisted the boxy apparatus onto the steel counter beside the sink and plugged it in. I eyed the fuming chamber dubiously. "How do you aim to fume this guy? Even without his arms and legs, he's a lot bigger than that box."

"One piece at a time," said Art. "I've got a chain saw out in the van."

I laughed. Bending down to the shipping case that the rig had been packed in, Art fished around and removed a flexible plastic hose that sported a boxy plastic attachment at one end.

"That looks suspiciously like the hose from my vacuum cleaner," I observed.

"It *is* the hose from your vacuum cleaner," he joked. "Used to be, anyhow. The hose connects to this port on the side of the fuming chamber, so I can apply fumes directly to the body through here." He aimed the hose at me, and I saw that the end of the boxy attachment was open. "This one's cut to fit the contours of the arm," he explained, tracing the curved edges of the box with one finger. "Not that our guy's got any arms to fume." He removed the attachment and returned it to the case. "I've got another one that fits the curve of the thigh and the neck, and this flat one fits the chest and back."

Taking the flatter attachment from the case, he pressed it onto the hose, then fitted the other end of the hose to the back of the fuming chamber. Next he took a plastic bottle from the case and squeezed a small amount of liquid into a metal tray in the center of the chamber. Closing the chamber, he flipped a switch, and I soon caught the acrid scent of superglue. "The trick," he said, "is to move the hose over the body slowly and evenly enough so that every part of the skin gets fumed for somewhere between fifteen and thirty seconds. Less than fifteen and the print doesn't get enough glue to show up; more than thirty and the difference between the ridges and the valleys tends to blur."

Art slowly, methodically swept the fuming hose over the face, chest, abdomen, taking care not to linger more than thirty seconds in any one spot. Unfortunately, the timing turned out to be irrelevant—there were no prints to be found anywhere on Willoughby's body. Culpepper was disappointed, but Art seemed unsurprised. "Embalming chemicals are strong solvents," he explained. "They can dissolve the oils in fingerprints really quickly. Thing is, there might not have been any prints in the first place. Anybody handling this body after death would have worn rubber gloves, unless he was an idiot."

"Here's to idiotic criminals," said Culpepper. "What was it the man said? 'Nobody ever went broke overestimating the stupidity of the average criminal'?"

"Not exactly," corrected Art. "I think the quote dissed all of us, not just the bad guys. 'Nobody ever went broke underestimating the intelligence of the American public,' or something along those lines. Apparently—at least according to H. L. Mencken, who said it—we're all idiots."

Culpepper smiled ruefully. "I guess I just proved his point by misquoting him, huh?"

While Art packed up the superglue unit and trundled it away, I dialed the nurses' station up on the hospital's seventh floor. "We're ready for him," I said.

THE WIDE, WINDOWLESS DOOR TO the autopsy suite swung inward. With the squeak of rubber tires on polished concrete, Eddie Garcia rolled into the morgue.

Unlike most people delivered on wheels, though, Eddie Garcia was very much alive. Actually, "very much alive" was a bit of a stretch. He arrived in a wheelchair, and he still looked weak. Six weeks earlier he was very nearly dead: A searing dose of radiation had destroyed his entire left hand and claimed all but the last two fingers of his right hand, as well as ravaging his bone marrow and immune system. He was still a patient here at UT Medical Center—Miranda had wheeled him down from his room on the seventh floor—but his wounds were healing and his immune system was recovering. When I'd told him about the limbless corpse Miranda and I had exhumed, though, he'd voiced an interest in seeing the body. Eddie—Dr. Edelberto Garcia—was Knox County's medical examiner, as well as the director of the Regional Forensic Center, so even if he was still on medical leave, he was certainly entitled to be present. He was also likely to be helpful, and I considered it an encouraging sign of his recovery that he was here.

I'd turned up the autopsy suite's exhaust fan to remove the smell of embalming fluid, but even so the acrid chemicals—a mixture of formaldehyde, methanol, water, and various additives—stung my nostrils and eyes. They seemed to have stung Miranda's, too, because she rubbed her face with a paper towel. The towel came away damp—her cheeks and the rims of her eyes were red and glistening—and I realized that it wasn't the harsh chemicals causing her pain, but the far harsher blow that had been dealt to Eddie Garcia.

Before his devastating injury, Garcia had been a handsome and elegant man. Tennessee's first Hispanic medical examiner, he'd come to the United States from a prominent family in Mexico City. His medical education was first-rate, and his English was polished and precise—better than the English most of my friends and colleagues spoke, probably better than my own, too. His wife, Carmen, was a Colombian beauty; not surprisingly, their two-year-old son was a lovely boy. A few doors down the hall, on the desk in Garcia's office, stood a family portrait, a black-and-white photo for which the family had posed in elaborate nineteenth-century dress. Carmen's thick hair was pinned up, with a pair of tight curls framing the sides of her face above a pleated, high-collared white blouse and a fitted black jacket; Eddie's wavy hair was slicked back, his mustache closely trimmed, a starched shirt buttoned tight; the baby, Tomás, wore a long white christening gown. With their aristocratic bearing and intelligent eyes, the people in the photo could have passed for old-line Spanish nobility, and for all I knew, they were.

Now, though, it was impossible not to focus on the damage he'd suffered. Garcia's right hand was a thin, scarred paw on which only the last two fingers remained; his left hand was simply not there. Destroyed by the radiation, the hand had been amputated just below the wrist. A pellet of intensely radioactive material, which he'd plucked from the body of a dead man, had seared both of Garcia's hands and decimated his immune system. It had taken only a moment's exposure—to a piece of metal the size of a ball bearing—to ravage his body, threaten his life, and jeopardize his career. Yet here he was now, against all odds, taking a first brave step back to the job that had nearly killed him.

Garcia allowed Miranda and me to help him rise from the wheelchair, but otherwise none of us acknowledged that anything was out of the ordinary. When I introduced Culpepper, Garcia bowed slightly in lieu of a handshake. Then he peered at Trey Willoughby's mutilated body, and we all shifted our focus to the corpse as well.

Willoughby's body looked freakish, a horror-movie version of a disassembled mannequin. I'd taught anatomy for two years during graduate school, and I'd worked several dismemberment cases during the past twenty years. This one seemed different, though, more thoroughly and precisely stripped of its limbs than the others.

The face and head had been injected with embalming fluid, and so had the abdomen; the efforts to preserve the head and torso were evident not only from the smell of the chemicals but also from the trocar, the large injection port in the stomach. But these steps at preservation seemed incongruous and absurdly irrelevant given the violence inflicted on the corpse.

Garcia leaned down and peered at the left shoulder, where the collarbone and the shoulder blade had once been connected to the humeral head, the ball at the upper end of the arm. The tissue there had softened and decayed, but not so badly as to erase the original contours of the cut. "Bill," he said to me, "could you take a probe and some pickups and expose more of that joint, please?" It pained me that he needed to ask someone to do a simple maneuver that would normally have been an automatic, five-second move for him. "The arms have been severed quite cleanly," Garcia observed. He looked at the hip joints—more difficult to cut cleanly, because of the tendon that anchored the ball of the hip into the socket. "This amputation was the work of a professional," he said. "It could have been done by a physician or a medical student. Or maybe," he added, his eyes looking at me with a sparkle I hadn't seen since his injury, "an anthropology professor who has a hidden dark side."

"Ha," said Miranda. "Who says it's hidden?"

AFTER WE'D POKED AND PRODDED at Willoughby's torso to the satisfaction of Garcia, I turned to Culpepper. "Okay if I pull a couple of teeth now for DeVriess's DNA test?"

Culpepper shrugged. "Dr. Garcia, do you see any reason why not?" Garcia shook his head. "Go ahead," said the detective. "I'd hate to stand between a plaintiff's attorney and his money—it's like standing between a dog and a steak bone."

Willoughby's lips had been glued together and his jaw sewn shut. Using a scalpel, I slit the lips open and cut the sutures. It took some digging to reach the stitches, as the embalmer had plumped the corpse's cheeks with mortuary putty, which by now had hardened to the consistency of plaster. Once I'd managed to wrestle the mandible open, I pulled two molars, using a pair of slip-joint pliers whose ridged jaws I cushioned with a bit of paper toweling. Then, with a Stryker autopsy saw, I notched a chunk of bone from the hip. I swabbed the teeth and bone samples with disinfectant and sealed them in a padded FedEx envelope, which I tucked inside a FedEx mailer addressed to GeneTrax, a Dallas DNA lab.

By the time I'd packed the samples and dropped the package at the forensic center's front desk, Culpepper was antsy to head back to KPD. I walked with him to the loading-dock door, where he'd parked, then detoured to the front desk, where I left the FedEx envelope with Amy, the receptionist. I met Garcia and Miranda in the hallway; Miranda was pushing the wheelchair, but it was empty, and Garcia was walking.

He seemed reluctant to leave the forensic center and head back upstairs to his hospital room, and I couldn't blame him for that. Down here in the basement, he was an authoritative professional; up there, despite the deference he received from the hospital staff, he was just a patient. Either place, his injuries were the same, but down here the trauma was incidental to his identity; up there the trauma *was* his identity. He was a patient, defined as—and reduced to—"the hand-trauma case in 718."

He invited Miranda and me into his office. Settling weakly into the swiveling leather armchair behind the desk, he said, "Please," and nodded to the two wing chairs that faced it. We sat. "Would you like something to drink? Perhaps coffee or tea?" We both declined quickly—too quickly, apparently, because he smiled sadly and said, "Please don't stop using your hands just because you're with me." His forearms had been resting on the arms of his chair, slightly below the level of the desktop, but now he shifted them to the desktop and stared at their ravaged ends.

"I can say this to you only because you are my friends. It makes me feel more conspicuous if you act incapable of picking up a coffee cup or pushing a button. That makes me feel almost as if I'm contagious—as if I've infected and destroyed your hands, too."

"I'm sorry, Eddie," Miranda said. Leaning forward, she reached across the desk and gently squeezed his left elbow. "Thank you for telling us." He smiled again, not as sadly. "Is there anything else we can do that would be helpful," she asked, "besides, you know, not acting weird?"

"As a matter of fact, there is." With the two fingers that remained on his right hand, he gestured at the computer occupying a table to one side of the desk. "If one of you wouldn't mind navigating the Web, I'd like to show you some sites I've been looking at. I'd show you myself, but I'm very slow on the keys, pecking with just one finger."

"That would be Miranda's department," I said. "I'd be as slow as you." As soon as I heard the words, I wished I could reel them back in, but when Miranda snorted and Garcia laughed softly, I relaxed.

Miranda moved to a rolling stool parked in front of the computer. As she swiveled into position in front of the keyboard, she made a big show of interlacing her fingers and cracking her knuckles. Then she rubbed her hands briskly together and wiggled her fingers rapidly. "At your service. What's your wish?"

"Let's start with toe-to-thumb transplants," he answered. Miranda's fingers clattered rapidly over the keyboard.

"Wow, look at that," she said. "Over a hundred thousand hits. Who knew that was such a hot topic?"

"This one." He pointed with his pinkie to one of the search results. "Click on that, please."

Miranda used the mouse to highlight the link. As it loaded, she remarked, "You know, Eddie, if you replaced this clunky desktop computer with a laptop, you might get pretty good with the touch pad."

Before he had time to respond, the page finished loading and a television news story began to play. The footage showed a teen-age boy—a New Jersey fourteen-year-old—who'd lost his thumb and first two fingers in a fireworks accident. A close-up showed the damage to the boy's right hand, which looked almost exactly like Garcia's right hand. Five months after the injury, a Philadelphia hand surgeon removed the second toe from the boy's right foot—the toe Miranda liked to call the "index toe"—and fashioned a new thumb from it. "The structures line up very well," explained the surgeon on camera. "You have two major nerves, you have a major blood vessel, you have similar tendons. The circumference is very similar." In the story's "after" images, the gap created by the missing index finger and middle finger remained quite prominent, but the reconstructed right thumb was a virtual mirror image of the boy's undamaged left thumb.

"Cool," Miranda commented. "Very cool. That would give you back an opposable grip on your right hand."

Garcia pointed her through a quick series of articles about toe-to-thumb transplants. The procedure might not qualify as "routine"—complex microsurgery was required to stitch together the network of delicate blood vessels and nerves—but it had been performed hundreds of times during the past few decades, with a success rate of well over 90 percent.

"Let's change the search," he said. "See what you find using 'myoelectric prosthesis' and 'bionic hand' as search terms." The technical term—a reference to the use of electrical impulses from muscles in the arm to trigger electric switches and motors in an artificial hand—produced about a hundred thousand hits. The much catchier "bionic hand" yielded over three hundred thousand, including thumbnail-size photos and sketches. Miranda clicked on one of the images, a robotic-looking prosthesis called the i-Hand.

Miranda leaned closer to the monitor. "Ooh, that's kinda sexy," she remarked, studying the photo. The i-Hand's fingers were formed of pale white plastic, translucent enough to reveal bonelike metal rods in the fingers, as well as hinges and tiny motors. According to several articles, the i-Hand was the first prosthetic hand to faithfully mirror the structures and movements of the human hand. One video clip showed a young woman with an i-Hand lifting bags of groceries, picking up a set of car keys, and typing on a computer keyboard. Her bionic hand was covered with a flesh-toned "skin" of rubber. "I like it better without the skin." Miranda frowned. "Much more futuristic-looking."

"Yes," Garcia agreed, "very Luke Skywalker. But I suspect that the rubber provides a better grip than the hard plastic. It probably also protects the mechanism from things that could damage it. Dirt. Sharp edges. Coca-Cola."

"Embalming fluid," I added, thinking of the body we'd just examined. "Blood."

"Oh, *fine,*" Miranda retorted with mock indignation. "Go ahead, rain on my style parade, see if I care." She wiggled the fingers of one hand, then folded all of them except her middle finger. "I assume the i-Hand is capable of making this gesture, with or without the skin." Garcia asked her to bookmark several of the i-Hand links, then asked if she'd search one more topic. "Sure," she replied. "What?"

"Total hand transplantation." He said it quietly, but I heard an edge of hope and anxiety in his voice that I hadn't heard earlier, when he'd asked for the other searches.

Miranda's fingers clattered. "Wow," she breathed, "almost a million hits." Garcia had her call up only a few of the million, but those were enough to confirm my prior impressions. Hand-transplant surgery was relatively new; the first total transplant had been attempted in Ecuador in 1964, but it didn't work, and the procedure had been attempted only a few more times until the late 1990s. Even now it remained incredibly rare—so far, fewer than fifty hand transplants had been performed in the entire world. The surgery was extraordinarily complex, requiring surgeons to connect dozens of nerves, tendons, veins, arteries, and muscles. The operation was both an intricately choreographed ballet and a brutal test of endurance, requiring delicate, nonstop work for twelve to sixteen hours. Even if the surgery itself went perfectly, the long-term outcome was far from certain. To keep their immune systems from rejecting the transplants, recipients had to take immunosuppressants—drugs to weaken their immune systems—for the rest of their lives, and the immunosuppressants increased their vulnerability to diseases.

Total hand transplantation looked like a medical miracle, no doubt about it. But I couldn't help thinking how much riskier it looked than either the toe-to-thumb reconstruction or the prosthesis.

"It's a big risk," Garcia said, as if hearing my thoughts. "But it would be worth taking a big risk to have real hands again."

His words stayed with me long after I drove back to the stadium and Miranda had wheeled him back upstairs to become the hand-trauma case in 718 once more.

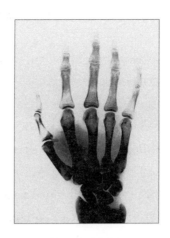

CHAPTER 7

I GRITTED MY TEETH AS I PULLED INTO THE PARKING lot in Farragut, the suburb to the west of Knoxville. I was headed for my spring dental cleaning, and like most people, I tended to be nervous about it. I would much rather be using my lunch hour to eat lunch than to have my teeth probed and scoured. "Sorry I'm late," I said to Barbara, the dentist's silver-haired office manager. "I just came from an autopsy. I figured y'all would appreciate it if I took the time to wash my hands afterwards."

"You figured right," she said. "Anyhow, Reuben's running a few minutes behind. How're you doing today?" Barbara wasn't just Dr. Pelot's office manager. She was also his wife—and she was a Knoxville City Councilwoman, representing the city's West Hills district.

"Dentally speaking, I'm fine," I answered, "unless your husband tells me I'm not flossing often enough. Professionally, though, I've got a big cavity forming in the Body Farm's budget, and I don't know how to fill it. I don't suppose the city's got any pots of money sitting around that could be tapped for educational purposes?"

She frowned. "Let me think about that," she mused, then she laughed. "The first thing that comes to mind is the Blighted Properties Redevelopment Program."

I laughed, too. "Well, 'blighted' does seem to be a shoe that fits the Body Farm. Truth is, 'blighted' would actually be a pretty charitable description of our residents."

She shook her head. "Unfortunately," she went on, "that money's all spent. Tell you what. City Council meets every Tuesday. At next week's meeting, I'll ask the Development staff if there's any way we could scrape up some funding for you."

I thanked her and took my seat in the waiting room. Forty minutes later, my teeth scoured slick and my flossing pronounced satisfactory, I headed back to UT, hoping that Barbara and the City Council might find a few thousand dollars to offset UT's belt-tightening.

I stopped by the Anthropology Department's administrative offices just long enough to retrieve a few messages from my secretary, Peggy. Then I'd retreated to this office—my private, preferred office at the far end of the stadium—to concentrate. This spring I was teaching Introduction to Forensic Anthropology, an upper-level undergraduate course, and I had thirty test papers to grade by tomorrow morning. Tucked beneath the north end-zone grandstands of Neyland Stadium, my sanctuary was a football field away, literally, from the constant distractions of the administrative office. But the hydraulic mechanism in the stairwell door had broken recently, and every time someone opened the door, it crashed into the concrete wall.

After six or eight crashes, I'd stopped cursing, and after a couple dozen I'd called the maintenance department to report the faulty door. Shortly after a window-rattling impact, Gary Culpepper appeared in the doorway.

"Hello, Detective. I hadn't expected to see you again today." I had just poured a large bag of M&M's into a one-liter glass beaker. Plucking out one for myself—red, my favorite—I offered the beaker to Culpepper. "M&M?"

He held up a hand by way of declining. "Doesn't mix well with the gum," he smacked. "Besides, I'm a little off my feed since this morning's session in the morgue."

"Feeling a bit squeamish?" He nodded sheepishly, and I laughed. "The last time I was in the morgue with Dr. Garcia, a detective from Oak Ridge was in there with us. First he threw up on me, then he fainted. You, by comparison, held up brilliantly."

"That Oak Ridge case," he said, "that's the one that injured Dr. Garcia, right? Where the woman murdered the old guy by slipping a radioactive pellet into his vitamin pills?"

I nodded. "He was a retired physicist—an atomic scientist. He died within hours after swallowing the pill."

"And Dr. Garcia's hands got cooked during the autopsy?"

I nodded again.

"What was the scientist's name?"

"Novak. Dr. Leonard Novak. He played a key role in the Manhattan Project during World War II. Dr. Garcia found the pellet in Novak's intestine. He held it for less than a minute, but that was enough to destroy his hands."

Culpepper shook his head. "Damn shame."

"It was—still is—but it could've been even worse. Garcia nearly died. Miranda got some burns on her fingertips, too, but not serious. Garcia's borne up pretty well, considering, but what a blow." I thought of his wife and child, Carmen and Tomás, whom he could not hold again in the same way. "Hard on the whole family."

"I don't get it, Doc. I mean, why single out one guy from the whole atom-bomb project? And why not just shoot him or stab him?"

I agreed that it was arbitrary to wreak vengeance on one scientist, but I did see the symbolism behind choosing radioactivity as the murder weapon.

"The killer was a Japanese-American librarian, right?" I nodded. "For chrissakes, why couldn't she have beaten him to death with the *Encyclopaedia Britannica*? What kind of wacko would use radiation? She could've killed or hurt dozens of people."

His comment pressed a bruised spot in me. "She was deeply disturbed," I acknowledged. "She was trying to settle Japan's score with the U.S. over the atomic bomb. Sounds crazy, I know, but that was how she saw it. And she got pulled under by it— she went off the deep end—and she took some other folks with her." I looked away from Culpepper, out through the grimy windows of my office. What I saw with my eyes was a spiderwork of filthy steel girders, the supports for the hundred thousand stadium seats and the plush skyboxes overhead. But what I saw in my mind was Isabella Arakawa Morgan, who'd purposely killed an old man and accidentally maimed a young physician. Isabella, who'd helped me research and solve a sixty-year-old murder in Oak Ridge, one that had been mysteriously connected to the creation of the atomic bomb. Isabella, who'd come to my house one night and made love to me. Isabella, whom I'd confronted when I realized what she'd done. Isabella, who'd run from me when I did, disappearing into the underground maze of Oak Ridge's lab-yrinthine storm sewers.

I looked back at Culpepper, who was studying my face closely. I realized that I had no notion of how long I'd stared out through the dusty pane and the dirty girders. Had it been a few seconds or many minutes? "Sorry, Detective. I seem to have spaced out on you there. Ghosts."

"I understand, Doc," he said. "I get blindsided by one every now and then, too. My first year on the force, there was this kid—a six-year-old girl—who'd be alive today if I'd been a little smarter, a little quicker. She'd be seventeen now, and I'd probably never think of her. But she's not seventeen and alive—she's six and she's dead. Always six, always dead, and often on my mind."

"I'm sure there are other people who are alive *because* of you. Don't forget to think about those."

"Funny thing," he said. "Those are harder to remember than the ones who aren't alive." He shrugged and turned his palms up. Maybe the gesture was expressing helplessness, maybe ac-ceptance. Maybe both. "So I remembered something I should've asked you this morning at the morgue—an old case of yours. You worked a dismemberment case some years ago, didn't you?"

"I've worked several, actually," I said, "but only one here in Knoxville. Ten or twelve years ago? No, longer—fifteen years, maybe more."

"Any similarities to this one? I mean, besides the fact that the victim was cut up? Any chance it was the work of the same killer?"

"Let's take a look at the file." I got up and crossed to an ancient four-drawer filing cabinet that stood beside an interior doorway. The olive drab cabinet, chin high, nearly blocked the doorway, which led to the collection: the series of adjoining rooms where nearly a thousand skeletons were neatly boxed and shelved.

Tugging open the balky top drawer—the top left corner of the cabinet had been dented years ago, possibly around the time I was born, and the drawer had an annoying tendency to stick—I took out a manila file folder at the front. The folder contained a listing of all the forensic cases the Anthropology Department had assisted with, arranged chronologically and with a brief description after the case number. Beside case 93-17—the seventeenth forensic case of 1993 (because it was a criminal case, not a donated body, the year was the first number in the pair)—was the notation "Dismemberment/mutilation of male victim." Squatting down, I slid open the lowest drawer of the cabinet and removed the case file, taking it to my desk. Besides my forensic report to KPD and the district attorney's office, the file contained brittle newspaper clippings about the case. The grisly crime and the sensational trial had made front-page headlines off and on for weeks: HUMAN BODY PARTS TOSSED IN DUMPSTERS. VICTIM'S SEVERED HEAD FOUND IN DITCH. SUSPECT ARRESTED IN DISMEMBERMENT CASE. LOVE TRIANGLE MOTIVATED MUTILATION. DUMPSTER KILLER SENTENCED TO LIFE.

The file confirmed my memory of the case. "That was a crime of passion," I said. "A stabbing, followed by a crude mutilation of the corpse. Partly a clumsy attempt to dispose of the body, but partly a chance to add postmortem insult to injury. Stab a guy to death, then stab him some more, then hack him to pieces. It sends a message: 'Mere murder's way too good for this guy.'"

I passed the file to Culpepper, who flipped through it wordlessly until he got to the photos of the severed body parts. "Yuck. This stuff makes Willoughby's body look pretty damn good."

"Doesn't it? As you can see, the cases are very different. Willoughby died of natural causes, and his arms and legs were cleanly amputated, not hacked off. Nothing personal about that. Hell, if it weren't for the paternity suit, the dismemberment wouldn't have been discovered," I said. Culpepper was nodding glumly. "Anyhow, the Dumpster killer was in prison when Willoughby was buried, so he's got a pretty good alibi."

Culpepper frowned. "Figures," he sighed. "Not my first dead end of the day either. I followed up on the people working at Ivy Mortuary. The former owner, Elmer Ivy, died in 2005, the office manager got married and changed her name and moved who-knows-where, and nobody knows a damn thing about the embalmer who was working there in 2003."

"*Sic transit gloria mundi,*" I said.

"Sick what?"

"*Sic transit gloria mundi.* Latin. 'Thus passes the glory of the world,' I think is how it translates. A highfalutin way of saying, 'We're nothing but dust in the wind.' Most of us leave fainter tracks than we'd like to believe. Doesn't take long for them to get covered over or swept away." I thought for a moment. "I know somebody who would probably be able to tell you more about Ivy Mortuary. Helen Taylor. She runs East Tennessee Cremation Services, a crematorium out near the airport. She's sharp and first-rate, and she's done business with all the funeral homes in the area. I'd be surprised if she didn't remember who worked at Ivy Mortuary seven years ago." I flipped through my Rolodex and jotted down her name and number.

The card tucked behind Helen Taylor's was sticking up slightly higher than hers, and out of curiosity I flipped to it. It bore the distinctive gold-and-blue logo of the FBI and the name "*Special*

Agent Charles Thornton." Underneath his name were the words *"Weapons of Mass Destruction Directorate."* Seeing his card, so close on the heels of my conversation about the Oak Ridge case, spooked me all over again. Did all roads—all tracks—lead me back to Isabella?

The stairwell door slammed again, jarring me back to the present and to Culpepper once more. I took another M&M from the beaker—green this time. Culpepper reached in and took one as well, a yellow. "Okay, I gotta go." He raised the M&M as if it were a tiny drink and he were proposing a toast. "To finding the tracks before they're swept away." Then he tossed the candy straight up, catching it in his mouth as it arced down. "And to not going off the deep end."

He closed the stairwell door gently on his way out. I let the green M&M dissolve slowly in my mouth, feeling the wall of denial I'd erected around Isabella's memory melt and crumble like the hard candy shell.

CHAPTER 8

I STARED AT THE SMALL DIGITAL RECORDER IN MY hand, paralyzed by the countless unspoken questions it posed, questions to which I had no answers. I was as paralyzed by the machine as I'd been by the man who'd loaned it to me: a Knoxville psychologist named John Hoover, highly recommended by my family physician. I'd phoned him for an appointment several weeks earlier, in hopes he could help me sort through some confusion and sadness. In doing so I was heeding the advice Miranda had given me, when she'd said to "take a sabbatical, write a book, see a therapist, get a dog—do whatever will help you heal." Seeing a therapist had struck me as more efficient than the sabbatical or writing options and as less work (and probably less expense) than the dog option. But sitting in his office, I'd spent forty-five of my allotted fifty-minute session avoiding the real reason I'd come. I'd chattered about my work and about my past, but not about my present or my pain—not about Isabella.

As the final minutes of the session ticked away, Dr. Hoover rose from his overstuffed chair, walked to his desk, and took out a small audio recorder. "Here," he said. "Maybe it would be easier to start by speaking what's on your mind into this. You don't have to share it with me; you can just erase it afterward if you want. But putting words to whatever's troubling you—naming the parts, telling the story of your sadness—might help you get a handle on it."

Now, at midnight, sitting in darkness in my living room, I realized I'd been staring at the recorder for forty-five minutes. Did that mean I had only five more minutes in the session with my digital therapist?

Summoning up my nerve, I pressed "record" and began to speak.

NOW IS THE TIME FOR all good men to come to the aid of their country.

I hate this. I don't know what to say. I feel like a blackmailer whispering into this thing. How do I tell the story of my sadness? Right now that would be the story of Isabella. But where do I begin the story, and how? Do I begin the day I met Isabella? The day I walked into the Oak Ridge Public Library and she asked if she could help me? Do I begin with the World War II photos she showed me, the ones that helped me find the buried bones of a murdered soldier? Or do I go all the way back to the war itself, the race to build the Bomb, the relentless momentum to drop it on Hiroshima and Nagasaki? Do I begin that day in August of 1945, when a B-29 took off from the island of Tinian, crossed a thousand miles of the Pacific, and destroyed the city where Isabella's parents lived? No. That would be her story of sadness, not mine, not ours.

Did our story begin the night we ate pizza and I walked her partway home and listened to the wind sighing in the treetops and felt the urge to kiss her? Or did it begin the night she came to my house bringing a DVD of Dr. Strangelove *and microwave popcorn and Coke? Perhaps it began the moment she pressed herself against me, took me into her arms, and gave herself to me.*

But what can I say about her? That she was beautiful? She was. She still is, if she's alive. Exotically beautiful, but in a way that was too subtle to pinpoint. One of her four grandparents had been Japanese; the others had been American missionaries who ended up in the wrong place at the wrong time: in Nagasaki in August of 1945, as American B-29s dropped the deadly fruit of the Manhattan Project.

Isabella's ethnicity matters to me; it interests me, not just because it's so entwined with her crime but also because of my habit of mind as an anthropologist. Knowing her ancestry gives me some skeletal context, something to latch onto when I reach out and try to grasp the enigma of her. Because she is one-quarter Asian, I know that most of her skeletal features are Caucasoid. Most—but not all. Some of the stories told in her bones are Mongoloid, Asian. Her cheekbones, as I picture them in my mind's eye right now, are slightly higher and wider and flatter than, say, Miranda's. Her skin is a few shades darker than Miranda's, too, but then again, almost everyone's skin is a few shades darker than Miranda's. I remember her teeth in two ways: I remember how dazzling they were when she smiled at me and how quickly hidden they vanished behind the curtain of her hair when she ducked her head shyly. And I remember how they felt when we kissed, smooth and hard and slick against my tongue, nibbling gently at my lip and then, later, biting into the meat of my bicep and the heel of my hand hard enough to leave bruises outlined in tooth marks. If I had thought to run the tip of my tongue along the backs of those front teeth, I might have felt indentations, concavities: the distinctive scooped-out curvature of shovel-shaped incisors, a signature skeletal trait of Asians and Native Americans. But what man in his right mind would think of dental details when a lovely woman presses her warm mouth and trembling body to his?

As I listen to myself say these things, I feel foolish and pedantic. And yet. And yet: I have so few things to hang on to as I try to grasp Isabella that I suppose it's understandable and forgivable that I should lapse into my comfortable role of professor and anthropologist—categorizer and explainer. Yet the truth is, I barely knew Isabella. Our lives intersected, briefly but powerfully, at two points—no, three. First when Garcia and Miranda and I were exposed to the radioactive pellet Isabella had used to murder Dr. Novak. Next when Isabella helped me discover the location where a murdered soldier had been secretly buried during World War II. And third when she offered her body and her passionate need to me. No, wait, there was a fourth time as well: when I realized that she was the one who had killed Novak, when I confronted her, and she disappeared into the labyrinth of storm sewers beneath Oak Ridge.

I followed her into the labyrinth. In hindsight maybe that was a mistake. In hindsight maybe confronting her was a mistake. In hindsight maybe making love to her was a mistake. In hindsight maybe hindsight itself is a mistake—what's the point of following the trail of regret back into the past? It's not possible to choose a different path from the very one *that brought me to the present, to this exact moment, where I hide in the darkness of my living room and the labyrinth of my heart, murmuring into the digital emptiness I clutch in my hand.*

I hate this. I don't know what to say. Now is the time for all good men to come to the aid of their country.

CHAPTER 9

the next morning on my way to campus, still feeling self-conscious and vaguely guilty about voicing my thoughts and fears into a microphone. When I walked into the bone lab, Miranda looked at me sharply and said, "What?"

"What do you mean, 'What?'"

"You have a funny look on your face. Embarrassed or something. Like a kid who's just peed in his pants."

"Thanks a lot."

"You okay?"

"Sure," I lied. "Just preoccupied."

"Whatever you say. Anyhow, Eddie called. He's got an appointment next week to get fitted for an i-Hand."

"The bionic prosthesis? Just for his left hand?" She nodded. "I thought he was more interested in a transplant."

"He was, but there's a big problem with that, apparently." She frowned. "It's virtually impossible to be approved for a hand transplant unless you're a double amputee."

"Eddie *is* a double amputee, essentially," I pointed out. "He's only got two fingers on his right hand."

"Apparently the hand surgeons consider those fingers more of a plus than you and I do," she said. "He does have some function in them, after all. And once he gets the toe-to-thumb transplant—in a month or so, he hopes—he'll have three digits on the right hand, including an opposable thumb."

"Still," I protested, "it seems harsh to rule him out for a transplant on the left side. It's like he's being punished for being not quite maimed enough, you know? Like that sick girl—what did she have, lupus?—whose insurance company refused to pay for her medical treatment until she was dying."

"Well, yeah, sort of," she hedged, "but on the other hand— ooh, remind me not to say that in front of Eddie—not everybody who wants a transplant can get one. If there aren't enough hands to go around, what's the best, fairest way to pick who gets one and who doesn't? If *you* were the one parceling out hands, how would *you* pick?"

I didn't have an answer to that. But I did have another question. "Are there really not enough hands to go around?"

She shrugged.

"How many kidney transplants were performed in the United States last year?"

She did a quick Google search. "Don't know about last year," she answered, "but over sixteen thousand were done in 2008."

"And how many hand transplants?"

"Not a fair comparison," she pointed out. "A lot of kidneys came from living donors—somebody's son or sister or friend who was willing to give one up for a person they love."

"You're right, not the same thing. How many heart transplants?"

The keyboard rattled again. "Wow. Two thousand, one hundred sixty-three. I would have guessed a hundred or so."

"Okay. So none of those heart donors got out alive. If my math's right, those twenty-one hundred heart donors had forty-two hundred hands, plus or minus."

"I don't think you can say 'plus' unless some of them started out with three hands," she said reasonably.

"Don't be a hairsplitter. We're talking about potentially four thousand transplantable hands, right?"

"Hang on," she said. "This is a really interesting database. All categories of organ-donation stats compiled by the federal government. You can sort by organ, by donor type, by state, all kinds of things. Okay, actually, there were about eight thousand deceased organ donors in the U.S. in 2008. So, in theory, sixteen thousand hands, if all of them had both hands when they died."

"And how many hand transplants in the U.S. in 2008?"

"No hand-transplant stats in the federal database. Let me try 'hand transplants United States 2008' and see if my friend Google can shed any light." A moment later she said, "I say again, wow."

"How many?"

"Two."

"Two thousand?"

"No," she answered. "Two, period. As in 'one, two, buckle my shoe.'"

"So the problem's not a shortage of hands," I mused, "but a shortage of hand-transplant experts? Not enough surgeons who've been trained to do it?"

She worked the keyboard again. "I believe you have sussed out the problem, Wise Master. Listen to this press release from

Emory University Medical Center, dated February 2008: 'The only physician in the United States formally trained in both hand surgery and transplant surgery is establishing a new program at Emory to train other experts and to conduct research on what is still an extraordinary procedure.' One formally trained hand-transplant surgeon in the whole U.S. of A.—that would appear to be a bit of a bottleneck." She turned to me and frowned. "I don't get it," she pondered out loud. "What makes a hand transplant a thousand times more complicated than a heart transplant? Hearts have lots of blood vessels and nerves, and the potential for the recipient's body to reject the transplant would appear to be the same, whether it's a heart or a hand, wouldn't you think?"

I considered that for a moment. "I'm not sure that it's the complexity that accounts for the difference," I answered. "A heart transplant's a lifesaving procedure—if you need a heart and you don't get one, you die. But there are a lot of people walking around minus a hand or two. So maybe refining the techniques in hand-transplant surgery isn't considered as high a priority."

"Hmm," she grunted, and did another search. "Guess how many boob jobs were done in 2008?" She didn't wait for me to answer. "Four hundred thousand. What does *that* say about priorities? Plenty of surgeons up to speed on that."

"There's a lot of money in plastic surgery," I said. "It's the free market at work."

"Swell," she retorted. "Life, liberty, and the pursuit of perkiness."

I sighed. "So the bottom line here, since it's a left hand Eddie needs, is that the bionic hand, the i-Hand, looks like his best bet?"

"Looks like," she agreed. "Be good to learn more about it,

though—get a review from somebody other than the manufacturer's own marketing department."

"I think I know just the guy to ask," I said.

THE GLEAMING WHITE PLANE TAXIING toward me was unlike any I'd ever seen. It had wings and a tail, true, as well as a pair of turboprop engines. But the engines were at the trailing edge of the wings and faced aft, so the propellers pushed the plane rather than pulling it. The fuselage wasn't cylindrical but slightly bulbous, like the sleek body of a seal or a killer whale. The wings were set far back, near the tail; up near the plane's nose was a much smaller pair of wings that angled slightly downward. As the plane turned its two-eyed, droop-winged nose directly toward the ramp, I realized that it bore a striking resemblance to a flying fish. A flying catfish, to be precise.

The props stopped, the engines spooled down, and a door just behind the cockpit swung open. A small folding stair unfolded outward and down, and Glen Faust, M.D., Ph.D., descended from the aerial catfish and strode toward me, a leather satchel slung over one shoulder. "Dr. Brockton," he called, "so nice of you to pick me up."

"Welcome to Tennessee," I said. "It was worth coming out here just to see that airplane. I've not seen one of those before."

He smiled. "It's a head turner, isn't it? It's an Italian design, which is why it looks so damn sexy. Nearly as fast as a jet—cruises at four hundred miles an hour—but a lot more efficient. Room for nine, and a high ceiling, thanks to that fat fuselage. Interesting thing is, the fuselage is actually an airfoil and provides part of the lift. That allows smaller wings—and therefore less drag. Clever, huh?"

"Clever," I agreed. "Sounds like you know almost as much about the plane as the pilot."

"I am the pilot"—he smiled—"about half the time, including today. When we were looking for a new corporate aircraft, I decided to meddle. 'I'm a pilot,' I told the CEO, 'and I'm also in charge of research. Let me research this.' He fell for it." His smile broadened into a grin. "You wouldn't believe the view coming down the Shenandoah Valley today at twenty thousand feet. I could see Knoxville all the way from Roanoke." Roanoke was 250 miles to the north, so what he was describing was impossible; still, the day was crystal clear—thirty miles to the east of the airport, the Great Smoky Mountains looked an easy walk away—so I could almost believe the claim.

I led him from the ramp and through the lobby, out to where my truck was parked in the small lot. "Nice thing about the corporate terminal is not having to go in and out of the parking garage," I said.

"Nice thing about having your own plane is not having to hassle with airport security. I swung through Starbucks and brought a big cup of coffee with me, I boarded two minutes before take-off, and I didn't have to sit through a safety demo." He patted his satchel. "Oh, and I stuffed my briefcase full of knives and guns."

"Smart move. Clearly this isn't your first trip to Tennessee."

We headed north on Alcoa Highway, past mobile-home dealerships and abandoned shopping centers and broad, rolling pastures. In ten minutes we rounded a bend at the base of a wooded hill and the main tower of UT Medical Center appeared. I bore right onto the exit ramp, looped behind the hospital complex, and traversed the employee parking lot that bordered the Body Farm. Pulling into the farthest corner of the lot, I parked in front of the facility's dual gates of chain-link and solid wooden planking. "I'm surprised your place isn't farther off the beaten track," Faust commented.

"It used to be," I said, unlocking the padlocks and opening the gates. "I first started with an old barn—a pig barn—out at one of the UT farms, but that was too far away. When I relocated to this spot, the parking lot wasn't here yet and the hospital tower wasn't even on the drawing board."

As I led him inside, he peered over his shoulder, across the top of the wooden privacy fence. "It looks like you might actually be able to see inside here from the top floors of the hospital."

"You can," I said. "Gives the patients a little added motivation to get well. *Memento mori* and all that."

"Does the hospital charge extra for that?"

"No, the view's free. Where they make their money is selling air fresheners to the patients on hot summer days, when the Body Farm's getting really ripe." He smiled at the joke, so I kept it going. "If the billing folks could just figure out how to get Medicare to reimburse them a hundred bucks for every air freshener, their financial worries would be over."

I gestured at the clearing inside the gate, a patch of brown grass and bare dirt that measured about sixty feet from edge to edge. "So this is it. We've got a little less than three acres here inside the fence now." I led him across the grass and slightly downhill, where a cube of chain-link fence nestled beneath the trees, its roof draped with a bright blue tarp. "Originally all we had was this chain-link enclosure, which measures sixteen feet square. Now we keep equipment and a meteorological station in here, but this was where the research began."

He nodded. "I've seen an old photo of you and some graduate students in here, with a body stretched out on the concrete."

"That was taken the spring of our first year," I recalled. "We got just four donated bodies that year, and they were all used to research a master's thesis—a study of which insects feed on bodies, and when."

"I've read it," he said. "That was a seminal piece of research. Helped jump-start the field of forensic entomology, didn't it? Laid the foundation for estimating time since death by collecting insects and maggots off a murder victim?"

"It did," I agreed, adding, "You've done your homework."

"I generally do, when we're planning to invest half a million dollars in a research project."

My eyebrows shot up. "Is that what you're planning to invest here?"

"Could be." The tripod with the camera caught his eye; he glanced from the equipment to the corpse of Maurie Gershwin. Most of the skin was gone from her skull, neck, and hands now; the fabric of her clothing hung loose and dark-stained on the bones of her torso and limbs. "Tell me about this?"

"Nothing too fancy," I said. "Just using time-lapse photography to document this woman's decomp. She's been out here for about two weeks now. If this were August, she'd be bare bones by this point. But the blowflies are dormant if the temperature's below fifty degrees, so there's less insect activity in winter and spring. And the bacteria and enzymes that digest the body work slowly at lower temperatures."

"Sure. Biochemistry 101: Heat accelerates almost every chemical reaction."

I pointed toward a lower corner of the fence. "There's some interesting research down this way," I told him. "You see these concrete pads?" There were five of them, each measuring seven or eight feet square.

"I recognize those," he said.

"Excuse me?"

"I've seen those. From space."

"I'm not following you."

"They show up in satellite images," he explained. "I peeked over your fence on Google Earth. It's amazing what you can see in those satellite images. These concrete pads show up very clearly." Pointing at a rumpled white body bag, which was draped atop a corpse, he added, "You can also see a couple of those. And I *think* maybe a body or two, but that might have been wishful thinking on my part."

"Amazing. But I'm not sure I like the idea that just anybody can look over my fence from up in the sky."

"You can only see it if you know where to look and what to look for. What sort of research is being done with those pads? Are there bodies buried underneath them?"

I nodded. "One of our graduate students was studying ground-penetrating radar and how the radar image—the signature—of a body changed as it decomposed. So she buried bodies at various depths, camouflaging some of them with debris, and then poured these concrete pads on top. She ran the radar rig across the pads once a week for several months. Looked sort of like she was using a floor polisher out here in the woods, but she was looking through the concrete, not cleaning the top of it."

"How'd the images change?"

"To be honest," I said, "to me they looked like clouds on a weather radar screen. Because I already knew they were bodies, I could see the outlines, and I could tell that they were collapsing as they decayed. But if I hadn't already known what I was looking at, I'm not sure I'd've known what I was looking at."

"Like me looking at the Body Farm from space," he observed. "Research is tough. If you already knew what you were going to find out, you wouldn't need to do the research. Sure does help to start out with an educated guess."

We'd reached one of the lower corners of the facility. "Here's our longest-running research project." I pointed to a cluster of small stainless-steel pipes projecting slightly above the leaves and dirt. One of my former Ph.D. students, Arpad Vass—now a research scientist at Oak Ridge National Laboratory—had spent the past six years analyzing the cornucopia of chemicals given off by decaying bodies, I told Faust. He'd buried three bodies in this corner of the facility, running a grid of perforated pipes through the graves. To collect and analyze the chemicals, Arpad used a vacuum pump to draw gases out of the pipes and through a gas chromatograph–mass spectrometer.

"And what's he found, after six years?"

"A lot." I stooped down to disentangle a strand of Virginia creeper from one of the pipes. "I figured maybe he'd pick up thirty or forty different compounds, but so far he's identified more than five hundred. Interestingly, some of the most prevalent ones are carcinogenic: cancer-causing organic compounds like toluene and benzene. Things the EPA regulates as hazardous chemicals when they're used in factories or chemical plants."

"And is this basic research he's doing by analyzing these postmortem compounds, or does he have an application in mind?"

"Oh, very applied," I assured him. "He's recently developed a 'sniffer,' he calls it—a handheld instrument that looks a lot like a metal detector—to locate buried bodies and clandestine graves. Just a couple months ago, he used it to help me with an old case—we found the bones of a soldier who'd been killed and buried in Oak Ridge back in 1945, during the Manhattan Project. He also used it on a modern case down in Florida—Caylee Anthony, the two-year-old who went missing in Florida. Arpad was able to show that the carpeting in the trunk of the car contained chemicals from a decaying human body."

"That reminds me of your electron-microscope case," he said. "Using high-tech science to solve real-world crimes and real-world problems. That's what I find most rewarding about my job. Well, that and the chance to fly that airplane every now and then."

I laughed. I liked Faust. He was funny, smart, and unpretentious.

I checked my watch. "Uh-oh. I need to get you to Engineering. You've got an eleven o'clock meeting there, don't you?" He nodded, so I steered him toward the gate and locked it behind us.

On the drive across the river to the main campus, I worked up my nerve. "Mind if I ask your advice about something?"

"My advice? Sure, ask away. Just remember, though, it's worth what you pay for it."

I hesitated, unsure how much background to give. "I have a colleague here," I began. "A pathologist—the medical examiner, actually. He suffered traumatic injuries to his hands recently. He lost the thumb, index finger, and middle finger of his right hand and all of his left hand."

He nodded. "I remember reading about this. Gamma-radiation burns, wasn't it?"

"Yes." I was surprised; he really *had* done his homework.

"That's a shame. Devastating blow for a physician. Would've been worse if he were a surgeon, though. At least he can't do any harm to his patients, since they're already dead." He made a face. "Ouch, that sounded harsh. I apologize. What I meant—"

I waved the apology aside. "It's okay. I've had the same thought a dozen times. I've even thought, 'Too bad he's not a psychiatrist. A psychiatrist could get by without hands.'"

"Could be," he said, "but every psychiatrist I know is already pretty strange. Can you imagine how it would mess with the mind of a shrink to lose his hands?"

I tried picturing it—a Freudian analyst on his own couch, staring at the empty cuffs of his tweed jacket—and in spite of myself I laughed. "We are both bad men," I said. "Both going to hell."

"If a little gallows humor is a burning offense, we'll have lots of company," he responded. "So tell me about your pathologist friend and about the sort of advice you think I might be able to give."

"One of the options he's considering is a prosthesis called the i-Hand," I said. "A bionic hand. If you take off the rubber skin, you can see a metallic version of bones through the fingers. They're made of some high-tech engineered plastic, and they're rigged to flexors and extensors and little motors that mimic the tendons in a living hand."

He nodded. "I'm familiar with the i-Hand," he said. "It's a good prosthesis, but I do have one thing against it."

My heart sank on Garcia's behalf. "What do you have against it?"

"The fact that we don't hold the patents on it." He laughed. "Kidding. Mostly. But myoelectric prostheses are a multimillion-dollar revenue stream, and the embarrassing truth is, this itty-bitty company got out of the gate ahead of OrthoMedica with a better product, and we're still playing catch-up." His expression sobered. "It's not just about money, of course—it's about need. Worldwide, thousands of people every year lose hands and feet and arms and legs. Did you know that in some parts of the world—Afghanistan, for instance—kids are used as human land-mine detectors? Taliban commanders send kids through areas they think might be mined, and if the kids don't get blown up, the soldiers know the area's clear. If the kids do get blown up, the soldiers send more kids through, till they've set off all the mines." He shook his head sadly. "A bionic hand or a carbon-fiber leg isn't an option for those kids in Afghanistan," he went on. "They get a cauterized stump and a crutch, maybe a hook in place of their hand, if they're lucky." He gave his head a harder shake. "But your friend Dr. Garcia, he's got some pretty good options, and the i-Hand might just be the best, at least for now."

"Why 'for now'—will his options be better later?"

"Sure," he said. "Prosthetic technology's always advancing. Today's prostheses—including the i-Hand—are controlled by consciously twitching various muscles in the arm. It works, but it's an extra step. Think about it: When you want to pick up a glass of water, you don't have to tell your muscles, 'Arm, extend. Now stop. Fingers and thumb, contract.' Your brain thinks, 'I want a drink,' and all the other steps follow automatically. Right now the Pentagon's putting a lot of R&D money into developing hands and arms that'll be wired into the brain like that. So a year or two from now . . ."

"Might be too long for Dr. Garcia to wait," I finished. "There's nothing else on the market now you'd recommend above the i-Hand?"

"For his left hand, that's about as good as it'll get. For his right, a toe-to-thumb transplant is probably the way to go. Have you heard of it?" I nodded. "It's an autograft, not an allograft—the toe comes from his own body, not a deceased donor's—so there's no risk of tissue rejection. And it doesn't burn any bridges to do the procedure, apart from making one of his feet look a little odd."

"But for his left hand, you'd recommend the i-Hand?" I pulled up in front of Engineering—housed in a modern building that put Anthropology's makeshift quarters to shame—where two of the Biomedical Engineering faculty awaited Faust at the curb.

He hesitated. "I'm not the doctor or the patient here, so I'm in no position to say. Any advice I offered would be worth exactly what you paid for it. Maybe less."

"But if you *were* the patient," I persisted, "what would you do, knowing what you know?"

"Knowing what I know?" He gave a slight, enigmatic smile as he opened the door and got out. "Knowing what I know, I'd get an i-Hand, and I'd get it pretty damn quick."

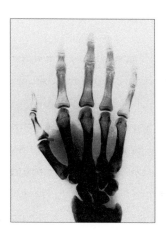

CHAPTER 10

banged shut, and thirty seconds later the second-floor door, just outside my office, noisily followed suit. The maintenance department still hadn't fixed the hydraulic mechanism, and my M&M's were long since gone.

This time the nearer slam was followed by a brisk knock on my door. Unlike the slam, the knock startled me. The identity of the two people in my doorway startled me even more. Angela Price was a supervisor in the Knoxville field office of the FBI, and Ben Rankin was an agent I knew from a case involving murder and corruption by officers in the Cooke County Sheriff's Office. Rankin's undercover investigation of a massive cockfighting ring in Cooke County had earned him the colorful nickname "Rooster," and it fit: He was a small man with a big strut, like a bantam fighting bird.

Rooster's boss and I had gotten off to a frosty start in the

Cooke County case. I'd contacted Price when it appeared that the sheriff might be shielding a murderer, but she initially treated me as a meddler. Our professional relationship later thawed, but it had never entirely warmed. I was all the more surprised, therefore, when she smiled as she reached out to shake my hand. "Dr. Brockton, so good to see you. I hope we're not catching you at a bad time."

I'd been just about to devour a sandwich, because I'd skipped breakfast and was feeling ravenous. The thought of postponing my lunch gave me a pang of disappointment that was nearly as sharp as my pangs of hunger. "It's a great time, Agent Price," I fibbed.

"Please," she said, "call me Angela."

I nearly laughed at the irony of that. Shortly after we'd met, I'd said almost the same thing to her: "You can call me Bill." Her response at the time had been a curt, "You can call me Special Agent Price."

I smiled and bowed slightly, acknowledging the compliment she was paying by finally allowing the first-name collegiality. Nevertheless, I remained apprehensive. "And what brings y'all deep into the bowels of Neyland Stadium today, Angela?" My fear was that they were bringing bad news about Isabella, or maybe unhappiness about the way I'd handled things in the Oak Ridge case. My stomach rumbled with a mixture of hunger and anxiety.

She held up a finger to pause the conversation, then eased my office door closed and spoke in a lower voice. "We're hoping you might be able to help us with an investigation." She smiled nervously.

I felt a measure of relief, and the next growl from my stomach was just plain hunger. "I'm always glad to help the Bureau," I said, and I meant it. "Is there something you need me to look at? A body? Some bones?"

"Not exactly," she said. Her nervous smile now gave way to a look of frank discomfort. "Actually, we need some bones and bodies *from* you."

I looked from her to Rankin and back again; neither of the agents seemed inclined to explain. "I'm not sure I follow," I said. "We've already planned this year's evidence-recovery class, and if I remember right, we're providing three bodies this time." Every spring, new members of FBI Evidence Recovery Teams from around the country came to the Body Farm for a week of training in unearthing buried bodies and finding scattered bones. "Are you talking about that, or do you need another training in addition?"

"No, it's not a training. It's more complicated than that." She looked at Rankin and nodded.

Rankin cleared his throat slightly. "Dr. Brockton, I know I don't need to tell you this," he began, "but the human body can be remarkably useful even after death."

"Indeed it can," I said. "It's kept me gainfully employed for decades now. And it's landed me in this lavish office." I made a sweeping gesture that encompassed the battered filing cabinets, the ancient desk, the filthy windows, and the grimy trusswork that supported the stadium.

"Good one." He smiled mirthlessly, then went back to his briefing. "There are roughly thirty thousand organ transplants every year in the U.S.—kidneys, hearts, lungs, liver, pancreas."

I couldn't resist tweaking him. "Me, I'm on the list for a brain transplant," I deadpanned.

This time he didn't even pretend to smile. Instead he fired back, "And who could be more deserving?" I had to laugh; he'd skewered me with my own joke. Price shot him a reproving look, though, so he got back to business. "Right. Of the thirty thousand organs transplanted, about three-fourths—roughly twenty-two thousand—come from deceased donors."

"Kinda hard for a living donor to give somebody a heart," I pointed out. Now Price shot the reproving look at me. "Sorry," I said. "Please go on. I'll quit interrupting."

"Thanks," he said. "As you probably know, the demand for donated organs far exceeds the supply. Over a hundred thousand people nationwide are on the waiting list for organ transplants; some of them will die before a matching donor is found for them. Almost half the kids who need transplants never get a matching donor in time."

For once I had a legitimate reason to interrupt. "There was a movie about that a few years ago, wasn't there? About a dad who takes everybody in a hospital hostage so he can force them to give his son a new heart?"

"Right. *John Q,* I think it was called. Kinda hokey, especially at the end, but they did a decent job of dramatizing the parents' anguish. So the point I'm making, in a roundabout way, is that the wait for an organ can be agonizing but the organ-transplant process itself—matching needy recipients with suitable donors through the Organ Procurement and Transplantation Network— is meticulous and rigorous. The donor and the recipient are scrupulously documented. It's illegal in the U.S. to buy, sell, or trade human organs for transplant. In short, human organs are closely monitored. That's *not* the case, though, with other forms of human tissue."

My stomach rumbled again, and I wished he hadn't just spent five minutes making a point that was really no more than throat clearing set to words. "You're talking now about corneas, tendons, and so on."

"Corneas, tendons, ligaments, blood vessels, skin, bone," he itemized. "There's very little oversight, especially in terms of where those tissues come from. The same is true, with all due respect, to donated bodies."

I felt my anxiety ratcheting up once more. Years before, a brief but intense political controversy had erupted when a Nashville television station reported that the bodies of low-income Vietnam veterans were being treated disrespectfully at the Body Farm. Nobody had told us that those particular men had been veterans; when we found out, we offered to send their bodies back to the Veterans Administration or to family members for military burials. A handful of state legislators proposed curtailing our postmortem research, but then a bunch of district attorneys rushed to defend the importance of our forensic work, so the storm blew over. I'd considered that issue long since dead, but perhaps it had merely been hibernating. I looked Price in the eye. "Is the FBI concerned about where we get our bodies for the Body Farm?"

"Not at all, Dr. Brockton. We have the utmost confidence in your program and in your professional and personal integrity. We're here because we hope you can help us bring down some people who are not as honest and ethical as you are."

"And how could I help you do that?"

She hesitated, but only for a second, and when I heard what she had to say, I wished she'd hesitated longer. I wished she'd hesitated forever, in fact. "By selling some of your bodies," she said. "On the black market."

I stared from Price's face to Rankin's. They stared back impassively. Finally I said, "That's unethical. Probably illegal."

"That's the point," she replied. "That's why we want you to do it."

"I'm sorry to be slow on the uptake," I said. "I don't, as a general principle, set out to break federal laws. What, exactly, are you asking me to do? And why?"

"We'd like you to help us run a sting," she said. "We've been building a case against a tissue bank—a company that receives bodies and then distributes the organs and tissues for transplants and medical research. The company's based in Newark, New Jersey; it's called Tissue Sciences and Services."

"Did you say it's a company? I thought all tissue banks were nonprofit organizations."

Price shook her head. "No, it's definitely a for-profit company. Emphasis on 'profit.' We have strong evidence that Tissue Sciences engages in fraud and conspiracy to obtain bodies and body parts, then profits illegally when it resells the cadavers or various tissues from them."

"So if you already have strong evidence, why not go ahead and bust them?"

"We were just about to," she said. "The lead agent in our Newark field office was writing up a criminal complaint against the company's president—a guy named Raymond Sinclair—when our key informant died."

"Did the informant die from being an informant, by any chance?"

Rankin shook his head. "He died from being overweight and underexercised. Massive heart attack." He shrugged slightly, then conceded, "It's possible he was experiencing some additional stress about this investigation."

I pressed. "Because . . . ?"

"Because we had enough evidence to charge him on several counts," he answered. "He was a target before he became an informant."

"So he was cooperating because you promised him a break?"

He shook his head again. "We never promise breaks. All we promised was that we'd tell the U.S. Attorney's Office how incredibly helpful he was."

I raised my eyebrows quizzically, but he didn't seem inclined to take the hint, so I put the question into words. "Who was this helpful fellow, and how'd he help before his untimely demise? Was he a disgruntled Tissue Sciences employee who squealed?"

He looked at Price and got another nod from her before answering. "No. The guy was the diener in the Anatomy Department of MacArthur School of Medicine, in Maryland. He prepped all the cadavers for the med students and faculty, and he ran the body-donation program. That meant he handled the intake and the disposition of every cadaver that came through the doors of the medical school."

"And how many cadavers came through the door?"

"Twenty-seven last year." He cocked his head. "How many'd you get last year, Doc?"

"A hundred thirty-five," I said.

He whistled. "That's a lot of bodies."

"Lots of people want to donate their body to science," I pointed out. "Partly that's because funerals have gotten so damn expensive, but mostly it's because people like the idea of doing some good after they die—helping train doctors or advancing medical research or forensic science. We're getting four or five times as many bodies now as we were just a few years ago. We're about to run out of places to put them."

His gaze sharpened. "So are you getting more bodies than you can handle these days?"

"We can always make room for an FBI agent or two," I joked. "In fact, I just happen to have donor forms here in this filing cabinet."

Rankin smiled and shook his head.

"It's true that we don't need a hundred thirty bodies a year for research," I said. "We don't have enough graduate students and faculty to do that many experiments. And our three-acre site is getting kinda crowded. And we're understaffed. It's not that we have too many bodies. We just don't have enough money or land."

He and Price exchanged a look. "I like it," he mused. "'We don't have too many bodies, we just don't have enough money.' What do you think?"

"Could be a good hook," said Price.

Suddenly I had a bad feeling: the feeling that I myself was about to become a tasty bit of shark bait.

"Before I say yes," I told Price, "I need to talk to a lawyer."

Her eyebrows shot up. "You want to talk to your *lawyer*?"

"Not my lawyer, UT's lawyer. Amanda Whiting, the general counsel—UT's top legal eagle. Before I can do something like this, I'd need to make sure the university knows and supports it."

Price shook her head. "Bureau policy is to keep a tight lid on our investigations," she said. "The fewer people in the loop, the less risk that something leaks out. I'd have real concerns about bringing people from the legal department into this."

"Not 'people,'" I countered, "one person. I'd have real concerns about *not* bringing her into this. Do you realize how bad it could look for UT if things go wrong?" She didn't answer, so I painted the picture for her. "If word got out that the Anthropology Department was selling donated bodies on the black market, that would do terrible damage. We could kiss most of our donations good-bye—not just body donations to Anthropology but financial donations to the entire university. A scandal like that could cost us millions of dollars, maybe tens of millions."

Price and Rankin made no move to respond.

"And then there's me," I added. "If I understand you right, the guy from the medical school who was selling off bodies and body parts was about to be indicted."

Price nodded reluctantly; she opened her mouth to speak, but I cut her off.

"Hang on, let me finish. The med-school guy was committing fraud, is that it? Altering donor charts or falsifying financial records to hide the fact that he was making a fortune off a post-mortem chop shop?"

"That's exactly what he was doing," she said. "He would indicate that a body was unsuitable for use by the school, report it as cremated, and then sell it to Tissue Sciences. He took cash under the table—seven thousand per body, and he admitted to selling thirty-one bodies over the past three years. He paid cash for a big boat and a Mercedes convertible. For a guy with no college degree and no formal medical training, he was living large."

"And you're hoping Tissue Sciences will offer me that same sort of deal? Big bucks for bodies? Payola for parts?"

She nodded. "Technically, this is still Newark's case, but if we can bring you in, a lot of the focus would shift to Knoxville, and Special Agent Rankin would serve as our lead agent. We'd begin gathering evidence here, starting with recordings of every conversation you have with Sinclair or anybody else at Tissue Sciences."

"You'd tap his phone lines?"

"Actually, what we do is ask you to record all your conversations with him," Rankin said. "We'd need a court order to do a wiretap, but in Tennessee, if one party to a conversation consents to recording the call—that would be you, we hope—it's legal to record it. So if you're willing, we'll attach a recorder to your office and home phone lines. All you have to do is hit a button when you get a call from the guy."

"What if he calls my cell phone?"

Rankin looked at Price, and she nodded, so he went on. "Actually, with your permission we can record your cell-phone conversations with him, too, by routing them through our engineering lab up in Quantico."

"So it gets you the same evidence as a wiretap, but you don't have to jump through the legal hoops to get it?"

"Pretty much," he conceded.

"And was your med-school diener recording his calls with this guy Sinclair?"

Rankin nodded.

"Any chance he made a deathbed warning call to Sinclair from some other phone?"

"Unlikely," he said. "We recorded a conversation they had only a few minutes before our source had the heart attack. Only other call he made before he died was to 911. He didn't have an opportunity to spill the beans. He was too busy dying."

"Any chance his heart attack was triggered by something other than fat and laziness? Maybe something somebody slipped into his coffee?" I thought of Leonard Novak, unsuspectingly swallowing the capsule that killed him. "Or into his vitamin pills?"

Rankin looked pained. "Also unlikely, but remotely possible."

"What does *that* mean?"

"No poisons showed up in the toxicology screen at his autopsy," he explained, "but his potassium level was abnormally high. And a massive dose of potassium can trigger a heart attack. But as I say, he was on the phone with Sinclair at Tissue Sciences shortly before he keeled over, and Sinclair talked like they'd be doing business for a long time."

"Maybe so," I pointed out, "but your snitch talked like that, too. Maybe they were both acting."

Rankin shrugged; there was no way to disprove that possibility. "Either way, Sinclair's a bad guy. Besides his med-school source, we think he's buying bodies from funeral homes and crematories. And we've got some indications he's buying kidneys from poor people overseas—living donors—then selling the organs to rich Americans and Europeans, patients who'll pay top dollar to jump to the front of the line for a transplant."

I felt my resistance weakening. "I can't help you bust him for that," I said, "since none of my donors have transplantable kidneys. But just for the sake of argument, let's say I'm willing to do this. What's going to set the wheels of the sting in motion? Do I just call up this guy Sinclair and say, 'Hey, the FBI tells me you need a new supply of black-market bodies'?"

"We'll figure something out," he said, "if you're game to help us. We have some experience in setting up undercover sting operations."

"Which brings me back to my big concern," I responded. "If things go the way you hope they'll go, I'll have the opportunity to betray the university's trust in me, betray donors' trust in the Body Farm, and break sundry laws of the state of Tennessee and the United States of America." I looked from him to Price. "You're sending me into battle unarmed and defenseless?"

"We prefer to think that we're protecting the integrity of the investigation," she countered. "I know, it's asking a lot."

"It's asking too much," I said. "I was accused of a murder a couple of years ago, and it damn near killed me to have my friends and colleagues think I was guilty. I want some reassurance that my reputation won't be ruined, and the university's image won't be destroyed, if I help you with this."

"And the Bureau's word isn't good enough?"

I looked out the grimy windows for guidance. The view reminded me where I stood, and where Anthropology stood, in the pecking order of the university. When I'd come to Knoxville to head the department, I'd been promised that the makeshift space in the stadium was only temporary and that we'd get bigger, better quarters soon. I'd also been promised, time and time again, that our shoestring budget would be increased. And yet, twenty years later, here I was, still stuck beneath the lavishly funded football program, still nickel-and-diming the bush-league budgets of my research facility and my faculty and graduate students. The university hadn't protected me when I'd been falsely accused of murder. Did I really need to worry so much about protecting the university?

I did, I decided. UT hadn't given me everything I'd hoped for, but along with the shoestring support and the makeshift space, it had given me the freedom and encouragement to build a program in forensic anthropology that was considered one of the best in the world. Without ever once questioning my sanity, UT had allowed me to haul in bodies by the hundreds and watch them rot, just for the sake of science. In a very profound way, the university was my home, and my colleagues and graduate students were my family. I had a responsibility to protect that home and family as best I could.

"Sorry," I said. "I won't do it. Not without bringing the general counsel into the loop."

Price's face was grim. "Dr. Brockton, I wish you'd reconsider. We will stand behind you if you help us," she assured me.

"No offense," I countered, "but if this backfires on me, and on UT, I want at least some paper trail here within the university that says I didn't crawl out on this limb without asking permission. Package deal: me and the general counsel."

"You're putting us in a very difficult position here," she said.

"Gee, welcome to the damn club, Angie. If the general counsel gives her blessing, I'm in. If not, I'm out. Simple as that. Sorry." Price and Rankin exchanged unhappy looks. "By the way, just so you know," I added, "if the general counsel says she'll keep it to herself, she will. Her word's as good as the Bureau's."

I expected them to leave. I figured they'd need to discuss my demand in private or run it up the chain of command. But Price didn't even look at Rankin before she spoke.

"Deal," she said, extending her hand.

I studied her eyes for a moment. I saw toughness, integrity, and maybe some weariness as we shook.

"The Bureau appreciates your help, Dr. Brockton."

"It's an honor to be asked, Special Agent Price. Even if I'm not thrilled about what you're asking me to do."

Suddenly someone rapped at the door. It opened before I had a chance to say, "Yes?"

"Dr. B.?" Miranda's head leaned around the edge. When she saw the FBI agents, she appeared startled. "Oops, sorry to interrupt. I'll come back later."

"You're not interrupting," said Price. "We were just leaving."

Miranda looked a question at me. "Please, come on in," I said. "I need to talk to you about something."

She stepped into the office, which now felt crowded and awkward. Her keen eyes swiftly sized up my two visitors: business suits, tidy haircuts, intelligent eyes, and the sort of physical confidence exuded by ex-marines and gifted athletes and skilled marksmen and FBI agents.

"This is my graduate assistant, Miranda Lovelady," I said. "She's the real brains of the outfit. Miranda, this is Special Agent Angela Price and Special Agent Ben Rankin."

She swapped quick handshakes with them, and then all three of them turned to me expectantly.

"Agent Price and Agent Rankin stopped by to ask me for some help." I sensed Price and Rankin tense up as I struggled for what to say next. "If they can get approval from headquarters, could we squeeze a few Knoxville field agents into the Evidence Recovery training?"

"No problem," she said.

Something in her eyes shifted ever so slightly, like the merest flicker in a steady candle flame, and I realized that lying to Miranda might prove to be the steepest challenge and the highest cost of the deal I'd just made with the FBI.

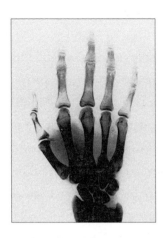

CHAPTER 11

THE VOICE IN MY EAR SOUNDED FRIENDLY, BUT IT HIT me like a fist.

"Hi, Doc, it's Jim Emert at ORPD."

Emert was the Oak Ridge detective who'd investigated the Novak murder. I hadn't spoken with Emert in weeks, not since shortly after Isabella had disappeared into the rushing maze of storm sewers beneath the city. That last conversation, two days after she vanished, had been brief. The detective had brought in a cadaver dog to search the tunnels, and the dog, Emert told me, had come up empty-handed, or, more precisely, empty-nosed. I knew the dog's track record at finding corpses, and it was impressive, so if he'd failed to detect death in the sewer, I felt pretty sure Isabella had escaped. What I felt unsure about was whether to be dismayed or relieved.

Part of me—the part that held fairly old-fashioned notions of right and wrong, of law and order—was frustrated and disappointed that the woman who had killed Leonard Novak and maimed Eddie Garcia appeared to be getting away. But another part of me—the part that felt compassion for the way her family's lives had been shattered by the dropping of the atomic bomb during World War II—figured she'd already suffered for years and would continue to suffer as long as she lived. She'd expressed anguish at the injury she caused to Garcia's hands, and she herself had sustained radiation burns to her own hands as well, though hers were less severe than Eddie's. Finally, although I was reluctant to admit it even to myself, my judgment was clouded by the fact that Isabella and I had made love once.

"Hey, Jim, what's up?" I hoped I sounded more casual than I felt. I had never told Emert—nor anyone else, for that matter—that I'd slept with Isabella. "Am I about to read headlines about a high-profile arrest in a bizarre Oak Ridge murder?"

"Not unless our friends at the FBI have made a breakthrough they haven't told me about," he said. "But there is something I think you should know. We've found something really interesting."

"Tell me."

"I'd rather show you," he said. "It's short notice, I know, but is there any chance you could head over this direction on the spur of the moment?"

"I'm on my way," I answered, scrambling to my feet. "I'll be in Oak Ridge in half an hour. Should I meet you at the police department?"

"No. Meet me at the Alexander Inn." The words sent a chill through me.

Thirty minutes later I turned in to the driveway of the boarded-up, run-down Alexander Inn, feeling as if I'd come eerily full circle. The inn was where the Novak case had begun, when I'd cut the elderly physicist's body from the scummy ice of a long-neglected swimming pool. Now, two months later, the pool was drained, its cracking walls and floor coated with slime in shades of black and green and brown. The building itself seemed to have aged by decades during the past two months. Sixty-five years earlier, the stately hotel, with its broad veranda and homey rocking chairs, had played host to the leading scientists of the Manhattan Project. Physicist Robert Oppenheimer, the father of the Bomb, had stayed at the Alexander during his wartime visits to Oak Ridge; so had Enrico Fermi, whose primitive atomic reactor under the stadium at the University of Chicago had produced the world's first controlled chain reaction. Ernest Lawrence, inventor of the cyclotron—harnessed to separate uranium fuel for the Hiroshima bomb—had likewise stayed at the Alexander.

Now, six and a half decades after Hiroshima, the historic hotel was crumbling virtually before my eyes. Glancing up at the white-columned façade, I noticed that several letters of the hotel's name had dropped off the building since I'd last seen it. ALEXANDER INN had now been reduced to ALE AND I. It was still possible to read the sign, because the blasted and blistered paint on the façade was less blasted and less blistered where it had been protected, until recently, by the missing letters. But the entire structure was one burning match away from irreversible destruction.

Surprisingly, I didn't see any ORPD vehicles parked in front of the hotel or beside the swimming pool. Then, glancing behind the dilapidated structure, I spotted several police cars, a crime-lab van, and an armored truck labeled SWAT TEAM parked near the back of the property. As I rumbled across fissured asphalt toward the vehicles, my eyes beheld a ghastly sight: the head of Detective Jim Emert rested, neck down, on a platter on the ground.

That at least was how it looked for a moment. Drawing nearer, I saw that a slight rise in the ground had played a trick on my eyes: What appeared to be a platter was in fact the rim of a manhole, seen edge-on. As I parked and got out of the truck, Emert climbed from the opening and walked toward me.

I reached out to shake the detective's hand, but he shook his head instead. As he did, a yellow-and-black headlamp on his forehead swiveled back and forth. "You really don't want to shake hands with me right now," he said, holding up his palms for me to inspect. He was right, I didn't: The purple gloves he wore were virtually black with sewer grime.

Half a dozen SWAT-team officers, in black fatigues and Kevlar vests, clustered near the armored vehicle. On the ground to one side lay helmets and what I took to be night-vision goggles. The men looked relaxed, though several of them held automatic rifles dangling from one hand, as casually as I might hold a hip bone or a laser pointer. With their combat-grade weaponry and uniforms, they resembled soldiers more than police officers. "Looks like you came loaded for bear," I said to Emert, "but it also looks like maybe you called off the hunt."

"We got a call from the guy who lives up there on the hill." He pointed. "He saw a woman climbing into the sewer, and he wondered if it might be our gal Isabella. I called our friends here for backup, and at the very moment these guys were pointing M16s at the manhole, out popped this skinny twelve-year-old boy with long hair. The kid let out a scream, which could've gotten him blown away. Lucky for him the guys with the guns don't have the hair-trigger problem that I have." Emert shook his head as he contemplated the near tragedy. "The kid peed his pants, but all things considered, he got off mighty lucky."

"Sounds like it."

"That's when it started to get interesting. The kid was sure he was in big trouble—he didn't know we were looking for someone else—and he started blubbering right away about how he wasn't the one who did it."

"Did what?"

"Exactly. 'Tell me what you didn't do, kid,' I said. 'Didn't put all that stuff down there,' he said. 'All what stuff?' I asked him, so he took me down there and showed me. Just like I'm about to show you." Emert sized up my khaki pants and button-down shirt. "You keep coveralls in the back of your truck, don't you, Doc?"

I nodded.

"Why don't you suit up, and let's go take a look."

I wormed into a jumpsuit and pulled on a pair of disposable gloves—mine were green, not purple—and joined Emert beside the mouth of the manhole. I'd brought a flashlight from the truck, but Emert frowned at it. "Here, try this instead," he said, offering me the headlamp. "So you can use both hands going down the ladder." I tucked the flashlight in the hip pocket of my jumpsuit, then tugged the lamp's elastic headband into place. Through my hair I could feel that the fabric was damp with sweat, or storm-sewer water, or both.

"Thanks," I said, wiggling the light to even out the tension in the headband. "How do I look?"

He studied me. "Very natty," he pronounced in a dreadful British accent. "The yellow and black of the strap complement the olive drab jumpsuit splendidly." He paused and made a face. "But . . ."

"But?"

"Well, you might consider accessorizing with an M16."

"If I did, would I look as studly as those guys?"

"Oh, more studly," he said. "Ever so much more studly." He dropped the accent. "You ready to climb down?"

"Sure." But as I swung a leg down into the opening and groped with my right foot for the first rung, I suddenly felt anything but sure. "You know, the last time I was in this position, things didn't turn out so well for me." The night I'd lost Isabella in the sewer system, I'd attempted to climb out of a manhole at a dead end in a tunnel, but when I reached the top rung of the ladder—a series of steel brackets set into the mortar of the sewer's brickwork—it had snapped off in my hand. I'd fallen six or eight feet into icy water, cracking my head on the bottom of the pipe. "I hope this ladder's stronger. Or the concrete's softer than last time."

From the darkness below me came a familiar voice. "Plenty of padding down here if you fall," said Art Bohanan. Art's fingerprint expertise had been requested in the Novak murder, so it wasn't surprising he'd been called back to Oak Ridge to help collect whatever new forensic evidence Emert was about to show me.

Gripping the metal rim of the opening, I tested the rung with my weight—it felt solid enough—and then eased my left foot onto the second rung. Ten rungs later I was standing beside Art Bohanan at the bottom of a small, conical room, roughly six feet across. "Fancy seeing you here," I said to Art. "Good of KPD to let you spend so much quality time in another jurisdiction."

Art shrugged, his headlamp bobbing slightly as he did. "They agreed to let me help with the Novak case. This is still the Novak case. And who could pass up a chance to spend a day in such a beautiful setting?" He played his light over the bricks and tendrils of cobwebs, drawing a laugh from me.

"Coming down," Emert called from above. Art and I backed away from the base of the ladder to give him room, and my shoulders brushed against the grime of the arched vault. Once Emert was down, the room felt crowded. He turned to me. "How's your back?"

"Fine," I said.

"Not for long." He chuckled. "Walk this way," he added, bending over and half crouching. Two pipes, each just big enough for me to wriggle into and get stuck inside, fed into the sewer junction on the uphill side; a larger pipe led out the downhill side, and Emert duck-walked into this one and disappeared.

"Age before beauty," said Art, motioning me ahead. Copying Emert's awkward posture, I hunched forward and ducked into the tunnel. With my face angled down, the headlamp illuminated only a small oval of pipe just in front of my feet, and I couldn't tell how much clearance I had between my head and the top of the pipe. Fumbling in the hip pocket of my jumpsuit, I wrestled the flashlight free and switched it on. I didn't much like what I saw. The pipe, roughly four feet in diameter, was corrugated steel—a series of concentric rings sloping downward. In the distance the pipe appeared to narrow and constrict. I realized that was just an illusion, since I saw Emert waddling onward, but the effect was disconcerting, as if we were voluntarily entering the descending colon of some immense metallic organism. Strings of dirty cobwebs dangled from the top and sides of the tunnel, though most of the ones hanging from above had been sheared off, doubtless by Emert and Art. Here and there, stray brackets and bolts projected from the roof, and I wished for a hard hat. Structurally, the pipe seemed to be in remarkably good condition, considering it had been laid in the early 1940s, when the U.S. Army had hastily built the top-secret atomic-bomb complex in Oak Ridge. As I took my first steps forward, though, I realized that it was only the upper parts of the pipe that remained strong; the metal underfoot felt thin and spongy, and I'd gone only a few feet before the metal gave way and my boot plunged downward several inches, scraping through a jagged fringe of rust.

"Duck!" Art called. I dropped my head just in time to avoid whacking it on an angle bracket jutting from the top of the pipe. "So is this the size pipe you chased Isabella into that night?"

"Lord, no," I said. "That one was twice this big. I could stand up straight in that one—hell, I could have jumped up and down. I probably wouldn't have followed her into something like this. Over by the library, where she went in, it's newer, concrete pipe, probably only ten or twenty years old. This stuff here ought to be on the National Register of Historic Sewers. I wouldn't be surprised to find shards of Roman pottery somewhere along here." My ear snagged a cobweb that Art and Emert had somehow missed.

"Yo, guys," Emert called from somewhere ahead. He'd disappeared around a bend or a drop in the tunnel—that, or he'd been digested by the beast we were inside. "We're burning daylight. Are y'all sightseeing back there?" Rather than echoing, as I'd have expected, the detective's voice sounded muffled, as if smothered by the weight of the earth above us.

"Coming!" yelled Art. "We just stopped to check out some dinosaur bones."

The slope of the tunnel increased sharply, and I wondered how difficult it would be to retrace our steps back uphill. Art and Emert had already done it, so clearly it was possible, but if the pipe had been wet and slippery rather than dry, the footing would have been perilous. After thirty or forty steep yards, the gradient flattened out, and not far beyond that the tunnel seemed to dead-end at a brick wall. Emert was nowhere to be seen. As I neared the brick wall, I saw why: The tunnel fed into a vertical shaft, easily twice the height of the manhole we'd entered. "Crap," I called down to Emert, who awaited us at the bottom. "You didn't tell me we were going spelunking."

"I wasn't sure you'd come if I did. Art said the two of you got trapped in a cave once."

"We did." The memory still sent me to the edge of panic. "A guy set off a stick of dynamite to cause the tunnel to collapse. Art and I found a side tunnel, but it necked down so tightly I got stuck—couldn't move, couldn't even breathe. Art finally shoved me through the bottleneck just as I was running out of air. My ribs and back were sore for weeks. I still have nightmares about that sometimes."

"I'm guessing my back and butt will be sore for weeks from walking in this bent-over crouch," Emert groused. "But we're almost there." He stooped and ducked into the tunnel that continued downhill from the base of the shaft. I followed, and after a short distance I saw him straighten up. Moments later I emerged from the tunnel into a square chamber. "Damn," I said as I took in my surroundings. Unlike the sounds in the tunnels, the word reverberated and hung in the musty air.

I was standing in a space nearly the size of the living room in my house, where half a dozen four-foot pipes converged and a pair of larger pipes, each five or six feet in diameter, exited on the far side. The ceiling must have been six feet high, for it allowed the three of us to stand upright, though I noticed that Emert—the tallest of us—had to spread his feet widely in order to keep from bumping his head. The room was lit by portable, battery-powered work lights, whose clusters of LED bulbs cast a cool, bluish-white light on the grimy concrete surfaces. The floor of the room was covered with layers of sand and mud, laid down and then scoured out and laid down again, sculpted and channeled by sediment-laden storm water.

The room's size was what initially startled me, but its contents were what truly astonished me. A folding camp cot was nestled against one wall of the room; a puffy down sleeping bag lay crumpled on top, the bag's red vivid against the blue of the cot's taut nylon mesh. At the head of the cot, on a plastic milk crate, stood a kerosene lamp and a box of matches; at the foot was a wire-mesh wastebasket, half filled with empty cans and bottles and food wrappers. "My God," I said, "someone's been living here."

"No shit, Sherlock." Emert chuckled, obviously pleased that he'd managed to surprise and impress me.

"Isabella?"

"Don't know," said Art. "Looks like plenty of prints on bottles and cans in the trash—the lamp, too, thanks to the kerosene and the soot—but it's better to bag everything and take it back to the lab, instead of trying to fume it here."

Emert caught my eye and pointed to the opposite wall—the one where we'd entered. Midway along the wall, between our pipe and another, a pair of plastic milk crates supported an unfinished pine plank, and on this plank stood an elaborately carved wooden artifact. "Get a load of the pagoda," he said.

"It's not exactly a pagoda," I corrected, "but close. I saw a presentation about these a few years ago by a cultural anthropologist from Asia. It's called a *kamidana,* if I remember right, and it's a Shinto shrine to the gods of the ancestors. You find them in a lot of Japanese homes."

Arranged on the plank in front of the shrine was a cluster of small glass bottles. I knelt and shone my flashlight into them and saw that they contained rice, salt, wheat, and what I guessed to be dried tea berries—traditional Shinto offerings to the gods. Emert played the beam of his light on the wall above the *kamidana,* where a Japanese symbol reached nearly to the ceiling. The black paint was fresh and bold; the concrete had obviously been cleaned shortly before the paint had been brushed on.

The room suddenly exploded with light. "Jesus H.," snapped Emert in the general direction of Art, whom I could no longer see. "Couldn't you have warned us before using the flash?"

"Sorry," said Art. "I didn't mean to take the picture yet. I was just trying to check the focus, but I guess I pushed the shutter all the way down."

"Man," grumped Emert. "I thought for a second there that Oak Ridge had just been vaporized."

"Really sorry," Art repeated. "But now that you're already blinded, let me take a couple more, just to be sure. We can send it to a translator and find out what it means."

"I know what it means," I said as I covered my eyes to shield them from the flash. "I've seen that symbol once before, on a pendant, and the woman wearing it told me what it meant. It's the Japanese symbol for 'remembrance.' Isabella wore it around her neck."

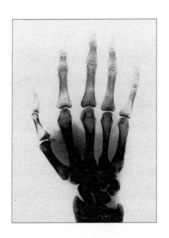

CHAPTER 12

Bohanan. A trash can appeared to have exploded there in the forensic lab. Empty cans and scraps of food wrappers covered every table and countertop in the room. The lab room smelled like an untidy teenager's room, one where pizza crusts and apple cores have accumulated under the bed for a week or two.

Art was bent over the red sleeping bag we'd hauled from the underground room. The bag was spread flat on a large piece of white paper, and Art was methodically coating the bag's entire surface with overlapping strips of clear evidence tape. He laid the last strip in place just as I entered, then began peeling the tape off the bag as a single patchwork sheet. Holding a section of the tape up to a lamp on the table, he studied the fuzz and fibers stuck to the adhesive. "Looks like some black hairs," he said. "We'll compare them to the ones we found in her house, but I'm betting they match. If we've got follicles on any of these and any of those, we can do a DNA comparison." Loosely wadding the tape, he dropped it into a plastic five-gallon bucket filled with water. The water-soluble tape quickly softened; once it had dissolved entirely, Art would strain the water to collect all the hairs and fibers.

On one corner of a table, clumped on a tray, I noticed several wads of dirty cotton gauze. Beneath the grime were crusted, reddish brown stains. "That looks like blood to me," I said.

"Looks like blood to the black light, too," Art observed. "Take a gander—the light's on the counter there." I held the portable ultraviolet lamp over the gauze, and the stains darkened; if not for the ambient light in the room, I knew, they'd appear completely black. I couldn't help wincing as I thought of Isabella's fingers, seared into open wounds—not as bad as Garcia's, but still serious—by the radiation source she'd handled before feeding it to Novak.

I surveyed the assortment of empty bottles, cans, and food wrappers. "Anything that indicates when she bought any of these items or when she consumed them?"

"Not that I've found so far," he said. "None of this stuff was perishable—bottled water, canned tuna fish, dried fruit— so there's no pull date, the way there'd be on a jug of milk or a pound of ground beef. Some of this stuff has a shelf life that's measured in decades. Look at this unopened pack of trail mix— 'Best when consumed by July 2017.' California might have slid into the ocean by then, but these nuts and raisins will still be lip-smacking good." He laughed. "The most interesting thing is that, though." He pointed to a small, wandlike object of white plastic, half hidden beneath a Hershey bar wrapper.

At first glance I thought it was a digital fever thermometer, but looking closer I realized the shape wasn't quite right; it was about as long and wide as a tongue depressor, but considerably thicker. "What is it?"

"Look but don't touch," he said. "Here's some tweezers."

With the tip of the tweezers, I slid the candy-bar wrapper aside for an unobstructed look, but I still couldn't tell what I was seeing. "Accu-Clear," read a word in small blue letters. To the left of the word was an oval-shaped indentation in the plastic, and within the indentation were two small cutout windows. One of the windows, an oval, was bisected by a crisp magenta line on a white background. The other opening, a small rectangle, also showed a line, a fuzzier, paler pink. "I still don't know what it is."

"Flip it over and read what's on the back."

Gingerly I grasped the object by the edges and turned it. This side was printed with instructions in the same blue ink. "Hold for five seconds in urine stream," read the first line. "Urine stream?" I asked.

"It's a pregnancy test, dummy."

A small illustration on the back depicted the two small cutout windows, complete with the colored lines I'd seen on the other side. The caption beside this illustration explained what the pair of lines meant.

The lines meant my life had just turned upside down. Unless someone else had taken the test, Isabella was pregnant.

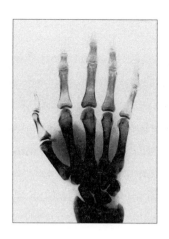

CHAPTER 13

"JESUS," SAID MIRANDA, "SHE'S ON THE LAM AND SHE'S knocked up to boot?" It was the morning after I'd seen the pregnancy-test kit in Art's lab, and I'd dropped by the bone lab when I first arrived on campus. I'd had a bad night of it, so I was eager to get out of bed and onto campus, and I'd been relieved to see Miranda's car parked beside the stadium when I arrived. When I walked into the lab, she was checking her Facebook page on the computer, but now—when I told her of Isabella's pregnancy—she closed the window on the screen and gave me full attention. Suddenly her eyes widened and she clapped a hand to her mouth. "Holy crap, Dr. B. Oh, my God. It's your baby, isn't it? Oh my God, oh my God, oh my *God*."

I shrugged miserably. "I don't know. It seems so far-fetched in so many ways, but then again, she doesn't—didn't?—seem like the sort to sleep around." I shook my head. "Then again, what the hell do I know about what sort she is? She killed a man to avenge the bombing of Nagasaki; clearly she's a bit unhinged. For all I know, she might've slept with a dozen other men in the past few months." But even as I was saying it, I knew it wasn't true.

"When you say 'other men,' I assume you mean besides you. I *knew* you were sleeping with her," she said, with what sounded like a mix of vindication and disapproval.

"Slept," I corrected miserably. "Just once."

"And am I right in thinking that maybe, just possibly, the topic of protection did not . . . um, arise, before or during the doing of the deed?"

"Alas, you are correct," I said. "Things happened pretty quick that night. I think we both got swept away."

"Swept away? Swept *away*? What are you, sixteen years old? Jesus, Dr. B., this isn't the Age of Aquarius, it's the Age of HIV. And herpes, not to mention—*duh*—unplanned pregnancy."

"You're right, of course. But you know what, Miranda? It's easy to be right in hindsight. Haven't you ever been wrong—wrong and headlong—in the heat of the moment?"

"Not since undergraduate—" She stopped midsentence, and her cheeks reddened. "Okay, okay, I see your point. But *fuck*, Dr. B." She snorted. "Oh, wait, you already did that, didn't you?" I was not amused, and she could tell. "Sorry. I don't mean to make light of your distress. But *fuck*, Dr. B.—you had sex with a murderer."

"I know that now," I protested, "but I didn't know it then. I mean, I knew I was having sex with her. But I didn't know she was a murderer. Murderess. Whichever."

"I prefer the term 'crazed killer,' actually," she said. "But don't let me sway you one way or another." She studied me, her face suddenly serious. "So if Isabella got pregnant after being exposed to gamma radiation, does that complicate things medically? Isn't there a big risk of birth defects?"

I shook my head. "I looked that up yesterday, and I don't think so. Handling the source burned her fingers—just like it singed your fingertips and cooked Eddie's hands—but apparently it wouldn't endanger a baby who was conceived a week or two later."

"Well, thank heaven for small favors," Miranda responded. "Still, if it's your baby, that's pretty heavy stuff. How are you doing with that?"

"I don't honestly know," I said. "I can't even imagine it. There might be a baby on the way that I've fathered, with a woman who's wanted by the police and the FBI? I have a grown son, Miranda. I have two grandsons. I don't know this woman. I don't even know where she is. And if I did, I'd have to turn her in."

"Wow. Makes worrying about a dissertation topic seem like small potatoes."

"What do I do about this, Miranda?"

She shrugged. "What *can* you do? She's a fugitive. It's not like you can get together and discuss the situation over coffee at Starbucks. I mean, if the FBI can't find her, you probably won't be able to. So unless she surfaces, I don't see how you can do anything except wait."

"But she's in trouble—deep trouble—and she needs medical care for her hands, and she needs prenatal care for the baby. For *my* baby. Jesus. What a mess."

"It is a mess," she agreed. She paused, looking uncomfortable, then added, "So . . . um, Dr. B.? Is there somebody else you can talk to about this? Because I'm probably not the best person. A therapist, maybe? Or your son?"

I didn't tell her that I was already talking to a therapist. She was right, of course, to feel uncomfortable about the conversation. It had been inappropriate to unburden myself to one of my students, even one with whom I'd worked for years, almost as an equal. "I'm sorry, Miranda. That was inconsiderate of me. You're right. I'll talk to Jeff."

Leaving the bone lab, I avoided the stairs that led up one flight to the departmental office. Instead I took a right, out the door at the bottom of the stairwell, and then skirted the base of the stadium on the one-lane service road that threaded between the girders and the columns. The day was chilly, and the cold felt good on my face for the two-minute walk to the north end zone. There I closed my door and dialed a call.

But it was not my son I called—it was the Oak Ridge Police Department, and I was pretty sure the call wasn't going to make me feel better.

"AND YOU DON'T WANT TO tell me what this is about before I call the feds?" Jim Emert sounded both intrigued and unhappy.

"Not really," I said. "I'd rather tell you and Thornton at the same time." Thornton—Special Agent Charles "Chip" Thornton—was assigned to the FBI's Weapons of Mass Destruction Directorate. When Novak had been killed by a radiation source, the Bureau feared that it was the work of terrorists. Thornton had been sent down to Tennessee to head the investigation.

Emert sighed. "Dr. Bill Brockton, man of mystery. Hang on a second. I'm putting you on hold while I conference Thornton in. If I lose you, I'll call you right back." I heard a click, then silence. A minute passed, then a couple more. I'd just about decided I'd been disconnected when the phone clicked again. "Doc, are you still there?"

"Yes, I'm here."

"Special Agent Thornton?"

"Yeah, Chip here. Hello, Doc."

"Hi, Chip. How's life in our nation's capital?"

"I miss Tennessee. I got spoiled down there."

"You know where to find us." I hesitated, unsure how to begin the discussion that I'd requested. "You guys still beating the bushes for Isabella?"

"We are. Nothing but leaves and branches so far, unfortunately. We'd thought she might turn up in Baton Rouge or Shreveport, since she grew up in Louisiana, but no trace of her there so far. Emert says they found a room in the Oak Ridge storm-sewer system where she holed up for at least a few days."

"Incredible," I said. "She must have stashed the food and stuff there before she killed Novak, in case she needed to lie low." I was stalling, I realized. "Did Jim tell you there were bloody bandages in the trash they found in the room?"

"He did," said Thornton. "He sent me an inventory of everything the forensic techs recovered from the scene."

I couldn't stall any longer. "Then you know she's pregnant. Or probably is. Or was."

"Yeah," he said. "Puts an interesting twist on things, doesn't it?"

The line went quiet. They were both waiting for me, the one who'd requested the conference call, to continue. "So," I began, "about that interesting twist . . ." I foundered, but neither one seemed inclined to help me out. "I need to tell you guys that I slept with Isabella. I'm probably the one who got her pregnant."

"Damn, Doc," said Emert.

"Go on," prompted Thornton.

"It was just once," I said. "A couple of weeks before we found out she was the one who'd killed Novak. She'd helped me find the place where the soldier's body was buried back in 1945. I . . . I *liked* her. She came over to my house one night. . . ."

"I know," said Thornton.

"What?" said Emert.

"What?" I echoed. "You know? You knew? How?"

"We had you under surveillance," he said.

"You *what*? Why the hell did you have me under surveillance?"

"Christ, Doc," said Emert. "Could it be because you were having an affair with a deranged killer?"

"Good grief, don't be stupid, Emert," said Thornton cheerfully. "You think we knew she was a deranged killer but decided to let the Doc get a little nooky before we arrested her? You think Dr. Brockton was weeks ahead of the Bureau and Oak Ridge's finest in solving the crime?"

"Okay," said the detective testily, "so why *did* you put him under surveillance?"

"Because we thought he might be at risk. Novak was dead from radiation exposure, Dr. Garcia was badly injured, and Dr. Brockton and his assistant were also exposed. Hell, Emert, *you* were exposed—we thought *you* might be at risk, too."

"So why didn't you put me under surveillance?" badgered the detective.

"Maybe we did," said Thornton.

"Shit," said Emert again. "Can I just say for the record that I'm feeling totally out of the loop here, in every way possible?"

"Sure you can," said Thornton, still cheerful. "Nothing personal, though. The Novak case was, and is, a very high-profile case. We put a lot of resources into it, especially early on, when we thought there might be a threat of terrorism with nuclear materials. There are all sorts of avenues we've pursued that we haven't felt the need to disclose to local law enforcement."

"Excuse me, guys," I said. "Fascinating as I find this juris-dictional discussion, and loath as I am to return to my personal shame, I'm wondering if you need to ask me more questions. Chip, since you already knew that Isabella had spent the night at my house, had you already figured out what I was calling about today?"

"I had a pretty good idea," he said. "Soon as I saw 'home preg-nancy test, positive,' on the inventory of stuff from the sewer, the lightbulb went on."

"How come you never asked me about that night she spent at my house? You knew about it months ago."

"At first it seemed like none of our business—even though we were keeping an eye on you. When we're doing surveillance, we learn a lot of details about people's personal lives. We had no idea Isabella was relevant to the Novak case. We thought she was just a random civilian. And, by the way, a totally hot librarian. By the time we realized she'd killed Novak, she was on the run. And she didn't run toward you when she ran. She ran away from you. It's not like you've aided and abetted."

"So you're not thinking I've done something wrong."

"Sexually risky, yeah. Criminally wrong? No. Not unless there's something else you haven't told us."

"No, that's it. What now?"

"We keep looking," Thornton said. "We're already check-ing medical clinics for female patients who came in with burned hands. Now we'll start checking for prenatal care, too. But there are a hell of a lot of clinics in the United States. Meanwhile, I trust you'll let me or Emert know if she contacts you."

"I'm not holding my breath," said Emert. "Nobody ever tells me anything."

"Good grief, Emert, don't be a baby," said Thornton. "I gotta go. Doc, give my regards to Price and Rankin." He clicked off, leaving me to wonder how much he knew about their body-brokering investigation—and how much they knew about my personal but not-so-private life.

"Hey, Doc?" Emert was still on the line. "Who are Price and Rankin?"

"Can't tell you," I said, and hung up.

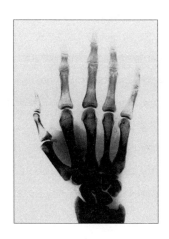

CHAPTER 14

BURT DEVRIESS'S LAW OFFICE OCCUPIED SOME OF the swankiest real estate in downtown Knoxville: the twentieth floor of Riverview Tower, a sleek skyscraper—tall enough to scrape Knoxville's sky at least—perched on the bluff near the headwaters of the Tennessee River. The streamlined oval building was clad in alternating horizontal bands of green glass and stainless steel. Early in our acquaintance, as we'd walked back to his office from a court hearing, Grease had nudged me and pointed to the building. "Just look at it, Doc," he'd said, "all green and silver. The color of money. No wonder I love it."

Today I was the only passenger in the elevator, which whisked me up without stopping, the air in the shaft whistling slightly during the ascent. DeVriess had phoned to ask if I wanted to drop by for an interesting tidbit about the Willoughby case. His call caught me on my way back to campus from my session with Dr. Hoover. I was still feeling antsy and anxious, so I was grateful for the distraction of an errand and an inside scoop.

I was also glad to have occasion to see DeVriess's assistant, Chloe Matthews, again. I'd first met Chloe a year earlier, the afternoon I'd walked in off the street, the taste of freshly swallowed pride rising bitter in my throat, and asked DeVriess to defend me against a murder charge. Chloe had greeted me that dark day with a welcoming smile and a warm handshake. I'd been grateful then, and I was grateful still.

She was on the phone when I walked in, but she flashed that same smile at me and held up a finger to tell me she'd be with me momentarily. As the call dragged on through several of Chloe's attempts to wrap it up, she rolled her eyes and made the universal hand-puppet motion for "yak, yak, yak" with her right hand. "Sorry," she said as she finally hung up with a head shake. "My mother, bless her heart, calling to complain about how long *her* mother keeps her on the phone. So now I'm complaining to you, and you can complain to Mr. DeVriess about me."

"And then Burt can phone your grandmother to gripe about me," I teased. "How've you been? And how's the speed dating working out?" The last time I'd seen Chloe, she was about to go on a speed date, a round-robin lunch gathering where single people spent five or ten minutes auditioning a series of other single people.

"Utter disaster," she laughed. "It took me twenty years to get over junior high school, and one hour of speed dating undid two decades of progress and self-esteem. I clammed up and turned into a total geek again."

I found it hard to imagine the attractive, articulate, and confident woman in front of me as a geek.

"Did you ever try it?" she asked.

"Actually, I did look into it once," I confessed, "but I got rejected even before I got in the door. Too old."

"You? Too old? No way," she scoffed.

"Seriously. You have to be under fifty. I've missed my chance by a year or three."

"Well, that's just speed dating's loss," she said. "Anyhow, I think Match.com or Facebook would be better for you. Those sites have zillions of women in their forties and fifties, and I'm sure they'd be fighting over you tooth and nail." She frowned. "The problem is, online dating can turn into a full-time job."

For an insane split second, I considered saying, "I'm about to be really busy raising an out-of-wedlock baby I accidentally fathered," but instead I opted for, "Heavens, Chloe, I can barely handle the job I've already got."

"Oh, nonsense." The phone rang, and she stuck out her tongue at the display. "Mr. DeVriess's office," she answered cheerfully. " . . . I'm so sorry, Judge Wilcox, he's taking a deposition right now. . . . I know, I told him, but he's been tied up all day. . . . I'll make sure he calls you as soon as he's free. . . . Yes, sir, I'll remind him it's important. . . . Thank you. Good-bye." She made a face as she hung up. "What a pompous ass. Thinks he was appointed by God Almighty." Her lips pursed. "Or thinks God Almighty was appointed by him. Let me tell Mr. DeVriess you're here." She lifted the telephone receiver and pressed the intercom button. "Dr. Brockton's here. . . . I'll send him right back." She hung up. "You know your way, right?"

"I do. But I thought you just said he was in a deposition."

"I did. He is," she laughed. "Every single time Judge Wilcox calls." She waved me through the frosted-glass door behind her.

Burt DeVriess's office was positioned in the eastern curve of Riverview Tower. A glass door behind his desk opened onto a private balcony overlooking the river, a marina, condos, the cozy runway of Island Home Airport, and a thirty-foot, ten-ton orange basketball, forever hanging in mid-swish, halfway through the forty-foot hoop atop the Women's Basketball Hall of Fame. Out the broad band of windows to the side, the dark green river spooled beneath the bright green trusswork of the Gay Street Bridge, Knoxville's bridge of choice for suicidal jumpers. Across the river, atop a kudzu-covered bluff stretching from the angular struts of the Gay Street Bridge to the graceful arches of the Henley Street Bridge, sprawled the vestiges of Baptist Hospital, torn down to make way for a new medical center that had been scrapped even before construction began.

DeVriess was seated behind a sleek glass table, which served as his desk. The glass—the same green as the building's windows—was spotless and empty, except for an art deco reading lamp, a thick file folder, and the silk-sleeved elbows of DeVriess. "Hey, Doc, have a seat." The two chairs facing the desk had slender, angular frames of glossy black wood; their backs and seats were strung crosswise with fine cords of nylon, thin as the strings of a violin.

I eyed the nearer chair doubtfully. "Are you sure this thing will hold me up?"

"Hell, Doc," he said, "that would hold up you and me both, with a couple hundred pounds of legal files sitting on our laps. If it breaks, sue me." I laid a hand on the seat and gave an experimental push. The taut cords scarcely moved. I plucked one with a fingernail, and it hummed like a guitar string. "Go ahead, try it." I sat, nervously at first, then with increasing confidence. I'd expected the cords to dig into me, but the chair was surprisingly comfortable. "Aren't they cool? Designed by a Canadian architect in the 1950s. Manufactured by a company that made tennis rackets. Simple but elegant."

"Don't you worry that somebody might sit down with something sharp sticking out of a back pocket? I'm guessing that if one cord got cut, the whole thing would implode."

"Hadn't occurred to me to worry about that," he said. "Remind me to frisk you next time you come in." He tapped the file in front of him. "I dug up some interesting history on Ivy Mortuary. They were sued in 1999 by the widower of a woman who died and was cremated. Seems the cremains came back with a shiny set of dentures tucked inside the bag, but the deceased had died with a jack-o-lantern handful of rotting teeth. Turns out the funeral home swapped her cremains with those of a guy who wore dentures. Needless to say, the toothless guy's family wasn't real happy about the mix-up either. They sued, too."

"Who won?"

"Both families settled out of court. The sum wasn't disclosed, but I hear it was around fifty thousand apiece. I could've gotten 'em a lot more."

It wasn't an idle boast. DeVriess had won a huge class-action lawsuit against a Georgia crematorium that had dumped bodies in the woods instead of incinerating them—a move that, in the short run, saved fifty or a hundred bucks' worth of propane per body but that eventually cost millions of dollars in legal claims, as well as incalculable emotional pain. DeVriess's own Aunt Jean, in fact, had been one of the 339 bodies the Georgia Bureau of Investigation had found amid the pines. I vividly remembered the day I'd identified her remains in a refrigerated semi trailer, one of five that served as makeshift morgues at the site of the gruesome discovery, and I also recalled the deep distress the discovery had caused DeVriess and his Uncle Edgar.

"There was a prior case against Ivy, in 1997," he went on. "Fancy funeral, open casket, the family's saying their final good-byes, and the widow faints when she sees maggots in the mouth of her dearly departed husband."

"Jeez. How long had the corpse been lying around at the funeral home? Was he embalmed? Didn't they have him in a cooler?"

"He'd only been at the funeral home for about twenty-four hours. But he'd died three days before that, down in Mississippi, fishing. Somebody found him floating in his fishing boat around midafternoon, and he'd launched his boat early in the morning."

"So the flies had plenty of time to lay eggs in his nose and mouth while he was drifting around outdoors. That doesn't sound like the fault of the funeral home."

"Ha," he said. "That might be true, but try telling that to a jury that's been reduced to tears by the traumatized widow. The funeral home—actually, their insurance company—settled for half a million, and they were lucky to get off that easy."

"I could've gotten 'em a lot less," I said, and he laughed at the topspin I'd put on his earlier comment. "So are you planning to share this with Culpepper?"

"Already have."

"My, my, aren't you helpful, Counselor?"

He lifted his hands in a magnanimous gesture. "Ain't it the truth, *ain't* it the truth? Plus, I figure it's probably wise not to blindside Culpepper with my next move."

I should have known that Grease would be working some sort of angle. "And what's your next move?"

"I want to exhume more of the people Ivy buried. Turn over a few more rocks, see what else crawls out."

"You planning another class-action suit, Burt? The funeral home's out of business, remember?"

"But their insurance company's not."

"And the insurance company's still on the hook for claims, years after their client's ceased to exist?"

"Arguable," he conceded, "but there's probably a case here. Statutes of repose cover how long the insurance company is on the hook. Of course, if it's a clear case of fraud, rather than a mistake, the insurance company will argue that they're not liable—fraud would be the action of an individual, not the mortuary. But I'll argue that there's a pattern of negligence, since there were multiple problems."

"Sounds like a lot of arguing," I said.

"It's not a slam dunk, but it's worth a try."

"Is it, Burt? No offense, but you're already rich. How much richer do you need to be?"

"This one wouldn't really be about the money, Doc."

I gave him a skeptical look.

"No, really," he insisted. "It still makes me madder than hell to think how shamefully my Aunt Jean's body was treated and how hurtful that was to my Uncle Edgar. I figure most funeral homes and crematories are honest and respectful. But I also figure it's healthy for those to see why it pays to stay honest and respectful."

"Like the instructive example of a public flogging, back in the good old days?"

"Something like that," he said. "But instead of the lash, it's the law, and instead of blood flowing, it's money. And instead of the cobblestoned public square, it happens in the marbled and paneled courtroom."

"Or the glass-walled office tower," I said, "with the art deco lamps and the tennis-racket chairs."

"There, too," he said.

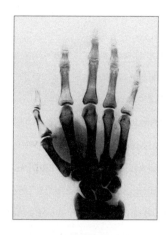

CHAPTER 15

I WAS JUST PULLING IN TO THE PARKING LOT FOR A noon session with Dr. Hoover when my cell phone rang with a call from the bone lab. "Miranda, is that you?"

"It's me." Her voice sounded glum.

"What's wrong?"

"Carmen Garcia just called. Eddie got some bad news this morning from the orthopedist."

"What kind of bad news?"

"It's about the i-Hand. He can't get fitted with one next week after all."

"Why not? When can he get it?"

"Maybe never. The i-Hand's just been taken off the market."

I was stunned by that news, but even more stunned by what she went on to tell me.

"The company that makes it was bought yesterday by Ortho-Medica for ninety million dollars, and OrthoMedica announced today they're suspending sales until further notice. Here, listen, this is from their press release: 'We will continue to provide parts and service to patients already fitted with an i-Hand prosthesis, but we believe that our next-generation bionic hand, currently in development, offers sufficient advances to warrant OrthoMedica's full, undivided attention.' What do you suppose *that* means?"

I had a sinking feeling, and the words "revenue stream" were part of the weight pulling me under. "I suppose," I said, "it means that OrthoMedica bought out the competition in order to kill it." I thought back to my conversation with Glen Faust. What was it he'd said when I asked his advice about the i-Hand? *I'd tell your friend to get an i-Hand, and get it pretty damn quick.*

I'd planned to spend my therapy session with Dr. Hoover making peace with the idea that somewhere out there Isabella was running from the FBI, nursing burned hands, and heaving her way through a trimester of morning sickness. Now, instead of peacemaking, I spent my fifty minutes warring against the injustice of the universe—a universe that seemed to be dealing from a deck stacked mercilessly against the Garcias. My own troubles seemed, for the moment at least, comparatively minor, and as I drove back to campus, I offered up prayers—I wasn't sure to whom or to what—on behalf of Eddie and his family.

Parking beside the stadium and drawing a deep breath to reorient myself, I headed into the Anthropology office. Peggy glanced up at me, then back down at her computer, then up at me again, sharply this time. "You look terrible," she said.

"Gee, thanks."

"Sorry, nothing personal. You just look . . . tired? Worried? Sick?"

"So many wonderful choices," I said. "Don't you want to add

'clinically depressed' or 'terminally ill' or something equally cheerful?"

"No, none of those. But crabby, maybe." She scrutinized me further. "Yes, crabby. Definitely crabby."

"Well, that's a relief," I said, surprised to find that I actually *did* feel relieved by this milder diagnosis. "Since I appear likely to pull through, I suppose I should ask if I've got any messages?"

"Two," she said. "The dean called; he wonders if you can meet with him Thursday to go over the budget numbers."

"Not again," I groaned. "Okay, now I feel tired, worried, *and* clinically depressed. What else? The IRS called to say my tax returns are about be audited?"

"Do they call? I thought they indicted first and asked questions later. Actually, the other call was from Dr. Garcia."

"Dr. Garcia?" I was suddenly on high alert, given what Miranda had relayed. "What did he say? How'd he sound? When did he call?"

"About ten minutes ago. He sounded pretty chipper, actually—not crabby, like some people I could name. He asked if you were in, and when I said you were at lunch, he said, 'I hope his lunch tastes better than mine. The medical care at the hospital is superb, but the food is not superb.' Then he asked me to have you call him when you get a chance."

Feeling my heart rate slow to something approximating normal, I stepped through the doorway that led from Peggy's office to my administrative office, the one where I scheduled meetings with peeved professors and stressed-out students. As a general rule, I preferred to make calls from the office at the other end of the stadium, but I didn't want to delay my call to Eddie by the five minutes it would take to walk there. Dialing the number at UT Hospital I'd long since learned by heart, I drummed my fingers through one ring, two, three. "Seven West," answered a familiar voice.

"LeeAnn?"

"Yes, this is LeeAnn. Who's this? Oh, Dr. Brockton, is that you? Hi there."

"Hi, LeeAnn. You've got a good ear."

"Well, you *have* called a few million times this past month. What can I do for you?"

"Dr. Garcia called me a few minutes ago. Can you transfer me to his room?"

"Sure, hang on."

After two rings I heard the hollow background sound of the hands-free speakerphone Eddie used.

"Hello, Eddie. Miranda tells me you got some bad news today."

"The i-Hand. Yes, it's disappointing, without a doubt. But that's not why I'm calling you. I wonder if you can do a large favor for me."

"Of course. How can I help?"

"By performing an autopsy for me."

"An autopsy? Eddie, I'm not a pathologist."

"I realize this, of course. But you taught anatomy when you were in graduate school, yes?"

"Yes. For two years." I had mentioned my teaching assistantship once, in passing, during a conversation shortly after Garcia and I had met. I was surprised he remembered it. "But that was a long damn time ago, Eddie. A pathology resident would be much better qualified, I'm sure." The phone fell silent except for the tinny background noise.

"Of course. I understand, Bill. I did not mean to impose." He suddenly sounded defeated, and I wished I could take back my words. In my rush to downplay my own abilities, I'd failed to consider how difficult it must have been for him to ask for help with an autopsy he was no longer capable of doing himself. He could have let one of the contract M.E.'s handle the case. After all, for the past two months his caseload—dozens of unattended deaths and even several murders—had been farmed out to contract pathologists or sent to the state M.E.'s office in Nashville. He'd finally been ready to take a step toward returning to work, and I'd failed to recognize the significance of what he'd asked of me.

"Eddie?"

I wasn't sure he was going to answer. If not for the background noise, I'd have thought he'd hung up. Finally: "Yes, Bill?"

"You're not imposing, Eddie. That's not it. I just don't want to let you down. If you think you can guide me through it—if you trust me not to make a mess of things—I'd be honored to help." The phone fell silent again, and I hoped what I'd said wasn't too little, too late.

"How many years since you were in graduate school, Bill?"

"A lot," I said. "Thirty? No, wait—only twenty-nine." I laughed. Where had the time gone?

He laughed, too, and the significance of this moment, at least, was not lost on me: It was the first time I'd heard him laugh since his injury. "Thirty, that would be too many," he said. "But twenty-nine? *Bueno. Perfecto.* You have got the job."

THE ENVELOPE IN MY MAIL bore the return address, "Barbara Pelot, Knoxville City Council," along with the City-County Building's street address. Inside was a handwritten note from Barbara. "Dear Dr. Brockton," the note read, "I'm sorry to say that we've not found any funding in the city's coffers that we can steer your way. Like UT, the city, too, is stretched pretty thin this year. I hope the enclosed will be of at least some help, however." Tucked into the envelope behind the note was a check for a thousand dollars—a personal check from Barbara herself—made out to UT and designated for the Body Farm. It wasn't enough to fill the cavity in my budget, but it was enough to fill me with gratitude. And it was a heck of a lot more than her husband's dental practice had made by cleaning my teeth. I made a mental note to eat more M&Ms and to floss less rigorously.

"SHALL WE BEGIN?"

I'd heard Dr. Edelberto Garcia begin half a dozen autopsies, maybe more, with those three words. Always before, though—before his hands had been destroyed—he'd said them as a statement, a command swiftly followed by a Y-shaped incision into a chest cavity or an ear-to-ear scalp incision, followed by a saw cut into a skull. This time, for the first time, he was asking the question as if he didn't know the answer. In fact, as I glanced across the autopsy table at Miranda, I guessed that as he was posing that single, simple question to us, he was asking himself a multitude of other questions, far more complicated: *How can I work as a medical examiner without hands? Will I be able to contribute anything here today? Am I an asset or a liability in this case? Am I an asset or a liability to my family, and in this world?*

And this time, for the first time, I was the one gripping the scalpel as Garcia posed the question. "I'm ready if you are," I said. I looked over my left shoulder at him, and he nodded. Across the table Miranda nodded slightly, too, and I followed her eyes down to the dead woman on the table. A sixty-one-year-old white female, she was fairly tall—five feet eight inches—with the sort of lean, willowy frame shaped by years of yoga or running or swimming. The hair on her head was long and wavy, an elegant silvery gray that contrasted sharply with the still-black triangle of pubic hair. Her face wasn't conventionally beautiful, but her coloring and features—olive skin, brown eyes, and a wide, full mouth—would have made her a handsome woman in life.

Her name was Clarissa Lowe; she'd died two days before, about a week after undergoing a cervical spine diskectomy and fusion—an operation to remove a damaged disk from her neck and then fuse the two adjoining vertebrae together. The surgery was performed at the regional hospital in Crossville, a town of about ten thousand people, sixty miles west of Knoxville. The procedure had gone smoothly, according to the neurosurgeon's notes, and the woman appeared to be recovering well by the time she was discharged the following morning. Then, three days later, she called the surgeon's office, complaining of nausea, weakness, and pain in her neck. The doctor saw her that same afternoon in his office; not surprisingly, her neck appeared inflamed around the incision, but she wasn't running any fever and her vital signs were normal, so he prescribed a stronger painkiller, recommended cold packs, and sent her home.

Eighteen hours later her panicked husband called 911. She'd vomited three times within an hour, he told the dispatcher—nothing but green liquid—and she was suddenly too weak to stand. By the time the ambulance arrived, she was going into shock; her pulse was fluctuating between 50 and 140 beats a minute, her blood pressure was alarmingly low, and her breathing was labored, though her temperature remained normal. An hour after arriving at the Crossville emergency room, she was fighting for breath, and within two she could no longer breathe on her own. The ER doc put her on a ventilator, started her on powerful antibiotics, and sent her to UT Hospital by ambulance. Ninety minutes later—as she was being wheeled into the ER in Knoxville—she died.

Garcia had briefed me on the woman's surgery, complications, and death, but being briefed wasn't the same as feeling prepared. Tightening my grip on the scalpel, I placed the tip on the woman's chest, at the edge of her left armpit. Her body had been in the morgue's cooler for the past twenty-four hours, so it was chilled nearly to freezing; beads of moisture were condensing on her clammy skin, and a few wisps of fog spooled upward from the corpse, pulled aloft by the morgue's powerful ventilation system. Miranda and I had wedged a body block into place beneath the woman's back; the curved block thrust the chest upward, as if the woman were offering herself to the scalpel as a sacrifice. I bore down, and the blade parted the flesh. Following the natural curve at the base of the left breast, I cut to the midline of the body, then made a mirror-image cut from the right side. The blade rose and dropped as it bumped across ribs. Where those two cuts joined at the breastbone, I began a new incision, this one running down the midline all the way to the pubic bone.

As the abdominal cavity opened, fluid—watery, almost clear but tinged with pink—poured from the incision. During my graduate training and my career, I'd seen twenty or thirty abdominal cavities opened, but I'd never seen one give off such a quantity of fluid. It sheeted down the sides of the abdomen, pooling at the foot of the autopsy table and then gurgling through the drain and into the sink below. "Copious peritoneal effusion," noted Garcia, confirming my sense that the amount of fluid was unusual. "Es-

timated volume approximately one liter. Miranda, would you be
so kind as to collect a sample?" Miranda took a small plastic vial
from the counter and held it beneath the drain, catching a bit of
the liquid as it dribbled through, then screwed the cap tightly in
place.

Garcia next asked me to peel back the chest flap. I did so by
pulling the skin upward with my left hand, using the scalpel to
extend the incisions from the armpits up to the shoulders so I
could peel the skin and breast tissue away from the ribs. Laying
the chest flap over the face, I swapped the scalpel for a rib cut-
ter—a sharp stainless-steel cousin of the dull pruning shears in
my garage at home—and cut through the ribs on both sides. The
chest cavity gaped open, exposing the spongy lungs and the heart
in its fibrous sac. Like the abdomen, the chest cavity oozed copious amounts of liquid. "No wonder she had trouble breathing," I
said, "with all this fluid pressing on her lungs."

"There appears to be considerable edema around the heart,
too," said Garcia. "Let's open the pericardial sac."

I used the scalpel to finish cutting out the chest plate—the
breastbone and the stubs of the ribs I'd sheared—and laid that
aside, then sliced into the tough, grayish-white membrane surrounding the heart. Once again fluid gushed from the incision.
Garcia was leaning in, his face practically in the corpse's chest
cavity. "Now let's check the pulmonary artery," he said.

I probed the tangle of tubing at the top of the heart, nestled
just beneath the arch of the aorta. The pulmonary artery was a
thick vessel that branched immediately into a T shape to carry
blood to the lungs. Slicing through its fibrous wall, I slid the end
of my little finger inside, feeling for a clot that might have choked
off the flow of blood.

"I don't feel anything," I said.

"I didn't think you would," Garcia said. "Her death was rapid, but not rapid enough to be the result of a blood clot." Next he asked me to check the retropharyngeal area, a cavity deep in the neck, directly in front of the spine. "She had no fever, irregular pulse, plummeting blood pressure—symptoms consistent with hemorrhage. Three or four liters of blood from a bleeding vessel could pool in the retropharyngeal area and nobody would know it unless they did a CT scan. But they didn't; the ER physician in Crossville says they didn't have time to scan her. So let's go in and look. We probably need to Roke out her chest; do you know how to do that?"

Miranda asked the question before I could. "How to do *what* to her chest?"

"Roke it out," he repeated. Miranda looked as baffled as I felt.

"Roking out a body is a dissection technique," he explained. "The Rokitansky technique. Named for Karl von Rokitansky, a pathologist at the University of Vienna a century ago. During his career Rokitansky performed or supervised a hundred thousand autopsies."

"Wow," said Miranda. "If practice makes perfect, ol' Karl must have been damn good. So 'Roking her out' is pathologist slang for what, exactly?"

"Gutting the corpse," he said. "The way a hunter guts a deer. Pulling out all the internal organs, from the chest all the way down the abdomen, in one long string."

"Yuck," exclaimed Miranda, who never showed any squeamishness around decayed or dismembered human corpses.

"I've never Roked out a body or gutted a deer," I said to Garcia. "You want me to go up to the hospital lobby and corral a hunter? There's probably a guy up there who's field-dressed dozens of deer. He might do a quicker and neater job than I can."

"You'll do fine," he assured me. Following his directions, I cut the carotid artery and tied it off, then did the same with the subclavian arteries, the pipelines carrying blood to the arms. Next, trading the scalpel for the long autopsy knife—the one Jess Carter always called a "bread knife"—I sliced through the windpipe and the esophagus and tugged them downward, peeling the lungs and the heart and other organs out of the body cavity and away from the spine.

As I pulled, the cavity behind the lungs became visible. This space, too, brimmed with watery fluid.

"Interesting," Garcia murmured again. "Pronounced effusions, but no real bleeding. I'm surprised." He took in a deep breath and exhaled heavily. "Also concerned."

I looked at him. "Concerned about what? Why?"

"Hemorrhage was my prime suspect, and it would have been a relatively benign explanation."

"Not so benign for the dead woman," Miranda pointed out.

"No, not for her, but for others," he responded.

I paused, resting the heart and lungs on the corpse's abdomen. I suspected I knew how he'd answer my next question, and I didn't much like it. "So if hemorrhage didn't kill her, what's the next-best possibility, or the next-worst possibility—infection?"

"Not just infection. Infection leading to toxic shock."

Miranda's eyebrows shot up. "Toxic shock? Isn't that what happens when a woman leaves in a tampon too long? This woman was, what, sixty? Surely she was past menopause."

"She was," he confirmed. "And you're right, tampons are what most people associate with toxic shock. But there are other causes. Toxic shock can occur after normal childbirth, after spontaneous or induced abortion, after injury, after surgery. Sometimes the bacteria that create the toxins are new invaders; sometimes they're already in the body, but at a harmless level. Then something in the body's chemistry shifts and they start multiplying like crazy, producing spores by the billions. When they do, they can overwhelm the host within a matter of hours."

"By 'host' I assume you mean the unlucky human," said Miranda, and he nodded. "But according to the ER chart, this woman got vancomycin," she persisted. "Isn't that like the hydrogen bomb of antibiotics?"

"It's powerful," he agreed. "It can kill bacteria that are resistant to other antibiotics. But by the time she got it, it was already too late. In cases of toxic shock, it's not the bacteria themselves that cause death. It's the poisons they produce—the toxins—that are lethal, and antibiotics can't destroy the toxins. Once toxic shock sets in, the mortality rate can range between fifty and one hundred percent, depending on which bacterium is involved. Some bacterial toxins are deadly; others are even deadlier."

"Should I be running away right now?" Miranda tried to make the question sound like a joke, but she couldn't hide the strain in her voice.

"If you want to leave, I understand," he said. "You, too, Bill. The face shield and the mask and the gown and the double gloves are good protection, but there are no guarantees. Does either one of you have any open cuts or scrapes?" Miranda and I both shook our heads. Miranda's eyes widened abruptly as her gaze dropped to Garcia's left wrist and mangled right hand, both still bandaged.

"Jesus, Eddie, you're the one who shouldn't be here," she said. "Your hands aren't fully healed, and your immune system's been compromised."

He shrugged. "I *am* at more risk here," he acknowledged. "I thought about that yesterday, and I decided to accept the risk."

I wondered if he was doing more than merely accepting the risk; was he actually *seeking* the risk, intentionally exposing himself to a potentially deadly infection?

"Don't worry," he said, "I'm not trying to commit suicide by sepsis." After a pause he added, "Shall we continue?" This time it was a request, not a question. "I don't think we need to Roke out the abdomen, though. Let's look at the neck now, instead."

I laid the chest flap back down into position. With the chest plate and organs now gone, the flap drooped deeply into the chest cavity.

The Crossville surgeon had made a two-inch cut in the neck, which he'd tied off with about fifteen stitches, around which the skin puckered. The thin black threads, whose clipped ends bristled stiffly at each stitch, reminded me of the legs of ticks, and I shivered at the image of ticks burrowing into the woman's neck. Odd: I wasn't at all squeamish about swarms of maggots, but ticks were different, scarier bugs altogether.

The blade sliced easily through the sutures and down through the incision, whose edges had barely begun to adhere to one another. I halfway expected yet another gush of pale fluid as I cut, but there was none. What emerged instead—and what I'd not expected—was the stench of human decomposition. The woman on the autopsy table had been dead for only two days and had been in the cooler that whole time, but if I'd been guessing from the condition of her neck, I'd have guessed that her corpse had been ripening at the Body Farm for a week or more. The tissue was spongy and mottled, riddled with gray and black patches of decay.

"Ack," said Miranda.

"Interesting," said Garcia. He leaned closer and inhaled sharply. "I suspect that localized necrosis began long before she went into toxic shock. Probably immediately after the surgery."

"So the surgery itself was probably the source of the infection," I surmised.

"It depends."

"On what?"

"On the person you ask. If you ask me, I say yes. If you ask the neurosurgeon, he says the procedure went flawlessly and the patient's death was an unrelated event, a freak coincidence."

"Well, duh," Miranda scoffed. "He's terrified that the woman's husband is going to sue him, right? Our friend Grease could probably get thirty or forty million for the guy, right Dr. B.?"

I nodded.

Above his mask, through the face shield, I saw Garcia's brows furrow. "Even if the surgery opened the door to the infection, it might be impossible to pinpoint the source. It could be improperly sterilized instruments, contaminated saline, strep or staph bacteria floating around in the hospital's ventilation ducts. But let's take some samples of tissue from the neck. If we can identify the bacterium that's responsible, we have a better chance of finding the source." We took tissue samples from the neck's tissues, including bone—slivers that required the Stryker saw to cut. Finally I took a sample of fluid, inserting a syringe between the third and fourth vertebrae to draw fluid from the spinal canal.

Garcia leaned down to take another look at the fused section of spine, with its dully gleaming bracket of titanium and the small block of added bone.

"Do you want it?" he asked.

"Want what? The orthopedic hardware?"

"The entire cervical spine. Would it be useful as a teaching specimen, once you've cleaned off the soft tissue?"

"Sure," I said. Gripping the mandible with my left hand, I tipped the head back as far as I could, slicing the ligaments that held the skull to the first cervical vertebra—the washerlike bone called the atlas—and then severing the spinal cord. Then, with the Stryker saw, I cut the seventh cervical vertebra from the first thoracic vertebra. The oscillating blade buzzed easily through the disk, the spinal cord, and the bony prong of the spinous process, which jutted from the back of the vertebral body. The cervical spine was now detached at both ends. Setting aside the saw, I used the scalpel to cut through the last of the tendons that linked the bones to the muscles in the neck. Then, sliding both my hands beneath the five-inch column of bones, I lifted. The cervical spine pulled free of the body with one brief slurp.

An hour later, after cutting slices of Lowe's major organs for Garcia to inspect and preserve in his "save jar" of formalin, I was nearly finished—and almost done for. Using a curved needle to sew baseball-style running stitches, I closed up her body—her Roked-out, virtually decapitated body—for shipment to a Crossville funeral home, which would doubtless be dismayed by the hollow-hulled, thin-necked, floppy-headed husk they received.

In the morgue's changing room, I shucked off my blood- and tissue-spattered surgical garb, showered, and put back on my morning's khakis and soft flannel shirt. On my way out of the morgue, I checked to see if my souvenir was simmering yet. I had set the cervical spine in a steam-jacketed kettle—essentially an oversize Crock-Pot—in the decomp processing room, a lab devoted to removing the last bits of soft tissue from skeletons that had decayed at the Body Farm. The steam-jacketed kettle, its thermostat set slightly below the boiling point, would cook off the tissue without harming the bones. To speed the process and improve the smell of the cleaned bones, I tipped a capful apiece of Biz detergent and Downy fabric softener into the pot.

I turned out the fluorescent lights and closed the door of the decomp room, leaving the hot water, Biz, and Downy to do their work in the dark.

Some people launder money, I thought. *I launder bones.*

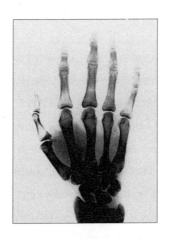

CHAPTER 16

Jeff the day I'd learned of Isabella's pregnancy, not the next, nor the day after that. I'd put it off for a week, in fact. Now, although I was exhausted from the autopsy—or perhaps *because* I was exhausted from the autopsy—I realized I couldn't avoid the conversation any longer. "Hey, Dad," he said, "what's up?"

"Oh, not much," I said. "How's it going?"

"Well, today's April first. How do you think it's going?"

"I don't know," I said. "That's why I asked."

"Christ, Dad, April fifteenth is only two weeks away," he said irritably. *Crap,* I thought, *I forgot about my taxes.* Jeff was an accountant with a small but growing practice in Farragut, an affluent bedroom community twenty miles west of downtown Knoxville.

"So you're sort of busy."

"Sort of. The way the pope is sort of Catholic. The good news is, I've got ten percent more clients than I had last year. The bad news is, I've got ten percent more clients than last year, and some of my new clients have really complicated tax returns. Speaking of which, when do you envision bagging up your financial debris and bringing it to me?"

"Soon, son. Very, very soon. I'm sorry to be such a bad client."

He sighed wearily. Every year since he'd opened his accounting practice, he'd done my return, and every year he'd had to nag me to gather up my records and bring them in. "I've got to have your stuff by Monday, Dad. No kidding."

"Sure." I hesitated. "So this probably isn't a great time to get together for a drink, huh?"

"A drink? You don't drink. Why would we get together for a drink?"

"Well, I don't, but I know you do every now and then. I thought maybe you might want to meet somewhere in Farragut on your way home and just catch up a bit."

"I'll be working till midnight, Dad. I just called Jenny to tell her that I couldn't meet her and the boys for pizza. I don't even have time to breathe, much less to hang out, until April sixteenth."

"Oh. Sorry. Of course not. I didn't mean to impose." They were the same words Eddie Garcia had said to me when I hesitated to perform the autopsy for him. Had he felt as stung by my reaction as I now felt by Jeff's?

A long silence hung in the air. Finally he said, "Dad, is something wrong? Are you in trouble again?" The "again" made me wince. I'd turned to Jeff for help when I was wrongly accused of murdering Jess Carter. He'd stood by me unquestioningly then, and he'd never made me feel like it had been a burden. But the fact that he'd said "again" just now embarrassed me; I felt like a kid who's gotten into trouble at school one too many times.

"No, I'm not in trouble," I said. "I'm not."

"Are you sick? My God, Dad, are you sick?"

"No, no, nothing like that. I'm fine. Well, not 'fine,' exactly, but not sick."

"What's on your mind? Is something troubling you?"

"I . . ." I felt my throat tightening. "It's just that there's something important I need to talk to you about, Jeff. Face-to-face."

There was a pause. "Okay, Dad. Sure. Tell you what. There's a Panera Bread pretty close to my office, out in Turkey Creek. Do you know it?"

"Is that the one that's inside the big Target store?"

"No, that's Starbucks. Panera is across from the movie theaters. Kinda near Borders Books."

"Oh, I remember," I said, though I didn't, actually—Turkey Creek was a huge, sprawling retail development, hundreds of stores and restaurants strung out along a two-mile, traffic-snarled boulevard. I avoided it whenever possible, which, luckily, was virtually always. I figured I could call Panera on my cell phone for directions if I had trouble spotting them amid the thicket of shops and signs.

"I forgot to bring anything to eat," Jeff was saying, "and they've got decent soups and sandwiches. How about I meet you there in an hour? Well, let's say fifty minutes; that would be seven-thirty. The dinner crowd will have slacked off by then."

Forty minutes and two cell-phone calls later, I spotted the striped awnings of Panera and pulled into one of Turkey Creek's gargantuan parking lots. *Turkey Creek my foot*, I thought. *They should call this place Asphalt Acres.* Then, *Yeah, and they should call you Grumpy Old Man.* I sat in the truck with the radio on—Sirius had a channel with 1940s big-band music I'd gotten hooked on lately—and watched for Jeff. Twenty minutes went by, and I was just about to call and check on him when his hybrid SUV whipped into the parking lot and lurched to a stop. Jeff jumped out, talking rapidly on his cell, and ended the call as we converged at the door.

"Sorry I'm late," he said. "One of my clients is a surgeon, and, being a surgeon, he assumes he's my most important client. So when he wants to discuss the draft tax return I e-mailed him, he assumes I'm at his beck and call."

"No worries. I know you're scrambling, and I appreciate your taking time to grab a bite with me. Let's order. I'm starving."

Jeff, health-conscious guy that he was, ordered a salad with grilled chicken; I got a chicken chipotle sandwich. At its center was grilled chicken like Jeff's, but it was drenched in a tangy, unhealthy sauce and served on crusty, buttery grilled bread. For his side item, Jeff chose an apple; I chose potato chips. The young cashier handed me what looked like a square plastic coaster. I must have appeared puzzled, because she explained, "It'll buzz when your order's ready." I had barely collected my change when the coaster practically leaped out of my hand, vibrating fiercely and flashing with enough red LED lights to serve as a road-hazard sign.

I held the buzzer up to the cashier. "What do I do with it now?"

"Leave it in the basket on the counter, down there where you pick up your order."

I followed her gaze and arrived at the pickup counter just as our food did. A large wicker basket occupied one end of the counter. Brimming with gadgets like the one vibrating in my hand, the basket buzzed like a flock of angry cicadas and flashed like a miniature disaster zone. It set me on edge, and I could understand why the young man putting our food on the counter looked far wearier than any twenty-year-old ought to look.

Jeff had gotten our drinks and claimed a vacant booth in the back corner of the restaurant. We slid onto the benches and squirmed into our conversation. Jeff asked polite questions about the classes I was teaching this semester, and about my forensic cases, and about Dr. Garcia's progress. Then, after a suitable amount of small talk, he ventured, "Sounds like you've got something on your mind."

"I do." I studied my hands. "I'm not sure how to tell you this, Jeff. A couple of months ago, I . . . uh, slept with a woman."

He laughed. "Good for you," he said. Then, "I sure hope you seemed more enthusiastic about it then than you do now."

I looked up, pained, and his expression changed to alarm.

"Jesus, Dad, what is it? Did you get AIDS or herpes or something?"

I shook my head.

"Wait, wait—have you gone and gotten married to this woman? Is that what you're worried about telling me?"

"No," I said. "I haven't married her. Hell, I haven't seen her since right after that night. She's gone, I don't know where." I drew a breath. "You probably heard about her in the news, son. Her name's Isabella Morgan. She's the one who murdered that Oak Ridge scientist, Novak—the old Manhattan Project physicist."

His eyes got wide. "The one the media called 'The A-Bomb Avenger'?"

I nodded.

"Christ, Dad." His eyes darted back and forth as he sorted through various possibilities in his mind. "Are you in some sort of legal trouble? Did you know she'd killed the guy when you slept with her?"

"No, of course not. I would never knowingly get involved with someone who'd committed murder." I splayed my hands, palms up, on either side of my sandwich, which was missing only one bite so far. "She was a reference librarian at the Oak Ridge Public Library. She helped me with some research. Historical research. I had no idea. . . ."

He reached across the table and took my left hand in his right. "Oh, Dad, I'm so sorry. It must've really pulled the rug out from under you when you learned the truth."

"It did," I said.

He gave my hand a squeeze.

"But there's more, Jeff. Feels like another rug just got yanked out from under me."

"What do you mean? Have they caught her?"

I shook my head.

"Have you found out where she is?"

"No. But I've found out she's pregnant."

Jeff's hand froze mid-squeeze. He stared at me, and then his eyes darted some more, and then he stared again. "She's pregnant?"

I nodded miserably.

"Are you telling me what I think you're telling me?"

I nodded again.

My son removed his hand from mine. He pushed his half-eaten salad away, slid from the booth, and walked out.

THAT NIGHT I HAD A dream, and in my dream I was helping Eddie Garcia autopsy a woman's body. But this was a young woman's body, and when I made the long incision that opened the chest and abdomen, her belly opened to reveal a full-term fetus inside: a baby boy whose face I recognized. It was the face I'd seen three decades before, when Jeff was born. Then I looked closer, and I realized the face was my own.

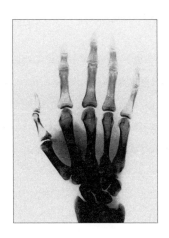

CHAPTER 17

"YOU DON'T LOOK SO HOT," SAID MIRANDA WHEN I walked into the bone lab the next morning.

"And yet I look better than I feel."

"Oh, my. So I guess I'd better start looking for a new Ph.D. adviser, huh?"

"Maybe," I said. "But first let's watch this DVD that Eddie got from the surgeon in Crossville." I slid the disc—a video of Clarissa Lowe's surgery—out of the envelope that had arrived the day before, while we were doing the autopsy, and Miranda loaded it into the computer's optical drive.

Watching the video was like opening a letter or hearing a voice mail after the sender has died: There was Lowe, anesthetized but still alive—and still healthy, except for a bum neck—just ten days earlier. "This is creepy," said Miranda, "but *so cool*. How'd they get this great camera angle?" If Lowe's eyes had been open, they'd have been staring almost directly into the camera lens. Besides her face, which was obscured by an oxygen mask, the image showed her neck and chest as well.

"Eddie said it's a prototype OR video system, designed by the surgeon's brother or cousin or something. The camera lens is built into the handle of the surgical light. So adjusting the angle of the light automatically adjusts the aim of the camera."

"Cool," she repeated. "Wish I'd invented that. Right after inventing the transporter beam and the perpetual-motion machine."

Early in the video—before the incision—a gloved hand reached up, filling the screen, and the image on the screen lurched wildly as the light was adjusted. Eventually the lurching ceased and the image stabilized; once it did, the angles of the light and the camera were—as best I could tell—exactly the same as they'd been before all the jostling and adjusting. A few seconds elapsed, and then the hand loomed into view again; again the image careened wildly, and again it returned to exactly the same angle. "Whee, *that* was fun," said Miranda. "Let's do it again. Dramamine, anyone?"

"Now, now," I chided. "Don't be snarky. If I were about to operate on your neck, wouldn't you want the light to be aimed just right?"

"If you were about to operate on my neck, I'd want someone to stop you." She moved the computer's cursor to an arrow labeled FF and clicked on the mouse. As the video scrolled forward, the camera zoomed in to a tighter shot of the neck, and the image lurched a third time—far more dramatically this time—and then, after it steadied, hands darted into the frame, a scalpel flicked swiftly, and the front of the woman's neck gaped open.

"Slow down, slow down," I said. "We actually want to watch the surgery, remember?"

"But the surgery lasted more than two hours, Dr. B. Do you really want to watch it all in real time? Can't we fast-forward till we see something interesting?"

"How will we know what's interesting if it zooms past in a nanosecond?"

"Tell you what," she offered. "If we get to the end and we haven't seen anything interesting, I'll back it up and we can watch it in slo-mo. Deal?"

"Deal." On the screen, two pairs of hands converged on the neck, steel instruments glistening in the light, and then withdrew. Once they were out of the frame, I saw that the incision in the neck had been spread apart with clamps; the opening was now as wide as it was long. "Slow down; this is getting interesting."

"Yeah, fascinating," she said, but her heart wasn't in the sarcasm, and once the speed slowed to normal, she leaned closer to the screen, drawn into the drama as the woman's trachea and esophagus were pulled to the side and the front of her spine was exposed to view. The surgery was accompanied by a sound track—country music, turned up loud—with an occasional indecipherable murmur of human voices underneath the drawling, twanging music.

With a series of tools—forceps, scissors, scalpel, forceps again—the surgeon attacked the disk, yanking and snipping and gouging out the crumbling cartilage that separated the third cervical vertebra from the fourth. The surgeon's gloves and the surgical drapes were soon spattered with blood and tissue. "Wow, I hadn't fully appreciated how much an orthopedic surgeon has in common with a butcher," Miranda remarked, adding, "Not much elbow room there in the neck."

"Not much," I agreed. "Back when I was teaching anatomy,

the surgery residents used to put pieces of tissue down in the bottom of Styrofoam coffee cups. They'd practice cutting and suturing without touching the sides of the cup."

She paused the video. "Like that doctor game for kids? Operation? The one where it buzzes if the tweezers touch the board while you're lifting out the funny bone or the brain or whatever?"

"Like that. The name of the patient was something-Sam, I think. Yosemite Sam? No, that was a cartoon character. Cavity Sam, maybe. Kathleen and I gave Jeff that game one year for Christmas."

"Did he like it?"

"Not so much. I thought it was fun, but Jeff was disappointed. What he really wanted was a BB gun."

Miranda snorted. "He wanted a BB gun, and he got Operation? Poor Jeff—he'll probably need therapy the rest of his life to get over the pain."

"We didn't want him to shoot his eye out, you know? But I felt so bad when I saw how sad he looked that Christmas morning that I got him a BB gun two months later, for his birthday."

"Did he shoot his eye out?"

"He never did. Not yet anyhow. I do seem to remember replacing a window or two, though." I laughed. "Oh, and the neighbor's cat stopped coming over and eating our cat's food. Which wasn't such a bad thing."

"Just think of all the money you could've saved on cat food if you'd gotten him the BB gun two months sooner," she said. "You ready to watch surgery again?" Without waiting for an answer, she hit "play," and the bloody fingers and tools resumed their assault on the spinal disk. The scraps of cartilage grew smaller and smaller; then, after a pause, I heard a high-pitched whine, like a dentist's drill. Gripping a small grinder, not unlike the Dremel tool I'd bought at Home Depot, the surgeon angled the tool into the opening in the patient's neck. "Yikes," said Miranda. "This is when you really don't want your spine surgeon to have the shakes. One twitch and you're a quad."

He laid aside the grinder and then, with a pair of forceps, held a small, white peg—a short, squat bone graft, roughly twice the diameter of a pencil eraser—in the neck, measuring it against the gap between the two vertebrae whose surfaces he'd just smoothed. The back of the surgeon's head leaned into the frame, bending down for a closer look, and then he withdrew the forceps and reamed out the gap between the vertebrae a bit more. After another inspection he reinserted the peg into the opening in the neck, wedged it between the vertebrae, and then tapped it deeper into the intervertebral gap, using a small hammer and punch, creating a snug fit: a fit whose snugness I'd noticed when I removed the section of spine from the neck of the corpse. Finally he took a silvery metal bracket and screwed it to the bones. The procedure he'd just performed was an anterior decompression and fusion; the "fusion" part would be completed by the patient herself—or would have been, if she hadn't died—as new bone grew from her vertebrae to surround and incorporate the grafted piece.

On the monitor the surgeon removed the retractors and clamps from Lowe's neck; once released, the skin contracted and the gaping incision half closed itself. With a curved needle and stiff black thread, the surgeon took fifteen neat stitches in the neck: the fifteen stitches that had so readily parted, only hours before, under the blade of the scalpel in my hand.

A different, smaller pair of hands entered the video frame. With brisk efficiency they scrubbed the dried blood off the patient's neck, then swabbed on iodine and applied a gauze dressing. The surgeon's hand reappeared; it waved to the camera, then gave a cheery thumbs-up.

Clarissa's surgery was finished.

Her swift death spiral was starting, and no inventor's high-tech video system could rewind that.

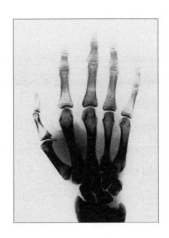

CHAPTER 18

"So here's another wild-ass guess. You think there's any chance Willoughby's dismemberment could've been cult-related?" The KPD detective had called just as I'd finished watching the video with Miranda. He'd offered to swing by a deli and pick up sandwiches so he could chat with me about postmortem mutilation over lunch.

I didn't answer the cult question right away—I'd just taken in a mouthful of smoked turkey and provolone cheese—so I shook my head to buy time. "You remember the Job Corps murder," he said as I chewed. I did. It had been committed by a teenage girl, who'd repeatedly stabbed and bludgeoned another girl, a classmate at the job-training center where they were enrolled. "*That* involved missing parts," Culpepper persisted, "and there was a cult connection there, right? Didn't she carve a pentagram into the chest of the victim?"

I nodded, wiping a stray blob of mayonnaise from my lip. "She did," I conceded. "She also kept a piece of the skull as a souvenir. But I don't think it counts as a cult killing. I think it was mostly about jealousy over a boy they both liked. I think the pentagram and the souvenir were drunken, stoned-out afterthoughts. And anyhow, Willoughby's limbs were amputated with surgical precision. Crazy cultists wouldn't have done such a neat job of it."

Culpepper chewed on this as he chewed on his egg-salad sandwich. For a man who chomped gum with such ferocity, Culpepper ate with surprising daintiness. He'd begun by nibbling the fringe of lettuce, pruning it to a neat, straight line, even with the edges of the white slices of loaf bread. From there he'd nibbled into the sandwich proper, starting at one corner and working his way around the perimeter of the crust. I watched in fascination as he spiraled slowly toward the center, one mincing bite at a time. He noticed me watching and stopped, the sandwich a few inches from his mouth. "What?"

"Nothing," I said. "I've just never seen anybody eat a sandwich like that."

"The egg salad squishes a little bit with every bite," he explained. "So if you start at one side and just go straight across, by the time you get to the other side, it's all squishing and dripping out the edge. This keeps it corralled."

"But you end up with a golf-ball-size wad of it in the center," I countered, pointing to the bulbous disk of sandwich clutched in his hand.

"No problem," he said. Opening his mouth wide, he popped it in, chewed briskly, and swallowed quickly. "So I went to East Tennessee Cremation to see your pal Helen. She remembered the name of the embalmer who was working at Ivy Mortuary back when Willoughby was buried," he mumbled. "A guy named Kerry Roswell. She thinks maybe he started working there in the mid-nineties. She said Roswell was sued, along with Elmer Ivy, by a woman whose husband's funeral service turned into an entomology science-fair project."

"Oh, the maggot case. Right. Burt DeVriess mentioned that."

He made a face, and I wasn't sure whether it was inspired by the mental picture of the maggot-infested corpse or the thought of DeVriess. "So I checked the court documents DeVriess sent me, and sure enough, there's Roswell's name as a codefendant." He popped a piece of gum into his mouth and began to work it. "Couple other tidbits from Helen. One, she said Roswell seemed kinda ambitious—talked about getting his funeral director's license, talked about someday opening his own funeral home—but then, poof, he just dropped off the radar screen. Two, she said Elmer Ivy was thinking about selling the business, back around that same time. She actually considered buying it herself, but Ivy was asking too much. Supposedly he had some other potential buyer whose pockets were deeper than Helen's. The other didn't follow through, but by then she'd lost interest."

"Who was the other buyer?"

"Dunno. Some guy from out of town, maybe with one of the national chains that's been gobbling up the mom-and-pop mortuaries."

"Could it be SCI?" SCI—Service Corporation International—was the eight-hundred-pound gorilla of the death-care industry, a multibillion-dollar company that owned thousands of funeral homes, crematories, and cemeteries worldwide. With its deep pockets and a reputation for ruthless competition, SCI tended to inspire fear and loathing among locally owned funeral homes, especially any that found themselves targeted in the giant's cross-hairs. SCI had been the subject of several lawsuits and scandalous news stories in recent years. One scandal was triggered by stories that National Funeral Home, an SCI facility in Virginia, had as many as two hundred unembalmed bodies stacked on racks in a big, unrefrigerated garage. Two other headline-making scandals—along with multimillion-dollar lawsuits—resulted from charges that graves and remains at SCI cemeteries in Florida and California had been secretly destroyed to make room for new burial plots.

Culpepper shrugged. "She didn't know what company. She never met the out-of-town guy, but she said she'd ask around, see if anybody else did. It was all just rumors, she said, but sometimes rumors have an underlying factual basis."

"Helen's plugged in," I said. "I'll be surprised if she doesn't dredge up something more for you."

"Let's hope." The detective folded another piece of gum into his mouth. He stood and headed for the door, then stopped and turned back. "By the way, I thought the ignition button was creepy but cool."

"Ignition button?"

"Yeah, the ignition button. The red button beside the family viewing window. The grieving widow or whoever can push it to light the furnace and send her loved one up in smoke."

"Oh, that button. Right." Helen had pointed it out to me when I'd toured her new facility. At the time I'd paid more attention to the three cremation furnaces and the six-body cooler, though I'd found the button intriguing and slightly amusing. Now I couldn't help wondering: If my body were the one in the furnace, who would push the button—and with what mixture of feelings?

With a casual wave of his hand and a loud pop of his gum, Culpepper left me to ponder the prospect of my own cremation.

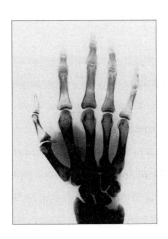

CHAPTER 19

Miranda over the roar of the backhoe as it tugged at another coffin—this one the blue-green of oxidized copper—deep in a grave in Highland Cemetery. A rolling, parklike cemetery in the Bearden area, Highland was the nearest burial ground to the moneyed manses of my richer Sequoyah Hills neighbors.

"Déjà vu all over again!" yelled Grease. "Did you see that movie? *Deja Vu*? With Will Smith? Think of me as Knoxville's Will Smith."

"Good God, man," Miranda scolded, "that was Denzel Washington."

"So think of me as Knoxville's Denzel Washington."

"Hard to do," she shot back. "You're not tall, dark, and handsome. You're not even tall, dark, *or* handsome."

He threw her a look of mock indignation. "But I gave an Oscar-worthy performance when I argued Judge Wilcox into signing the order for this exhumation."

"Tell me about that," I said, pulling on my gloves. "I was surprised when you called."

"I used the old lawsuits I dug up—the complaints I exhumed, you might say—to convince him that Ivy Mortuary was engaged in a systematic pattern of fraud. He was willing to grant me one additional exhumation. I figured it made sense to go for another body that was buried around the same time as Willoughby's."

"Conspiracy theory meets fishing expedition," observed Miranda.

"Like the Tom Waits song says," DeVriess added, " 'Fishin' for a good time starts with throwin' in your line.' "

"Looks like you've snagged a big one," I said as the backhoe hoisted the coffin out of the grave. The operator swung the arm to one side of the grave and set the coffin on a rectangle of artificial turf. Then he throttled the machine to idle and clambered down to unhook the cable sling.

This time the backhoe had reeled in Gill Pendergrast, a thirty-nine-year-old white male who'd been killed in a motorcycle wreck a week before Trey Willoughby's death. Both the accident report and the newspaper story DeVriess had found indicated that Pendergrast had died of massive head injuries sustained in the crash—he hadn't been wearing a helmet—so I was braced to see a crushed skull when I cranked open the lid of the coffin. I was also prepared to see another limbless corpse.

I was not, however, prepared to see what the coffin actually contained: four pillow-shaped paper bags, each labeled PLAYGROUND SAND 50 POUNDS.

"KNOXVILLE POLICE ARE INVESTIGATING two bizarre cases of grave robbing," began WBIR anchorman Randall Gibbons in that evening's television newscast. "We should warn you, this story is disturbing and some of the images that follow are graphic." I wasn't sure whether the warning was meant to deter viewers from watching it or deter them from switching to another channel.

Gibbons had coanchored the broadcast with Maureen Gershwin until her on-camera death a few weeks before; his transition to solo anchor had been smooth, though I noticed that I still missed Maurie. "One of the bizarre body thefts came to light today," Gibbons continued, "when a coffin exhumed at Highland Cemetery was found to contain four bags of sand instead of a body. The other theft—discovered last week at Old Gray Cemetery—was more gruesome: The corpse of a man exhumed for a DNA paternity test was found to be missing both arms and both legs. Police say both thefts occurred before burial, not afterward; they also say both bodies were buried in 2003, after funeral services at Ivy Mortuary." The footage included wide shots and close-ups of Pendergrast's copper coffin and its sandy contents, as well as deliberately blurred KPD crime-scene photos of Willoughby's limbless body.

The story included brief bios of the two men, as well as a few sentences about the life and death of Ivy Mortuary. Then it segued to a brief interview with me, in which I said that whoever amputated Willoughby's limbs seemed to know what they were doing, and a longer interview with Burt DeVriess, who denounced exploitation and dark misdeeds in "the death-care industry" without ever quite accusing Ivy or any other funeral home of specific crimes.

The footage also included a gum-smacking Culpepper, who asked anyone with information about the thefts or Ivy Mortuary to contact KPD.

The anchorman ended the story with a dramatic flair Grease himself might have envied—or might, I realized, have suggested: "Police investigators and the colorful attorney say they won't rest in peace until those responsible for the skullduggery have been brought to justice."

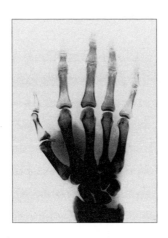

CHAPTER 20

AMONG THE VIEWING AUDIENCE FOR WBIR'S GRAVE-robbing story was my new therapist, Dr. Hoover. I learned this the morning after the newscast, when I arrived for my nine o'clock appointment.

"Fascinating," said Dr. Hoover. "Life and death, crime and punishment, justice and injustice—your work really does wrestle with the Big Questions, doesn't it?"

I allowed as how perhaps it did, but that my own personal wrestling match had taken the limelight, especially since my talk with Jeff had ended so abruptly and painfully.

"Any thoughts on why he walked out on you?"

Dr. Hoover's hands were clasped in his lap, his elbows resting on the arms of the wingback chair. He seemed relaxed but intent, focused on taking in whatever meaning I could put into words. His openness and attention seemed to wick word and thought out of me; it made me think of osmosis and the way a difference in pressure allows nutrients to flow through a cell's membrane.

"I think he was surprised," I began. "No—shocked."

"What would have been shocking to him?"

"Maybe the idea that he might be about to acquire a half brother or half sister thirty years younger than he is. Or maybe the idea that his dad could be so incredibly irresponsible as to impregnate a virtual stranger."

"Is that what you were? Incredibly irresponsible?"

"That seems pretty obvious, doesn't it?"

He shrugged. "'Irresponsible' is one word you could use. What are some others?"

"I don't know. 'Foolish'? 'Immature'? 'Naïve'?"

He bowed his head slightly, a gesture that was becoming familiar to me; it meant that he'd heard what I'd said but didn't necessarily agree with it. "I'm remembering the recording you brought me a couple of sessions ago, the one where you described the night that Isabella came to your house." He opened a manila file that had been tucked into the chair beside him. Flipping through it, he pulled out a page. "This is a transcript of the recording. May I read you a few of the things you said?"

I nodded, and his eyes scanned down the page.

"You said, 'She was beautiful.' You said, 'Our lives intersected, powerfully but briefly.' You said, 'She opened her arms and her body and her desire to me.' Do you remember saying those things?"

"I do."

"Were you telling the truth when you said them?"

"I was."

"So what kind of man, Bill, might make love to a beautiful woman whose life has just intersected with his in a powerful way? What kind of man might make love to a beautiful, intelligent woman who offers him her body and her desire? Can you think of any other words? Words that might be less harsh, less judgmental?"

I tried to summon other adjectives, but without success.

"How about 'passionate,' Bill? How about 'appreciative'?"

I looked up into his eyes and felt them drawing me into a space of kindness.

"How about 'lonely,' Bill?"

I felt myself take a quick, ragged breath, and I realized that I was crying.

"How about 'imperfect'? How about 'human,' Bill?"

We sat without speaking for a while, tears pouring from my eyes, compassion or acceptance or understanding emanating from his. My nose began to drip, and I pulled a sheaf of tissues from the box on the table beside me. I mopped my face, then blew my nose, messily and loudly. "God, what should I do about this mess?"

"Which mess?"

I laughed through the tears. The word "mess" could apply with equal aptness to the accidental baby in Isabella's womb, the unresolved tension with Jeff, or the wad of snotty tissues in my hand. "Well, this one here's pretty easy to deal with," I said, plopping the tissues into the wastebasket beside my chair, "but what should I do about the others?"

Hoover smiled. "Instead of talking about what you *should* do, Bill, can you think about what you *want* to do, what you *choose* to do, as the intelligent and kind person that you are?"

"What's the difference? Isn't doing the right thing all that really counts?"

"Doing the thing *right* also matters," he said. "When you do something because you 'should,' there's a way in which you're not doing it wholeheartedly, a way in which you're not completely owning it. There's a little bit of martyrdom in it, a smidgen of resentment or grudge—sort of 'Look what you made me do; look how you're making me suffer.' I had a client once who went to his wife's family's Thanksgiving dinner every year, not because he wanted to but because he 'should'—because that's what a good husband has to do, right? And every Thanksgiving he felt trapped and resentful, and so his relatives felt a lot of discomfort around him, because who likes to spend Thanksgiving with somebody who's pissed off? Finally one year his wife sat him down and said, 'You're not invited this year. You radiate resentment the whole time, and that spoils it for everyone else. Do us all a favor by spending the day at home or hunting or hiking, doing something you'd rather be doing.' Complicated story—they had other issues to work on, not surprisingly—but eventually, once she'd let him off the hook, he decided that he actually *wanted* to go. And for the first time ever, he had a good time. He discovered interesting things about his in-laws; they discovered that he was a nicer guy than the grouchy husband who'd suffered through all those turkey dinners. What made the difference was that he wanted to go, he chose to go. He went out of 'get to,' not out of 'have to.' Does that make sense?"

I nodded.

"So as you think about yourself, and your life, and the people you care about, and these things that are swirling around all of you—these messes, if you wish to call them that—what do you want to do, Bill? What do you choose to do, and why?"

I drew one deep breath and then another. "Isabella, that one's complicated," I said. "I'm concerned about her."

"Do you still care about her?"

"Yes." I was surprised how deeply true the word rang. "I do, but most of that situation is out of my control. As Miranda said, there's not much I can do, besides wait for the other shoe to drop." I grimaced. "The baby shoe. *My* baby shoe."

"Are you sure it wasn't another man who got her pregnant?"

"No, not a hundred percent sure. But I am a hundred percent sure that I *might* have gotten her pregnant. That information is relevant to the FBI investigation. That's why I had to disclose it. No, wait—that's why I *chose* to disclose it."

He smiled. "That does seem the sort of disclosure a responsible man would make." He cocked his head slightly to one side. "Why do you think your son is so angry with you?"

"Maybe his feelings are hurt," I suggested.

"Hurt? Why? Because you didn't consult him before going to bed with a beautiful woman?"

I imagined myself dialing Jeff's phone number that night with one hand while ripping off my clothes with the other hand. The image made me laugh again, and the relief of laughter felt like balm to my soul.

He leaned toward me and repeated the question. "Why do you think your son is so angry with you?"

I sighed. I'd hoped I had laid this issue to rest, hoped I'd cleaned up this mess. "Because I was angry with Jeff, I think, after his mother died. Kathleen died three years ago of cancer. Uterine cancer. She'd had a very difficult pregnancy with Jeff, and she had three miscarriages after he was born. When she got cancer—even though it wasn't until Jeff was grown—I think I associated uterine cancer with childbearing, and with our child. Stupid, and maybe I'm imagining the reason for it, but I did pull away from Jeff after Kathleen died. Truth is, I pulled away from everybody—I pretty much shut down emotionally for a couple of years—but the only person I feel serious regret about pulling away from is Jeff. I wasn't as warm a father to him as I might have been during that time, and I wasn't as loving a grandfather to his boys as I wish I'd been."

"You said 'for a couple of years.' So you'd gotten closer to him again?"

"Yes. When I was accused of murder, Jeff stood by me."

"And the woman you were accused of murdering—you were romantically involved with her, is that right?"

"Yes. Briefly. Her name was Jess Carter. She was the medical examiner in Chattanooga. We were working together on a case, and I had just started to fall for her when she was killed."

"Was that a sexual relationship?"

I hesitated. "Yes. Barely, but wonderfully. I was falling in love with Jess—I *knew* Jess—and if she hadn't been killed, we might have made a life together."

Dr. Hoover looked startled, and I guessed that he was pondering the bizarre, mirror-image symmetry of my last two lovers: a woman who was murdered, then a murderous woman.

"Anyhow," I went on, "when I was framed for Jess's murder, Jeff ended up helping me, and I appreciated it. Over the past year or so, it felt like we'd regained most of the ground we'd lost. Until the night before last."

"When he walked out on you."

I nodded.

"Any more thoughts on why he got so angry?"

"Maybe because he had to work pretty hard to get my attention for a while. Maybe because I've always not been the most attentive or openhearted dad to him."

"And yet here you go . . . ?"

"Diverting my limited fatherly resources to some total stranger's baby. To a murderer's baby at that."

"And that might make him feel . . . ?"

"Slighted. Unimportant. Resentful. Afraid that this new baby could be a higher priority, could displace him somehow."

"You think Jeff fears that another child could cut into his inheritance? That it might diminish his prospects, or his children's prospects?"

That implication hadn't even occurred to me. "I don't know. I wouldn't think so."

"What sort of work does Jeff do?"

"He's an accountant."

"And you don't think he's imagined how the ledger sheet could change somewhere down the road?"

I shrugged. "I don't know. That might occur to him at some point, but I don't think it would've popped into his head first thing, in the thirty seconds between the moment I told him and the moment he walked out of Panera."

He nodded, conceding the point. "So how did you feel when he walked out on you? And how do you feel now?"

"Surprised. Confused. Embarrassed. Sad. Mad."

"Mad then or mad now?"

I felt a flush of shame. "Both."

"So what sorts of words might describe a son who reacted the way Jeff reacted?"

I looked into the cluster of oil lamps burning in the fireplace. "Same as me. Surprised. Confused. Embarrassed. Sad. Mad." I looked into Hoover's face. "Imperfect. Human."

"And what do you want to do now, Bill?"

I smiled a slightly rueful smile. "I want to call my son and tell him I love him."

He nodded.

"I want to tell him I didn't mean to pull the rug out from under him. Ask for his understanding and forgiveness."

He nodded again.

At the end of the session, I called Jeff to say those things. He didn't answer, but I said them anyway, telling them to his voice mail.

I hoped he'd hear the voice mail right away and call me back soon.

He didn't.

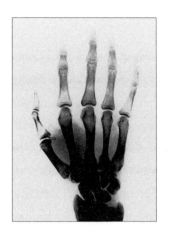

CHAPTER 21

THE STEAM-JACKETED KETTLE HAD DONE ITS WORK
well: Thirty-six hours in scalding water, Biz, and Downy had
turned the soft tissue surrounding Clarissa Lowe's cervical vertebrae into shreds of tissue and a slick of grease. If not for the
orthopedic hardware and the rank odor, the pot might have contained beef soup bones, simmering their way toward broth.

I fished the spine out of the pot with a large pair of tongs and
laid it in the deep, stainless-steel sink of the forensic center's decomp room. Gripping the hot bones with the tongs, I slipped a
scalpel between the vertebrae. Five of the seven parted easily;
the other two remained joined by the titanium bracket and the
tightly fitted wedge of bone.

I turned on the sink's faucet—warm, not cold, so as not to
risk fracturing the hot bones—and scrubbed the vertebrae with
stiff brushes, including a bottle brush to swab out the circular spinal canal. The last shreds of tissue let go easily, swirl-

ing down the drain into the hospital's sewer system. I saved the fused section for last, because I knew it would take more scrubbing, with a smaller brush, to clean the crevices and corners around the metal bracket and the bone graft. When I was satisfied that I'd removed all the soft tissue, I turned off the faucet, shook the water from the bones, and laid them on absorbent surgical pads on the counter. Then, switching on a lighted magnifier, I held the fused segment under the lens. What I saw was a juxtaposition of the familiar and the foreign: the natural curves and planes of the vertebrae, with a trapezoidal wedge of lighter bone—a shape that looked more like a machined part than a human bone—jammed between them, locked into place by lustrous metal and screws.

I was rotating the assembly beneath the light, studying it from the left side, when the phone on the wall began to ring. I ignored it, and after half a dozen rings it fell silent. A few seconds later, it jangled again; again I ignored it. Then, after a few seconds more, the door of the decomp room opened and Amy, the forensic center's receptionist, leaned in. "Dr. Brockton? I hate to disturb you, but Dr. Garcia's on line two for you, and he says it's important."

"Oops. Let me just get these gloves off and I'll pick up. Thanks, Amy."

Laying aside the bones and peeling off the gloves, I picked up the handset and pressed the blinking button. "Eddie, sorry to keep you waiting. I was just looking at Clarissa Lowe's cervical spine. It cleaned up very nicely."

"Don't look too closely," he said.

"Why not?"

"I just got a call from Calvin, my lab technician," he answered.

"Is Calvin the guy who's three doors down from me? The guy I saw looking into a microscope when I walked up the hall a few minutes ago?"

"Yes. Calvin. I think you should go look also. Can you go down to the lab and put me on the speakerphone?"

"Sure. If I lose you, call me back. Talk to you in a second." I pressed the "hold" button, and the light for the phone line began to blink again. Twenty yards from the decomp room was the forensic center's lab, a large room whose countertops bristled with petri dishes, culture incubators, and microscopes.

Calvin, a pale, stooped young man whose name I would never have recalled if Garcia hadn't mentioned it, glanced up from the microscope when I walked in. "'Lo, Dr. Brockton," he greeted me.

"Hi, Calvin. Dr. Garcia tells me you've got something I should see."

He flipped a switch on the scope; a monitor beside it lit up, and the screen filled with circles and ovals of gray and black. Their shapes reminded me of cross sections of tree trunks: circles within circles, crossed by faint lines radiating from the centers like wheel spokes.

I pressed the "speaker" button on the phone and was rewarded with a loud dial tone. "Oh, crap, I've lost Dr. Garcia," I said. Then I noticed the button for line two, still blinking. "Oh, wait." I pressed it, and the dial tone was replaced by hollow background noise. "Eddie, are you still there?"

"Yes. Are you in the lab with Calvin?"

"We're here," Calvin announced. "I've got the unstained slide on the monitor."

"Good," said Garcia. "Bill, do you recognize what you're seeing there?"

"I do." I'd seen hundreds of similar images over the years. Known as osteons and osteocytes, they were the microscopic framework of human bone—the skeleton's own inner skeleton, so to speak, magnified hundreds of times. "That must be from the sample we took from the cervical spine."

"Exactly," said Garcia. "Calvin, now show him the sample you treated with Gram's stain." Calvin twisted the stage of the microscope. The image on the screen spun dizzyingly, and a new slide clicked into place. This slide also showed bone, but the colors had changed to shades of beige and brown, with a sprinkling of tiny purple cylinders amid the structures of the bone.

"Um, remind me what Gram's stain is?"

"It's a stain, a dye, that certain bacteria absorb," Garcia answered. "It's named for Hans Christian Gram, the Danish microbiologist who developed it. Gram's stain distinguishes between two groups of bacteria, called Gram-negative and Gram-positive. Gram-positive bacteria absorb the stain and turn purple. Some species of Gram-positive bacteria are harmless; others are quite deadly."

"And how do you tell whether the purple stain Calvin's got here is a friendly species or a deadly strain?"

"The most precise way is a DNA analysis," he answered, "but that takes time. So I had Calvin do a two-stage stain. Calvin, could you show Dr. Brockton the next slide?" Calvin obliged, bringing up a slide showing small specks of red and black. "This second stain tells us that the bacteria in Lowe are from the genus *Clostridium*."

"Go on," I prompted.

"*Clostridium* is an interesting study in contrasts," he said. "There are about a hundred species of it. Some of them are very useful—they have the potential to convert wood into ethanol or to target therapeutic drugs at cancer tumors."

"So the good news is biofuels and magic bullets," I said. "What's the bad news?"

"Food poisoning. Tetanus. Botulism. Gas gangrene. Toxic shock. *Clostridium* produces some of the deadliest toxins on the planet. One thing about it that's interesting," he added, "is that we're exposed to these bacteria all the time. *Clostridium* lives mostly in the soil, in dirt and rotting organic material—there's probably a lot of it out at the Body Farm—but we also carry some species of it in our gastrointestinal tract. The vast majority of the time, our bodies manage to keep it in check."

"So something tipped the scales in Lowe's body after surgery," I said, "allowing the bacteria in her gut to multiply like crazy and spread throughout her body?"

"Actually, no," he answered. "I don't believe her GI tract was the source. Remember, these slides you're seeing are tissue samples from the allograft in her cervical spine. I think she received a graft of contaminated cadaver bone."

I stared at the images on the microscope monitor. If Garcia was right, the surgeon had unwittingly put a ticking bacteriological time bomb into his patient. And that bomb was sitting on a countertop a few doors down the hallway. And I'd been handling it casually—gloved, but not masked—for the past hour. "What should I do with the cervical spine? Should I boil it? Sterilize it in an autoclave? Incinerate it?"

"I'd like to do more testing on it. Maybe contact the company that supplied it. I checked the operating notes, but there's nothing that indicates who made it. I'll call the surgeon and find out. Meanwhile, would you bag it and freeze it?"

"Sure."

"And, Bill? Be sure to cover it with biohazard labels."

For once in the conversation, I was already way ahead of him.

TWO HOURS AND HALF A dozen hand washings later, Special Agent Ben Rankin phoned me. "Hello, Rooster," I said. "Are we still on for our meeting tomorrow morning?" We were scheduled to talk with Amanda Whiting, UT's general counsel, about the proposed sting operation.

"No. We need to reschedule it."

I was disappointed to hear that. We'd scheduled the meeting at eight at the FBI's main office, located downtown in the John Duncan Federal Building. The part I'd been looking forward to wasn't the meeting itself but the breakfast we'd decided to grab beforehand at Pete's, a downtown coffee shop just around the corner.

"You need to be someplace else in the morning?"

"I do. So do you."

"Me?" I checked my pocket calendar. According to it, my morning was open, except for the FBI meeting. "Where do I need to be in the morning?"

"Las Vegas. And actually, you need to be there tonight. Your flight leaves in two hours."

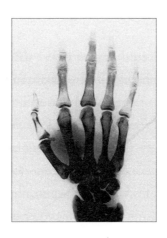

CHAPTER 22

I AWOKE TO THE THUNK OF THE 737'S LANDING GEAR cycling down on approach to the Las Vegas airport. As the plane banked in the night sky, the city glittered and flashed like the world's biggest carnival, full of dazzling promises, dizzying rides, and rigged games of skill and chance.

The trip itself was a high-stakes gamble, I reflected as the plane eased down to the runway. Las Vegas was not my dream destination; I'd far rather have been headed two hundred miles to the east, to the stark, rugged landscape of the Grand Canyon. But Vegas, not the Grand Canyon, was hosting the annual meeting of the National Consortium of Tissue Banks. At Rankin's last-minute request just ten hours earlier, I'd filled out the online registration form, dashed home to pack a bag, and then raced to catch a hastily arranged flight.

As the jet angled off the runway and onto a taxiway, I switched on my cell phone, which beeped to tell me I had a new voice mail.

"Call me," said Rankin's voice. I didn't call him back until after I'd caught the monorail to the main terminal—even the airport had the feel of a theme park—and hailed a cab for the hotel. Rankin picked up on the second ring. "Hey, how was the flight?"

"Long," I said. "I sure wish Knoxville were an airline hub. It makes no sense to me to fly two hundred miles east to Charlotte to catch a westbound flight. Hell, the plane from Charlotte to Vegas probably passed right over Knoxville. It's maddening to fly four hundred miles just to get back to the same place you started from two hours before."

"Sorry, Doc. I'd have let you fly out tonight on the Bureau jet with me and the other guys from Knoxville and Newark, but that would've blown your cover. We appreciate your going on such short notice."

"While you're feeling appreciative, be grateful that Amanda Whiting worked us in on a nanosecond's notice." Whiting, UT's general counsel, had actually cut short a meeting with the university president in order to hold an urgent conference with Rankin, Price, and me. She hadn't been happy about it, but before we left her office, she hand-wrote a confidential memo of understanding, signed by herself, the agents, and me, outlining and endorsing the role that the Body Farm and I would play in an undercover FBI sting. Now, as the wheels of the jet stopped on the tarmac in Las Vegas, the wheels of the sting—the wheels of justice, I hoped—began to turn.

"Great timing," Rankin was saying. "This tissue-bank convention's the perfect opportunity to make contact with Sinclair."

Raymond Sinclair was the founder and CEO of Tissue Sciences and Services, the New Jersey tissue bank that the FBI believed had obtained dozens of bodies from the MacArthur School of Medicine. "And you're sure he'll be here?"

"Well, I'm sure he flew from Newark to Las Vegas yesterday, and I'm sure he's scheduled to give a talk tomorrow morning. 'Enrolling Donors: Thinking Outside the Box.' I guess he means thinking outside the pine box." Rankin snorted. "You think the irony in the title was intentional?"

"Ask me after I hear his talk. What time and where?"

"Ten A.M., Nottingham Room."

"Nottingham? As in 'Sheriff of,' from Robin Hood? I thought the hotel was all about King Arthur. The hotel's called the Excalibur, right?"

"King Arthur, Robin Hood, same difference," he said. "Merrie Olde England. You were expecting rigorous historical accuracy at a casino hotel with red and blue plastic turrets at each corner?" He had a point there.

As Rankin went over the plan for tomorrow once more, the taxi left the airport and turned onto Sunset, then made a right onto Las Vegas Boulevard. To the left rose the three-winged tower of Mandalay Bay, its dark glass façade split by vertical shafts of golden light. Up ahead glittered a compressed version of New York City's skyline, where a roller coaster corkscrewed past a replica of the Empire State Building and the Statue of Liberty. Farther up the Strip, the Eiffel Tower blazed with light; it was only half the size of the real one, in Paris, but I had to admit, even a half-size Eiffel Tower was impressive. Although I wasn't fond of the noise or the crowds—or the traffic or the gambling or the drinking, for that matter—as an anthropologist I found Las Vegas fascinating. Plunked down in the middle of a hot, barren basin—Vegas averaged just four inches of rain a year, less than one-tenth Knoxville's amount—the city had no logical reason to exist, or at least no logical reason to exist where it did. Yet somehow, in the sands of the desert, it had carved out a unique, neon-lit niche for itself in the life and lore of the nation.

The taxi slowed as it passed the tawny sphinx guarding the Luxor, a black-glass pyramid of a hotel. From the pyramid's tip, a column of blue-white light soared into the sky: a searchlight that sought nothing, an eye staring blindly, blindingly upward. Years before, on a trip to the Middle East, I'd traveled to Luxor, the Great Pyramids, and the Valley of the Kings; seeing the comic-book replicas, I found myself appalled and amused in equal measure.

Just beyond the Luxor, the cab turned in at the Excalibur, its castle turrets topped with crayon-colored cones. I bid Rankin good night, paid the taxi driver, and stepped into the hotel's dark, mazy lobby, with its relentless *ching-ching-ching* of electronic slot machines. I checked in, rode the elevator up the vast tower of featureless rooms, and tumbled into bed to rest up for tomorrow morning's gambling, when—if luck was with me—I'd be betting with chips of flesh and bone from the Body Farm.

"ENROLLING DONORS: THINKING OUTSIDE the Box" was a more interesting talk than the clunky title had led me to expect. Raymond Sinclair—and the talk he gave—reminded me of Las Vegas: loud, flashy, and repellent, yet also equally fascinating. He began with a rapid-fire review of the history and growth of allograft transplants, transplants from dead bodies to living patients. First attempted a century and a half ago—a French surgeon transplanted skin from a fresh cadaver to a patient—allograft transplants had remained rare for decades but had soared during the second half of the twentieth century. By 2008 the number had risen to 1.5 million a year, and it was still rising fast.

Surgeries that had once been risky experimental procedures— transplanting corneas and rebuilding knees with cadaver cartilage, for instance—were now routine; meanwhile, new transplant surgeries were being developed all the time.

"So when the number of tissue transplants reaches two million a year," Sinclair said, "or five million a year, or *ten* million a year—and trust me, that'll happen in the blink of a laser-corrected eye—where will we get all those corneas and tendons and ligaments?" He paused to let the hundred people in the room consider the problem. "I'll tell you," he went on. "The government in Washington is gonna merge the IRS and the FDA to create a new federal agency that combines revenue collection with medical oversight. And if you think you pay an arm and a leg in taxes *now* . . ."

He left it unfinished, and as the joke slowly sank in, a few people laughed, and a chubby guy in the second row groaned.

"Hey, buddy, don't piss me off," Sinclair warned, "or I'll tell my amputation jokes, and those are really, really lame."

This time half the audience groaned, but the other half—and Sinclair himself—laughed at the outrageous political incorrectness. The bleary-eyed, jet-lagged crowd was warming to Vegas Ray.

And then he turned on a dime. "Seriously, folks, how do we, as tissue banks, keep pace with the rising demand? The organ-procurement network has made huge progress on that front, by a very simple mechanism. Millions of people in the United States every year are now routinely asked the question 'Do you wish to be an organ donor?' when they renew their driver's license. The number of people who've said yes to that question—the number who opt in—is incredible: eighty million. *Eighty million people* have said, 'Yes, I do.' If you've got a spouse or a son or a daughter wait-listed for a kidney, the suspense is pure hell. Still, at this moment hundreds of millions of human organs are flowing, at whatever speed fate decrees, toward the mouth of the donor pipeline. Isn't that amazing?"

He looked around the room, and heads nodded, including mine.

"But. *But*," he went on, "even with all the public support for organ donation, it's not enough. Thousands of people on the organ waiting list die every year for lack of a matching transplant. And whole-body donation faces far bigger challenges. People are good at denying the finality of death if they're signing over just a few parts. But the clerks at the DMV don't ask about whole-body donation, and—somebody correct me if I'm wrong—Hollywood isn't rushing to make blockbuster movies about cadaver tendon or bone paste."

Damn skippy, I heard myself thinking. It was an expression I'd picked up from Miranda, which I understood to mean "Amen, brother," or "You got that right."

"There are two things we absolutely must do," he went on, "if we're to have any hope of enlisting enough whole-body donors to meet the growing need for tissue. First, we have *got* to do a better job of storytelling. People connect with human stories— stories of wrenching need, stories of inspiring generosity. If all we say is, 'Give the gift of life,' we're doing a piss-poor job of educating the public about the importance of whole-body donation. It's crucial that we tell the stories of real-life people—flesh-and-blood people—whose broken lives could be mended with tissue from whole-body donation." He raised his arms and spread them wide, a gesture that reminded me of paintings of Jesus. "We are modern-day miracle workers, folks: healing the sick, helping the lame walk, and making the blind *see*. And we have a duty, to donors and recipients alike, to share those stories proudly with the world." His fervor surprised me, and so did the enthusiastic applause it inspired.

He nodded a couple times in humble acknowledgment, then held up a hand to quiet the room. "You might not feel so kindly toward me when I make this second point," he said. "The other thing we've got to do, to start thinking outside the box, is to get more realistic and more creative about incentives for whole-body donation. Tissue Sciences, like many tissue banks, now covers the cost of cremation for whole-body donors. We harvest and process everything we can, we cremate the remains, and—if the family wishes—we return the ashes to the family. For people who are planning ahead, we offer the opportunity not just to help the sick but also to help their own families, by sparing them the cost of a funeral or cremation. For a grieving family, we lighten the financial burden of death. But that's too little, too late. We need to expand the incentives we offer families who donate their loved ones . . . and we need to create substantial financial incentives for individuals considering becoming whole-body donors."

Several hands went up at the phrase "substantial financial incentives." He pointed to an attractive young blond woman in the center of the room, who asked, "Are you suggesting we pay prospective donors?"

"You betcha."

"But isn't that prohibited by law?"

He beamed. "You betcha," he said. "Sort of. But not really. The Uniform Anatomical Gift Act and the National Organ Transplant Act do prohibit the buying and selling of human organs and tissues, but there are a couple of gray areas. As all of you who work at tissue banks already know, we're allowed to recover costs associated with procuring organs and tissues. And defining 'costs' can be an exercise in creative writing—just ask any accountant at a Hollywood film studio. The reality is, tissue banks and anatomical-supply companies buy and sell bodies all the time; we just don't directly, openly pay the body donors or the families who donate. And that, I believe, is the step we must take if we're to meet the growing need for tissue and tissue-based products."

More hands shot up, but the blond woman who'd asked the first question fired off a follow-up before anyone else got a chance to. "But isn't the problem that paying donors—organ donors or whole-body donors—exploits the poor for the sake of the rich?" Her question prompted murmurs of assent throughout the room.

Sinclair shrugged. "Does it? Funny how it's always people with money and power who say that. Anybody polling the poor about this issue? Case in point: Say some peasant in Pakistan sells a kidney to some rich American for twenty thousand bucks. I pick Pakistan because organ selling is pretty common there. Twenty thousand dollars is twenty *years'* worth of income for the average Pakistani. Sure, he's taking a huge health risk, but are his other options any better? Which is worse, taking a health risk for twenty grand or watching his kids starve to death for nothing?"

Half a dozen hands shot up, and several people tried to interrupt him with objections, but Sinclair plowed ahead.

"Hang on, hang on, everybody gets a turn, but let me finish making my point. I know a dozen bioethicists who say it's exploitative to buy a kidney from a poor person, but I know three or four who think a mentally competent adult has a basic right to self-determination. Isn't that one of the fundamental principles of America—life, liberty, and the pursuit of happy, free-market dollars?"

A lot of faces were frowning.

"Fertility clinics pay sperm donors and egg donors. Couples pay surrogate mothers to bear children for them. It's illegal to buy or sell a baby, but any honest attorney or social worker who's spent much time in the trenches can tell you it happens."

He paused for breath, and the hands shot up again.

"Wait, I'm almost done," he said. "Seriously, we actually *can* buy bodies legally today, we just can't *call* it 'buying bodies.' What we're allowed to call it is 'sparing you or your family the expense of a funeral.' Talk about dancing around the truth. The average funeral costs six or seven thousand bucks, so what that means is we're allowed to buy bodies for six or seven grand, provided we don't own up to what the transaction really is. What a hypocritical crock. Insurance companies are willing to negotiate what they call 'life settlements'—cash payments for insurance policies owned by old folks and sick folks. Not the full amount of the policy—that's why the insurance companies are willing to do it—but at least you don't have to be dead to collect. A woman with ovarian cancer who's worth a hundred thousand dollars dead might rather get fifty thousand while she's still alive. Shouldn't she have that right? The right to cash in on her mortality? Shouldn't anyone? People mortgage assets like houses all the time. Why not let them mortgage their bodies? Isn't the body an asset, a very personal asset? How come, in the whole chain of organ and tissue transplantation—a multibillion-dollar enterprise—the one person who can't make money off the damn deal is the donor?"

He shrugged again, an olive-branch, peacemaking kind of smile. "These are complicated legal and ethical issues, sure. But we need to grapple with them. And we need to get more honest, more creative, and more aggressive about offering financial incentives for whole-body donation. Otherwise we simply can't expect to keep pace with the growing need for human tissue."

"Bullshit."

The comment came, in a confident, strong voice, from a darkened rear corner of the room. Sinclair looked startled; so did everyone else in the room. The speaker stepped out of the shadows and into a pool of light near the room's rear door. I was shocked to see that it was Glen Faust of OrthoMedica.

"I think you're selling people short. I think you're seriously underestimating the generosity of the human spirit."

At the podium Sinclair reddened. "I'm just saying we need to find realistic financial strategies for encouraging whole-body donations."

"No, you're saying people are greedy or stingy, that they have to be bought. I don't agree, and I see one other person in the room who I suspect might back me up on this point." He looked in my direction and pointed at me. "Dr. Brockton, forgive me for putting you on the spot, but have you had difficulty recruiting whole-body donors for your program?"

His question caught me utterly off guard. Price and Rankin had stressed the need to keep a low profile at the conference—the plan we'd agreed on was that I'd introduce myself to Sinclair after his talk and look for ways to bond with him—but it suddenly felt as if a spotlight as bright as the Luxor pyramid's beacon was shining directly on me.

I stood up slowly, buying a few seconds of time, and cleared my throat. "Well, I reckon I'd have to say no, we haven't had a lot of difficulty."

Sinclair eyed me dubiously. "And your name and affiliation?"

"Bill Brockton. I'm the chairman of the Anthropology Department at the University of Tennessee in Knoxville. The program Dr. Faust mentioned is our decomposition-research facility. Most people call it by its nickname, the Body Farm. We study postmortem human decay and the way the rate of decay is affected by factors like temperature, humidity, presence or absence of clothing, and so on. We also do a lot of trainings for crime-scene investigators, teaching them how to find buried bodies, how to search for scattered bones, that sort of thing."

Sinclair considered this. "And you use donated bodies for this work?"

"We do. Mostly. Some of our specimens are unclaimed bodies from the medical examiner's system, but the majority are donated bodies. About a thousand people have donated their bodies so far, and we've got another sixteen hundred donors on our version of a waiting list." I heard a few chuckles at my spin on the term "waiting list."

Soon I found myself answering a string of rapid-fire questions. People asked about our research, asked how we cleaned the skeletal material, asked for details on the donation program. Finally someone asked where we'd put the sixteen hundred donors on our waiting list. "I honestly don't know," I said. I decided there'd never be a better opportunity to dangle the line that Price and Rankin had liked, though this wasn't exactly the way I'd envisioned casting it. "It's not exactly that we have too many donated bodies," I said. "We just don't have enough space or enough funding."

More questions followed. I felt bad for Sinclair. I hadn't even planned to say anything, let alone steal the limelight, but once it shifted in my direction, I didn't know how to get out of it.

To his credit, he didn't seem to mind. When the session ended at ten forty-five, he made a point of coming over to speak to me. Faust, on the other hand, gave me a brief wave from the back of the room, then darted out the door like a scalded cat. There appeared to be no love lost between him and Sinclair, and I wondered what had originally caused the tension.

Sinclair hung back till a few people had finished chatting with me, then offered me a smile and a handshake. "Dr. Brockton, you certainly livened up the discussion," he said. "It was fascinating, and I appreciate it. I have to say, you make me wonder if I've been too quick to resort to the 'throw money at it' solution to the problem of motivating donors."

"Well, we've been really fortunate," I said. "The university is very supportive, the local media seem to like us, and we've benefited from the *CSI* craze. A rising tide lifts all boats, and we're happy to be bobbing along at the high-water mark."

Suddenly he frowned, aiming a finger. "I have a suspicion about you," he said, and I felt my stomach clench. Had I been so clumsy, so obvious, that I'd already botched things? "I suspect," he went on, "you're far too modest."

So perhaps I hadn't failed after all—not yet at least.

My relief turned to delight, followed swiftly by panic, when he added, "If you've got time, I'd love to hear more about your program over coffee."

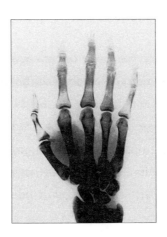

CHAPTER 23

"SHERWOOD FOREST CAFÉ OR SIR GALAHAD'S PUB?"
Sinclair offered the hotel map for my perusal.

"Tough choice," I mused. "If I were going just by the names,
I'd go for Sherwood Forest, but it looks like it's right off the casino floor, so I'm guessing it's pretty noisy. Sir Galahad's is on the
second level, so maybe it's quieter."

"Sir Galahad's it is." He motioned toward the escalator, and
we headed down a floor from the meeting rooms. "Who the hell
was Sir Galahad? Got any idea?"

"Hmm. One of the Knights of the Round Table." I dug around
in my memory banks. As a boy I'd read some of the Arthurian
legends, but tales of chivalry were a far cry from blunt-force
trauma and knife marks in bone. "Seems like Galahad was the
squeaky-clean knight," I ventured. "Raised by nuns. Chaste
and very pious, when he wasn't busy hacking foes to bits with
his broadsword." I fished around for any additional factoids I'd

stored about Galahad. "Spent a lot of time on a quest for the Holy Grail. That's about all I recall."

"That's a lot. I don't recall that much about the talk I just gave."

The escalator deposited us in front of a shuttered Italian restaurant and, beside it, a theater whose nightly show was "Thunder from Down Under," billed as "Australia's Hottest Hunks" and "Las Vegas' Best Male Strip Show." It struck me as interesting irony that the male strippers were performing a stone's throw from an establishment named for the Arthurian knight who embodied chastity and purity.

Sir Galahad's was closed, too, so we ended up buying coffee from a Starbucks stand and doughnuts from a Krispy Kreme counter. I suspected that the Krispy Kremes were not what had sustained Sir Galahad on his search for the Grail, but they did taste divine: warm, cloudlike puffs of dough, deep-fried to airy perfection, then varnished with a crisp, delicate sugar glaze. "That's tasty," I marveled. "*That* would be worth a serious quest."

Sinclair shook his head. "I gotta disagree with you there. I've never been a fan of the Krispy Kreme. I'm a die-hard Dunkin' Donuts man myself."

"Dunkin' Donuts? But they're so cakey."

"Exactly," he said. "That's what makes 'em good." He shrugged. "You're from Tennessee, I'm from Jersey. Maybe it's a geographic thing."

"Maybe that's it," I conceded. "It did take a while for Krispy Kreme to cross the Mason-Dixon Line."

He laughed. "There was a big article in the *New York Times* when the first Krispy Kreme opened in Manhattan. The barbarians were at the gates."

"If you think Krispy Kreme is culture shock for New Yorkers," I said, "just wait till Cracker Barrel hits town."

"Hey, bring it on. The more biscuits and gravy and fried okra people eat, the better it is for my business, and yours." He offered me his half-eaten doughnut. "You want the rest of that?"

"No thanks. One's my limit. When I was in my thirties, three was my limit. In my forties it dropped to two. Now, in my fifties, it's one."

"Their business is gonna go down the crapper when you hit your sixties," he said. "Remind me not to invest in Krispy Kreme stock." He pushed the doughnut aside and leaned forward. "So you said you use donated bodies for research, but also for training, right?"

I nodded.

"Tell me about the training. Who trains with bodies from the Body Farm, and how?"

"We work most often with the National Forensic Academy," I told him. "They offer a ten-week course for crime-scene and crime-lab techs, four times a year. The NFA brings in experts on fingerprints, blood-spatter analysis, hair and fiber evidence, that sort of thing. Our piece of the curriculum is teaching them how to find clandestine graves and skeletal remains." I nearly added that we spent a week every spring teaching those skills to FBI agents as well, but I was afraid I might give myself away if I mentioned the FBI—like a nervous poker player whose eye twitches when he tries a big bluff.

"Ever do any training with surgeons?"

"Surgeons?" I scanned backward through the talks I'd given during the past few years. "I don't think so. I do continuing-education lectures every year for lots of dentists and nurses, but no groups of surgeons. You know how surgeons are—one rung above God Almighty in the cosmic order. They're not going to sit through some lecture by a lowly anthropologist."

"True," he laughed, "but I wasn't thinking of a lecture. More like an intensive, hands-on approach. Small sessions—ten or twenty docs—working on actual human material, the real deal. To learn a new procedure, you have to *do* it, right? But what patient in his right mind would want to be the guy whose pancreas or pecker you practice on?"

"Not me," I agreed.

"So that's another way tissue banks provide a huge service. Sure, providing tissues for transplants is our primary role, but providing material for research and medical training—absolutely crucial."

I didn't need convincing on that point, but he wanted to talk, and I wanted to keep him circling the bait, so I nodded enthusiastically.

"We helped with an interesting training a couple months ago," I said. "Not a medical training, but similar—a disaster training, simulating mass fatalities from a radioactive 'dirty bomb.' We provided fifteen bodies, and the disaster teams practiced finding the radioactive contamination and cleaning the bodies."

"I hope they wore their lead-lined undies. Was that for FEMA?"

"Not exactly." FEMA, the Federal Emergency Management Agency, had sent a few representatives to the training, as had the U.S. Army, but those weren't the lead organizations. "It was organized by DMORT, the Disaster Mortuary Operational Response Team. Mostly volunteers—forensic dentists, EMTs, funeral directors, cops—who have some experience with death and are willing to help identify the dead after airplane crashes and hurricanes."

"Sure, I know DMORT. I've done trainings for 'em. How to improvise cold-storage facilities at remote sites. How to protect yourself against hepatitis C."

As he talked, I noticed that his chin was flecked with crumbs of sugar and doughnut.

"Hey, here's a joke I used to tell DMORT people heading down to Louisiana after Katrina: What's the best way to keep from getting hep C in New Orleans?"

I shrugged.

"Stay in New Jersey." He chuckled. "Hey, here's another one: What do you look for when you're looking for a DMORT team member?"

Again I shrugged.

"You don't need to look for anything; you just sniff—you can smell 'em a mile away."

Mentally I was cursing Price and Rankin for roping me into this, and kicking myself under the table for agreeing to help. "That's terrible," I said.

"I know." He grinned. "But hey, if we can't find a little humor in our line of work, we'll go nuts or slit our wrists, right?"

"Right." At the moment I was feeling a powerful urge to walk away. Instead I shifted the conversation to something I was actually curious about. "I was surprised when Glen Faust interrupted you the way he did."

He made a face. "I wasn't."

"So you know him?"

"Unfortunately."

"Is there a story there?"

"Not really. He's just a little full of himself for my taste." Sinclair reached inside his jacket and took out a folded program, which he opened to the next day's schedule. "He's giving a talk this afternoon—'Tissue banks are obsolete' is the message, though he's calling it something fancier. It's his manifesto about rebuilding the body with stem cells and cloning and bioengineering. You should go hear him."

"Are you going?"

"Don't need to. I've heard the spiel before." He pointed to Faust's name on the agenda. "See how he lists himself? 'Dr. Glen McFarland Faust, M.D., Ph.D., Fellow, BMES'? Let's all bow down. And then barf."

His hostility startled me. "Have you two clashed before today? Is there bad blood between you?"

"Bad blood? Naw. I just think he's a self-important prick, that's all."

His eyes locked onto something over my shoulder, and as they shifted and his head swiveled, I saw that he was tracking a young woman—a girl, really, probably eighteen or twenty. She was tall and curvy, wearing tight jeans and a low-cut top that called attention to her figure, and she walked in a way that suggested she liked the attention.

Sinclair sucked in a breath and shook his head abruptly, as if he were snapping out of a dream. "Hot damn, that is one fine woman. I'd love to make a little donation to her tissue bank, wouldn't you?"

I felt myself blushing. "She's a bit young for me," I said. "Looks like one of my undergraduate students."

"Your students look like that?"

"Some of them."

"Well, shit," he said. "I need to go back to school and get a Ph.D. in anthropology, so I can teach at the University of Tennessee."

"Bad idea."

"How come? You think I'd get caught messing around with a student?"

"I think you'd get all self-important if you had that 'Ph.D.' after your name."

He laughed. "Touché. So what were we talking about, before I got distracted by that gorgeous young thing?"

"Faust, I think, but I think we were done with him. Before that, I'm not sure. Trainings?" I hoped I wasn't being too obvious in my attempt to set the hook.

"Bingo." He thought for a moment. "I know what I wanted to ask you about. Consent forms. We're in the process of overhauling our donor consent forms right now, and we're wrestling with how much detail to include. On your forms do you spell out all the things you might-do to bodies in the course of your research?"

"We don't," I said. "Our consent form is just two sentences long. It starts out, 'I do hereby dispose of and give my body, after my death, to The University of Tennessee, Knoxville, for use by the Department of Anthropology or its designee for educational and research purposes.' The second sentence asks family members to notify us immediately when the donor dies."

"Short and sweet," he mused. "And very broad. That phrase 'or its designee' gives you a lot of latitude."

"It does. It frees us up to let DMORT or the National Forensic Academy or the FBI use our donated bodies."

"The FBI?"

Oh, crap, I thought, *I've just blown it.* I nodded, hoping my face hadn't turned crimson. "They were testing sonar as a way of finding submerged bodies, so they asked us to loan them a couple of cadavers."

"How'd it turn out? The sonar experiment?"

"They didn't tell me. Just brought back the waterlogged bodies a couple weeks later. The FBI tends to hold its cards pretty close to the vest."

"Even though you provided the bodies?"

I nodded.

"For free?"

I nodded again, and he shook his head at the injustice of it. He pressed his index finger into a pile of crumbs on his paper plate, then raised it to his mouth and sucked off the crumbs. His eyes swiveled up to me.

"You work with them often?"

I felt myself tensing—was he onto me? was he possibly even toying with me?—but I willed myself to relax. "I wouldn't say 'often.' More like 'occasionally.' A handful of cases in the past ten years."

"Hmm," he grunted. I was bracing myself for a barrage of follow-up questions when he shifted in his plastic chair and held up a finger. "Excuse me just a second." He pulled a vibrating BlackBerry from his pocket and scrolled down the display, frowning. "Well, hell," he said. "Dr. Brockton, I'm sorry, but I need to go put out a little brushfire."

He stood to go, so I did likewise, feeling a mixture of relief and disappointment: relief at escaping further interrogation about my dealings with the FBI, disappointment that I hadn't managed to set the hook and land the fish.

I was just about to offer a handshake and a good-bye when he stopped me. "I'd love to continue our conversation about trainings, if you've got time and any interest."

I felt my face breaking into a smile, which I hoped wasn't

transparently triumphant. "Sure," I said. "I've got an early flight in the morning. The ivory tower calls. But I'm free late this afternoon or early this evening, if that works for you."

"Perfect. How about seven o'clock? And how about we get out of this cheesy hotel?"

"Fine with me," I said. "Do you know the restaurants? Is there someplace you'd recommend?"

"Actually," he said, "I had a slightly different idea just now. How would you feel about getting together at the library? I try to go there anytime I'm in town."

"The library?" It was an unexpected suggestion, but I liked it. The quiet and calm would be a welcome contrast to the relentless barrage of noise and lights that filled the public areas of the hotel and the streets. "That's my kind of place. Is it walking distance from the hotel?"

"I'm afraid not, but it's worth a trip. I'd share a cab with you, but I've got a meeting at a hospital late this afternoon, so I won't be coming straight from the hotel." He reached into his coat pocket again and took out a business card, then scrawled on the back. "The driver's bound to know where it is, but here's the address, just in case."

"And they'll be open at seven?"

"Oh, for sure. I've been there plenty of times at seven."

"Okay, sounds good," I said. "I'll let you get back to your brushfire. See you at the library at seven."

He smiled broadly. "See you there. Looking forward to it."

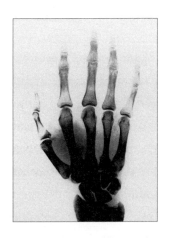

CHAPTER 24

a phrase bound to draw a crowd—an interested and potentially nervous or hostile crowd—at a tissue-bank convention.

He began with a brief PowerPoint tour of OrthoMedica's R&D complex in Bethesda. The facility was easily twice the size of UT's biomedical engineering building. It bristled with medical-imaging equipment, robotic surgical tools, and computer-controlled machine lathes. I was impressed: OrthoMedica looked like a cross between a research university, a teaching hospital, an automotive assembly line, a NASA clean room, and a computer factory.

The subtitle of Faust's presentation—"Rebuilding the Human Body"—gave him a launching pad to showcase the company's many products: artificial hips, knees, shoulders, elbows, and orthopedic hardware, as well as a line of surgical tools, developed to allow surgeons to install OrthoMedica parts—and only OrthoMedica parts—with precision and ease. "Our next generation of products and procedures will be custom-fit to every patient," Faust said. "We're developing interfaces that can translate a patient's CT scan into specifications for computer-controlled fabricating systems—lathes and molds and laser cutting systems—to create parts and assemblies in better, stronger alloys and ceramics and plastics. We'll custom-build replacement parts—synthetic bones and artificial joints—accurate to within one ten-thousandth of an inch." He capped off the brief sales pitch with a swift series of 3-D animations, showing diseased and damaged human joints and limbs undergoing robotic surgery, their flaws fixed with the new, improved products and procedures being pioneered, at that very moment, by OrthoMedica.

Moving on, he discussed synthetic scaffolds: fine meshes of carbon, collagen, and other fibers that provided frameworks for bone or cartilage to grow into. He showed micrographs and animations of nanomaterials—tiny rods and tubes only a few molecules in diameter—that could, in the not-too-distant future, be delivered to an injured bone or ligament with a syringe, whereupon they'd assemble themselves into a precisely shaped scaffold. They reminded me of tiny Tinkertoys, these nanomaterials around which a patient's body would mend itself. "Rebuilding the body," Faust reminded us.

Next came bone. "Chemically, bone is mostly calcium phosphate," he said. "When we think about creating synthetic bones, one of the first materials that comes to mind is ceramic." He lifted a white coffee mug from the podium—one of the mugs from the tables at the back of the room—and tossed it upward six inches. He watched it spin end over end, then caught the base in his palm, as if he'd flipped a flapjack in a skillet. "This mug's made of aluminum oxide. Aluminum oxide's cheap and easy to mass-produce. It can withstand heavy static loads"—he bent and set the mug on the floor, upside down, then placed one foot on it and stood—"such as the weight of the human body." He retrieved the mug from the floor, flipping and catching it again. "But the human skeleton has to withstand more than just static loads." He tossed the mug a third time, but this time he made no move to catch it. The mug tumbled end over end past his hand, past the end of the podium, then shattered on the marble floor below the stage. The sharp crash made me jump, even though I'd seen it coming, and I wasn't the only one in the ballroom who did.

"This is ceramic, too," he said, taking a gleaming white sphere from his hip pocket. The sphere measured about an inch and a half in diameter; he rotated it in his fingertips, and as he did, the PowerPoint screen displayed a three-foot image of the same glossy object, also rotating. A small portion of the sphere had been sliced off, creating a flat spot the size of a quarter, pierced by a hole the diameter of my little finger. "This is the femoral head—the ball—from our best hip replacement. It makes a great ball bearing, because it's harder, smoother, and more corrosion-resistant than titanium or other metals." He tossed it into the air a foot, then caught it. "Like the coffee cup, this is made of aluminum oxide." He lofted it ten feet into the air and let it fall to the marble floor. Instead of shattering, it bounced several times, then rolled to a stop against the front of the stage. Faust retrieved it and tossed and caught it a third time—the man liked threes—then held it up again. "But the difference between the fifty-cent mug and the hundred-dollar femoral head is that the femoral head has microscopic fibers embedded in the ceramic. It's reinforced, like concrete with steel rebar, on a much finer scale. So is human bone: The load-bearing, brittle minerals in bone are rein-forced with collagen fibers. Bone's better—lighter, stronger, and far more flexible—than reinforced concrete. And though it pains me to admit it, bone's better than any synthetic substitute we've been able to engineer at OrthoMedica." He smiled. "So far, that is. But I hope not for long."

He ended the talk with a brief discussion of stem cells—the simple, undifferentiated cells in the early stages of the human embryo, from which every specialized cell, tissue, and organ in the body eventually develops. Stem-cell researchers were already conducting clinical trials in which stem cells were being used to patch damaged hearts and repair spinal-cord injuries, he noted. "This isn't just pie in the sky," he stressed. "In Spain in 2008, a tuberculosis patient with a damaged windpipe got a new one, grown from stem cells and airway cells. Stem cells created a true replacement part for her." As he flashed up graphics showing how the windpipe had been created in the spinning chamber of a "bio-reactor" and then transplanted into the patient, I heard murmurs of amazement from the audience.

Faust stilled the murmurs with a rhetorical question. "So is this the beginning of the end for tissue banks? The dying days of allograft tissue transplants from deceased donors?" He shook his head decisively. "Not in our lifetimes anyway. Case in point: That windpipe created from the patient's own stem cells? The stem cells needed a scaffold, and where did that scaffold come from? From the windpipe of a deceased donor. A cadaver. Everything but the collagen matrix of the cadaver windpipe was removed—dissolved and washed away—and the patient's cells were cultured around that collagen matrix. So the stem-cell magic couldn't have happened without cadaver tissue. That won't always be the case;

maybe someday cadaver tissue will no longer be necessary. Unlikely. But if that day ever dawns, it will bring with it a new era of medical miracles, and won't that be a great day for humanity?" He paused to let us contemplate that. "Thank you for your time and attention."

I stayed around to speak to him after the Q&A session. "Very interesting," I said. "Impressive research and production facilities you've got. No wonder OrthoMedica's doing so well."

"We try." He smiled.

"But you're not on the verge of turning stem cells into replacement hands."

"I wish," he said. "You're thinking about your friend? What's his name? Dr. Garcia?"

I nodded, surprised he remembered.

"Someday we might be able to grow a new pair of hands for Dr. Garcia. Start with a few of his bone-marrow cells, reverse-engineer them into stem cells, and then program those stem cells to turn into a hand-shaped assembly of bones and muscles and nerves and blood vessels."

"But that's not six months or a year or even five years away," I speculated.

"More like fifty," he said. "In my most wildly optimistic moments—my delusional moments, my colleagues would probably say—I'd guess that we're five years from being able to grow livers or kidneys, twenty years from hearts, and half a century from hands or feet. Reality is, we'll probably never be able to grow hands and feet in the lab." He smiled again. "I grew up on *Popular Science* magazine, and every month the cover showed some incredible invention that was about to change our lives forever. Flying cars. Personal jet packs. Elevators to the moon. Colonies on Mars. Limitless power from a gallon of seawater." He shook his head good-naturedly. "I don't much care about the elevator to the moon, but I'm still disappointed I don't have the flying car or the jet pack."

I returned the smile. I, too, had spent many youthful hours anticipating *Popular Science* breakthroughs that never quite materialized.

"On the other hand," Faust went on, "sometimes they got it right. I seem to recall stories about heart transplants and microwave ovens and this clunky-looking gadget called the personal computer. Surely stem cells, too. But growing replacement hands and feet? I doubt even *Popular Science* is that optimistic."

"So could I circle back to something we talked about on your visit to Tennessee? The i-Hand? You recommended that for Dr. Garcia, and he was all set to get one, but now he can't."

He winced. "I'm sorry about the timing of that. The decision to withdraw the i-Hand was made by our board of directors," he said. "I was opposed to it. Still am. But OrthoMedica's a multibillion-dollar company, and the people in the boardroom are the ones responsible for making the tough business decisions."

"Any chance there's a spare i-Hand still tucked in a warehouse somewhere? A leftover left hand?"

"I'll check," he said. "I hate to sound discouraging, but don't hold your breath."

I nodded, disappointed.

"On the bright side, though, the lawyers don't seem to be finding anything too objectionable in the research collaboration I'm proposing with UT. You still want that CT scanner we've been talking about?"

"Absolutely. I've been talking to the facilities people about putting it in the spot I showed you, right by the gate of the Body Farm."

"Sounds perfect." He flashed me a thumbs-up. "If you'd put those people in touch with my assistant, we'll see if we can get those wheels in motion." He clapped me on the shoulder and shook my hand. "Now, if you'll forgive me, I've got a conference call to make to my masters back in Maryland." He turned to go, then stopped and reached into his pocket. "Here," he said. "For good luck." He handed me the ceramic femoral head.

The sphere's perfect smoothness and heft felt reassuring in my hand at first. But soon I found my fingers worrying at the flat spot and the hole at its center. The hole, my rational mind knew, was simply the attachment point for the metal neck of the artificial hip implant. But somehow, in my mind, the cavity evoked something else: the dark, hollow place into which I was about to crawl with Raymond Sinclair of Tissue Sciences and Services.

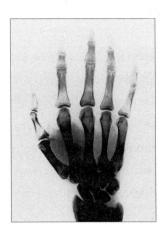

CHAPTER 25

cabdriver I was heading to the library, he pulled away from the hotel. The sun was going down in the distance, and the neon was coming up all around me. "Do you need the address?"

"Naw, I know where it is," he said, waving off the card Sinclair had given me. The cab headed east on Tropicana Avenue. In a few short blocks, the bustle and blare of the Strip receded and I felt myself sink into the seat. The cab smelled of stale cigarettes and stale coffee and soured sweat, but I was too tired to care. I was just beginning to doze off when I heard the driver say, "Sir, we're here."

I opened my eyes and looked out the window. At first I felt half sleepy and half confused, but then I felt merely totally confused. The cab had stopped in front of a low cinder-block building that pulsed with music. I tapped the cabdriver on the shoulder. "Excuse me," I said. "I think you misunderstood. I need to go to the library. Here's the address." I thrust the card at him; he took it grudgingly and gave it the briefest of glances.

"Yup, that's the address. And yeah, that's where we are." He pointed to a sign above the building's entrance. I had to lean to the side and look overhead to see the red neon letters: THE LI-BRARY. Another large, flashing sign at the edge of the road pro-claimed GIRLS! GIRLS! GIRLS! Underneath those words was the line CHECK OUT OUR SEXY LIBRARIANS!

I felt a sinking feeling in my stomach. "Listen, I need to make a phone call," I told the driver, "and I might need you to take me back to my hotel. Can you give me some privacy for a couple min-utes? Maybe stretch your legs or take a smoke break? You can leave the meter running."

"Sure, no sweat." He pulled forward, away from the entrance, and angled the cab into a parking spot. Leaving both the meter and the engine running, he got out and lit up.

I leaned down and spoke to my chest, waving my hand in front of my tie. Strapped to my chest was a tiny microphone, with a digital recorder and transmitter tucked under my armpit; my tiepin was actually a miniature video camera, feeding images to a tiny flash drive. Two hours earlier Rankin and a New Jersey agent named Spellman had slipped into my hotel room and fitted me with the surveillance gear. "Rooster, are you there? Spellman? Where are you guys?" Through the fabric of my shirt, I tapped the microphone three times. "Can you hear me? Call me on my cell right away. This is not good."

Nothing happened, so I scrolled through the recent calls on my cell phone and hit "send" when I got to Rankin's number. *Pick up, pick up, pick up,* I prayed. Rankin's voice answered my prayer. "Christ, Doc, what's wrong? He's not even here yet.

And don't thump the mike—you damn near blew out our eardrums."

"Sorry; it was an SOS signal," I explained. "Sinclair wasn't talking about the place where you borrow books. He was talking about a strip club called The Library." Suddenly it hit me: Rankin had used the word "here." I scanned the parking lot. "Where are you?"

"Across the street in a panel truck. Six of us. But don't look."

I looked anyway. There it was, a carpet-cleaning van. "You knew," I said. "You knew he was bringing me to a strip club."

"I didn't know at first, but I did know before you got in the cab," he admitted. "We can't send an informant someplace we haven't checked out ahead of time. That'd be dangerous. And shoddy." He laughed. "A strip club called The Library. Only in Vegas, huh, Doc? You gotta love it."

"No I don't," I snapped. "I hate it."

"Don't worry. We'll be watching and listening, and we're close enough to come in and get you if we need to."

"Crap, I wasn't expecting a strip club. What do I do?"

"What do you mean, 'What do I do?' I believe look but don't touch would be a good plan to follow. Unless you want to get to know the bouncer really quick."

"I'm not asking about etiquette. I'm asking if you actually think I should go in there. It seems pretty tawdry."

"Of course it's tawdry," he said. "I mean, I'm not the anthropologist here, but isn't the tawdriness the _point_ of a strip club?"

"I don't know. I've never been in one."

"Honest?"

"Honest."

"Well, then, this should be interesting. Listen to this. This is the description of the place that's posted on the Web. 'This gentlemen's club isn't just for bookworms. The club actually does have volumes lining the entrance, but the clientele comes here for a different type of learning experience. And they visit often enough to keep The Library busy even on school nights.' That's hilarious."

"Not to me," I said. "I really don't like this."

I heard him sigh. "I'm sorry you don't like it, Doc. I'm not asking you to like it. But I am asking you to *do* it. Remember, this guy's gonna want you—at least we *hope* he's gonna want you—to break federal laws for him. If you balk at setting foot in a strip club, he might have deep doubts about your scofflaw sincerity."

"So if he wants me to hire a hooker or snort cocaine, am I supposed to do that, too, Rooster? How much of me's for sale here?"

"Not that much," he said. "So no, don't do hookers or cocaine. But do this meeting. Please."

"Hang on while I think about this." The meter's digits glowed bright red in the darkness below the dashboard; currently it read $17.50.

A finger tapped my window, and I fumbled for the button to roll it down. "Sorry, I'm almost done," I turned to tell the driver.

But it was not the driver. "Take all the time you need," said Raymond Sinclair. The cab's meter flipped to $18.00.

"I need to go," I said into my cell phone. "I'm meeting a friend, and he just got here. I'll talk to you later." I snapped the phone closed, got out of the cab, and walked into The Library with Raymond Sinclair.

The front door opened into a short hallway with a counter along one side; behind it sat a burly man wearing a bored expression, a tight black T-shirt, and a dusting of ashes from the cigarette that dangled from his lips. Sinclair flashed the man a plastic card labeled VIP PLATINUM MEMBER, which he acknowledged with a nod. A battered clipboard lay on the counter. The man nudged it toward me.

"Sign in," he said, "and I need to see a driver's license."

I added my name to the list of other men and then fished my license out of my wallet and handed it to him, feeling embarrassed and vaguely guilty. He compared the names, handed my license back across the counter, then pressed a button beside the counter to buzz us into the main room.

The room was loud and dark, with a lighted square stage in the middle. A few men sat on low stools surrounding the stage, a handful more sat at tables dispersed throughout the room, and several others were tucked into booths with flashy young women beside them. A pair of waist-high bookshelves, lined with battered paperbacks—presumably the "volumes" Rankin mentioned—flanked the doorway through which we'd entered. Clearly The Library had pulled out all the stops in its effort to provide a highbrow experience.

As we entered, a tall young blond woman—naked except for a tiny G-string and a lace garter encircling one thigh—shinnied up a brass pole at center stage. Once she was at the top, she let go with her hands and leaned back, extending her arms and arching her torso to accentuate her breasts. They were, I had to admit, quite impressive. Then, extending one willowy leg, she hung by the other and began to slide downward, spiraling slowly around the pole, her descent set to throbbing music and strobing lights. During her final spin, timed to coincide with the end of the song, her long hair swept the stage, then fanned out behind her head as her body came to an artfully posed stop at the base of the pole.

"That's Desirée workin' it for you, guys," intoned a DJ's unctuous voice. "Give her a big hand, fellows, and don't forget to tip. These girls dance only for tips." I felt obliged to applaud, but no one else did, so after a few self-conscious claps I stopped. One of the men sitting stageside extended a folded bill in the dancer's direction; she squatted in front of him, hooking a finger under the garter to raise it off her thigh, and he slid the bill beneath the elastic band. The two men sitting beside him studiously looked away, their hands cupped around their beer cans. I wondered how much detail the tiny camera clipped to my tie was relaying to the FBI agents in the van.

Something about the woman's face looked familiar, and I realized with a start that I'd seen her before—only hours before—in a drastically different light. I tapped Sinclair on the arm. "Isn't that the woman who asked you the first couple of questions this morning?"

"In the flesh." He smiled at my obvious bafflement. "Sometimes it's a good idea to frame the questions the way you want 'em framed," he explained. "Gives you a little more leverage over the discussion. A bit of spin control. Politicians do it all the time—salt the audience at town meetings with friendly folks who'll lob some easy questions over the plate."

I thought back to the end of Sinclair's talk. "So when Glen Faust interrupted you—was that scripted, too?"

Even in the club's dim light, I could see Sinclair flush. "It sure as hell wasn't scripted by me," he snapped. "If I'd been scripting it, he'd have made some lame-ass point and I'd have demolished him. He caught me by surprise, and once he brought you into it, it got away from me." As he spoke, he watched the woman onstage wriggle into a tight tube dress and descend a short set of steps to the main floor.

"That lovely lady was Desirée," the DJ oozed. "Next up is Mandy. Mandy's going to do two numbers for you. Don't be shy, fellows. If you like what you see, come up and tip the ladies. They're available for table dances and lap dances, too."

A petite redhead wearing a push-up bra, lace panties, and stiletto heels took the stage. As soon as the song began, she unhooked the bra and let it fall, then slid down the panties and stepped out of them, snagging one heel briefly on the lace. I wondered when the striptease—the slow, tantalizing removal of layers of clothing—had been replaced by brutally efficient stripping.

The gymnastic blonde, whom the DJ had called Desirée, sidled up to Sinclair and kissed him on the cheek. "Hi, doll," he said. "Dr. Brockton, this is Melissa. Melissa, Dr. Brockton."

"Hi," she said, offering me a hand to shake. "That was very interesting, what you were saying this morning."

"Oh, hell, not you, too." Sinclair groaned. "Everybody loves this guy. What am I, chopped liver?"

"Aw, don't get jealous on me," she cajoled, kissing his cheek again. "You're the one that's out on a date with him." She looked at me naughtily. "I hope you're not the kind of guy who puts out on the first date."

I felt myself turn crimson and was grateful for the darkness of the club. "Not to worry," I said, unsure what to say next. Maybe, *I didn't recognize you without your clothes.* Or, *How'd you get so good at gymnastics?* Or maybe, *Doesn't it bother you that strange men come in to stare at your body and don't even clap or tip?* I settled for the lame safety of, "Nice to meet you, Melissa."

Sinclair nudged me. "Where you want to sit? Up by the stage?"

God forbid, I thought, but what I said—shouted, practically—was, "A booth, if that's okay with you. Be a little easier to talk."

He nodded. "Sweetheart," he said to Melissa/Desirée, "could

you excuse us for a few minutes? We need to talk a little shop."
She mimed a smooch at him, waved her fingertips at me, and sa-
shayed away in her short dress and tall heels.

Sinclair led us to a booth in a far corner of the room, mercifully far from the stage. As soon as we were seated, a pretty
brunette—not as young as the two twentysomething dancers—
came to take our drink order. She wore a simple white blouse,
a straight gray skirt that reached below her knees, and a pair
of wire-rimmed reading glasses. Her hair was pinned back in a
loose bun, skewered by a #2 wooden pencil. Despite how completely clichéd the costume was, I found the librarian-waitress
far more attractive than I'd found either of the topless, gyrating
dancers.

Sinclair ordered a scotch, a single-malt whose name I didn't
know and probably couldn't pronounce. He lifted an eyebrow at
me when I ordered a Diet Coke. "I don't drink alcohol," I explained across the table. "I have Ménière's disease—occasional
spells of vertigo—so I'm pretty careful to steer clear of dizziness."

He nodded, looking slightly amused. "Think of all the money
you've saved by not drinking. If I didn't love scotch so much, I'd
be a billionaire." His gaze drifted from me to the redhead on
stage, then back to me again. "Did you go hear Faust's talk this
afternoon?"

I nodded.

"What'd you think?"

"I thought it was interesting, especially the stuff about nanomaterials and tissue scaffolds for bone and cartilage. Sounds like
five or ten years from now we'll be able to limp into the doctor's
office and sprint out an hour later with a rebuilt knee."

"Don't hold your breath," he said.

"You think Faust is overstating the potential?"

He shrugged. "I think he's underestimating the difficulties. Guys like him always do. They think they're smarter than the rest of us. Smart enough to fix anything, solve anything. Smart enough to cheat death." He picked at the edges of a fingernail. "You remember all the buzz about cryonics a few years back? Deep-freeze your way to immortality?"

"Vaguely. Wasn't it Ted Williams, the baseball great, who had his head cut off and frozen when he died?"

"Right. Theory is, the brain—and memory, and personality, all that shit—can be preserved in liquid nitrogen and then thawed out and revived and spiffed up in a few decades or centuries and grafted onto a cloned body. Give me a break."

I smiled. "It does sound like they're selling water from a high-tech Fountain of Youth, doesn't it?"

"Faust's given money to those guys," Sinclair said, studying my reaction as he played that card. "He's funneled research funding to Alcor, the outfit in Arizona that has Ted's head on ice. He's on their scientific advisory committee, too."

He was probably gratified by my look of surprise. "Well, that's certainly interesting," I said. "Plant enough seeds, some of them bear fruit someday. Probably not the cryonic immortality seeds, but maybe carbon-fiber bone scaffolds."

He shook his head.

"So . . . clearly you're not worried that the biomedical engineers are going to put you out of business."

"Not a chance. People used to claim that the computer revolution would lead to the paperless office. Instead we use more paper than ever before. Same with human tissue. Even if Faust manages to create synthetic tissues—shit, *especially* if he manages to do it—the need for the real deal will always increase. Always."

Our drinks arrived. I reached for my wallet, but Sinclair

stopped me. "They're running a tab for us," he said. "We'll settle up later." As the waitress set his scotch down, Sinclair laid a hand on her wrist. "We're trying to talk some business here," he said, "and we're having to shout over the music. Is there a quieter room where we could talk?"

"There's the Archives Room," she said. "Nobody's in there right now."

"Sounds perfect." Sinclair slid out of the booth. "Lead on."

She took us through a wide door and a short hallway at one side of the main floor and showed us into a smaller, curtained-off room, ten or twelve feet square, with leather couches lining three of the four walls. In the corners between the sofas, end tables held potted ferns, leather-bound books, and brass lamps with shades of deep green glass. A waist-high stand in the middle of the room held a massive volume, which I recognized as *Webster's Unabridged Dictionary*. I revised my earlier opinion of The Library's lame literary décor; originally I'd given it two stars, but now I decided it might rate three. Sinclair sank into the corner of one sofa, gesturing with his glass to the adjoining sofa for me. In the background I could still hear the relentless throb of the music, but the volume had dropped by three-quarters, and I felt sure the audio recording would be much clearer here than in the main room. I also felt far more comfortable in here, away from the nonstop parade of exposed breasts and buttocks.

"This is much better," I said.

He took a sip of the scotch. "Ah, mother's milk," he breathed. "How's your Coke?"

I tasted it; it was flat and watery. "Fine. Hits the spot."

He shook his head. "You are a party animal," he said sarcastically. He was right. "Wild" was probably not the word my colleagues would use to describe me, but I didn't care. "Relax, Bill. Loosen up. Take off your tie."

I felt a flash of panic. Was he suspicious about the tiepin? "If I take it off, I'll forget and walk out without it. But it would feel good to loosen it." I unclipped the pin, slid the knot down a couple of inches, then reclipped the pin.

"Nice tiepin, by the way."

"Thanks. It was a Father's Day present from my son last year."

"What's the stone?" He leaned toward it, and my blood pressure zoomed.

"Uh, not sure. Maybe onyx?"

He shook his head. "I don't think so." He studied the pin closely. My palms began to sweat. "Looks more like moonstone to me." He sat back, and my panic eased. "Listen, Bill, I'd like to bounce an idea off you. Feel free to say no. I'm not shy—I'll ask anybody anything—but I never take it personally if the answer's not the one I was hoping for."

"Fair enough," I said. "Shoot."

"I think we've got a lot in common, you and I," he began. "We're both outsiders, in a way. We work in fields that most people consider morbid or gruesome. The public benefits tremendously from what we do, but they don't always appreciate us or reward us for doing it."

I shifted in my seat. "I might have to disagree with you on that," I said. "I like teaching, and I like the forensic work—identifying bodies, figuring out how or when somebody died. I find those rewarding."

He wagged a corrective finger at me. "Ah, but those are internal rewards," he said. "That's your own inner sense of satisfaction, not external reward. How much did you make last year, Bill? What do they pay you to do what you do?"

"Less than I want," I hedged, "but maybe more than I deserve."

"Not a chance," he said. "Okay, it's none of my business, but I bet the university doesn't pay you half as much as it pays the football coach." In fact, UT didn't pay me one-tenth as much as it paid its head coach, whose salary was more than $2 million a year. What's more, UT was also paying $2 million a year to a coach it had recently fired. One year after signing a four-year, $7 million contract with coach Phil Fulmer, UT asked him to step down . . . and agreed to pay his salary for the remainder of his contract. In other words, Fulmer was being paid $6 million not to work for three years. I didn't say all that to Sinclair, but I did say, "It would be nice if anthropology professors were considered as valuable as coaches or medical examiners or lawyers."

"Hear, hear," he said, raising his glass in toast. "To prosperous anthropology professors." I clicked my Coke against his scotch, hoping my strained smile didn't look too phony. "So I'm wondering if you do any consulting on the side? The university doesn't prohibit that, does it?"

"Generally not," I said. "Not unless it's a conflict of interest, or unless it averages more than two days a month. But they don't have to approve honoraria at all, so if you wanted me to do a lecture for you . . ."

"Hmm. We might be able to work it that way," he mused. "This morning I mentioned putting on small trainings for surgeons. We actually get a lot of requests for those. Would you be interested in working with me on something like that?"

Careful, I told myself. *Don't look too eager.* "I'm sure it'd be interesting, but I'm not qualified to teach surgeons. Not unless they want to know about postmortem decomposition and time since death."

"You're far too modest," he said. "I'm sure surgeons could learn a lot from you. But not to worry. We'd also have a surgery consultant there, an expert in the procedure we'd be teaching."

"I don't mean to seem dense, but if you have a surgery consultant and you're teaching surgeons a procedure, why do you need me?"

He raised his glass in a slight salute. "I do like a man who cuts to the chase, Bill. What I'm hoping is that you might be able to bring along some material."

"What did you have in mind?"

He leaned across the end table toward me. "We have a one-day training for orthopedic surgeons coming up in a few weeks in Asheville," he said. "Just across the mountains from Knoxville. We're teaching microsurgery techniques for reattaching small blood vessels and nerves in the arm. He swirled the glass in one hand, frowning slightly at how little of his scotch remained. "Right now we've got the enrollment capped at ten, and we're turning people away. If we had enough specimens, we could double or even triple the class size."

"So you're asking if I could haul ten or twenty arms to Asheville?"

"Like I said, I'll ask anybody anything. Is that an impossible thing to ask?"

"Possibly impossible," I answered, "but maybe just complicated. So the surgery consultant demonstrates the technique, then each of these surgeons practices it on an arm?"

He nodded.

"And where does this take place?"

"In a ballroom at the Grove Park Inn."

"The Grove Park?" It was the most elegant hotel in Asheville, a massive stone lodge built in the 1920s. Several U.S. presidents had stayed there, as had dozens of Hollywood stars. "The Grove Park lets us waltz in with a bunch of cadaver arms and carve them up?"

"Well, we don't exactly pile them on a baggage cart at the front entrance," he chuckled, "but basically yeah. I've done this at convention hotels plenty of times. We pack the material in leakproof shipping cases, on ice, and bring it up the service elevator. We don't allow hotel staff into the room, so nobody but the docs sees anything. End of the day, we pack everything up, haul it down the freight elevator and out the service entrance and back to where it came from. Piece of cake."

"And you're envisioning that I'd bring the material over just for the day, then take it back to Knoxville?"

He shrugged. "Your choice," he said. "You want to send it home with me, great—we'd be glad to be the 'designee' your donor consent form mentions."

I sipped my watery Coke and frowned. "I'd need to take it back with me. It would look pretty strange if a dozen skeletons in the collection were missing their arms." As I said it, I thought of Trey Willoughby's limbless corpse.

"Then take 'em back at the end of the seminar. If we can borrow or rent them for a day, that's great. So you're saying this is possible?"

"Possible. Wouldn't be easy. We'd have to stockpile the material in a freezer." *What else?* I asked myself. *What else do I need to do to reel him in?* "And those arms aren't going to amputate themselves."

"It would be a lot of work," he conceded, "but I think you'd find that the honorarium would make it worthwhile."

I stalled, studying the last of my drink. "How worthwhile?" I took another small sip.

He didn't hesitate. "A thousand an arm. Twenty arms, twenty grand."

A stray droplet of Coke water went down my windpipe, and I found myself coughing convulsively. The coughing fit was so intense it brought tears to my eyes.

Once the coughing finally subsided into throat clearing, Sinclair added, "Does that mean you'd consider such an arrangement worthwhile?"

"That's . . . quite worthwhile," I managed to say.

He reached a hand across the corner of the end table. "Bill, this could be the start of a beautiful friendship." As we shook hands, he smiled a broad, slow smile, and it made my flesh crawl. He stood up suddenly. "This calls for a toast. Our lovely waitress seems to have forgotten us. Let me go get us a fresh round. You sit tight; I'll be right back." He stepped through the curtains and out the doorway before I could protest.

I slumped back in the sofa, spent from the coughing and dismayed by the deal I'd just made. It wasn't that I disapproved of the surgical training—quite the contrary, in fact. It was myself I disapproved of: I had just agreed to exploit donated bodies for my own personal gain. I rested my head against the back of the sofa and closed my eyes.

"Jet-lagged?"

I jerked my head up and opened my eyes. It was the pretty waitress in the librarian outfit.

She set down a fresh Coke and another scotch on the end table. "Sorry. I didn't mean to disturb you."

"It's okay. I've just had a long day."

She smiled. "You do look like you could use something to

perk you up." She turned and took a few steps, then stopped at the wooden stand holding the massive dictionary. Reaching out a hand, she touched the back of the stand. The lights dimmed, and the room filled with the driving beat of dance music. The young woman was standing with her back to me, her feet slightly apart, the skirt stretched tight. One leg began to keep time to the music, and then—as the Pointer Sisters burst into the lyrics of "I'm So Excited"—she spun to face me. She widened her stance, and a slit in her skirt parted all the way up her left thigh. With one hand she removed her glasses and laid them on the dictionary; with the other she reached up and unpinned the bun, giving her head a toss that flipped her long hair into a high, sweeping arc. Then she began to move toward me, undulating and shimmying across the few feet of space that divided us.

"Wait," I said.

She held one finger to her lips and pursed her mouth in an exaggerated "shush" expression. Then she yanked the white blouse open—I heard the sound of Velcro letting go—to reveal a sheer, low-cut black bra underneath.

"Wait, stop," I said. "What are you doing?"

Instead of answering, she planted her right foot between my own feet, then wedged her left leg between my knees and levered them apart. Next she tugged at the top of the slit in her skirt, and the garment came off in her hand and fell to the floor. She was completely nude underneath. *Dear God,* I thought desperately and absurdly, *what would Sir Galahad do?*

"Stop," I said. "Please stop now."

She turned her back to me again, bent her knees, and arched her back, pushing her bare bottom toward me, swirling and swaying closer and closer in a sensual, primal rhythm.

"*Stop!*" I shouted. "Stop dancing and put on your clothes. Right now."

She froze in mid-sway, inches away from me.

"I'm serious," I added. "You're a beautiful woman, but I didn't ask for this, and I'm not comfortable with it."

She stood up straight and spun to face me, looking skeptical and confused and maybe a little mad. "You're saying you didn't ask for a lap dance from me?"

"No," I said, "I really don't want a lap dance," though that was no longer quite as true as it had been two minutes before. "Thank you, though."

Suddenly she looked embarrassed. She took two steps backward. With one hand she pulled her blouse closed, then stooped to pick up the skirt with the other. She wrapped the fabric around her hips and fastened it, then smoothed the blouse's Velcro fasteners into place

Just then the curtains in the doorway flew open. I was expecting—hoping—that Rankin and the rest of the FBI cavalry was riding to my rescue, but I was wrong, and disappointed, and very nervous: The burly man from the club's entrance rushed toward me. Planting himself between the dancer and me, he held a meaty hand six inches from my face, opening and closing his fist like some beating heart of violence and menace. "What's going on, Brenda? Is this guy giving you trouble? Did he paw you?"

"No, it's okay, Vic," she answered.

"I heard shouting," he said. "What happened?"

"Really, it's okay, Vic," she said. "He . . . he was on the phone, talking loud over the music."

Vic looked dubious. He lowered his hand, though it continued to clench and unclench.

"Really. He didn't do a thing. He's a good guy." Her face filled with sadness suddenly—sadness about this misunderstanding? sadness about the things she had to do for money?—and in her sadness she seemed more exposed than ever. "He's a good guy," she repeated with a shake of her head, making for the doorway.

Just as she reached it, Sinclair walked in, carrying a drink in each hand. He stared at her as she brushed past, then stared at the bouncer, then at me. "What the fuck just happened?"

"Nothing," I said, and when I said it, I realized that Sinclair must have arranged the whole thing. When he'd gone to get the drinks, he must have told the waitress I'd requested the dance. I had the distinct feeling that I was in over my head. "Nothing happened. I just got a little woozy, and I need to go. I've got to get up in six hours to catch my flight anyway."

I sidestepped the bouncer and headed for the doorway. Sinclair made to follow me, but I waved him off.

"You stay and enjoy yourself. Don't let me put a damper on your evening. Give Melissa my regards." As I parted the curtains, I looked back over my shoulder. It took everything I had to add, "Call me when you have a final head count for the training."

Would he call, or had I just lost the fish I'd been sent here to reel in? I didn't know, and I didn't much care.

I snagged a cab that had paused at the club's entrance to disgorge three rowdy young men sporting military haircuts. I hoped they were generous with their applause and their tips. I hoped they were good guys. I yanked off my tie, halfway hoping that I'd banged the microphone a few earsplitting times in the process.

Rankin called to praise my performance, but I cut him off quickly. I went back to my tacky turreted hotel, stripped off my smoky clothes and the FBI's recorder, and stood under a long, hot shower, trying to wash away the shame of having put out on my first date with Ray Sinclair.

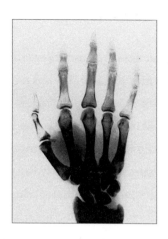

CHAPTER 26

"SO HOW WAS YOUR VEGAS TRIP?" MIRANDA'S TONE was casual. She was hunkered over a table in the bone lab, touching the tip of a 3-D digitizing probe to landmarks on the skull from donor 77-08, a skeleton that had spent the fall of 2008 by the foot of an oak tree at the Body Farm. Her back was turned to me, and she didn't even bother to look over her shoulder at me as she asked.

Her casualness, I suspected, masked something serious. Normally Miranda was the queen of eye contact. She could ask the most trivial question—"What'd you have for lunch?" or "What time is it?"—and the directness of her gaze would make the question seem profound. Asking about my abrupt departure and swift return without so much as glancing in my direction was a storm warning.

"Quick," I said. "Strange. Las Vegas—at least the parts I was in—is a bizarre place. A theme park disguised as a city. I'm sure hundreds of Ph.D. dissertations have been written about the odd cultural anthropology of Las Vegas."

"And wouldn't *that* be a waste of perfectly good trees." She glanced at the numbers that the probe was feeding into her laptop computer. "Man, this guy had some wide-set eyes. The intraocular distance is eighty millimeters. That's way wider than anything I've measured before. His depth perception must've been incredible." She touched the probe to other landmarks on the skull: the high points of the zygomatic arches, the widest points of the nasal opening, the contours of the chin. "That's a long haul to make in a day and a half. Was it worthwhile?"

Worthwhile. Her echo of Sinclair's word gave me a pang. "I hope so," I said.

She didn't respond, and in the silence a host of unasked questions and withheld explanations seemed to hang in the air.

"Glen Faust was giving a paper at a tissue-bank convention," I said.

"I know."

"You know? How do you know?"

"Peggy said you'd gone to a conference in Las Vegas on short notice. I Googled to see what was going on there this week, conference-wise. I figured you must be at either the cosmetology convention or the tissue-bank meeting."

"Cosmology? What do I know about cosmology?"

"Not cosmology, the nature of the universe," she said. "Cosmetology. Hair and makeup. A thousand cosmetologists are in Vegas this week."

"Hair and makeup? What do I care about hair and makeup?"

She finally looked in my direction, sizing up my appearance. "Not much, clearly."

I laughed. I'd lobbed that one right over the plate for her.

"I was hoping maybe you'd pick up a few style pointers," she added, meeting my gaze for the first time. "Then I saw Faust's talk on the agenda for the tissue-bank meeting, and I abandoned all hope for your stylistic salvation." The sarcasm, like the eye contact, was a relief—a hopeful sign that the invisible electrical charge in the air between us might dissipate, the way the static in the sky eases after a thunderhead passes over.

"He's a good speaker," I said.

"The abstract looked interesting. I can see why you felt moved to spend a thousand dollars and thirty-six hours to hear the talk, live and in person."

Ouch, I thought. The thunderhead appeared to have circled back.

"I didn't really go to hear his talk," I admitted. I vaguely recalled an old saying about the best lies being partly true. I'd never aspired to be a good liar, but at the moment I wished I felt slightly more fluent in falsehood. "I wanted to talk to him face-to-face about expanding their research funding, because we're looking at more budget cuts."

That, too, contained truth. The UT board of trustees had met six days earlier in emergency session to deal with the worsening budget crunch. Higher tuition—an increase of nearly 10 percent—had been expected to raise an additional $20 million in revenue for the current academic year. Unfortunately, the same economic bind that was squeezing UT itself was also squeezing the families of students; as a result the higher tuition had been largely offset by lower enrollment, and so more cuts were required. Miranda looked pained, and I felt bad for pressing on a sore spot—she knew I'd been struggling to protect the funding for her assistantship, and she was already feeling stress about that. But short of disclosing my role in the FBI's investigation, I could come up with no other credible pretext for my trip.

"He didn't make any guarantees," I added, with as much cheeriness as I could muster, "but he promised to try."

She returned her attention to the skull, which meant turning her back on me. "Well," she said hollowly, "I hope he succeeds." I was just opening the door to leave when she said, "Oh, we got a body while you were gone. Family donation—a white male, age sixty-seven, died of cardiopulmonary disease. His number is 37-09. He's still in the cooler at the morgue. I'll get him out to the facility sometime this afternoon."

Reluctantly I stepped back into the lab and closed the door. "Actually, let's leave him in the cooler for a while," I said.

She swiveled the chair 180 degrees to face me. "How long? And how come?"

I'd spent much of my flight from Las Vegas to Knoxville dreading these very questions. "Two or three weeks," I said, drawing a raised eyebrow that looked simultaneously curious and disapproving. Her second question was tougher: *Why?* I wasn't dazzled by the answer I'd come up with during the plane ride, but it was the best I could do. "I'm thinking of doing a research project of my own," I said. "I'd need at least five bodies to do it, maybe ten."

She stared at me. "Are you kidding? How long since you've done research of your own?"

"Too long. Feels like I'm losing touch with what life is like for you overworked, underpaid graduate students."

"Good of you to walk a mile in our moccasins, kemosabe," she said. "Does this mean you'll be giving up your salary for a while, too?" She laid down the probe. "I need to go check on some bones I put in to simmer while you were gone. I'll be back in an hour or so. Make sure the door's locked when you leave."

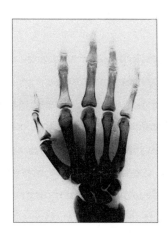

CHAPTER 27

TWO HOURS LATER THE STAIRWELL DOOR OUTSIDE MY office banged open, hard enough to send a slight shiver through the columns and girders of the stadium. Then my own office door was flung open with equal force.

Miranda burst into the room, wild-eyed, out of breath, and weeping.

"Miranda, what's wrong?"

"It's Eddie, it's Eddie." The words were barely discernible amid the sobs. "His right hand—it went septic."

"When?"

"I don't know. Now. Carmen just called me from the ER. She said they're taking him into emergency surgery." She shook her head in sadness and shock. "They're amputating the last bit of his hands right now."

WE FOUND CARMEN IN THE surgery waiting room, slumped in a chair, her face cradled in her hands. She looked up when Miranda called her name, and the face she raised to us had aged twenty years in the past two months.

"Oh, Carmen," said Miranda, "I'm so, so sorry." She sat beside her, taking Carmen's right hand in both of hers. I sat on the other side, holding her left hand. We sat in silence for what seemed hours, our six hands entwined. Eventually I lost track of where my hands ended and Carmen's began. I watched a finger twitch, and for a moment—until I noticed the small, manicured tip at the end of the nail—I thought the finger was one of my own, numb from lack of movement and blood.

As the time inched by, I became aware of a thought tugging at the sleeve of my mind. I tried ignoring it, then tried actively banishing it, but it returned to tug again and again, with increasing insistency. Underneath my worries about Eddie and Carmen—would he live? would he recover from this latest setback? would she?—swirled a cluster of darker questions: Had Eddie brought this on himself deliberately? Had he undertaken Clarissa Lowe's autopsy not in *spite* of the risk but *because* of the risk? Had he decided that a toe-to-thumb transplant wasn't good enough? Had he contrived to sacrifice his remaining half hand so he'd be a double amputee, and therefore a more compelling transplant candidate? I remembered the frightful, hopeful words he'd spoken the day Miranda had researched his options, when I pointed out the difficulties of transplantation. "It's a big risk," he'd said. "But to have hands again would be worth taking a big risk." Had he taken that risk, gambling with his very life?

Finally a scrub-suited doctor came to deliver the ritual postoperative news. "Mrs. Garcia?" Carmen stood, helped out of her chair by Miranda and me. "I'm Dr. Rivkin; I'm the hand surgeon on call. First, most important, your husband's in Recovery, and he's doing well." Carmen waited, knowing there was more. "Unfortunately, we did have to amputate the hand, just below the wrist. The good news is, we're confident we got all the decayed and infected tissue, and we've put him on a strong course of antibiotics. So his prognosis is very good." Carmen nodded numbly.

"Excuse me, Doctor," I interrupted. "You might already know this, but Dr. Garcia was exposed to *Clostridium* bacteria last week during an autopsy." I felt Miranda's eyes on me, and I wondered if she'd been pondering the same dark questions as I had. "The autopsy subject died of toxic shock a week after surgery." Carmen drew a sharp breath. "Does that exposure affect how you need to treat Dr. Garcia?"

He gave a noncommittal shrug. "Dr. Garcia mentioned that when we admitted him, so we'll certainly check for it when we do the tissue pathology. But he's not showing any symptoms of toxic shock. His vitals are stable and strong, and his blood work's good—normal pH, normal red-blood count, normal white-cell count."

I glanced at Miranda; her eyes were locked on the surgeon's with laser intensity, but I thought I saw traces of relief in her face, mirroring what must surely be showing in my own.

"We'll keep a close eye on those," Rivkin was saying, "but to me this looks like a textbook case of gangrene—localized necrosis, caused by poor circulation. I suspect the blood vessels in that hand were just too badly damaged by the radiation burn to recover."

"And does the amputation resolve the problem," Carmen asked quietly, "or will he need additional surgery?"

The surgeon shifted, visibly uncomfortable, and I had the feeling another shoe was about to drop. "We needed to provide blood

supply and skin for his . . . wrist," he said, sidestepping the word
"stump," which my mind had instantly plugged into the awkward
pause. "So what we've done is a procedure called a pedicle flap."

"I don't know what that procedure is," she said. "Tell me,
please?"

"We've grafted his forearm to his abdomen," he explained,
"here, just beneath the skin." Curling his right hand tightly, he
jammed his wrist into his lower belly. "New blood vessels will
grow from the abdomen into the wrist. Once they do—two or
three weeks—we can reverse the procedure and detach the arm.
Then we'll take a flap of skin from the abdomen to cover the
stump." This time he didn't flinch from the word.

If Carmen was taken aback by the news that her husband's
arm was now surgically grafted to his belly, she didn't show it.
She simply asked, "When can I see him?"

"He should be waking up soon. I can take you back to Recovery now."

She nodded, hugged Miranda and me, and left with the surgeon.

On the drive back across the river to the stadium, my thoughts
circled back to the idea I'd found so worrisome: the idea that
Eddie had contrived to lose his hand, as a way of angling for a
transplant. If the surgeon was right—if Eddie's infection wasn't
caused by the deadly strain of microorganism that had killed Clarissa Lowe—my worry had been unfounded. That knowledge
was a relief, but the relief was mixed with shame—shame at having suspected Eddie of recklessness and manipulation.

I also felt a fresh surge of sorrow and compassion. No matter
how much moral integrity he might have, Eddie Garcia no longer
possessed even a remnant of his hands.

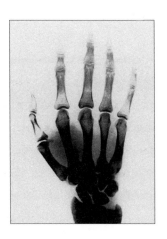

CHAPTER 28

THE MARKER AT THE HEAD OF THE GRAVE WAS A SMALL, weather-stained slab of unpolished marble, far less ornate than Trey Willoughby's monumental obelisk or even Pendergrast's granite slab. The chiseled letters read, MISS ELIZABETH JENKINS, B. JAN. 22, 1916, D. OCT. 4, 2003. CARPE LIBRUM. The death date was within three days of Pendergrast's and two days of Willoughby's. DeVriess's fishing expedition was expanding, but in very small outward ripples. In going back to the judge for additional exhumation orders, DeVriess had contended that mischief was clearly afoot at Ivy Mortuary in early October of 2003, and that the path of common sense and civil justice was to exhume other bodies from that same time period. His plan was to exhume other bodies buried by Ivy at that same time and then gradually work his way both forward and backward from there, in order to determine when the mischief had begun and when it had ended.

This time the television and newspaper reporters were already present, although Culpepper had corralled them into an area fifty feet away, behind a strand of yellow-and-black police tape.

Miss Jenkins—a former English teacher who'd lived and died alone—was buried in the simplest of steel coffins within a concrete vault. The coffin, like the headstone, had been purchased with donations from former students; the Latin inscription, *Carpe librum,* meant "Seize the book." I groped at the foot of the coffin for the crank that would open the lid, then swiveled it outward and began turning it. "So," I said, "predictions?"

"Four bags of sand," Grease said.

"She's a little old lady," Miranda said. "Only two bags of sand."

"Arms and legs, but no torso or head," predicted Culpepper.

As the lid pivoted up, the tripods of the TV and newspaper photographers leaned against the police tape, straining to get a few inches closer to the graveside. The lid of the coffin blocked the cameras' view of its interior, but it didn't block their view of the four faces peering down in astonishment.

Miss Elizabeth Jenkins was a tiny, white-haired woman, her aged features well preserved, her wrinkled cheeks slightly rouged with mold.

And Miss Elizabeth Jenkins was wrapped in a macabre embrace with the rotting remains of a large human male. His left temporal bone—the oval of thin bone above the ear—had a one-inch circle punched in it, a blow delivered with enough force to drive the disk of bone deep into the brain.

"NOT EXACTLY THE LOVERS OF Valdaro," commented Miranda as we extricated Miss Jenkins from the arms of her coffinmate. To escape the media circus, we'd loaded the coffin into my truck and taken it to the forensic center, tailed by a caravan of reporters. Culpepper had eventually dispersed them with the promise of a news conference and photos later in the day.

"The lovers of who?" asked Culpepper, clearly feeling squeamish.

"Not who," Miranda corrected as I handed her one of the man's arms. "Where. Valdaro. A village in northern Italy." She laid the arm on an autopsy table we'd positioned beside the coffin. "Archaeologists excavated a pair of skeletons—a man and a woman—near Valdaro in 2007. They were buried together about five thousand years ago, wrapped in each other's arms."

"I remember that," said Art, who'd already patted the two corpses with tape to collect stray hairs and fibers. "I saw something about it on Discovery or National Geographic. 'The world's longest hug,' I think they called it. But didn't somebody else dig up an even older couple someplace else just a few days later?"

"Dubious," she answered. "Somebody did find an older pair of skeletons in Turkey—around nine thousand years old. But it's not at all certain that those two were buried together. Could be just a case of commingling—mixed bones, one body dumped into the same patch of ground as another, maybe centuries apart. The Italian couple definitely had their arms wrapped around each other, though. Sweet, huh?"

"Very sweet," I noted, "unless it was a double murder, or a murder-suicide."

"Which this case could be," offered Culpepper.

"Sure." Miranda snorted. "Murder-suicide. Little Miss Jenkins whacks this big ol' man upside the head, then takes a bottleful of sleeping pills and dies—but not before she embalms herself, climbs into the coffin, and hauls him in with her."

"Okay, so maybe we can rule out murder-suicide," Culpepper said sheepishly.

Unlike Trey Willoughby, whose lips were quite literally sealed, this man's corpse was openmouthed; in fact, as I pulled gently downward on the lower jaw, so I could see the teeth, the mandible came loose in my hand. "Oh, man," groaned Culpepper, turning away, "I wish I hadn't seen that."

Miranda and I studied the mandible, while Art fished around in the pockets of the dead man's pants, which were greasy with fatty acids from the decaying corpse. Culpepper, still averting his eyes, asked, "So what's the best way to ID him? Fillings? Bridgework? Dental X-rays?"

"We could go the forensic-dentistry route," I said. "Means we'll need to check with a lot of dentists once we chart his teeth."

"Or we could go this route instead," said Art, who had fished a wallet from the corpse's left back pocket. Culpepper whirled around just as Art flipped opened the stained wallet and removed a driver's license. "I believe we just found Kerry Roswell, our missing embalmer."

The wallet wasn't all Art found in the coffin with Roswell and Miss Perkins. Tucked behind the fabric liner of the coffin was a clawhammer. Its head—which matched the size and shape of the skull fracture—was smeared with a thin coating of scalp tissue, hair, bone fragments, and brain matter. And its handle showed what appeared to be a partial fingerprint, etched in blood.

"Well," Culpepper said after a collective silence. "Maybe we need to dig up Elmer Ivy now and see if he's got any fingerprints we can compare to this."

"If he's got fingers," said Art.

"Or if he's really in his own coffin, not somebody else's," said

Miranda. "At this rate we're gonna have to dig up everybody— every last body—in Knoxville."

"KNOXVILLE'S GHOULISH GRAVE-ROBBING mystery has taken a bizarre, deadly twist," said WBIR anchor Randall Gibbons in that night's top story, "with grave robbing giving way to murder and grave stuffing." Like the station's earlier stories on the Pendergrast and Willoughby exhumations, this report stressed the shocking nature of the subject matter and images. In addition to video footage showing the coffin being hoisted from the grave and the lid pivoting upward—as Miranda, Culpepper, DeVriess, and I stared in shock—the images included several KPD photos of the coffin's embracing inhabitants, purposely blurred to render them less gruesome. My phones rang continuously throughout the late-night newscast and beyond. I ignored the calls, since I didn't recognize any of the numbers and didn't want to spend hours on the phone with reporters. But by the time I switched off the phones for the night, I'd counted more than a dozen different area codes and several international country codes.

Must've been a slow news day, I thought as I settled into bed. *They'll move on to something else tomorrow.* I was wrong.

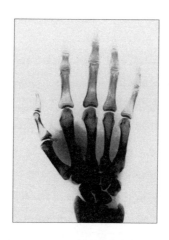

CHAPTER 29

BY THE NEXT AFTERNOON, THE MEDIA CALLS HAD driven me nuts—I'd dodged dozens of long-distance reporters but had talked with half a dozen local ones. Elmer Ivy had fingerprints on file, it turned out—he'd served in the military—and Art was able to get a scan of them. None of them matched the bloody print on the hammer. The mysterious coffin killer, as some of the reporters dubbed the hammer swinger, was suddenly big news, far bigger than the war in Afghanistan or nuclear talks with Iran and North Korea. It was a relief to drive away from the jangling phones in my office at the end of the day, even though I deeply dreaded what the evening's errand was likely to hold in store.

Out of the corner of my eye, I saw Miranda studying me from the passenger seat, so I turned toward her and asked, "What?" The right-front tire teetered on the edge of the pavement, and I twitched the steering wheel to avoid hurtling into the ditch. Duncan Road meandered along ridges and hollows about ten miles west of downtown Knoxville and UT. Decades earlier Duncan had been a rural farm road, but lately weathered farmhouses had given way to sprawling estates and cul-de-sac housing developments, with just enough shacks and rusting trailers to impart a tumbledown, seedy charm.

"What do you mean, what?"

"You're looking at me funny. What is it?"

"Nothing," Miranda said, "except watch the road. And slow down." After a pause she added, "And are you okay?"

I chose not to comment on the driving advice. "Not really." The truth was, I dreaded what lay ahead. I'd rather be fishing a bloated, slimy corpse from the river, I realized—and floaters were about as unappealing as corpses got, in my opinion—than embarking on this errand with Miranda.

"Slow down. It's on the left. There." She pointed into the twilight. "*There.*"

"Where? I don't see it."

"You just missed it."

I stopped. "I missed it?" Looking out the window, I glimpsed rectangles of golden light slightly below us, crosshatched by bare branches, pine foliage, and glossy rhododendron leaves. "Where the hell's the driveway?"

"You passed it."

"Are you sure? I didn't see one."

"It's hard to see in the dark. That's why I told you to slow down. Twice." One of the interesting features of my relationship with Miranda was that our interactions ranged so widely across the spectrum: Sometimes I dispensed knowledge as her professor and mentor; sometimes we teased each other mercilessly and happily; occasionally we bickered like an old married couple. "I've been out here half a dozen times," she added, sounding less snappish, "and I have trouble spotting it even in the daylight. It's just a tiny gap in the tree line. If you blink, you'll miss it."

I backed up twenty feet, grateful there was no other traffic on the winding road. Sure enough, the forested darkness on the left was broken slightly by a narrow opening, barely wide enough to accommodate my truck. I cut the wheel and eased into the notch. The headlights illuminated branches and treetops, and the earth seemed to drop off beneath us into the night. "Whoa. Is this a driveway or a cliff?"

"It's definitely an oh-shit experience the first time or two." She laughed. "If you think careening down it now is interesting, you should try slithering up it on a rainy day in the fall, when it's coated with wet, slippery leaves. We had to call a tow truck to get me out of here one night. And then we had to call a bigger tow truck to pull me *and* the little tow truck out."

The vertiginous ribbon of concrete was no more than a hundred feet long, but it dropped fifty vertical feet in that distance. It was flanked by a pair of contemporary houses, storklike in their slender verticality; they perched on the steep hillside on stilts, as if they, like the trees themselves, were rooted in the ground and reaching for the sky, stretching toward the top of the forest canopy.

The driveway's pitch lessened toward the bottom, and Miranda pointed me to a broader, flatter parking pad notched into an embankment. English ivy—some of it freshly nibbled, perhaps by deer—cascaded down a waist-high retaining wall. A black Subaru wagon was tucked alongside the wall; in front of it was a Nissan Xterra I recognized, its yellow paint mottled by brown leaves and dead twigs the size of finger bones. Eddie's car hadn't been driven in a while. I drew a deep breath and asked, "Ready?"

"What do you think?"

"Me neither. But let's do it."

Our doors opened and closed in unison. They swung slowly, reluctantly. "It's the house on the left." A long wooden ramp, a cross between a boat dock and a drawbridge, angled from the parking area up to a decklike front porch. The front door was a large panel of insulated glass, framed by honey-colored wood; the entry hall was floored in pale oak covered by a long runner, a rug of wool woven in diamonds and stripes of black, red, gold, and green—Central or South American, I guessed. The rug ran down a lighted hall to the doorway of a dark room. Miranda reached up to a bell beside the door and gave a tug on a braided cord dangling from the clapper, and the bell pealed with a high, clear tone. Inside, I heard a clatter and then the thud of footsteps on wood and wool.

The door was opened by a sad, haggard woman with a toddler slung on her left hip. "Please come in," said Carmen Garcia.

She'd asked me to come talk with her at home about her husband's treatment and recovery and job situation—all serious concerns, I knew—and I'd brought Miranda along for moral support. It was cowardly on my part, maybe, but also potentially helpful. Miranda knew the Garcias far better than I did; in fact, several months before Eddie's injury, Miranda had begun volunteering to baby-sit occasionally for the Garcias' toddler, Tomás, so Eddie and Carmen could have a date night now and then. It wasn't as if they couldn't afford to hire a teenager to baby-sit; Garcia was a physician, after all, and clearly they lived in a large, interesting house, but for whatever reason—because they were new to Knoxville, or because their house was hard to find in the dark, or because they worried about entrusting their baby to a young stranger—they'd not had many evenings out until Miranda started the date-night plan. Truth be told, she wasn't just thinking of the Garcias when she made the offer. She'd had them over for dinner about six months earlier, to welcome the new M.E. and his family to town, and she'd been instantly smitten by the sweet, dark-eyed, dark-haired boy. The attraction was clearly mutual, for when he saw Miranda at the door, Tomás stretched out his arms and practically dove off his mother's hip. "Randa, Randa, Randa," he chirped, his face beaming.

Miranda hoisted him off Carmen's hip and transferred him to her own, nestling him there as naturally as if he were her own child. *"Hola, muchacho,"* she said, and then repeated the greeting in English: "Hey, dude. How's my little dude, huh?" She punctuated each word with a wet, smacking kiss, and laughter burbled up out of the boy. The pure, musical sound brought a smile to my face and, I was happy to see, to Carmen's as well. Tomás pointed at a staircase in the hallway, and Miranda clambered over the safety gate and headed upstairs with him.

"I just made a pot of tea," Carmen said. "Would you like a cup? Come, let's sit." She turned and led us around a corner into a large, open room in the shape of a semicircle. A galley-style kitchen ran the length of the one straight wall; on the other side of a full-length butcher-block counter, a long, curving wall of windows defined the living room. I walked to the center of the room and looked around me. It was now fully dark outside, so the arc of windows acted as mirrors, reflecting ten images of myself back at me.

"What an amazing house," I said, and when I spoke, my voice sounded as if it were coming not just from within me but from slightly in front of me, too. "And the acoustics are interesting." The effect was similar to hearing my voice amplified by a micro-phone and a high-fidelity speaker.

"Yes," said Carmen. "It's because you're standing right at the center of that curve. It's like the—oh, what's the English term for *punto focal?*—the focal point of a lens. A lens of sound. Eddie and Tomás love the way it makes the sound big. I find it a little bit . . . um, haunting? Spooky?"

For someone born and raised in South America, Carmen spoke English with remarkable fluency. "Spooky sounds right. Sorry to spook you."

She fluttered her fingers at me to dismiss the apology. "No, don't be silly, Bill. If you stand there and talk for an hour, you will make me crazy, but for now enjoy it."

I hummed, changing position slightly to move in and out of the acoustic sweet spot at the center of the semicircle. As I did, my voice got louder and softer. I switched from humming to clap-ping, and Carmen laughed. "That's just what Eddie and Tomás love to do," she said. Then, suddenly, Carmen was weeping, star-ing stricken at my hands. My hands froze in the air, and my heart went out to her as I saw a wave of grief crash over her. "Oh, Car-men," I said, "I'm so sorry about all this." I reached out to give her shoulder a squeeze, and when I did, she crumpled against me like a child.

Her breath was ragged, half choked. "Oh, Bill, I don't know if I can bear it," she cried. "What will become of Eddie? What will become of me? How do we go on?"

"I don't know, Carmen," I said. "I wish I did, but I don't." She began to sob—keening, shuddering sobs—and she clung to me. "I'm so sorry," I repeated, wrapping my arms around her slight frame, stroking the back of her head with my right hand, the way I'd soothed my son when he was small. "So very sorry."

As her sobs subsided, she reached up and took hold of my right hand with both of hers. I thought she was starting to disentangle herself, but instead her fingers began to trace my own, one after another, as if she were a blind woman taking the measure of an unknown object. *My God,* I realized, *these are exotic things to her now: the hands of a man.* The realization saddened me for both her and Eddie.

"Your husband is a very fine man," I said. "And a very brave one, too." I locked eyes with her. "I'm proud to be his friend," I added. "And yours." I kissed her on the forehead, then eased away. "I don't know exactly how, but I believe that Eddie can get past this, and I believe you can, too. One thing I'm sure of: He has a lot better chance of reclaiming his health and his work—of reclaiming a life that's worth living—with his family standing beside him." Her eyes pooled again. "I see the light and the pride in his eyes whenever he talks about you and Tomás, Carmen. You both mean so much to him."

She drew a deep breath, then another, blowing them out through pursed lips. She rubbed her face with her hands, then wiped her hands on her jeans. Stepping to the kitchen counter, she took a paper napkin from a stack and dabbed at her eyes, then blew her nose. It honked, and she laughed tiredly. "God," she said, "I didn't know I had any tears left in me. I was so afraid when he nearly died, and so sad when he lost so much of his hands." She wiped and blew again. "I've cried so much, I hoped I was finished."

I thought about the deepest losses in my own life, Kathleen and Jess, and about how suddenly and strongly the wounds could be reopened by some slight, unexpected trigger—catching a whiff of the perfume Kathleen wore for years, or seeing Jess's signature on an autopsy report in a case file.

"I don't think we finish crying until we finish living," I said. I was reminded of something I'd read about joy and sorrow, about how the two are inseparably linked, like the opposite sides of an old-fashioned balance scale, one rising as the other falls. "But if we're lucky," I added, "we don't finish laughing until then either." I nodded at the teapot on the counter, a sleek, glossy vessel that would have looked at home in an art gallery or the Museum of Modern Art. "Any chance we could have that cup of tea now?"

She smiled, and I thought I saw a mixture of relief, gratitude, and sadness in it. "Of course. I didn't mean to make you work so hard for it."

"Nonsense, Carmen," I said. "I'm proud to be your friend, too. I'll go see if Miranda wants to join us for tea." Retracing the path to the front door, I turned down the hallway and then called up the staircase. "Miranda?"

"Yes?"

"You want some hot tea?"

"If there are juice boxes, Tomás and I would prefer juice boxes," she called down. I heard her make loud smacking, slurping noises as she clumped down the stairs, and Tomás giggled as she rounded the landing with him slung on her hip again, his head thrown back in burbling delight as she nibbled noisily on his neck. Miranda would make a splendid mom, I realized, and the notion hit me with surprising force. In all the years I'd known her, I'd never imagined Miranda having a baby or raising a child. Graduate assistant, Ph.D. candidate, promising young forensic anthropologist—these were all hats I regularly pictured on Miranda's head. But the mantle of motherhood, that was a new one. It was an idea I should probably get used to, I decided.

Miranda froze with one leg in midair over the safety gate and looked at me sharply. "What?"

"What do you mean, what?" It was the very question she'd asked me half an hour earlier in the truck.

"You're looking at me funny," she said, echoing my earlier response. "What is it?"

"Nothing," I said, my face breaking into a big smile.

Over tea and juice boxes, Miranda and I talked with Carmen about Eddie's weeks in the hospital and his despair over the latest damage to his right hand. "He's very discouraged again," Carmen said. "He tries to sound positive when he talks to me, but of course he is devastated by this." She hesitated. "And afraid."

Miranda posed the question I was loath to ask. "Afraid of what?"

"Afraid he is too damaged to be whole again. Afraid he cannot accept his disfigurement and limitations. Afraid he cannot do his job adequately." She looked down, studying the contents of her teacup. "Afraid he cannot love me adequately." She closed her eyes. "Afraid I cannot love him still."

Miranda reached across the table and took one of Carmen's hands in both of hers. "Can I tell you something, Carmen? I admire you tremendously. You have such a big, brave heart. No wonder Eddie loves you so."

Carmen gave Miranda's hands a squeeze, then refilled her cup and my own and then turned the conversation to more pragmatic talk of Eddie's job. She asked how critical his absence was becoming, and I did my best to reassure her. The state medical examiner's office in Nashville had contracted with several pathologists in Johnson City and Nashville and Chattanooga—Jess's former office—to perform the autopsies that ordinarily would be done in Knoxville. "They'll be glad to have Eddie back whenever he's able to return to work," I told her, "but they're fine for now, and for months, if need be. If he wants to ease back into it, even for just a few hours a week, that'll be fine. Eddie was injured in the line of duty, so his insurance and worker's compensation benefits will take care of him and the family. His job is safe, so you can cross that off your list of worries."

Talk turned to the Garcias' house, and to a few maintenance needs that had arisen during the past month. The tall cedar structure tended to take a beating from the sun, the rain, and the wildlife—the high, heated walls made it an attractive nesting place for squirrels and woodpeckers, Carmen explained—and the structure's height, forty or fifty feet at the roofline, tended to scare away contractors. Miranda recommended a handyman she'd used for various carpentry and plumbing jobs. "He can fix anything," she said, "and he goes rock climbing and rappelling for fun. He'll love working on this house."

Soon Tomás grew sleepy, so Miranda and I said our good-byes. Carmen walked us out to the driveway. "Drive boldly," she advised as we clambered into the truck. "Get a good, strong start down here, because it gets steeper as you go up."

The tires shrieked as I gunned the throttle and fishtailed out of the parking area. "Boldly done," said Miranda.

"Damn skippy," I answered, rocketing up the narrow band of concrete and whipping onto the road, grateful that no one was coming from either direction. "That Tomás is a cutie," I added. "And he clearly thinks you hung the moon."

"Mutual, I'm sure. He's a sweet boy." She sighed. "He misses his daddy."

"Yeah." We made the rest of the drive back to UT in silence.

Threading my way down to the one-lane service road ringing the base of the stadium, I pulled in behind Miranda's white Jetta and put the truck in park, the engine idling. "Thanks for going with me, Miranda."

"You're welcome." She opened the door and got out, then leaned her head back in. "By the way," she said, "you're right. Eddie is a very fine man. I'm proud to be his friend, too."

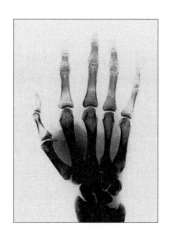

CHAPTER 30

THE GLEAMING WHITE TRACTOR-TRAILER INCHED along the edge of the parking lot, parallel to the fence of the Body Farm. The truck's gears clashed when the driver wrestled the transmission into reverse, and then the clutch caught and the rig eased backward, scraping a few low branches that overhung the chain-link and the inner wooden fence. The driver stopped when the trailer's rear end was just below the facility's main gate. He got out, checked his parking job, and unhooked the connections between tractor and trailer. That done, he fired up the large diesel generator attached to the front of the trailer and began raising the front end of the trailer slightly, with a pair of powered jacks built into the trailer's frame, to compensate for the slight grade of the parking lot.

Calling up the contacts stored in my cell phone, I punched in "F" and dialed the first number there. The call went to voice mail; there was no personal greeting, simply a computer voice telling me the number was not available and offering me the chance to leave a message. "This is Bill Brockton," I said, "calling from Knoxville to say thank you. It feels like Christmas came early to the Body Farm this year. "

I hadn't fully allowed myself to believe it would happen, but Glen Faust had followed through on his pledge: The trailer contained a mobile CT scanner, housed in a sleek, modern imaging suite—not that the Body Farm's "patients" were in any shape to notice or care about the ambience or décor, of course. My only hope was that the smell of decomp wouldn't follow the scanner from Knoxville to its next assignment, wherever and whenever that might be. Faust had committed OrthoMedica to a collaborative research project for the next three months, with the strong possibility of renewing it for a year beyond that if the data proved useful.

We'd barely begun to plan how we'd use the data from the scanner. One thing I knew, though, was that we'd scan every incoming body donated to the research facility, capturing three-dimensional images, inside and out, while they were still fresh corpses. Then, months later, we'd rescan their bare skeletons. Comparing the before and after scans would offer valuable insights into the intricate architecture of flesh and bone, their intimate entwining. We'd agreed to share the data with both OrthoMedica and UT's Biomedical Engineering Department. Biomedical Engineering had asked its faculty and graduate students to submit draft proposals for using the scanner to help design high-tech artificial joints and advanced surgical tools and techniques—what one of the faculty called "the operating room of the future." We'd also received an inquiry from the FBI Laboratory in Quantico, Virginia. One of my former students was working there on a team developing facial-reconstruction software: a way of restoring faces to the skulls of long-dead murder victims, using computer calculations rather than the sculptor's clay used by traditional forensic artists. Our scans could allow them to see the skull beneath the skin of dozens or even hundreds of donor faces—and thus help improve the computer's ability to model the skin atop the skulls of unknown murder victims.

Besides providing the scanner, OrthoMedica was funding two half-time assistantships. One of the half-time slots was for a graduate student in biomedical engineering, Eric Anderson, who already had training and prior experience as a scanning technician; the other slot was for Miranda, who would coordinate the arrival of the bodies with the arrival of the scanning tech. "Drop the kids off in the morning, pick 'em up after school," she'd joked. I worried that assigning her the scanning project would spread her too thin—she was already running the bone lab and helping me on cases in the field—but after the dean's latest call for budget cuts, it was the only way to keep her position fully funded.

The truck driver seemed to have countless adjustments to make. In addition to leveling the trailer itself, he needed to attach and level a set of metal steps, as well as a hydraulic lift that hoisted patients on gurneys—or cadavers in body bags—into the imaging suite. The fellow seemed capable, so I decided to let him get by without my supervision long enough to pay a visit to Eddie Garcia. Parking my truck at the loading dock, I punched in the combination code to let myself in the back door of the Regional Forensic Center.

I took the elevator to the seventh floor. Passing the nurses' station, I nodded and continued a few doors farther down the corridor to Eddie Garcia's room. Knocking gently, I pushed open the door to his room and walked in, hoping I wasn't waking him up.

I wasn't waking him up. The room was empty. Garcia was gone.

"WHAT DO YOU MEAN, HE signed himself out?"

"Just that," said Arlene, the duty nurse. "He signed himself out an hour ago."

"The man's got no *hands*," I said. "His right arm's grafted to his belly. How the hell did he sign himself out?" The nurse flushed, her eyes narrowing in anger or shock at what I'd said. "Oh, hell, I'm sorry, Arlene. I didn't mean that as harshly as it sounded. What I mean is, where did he go? And why? Did Carmen check him out?"

"No." Suddenly she began to cry. "I'm so worried about him, Dr. Brockton. I begged him not to leave. I begged him to let me call his wife. But he refused. He insisted on being discharged, and he left with that man."

"What man? Did you know who it was?"

She shook her head, and I racked my brain, trying to remember anything Garcia might have said about friends he'd made during the year he'd lived in Knoxville. I drew a blank. As far as I knew, the M.E. and his family kept mostly to themselves, and Miranda and I were as close to them as anyone. "Was it a relative? Did the man look or sound Mexican?"

"No, he had red hair. And he sounded like he grew up around here. Said, 'Y'all have a good un,' as they were leaving."

"What else do you remember about him?"

She thought for a moment, then once more shook her head in frustration. "Not much, I'm afraid. I wouldn't be any good as a crime-scene witness." She furrowed her brow and scrunched her mouth with the effort of concentration. "He was wearing a white shirt and a skinny black tie."

"You mean, like a Mormon missionary? One of those bike-riding kids with a plastic name tag?"

"No, he was older than that. Thirty-five, maybe forty. And not as clean-cut as those Mormon boys."

An alarming thought occurred to me. "Do you think Dr. Garcia might be in danger? Was he coerced into leaving with this guy?"

"No. No, it didn't seem that way at all. Dr. Garcia acted eager to go, almost happy. The closest I've seen him to looking happy the whole time he's been here." She looked puzzled. "But it didn't seem like the guy knew Dr. Garcia. I mean, he came to get him, and he told me that the doctor was expecting him—'The doctor's expecting me,' that's exactly how he put it—but he seemed surprised when I told him we'd need a wheelchair and really startled when he saw Dr. Garcia with his hands all bandaged and grafted."

"Arlene, could I make a quick call?" She motioned toward the phone at the nurses' station, and I lifted the handset and dialed 0. "Hello, this is Dr. Bill Brockton," I told the operator. "Yes, ma'am, the Body Farm guy. . . . I'm just fine, thank you for asking. . . . Well, I'm glad you liked it, Mary Louise; I always enjoy giving those lectures for the hospital staff. . . . No, of course I remember you. . . . Listen, Mary Louise, you reckon you could put me through to the hospital's police dispatcher, please? . . . No, it's not an emergency call. At least I don't think so. . . . Thank you, Mary Louise."

I heard a click, then a pause, and then a male voice came through the receiver. "Dispatch, this is Grimes," he said. "What can I do for you, Dr. Brockton?"

"Officer Grimes, I'm hoping you might be able to shed some

light on something for me. Dr. Garcia, the medical examiner—. . .
Yes, that's right. Well, Dr. Garcia had himself discharged from
the hospital about an hour ago. . . . I know, I know he wasn't
really healed up yet, but he wanted to go. . . . Yes, doctors can
be strong-headed. Anyhow, I . . ." My voice trailed off. I what? I
was being nosy when I should mind my own business instead? "I
was just worrying about him, and I wanted to make sure he got
down to the entrance and got into the car okay. You reckon there
might've been an officer down at the entrance who could ease my
mind about that?"

"Hang on a second, Doc." He put me on hold for what seemed
several minutes. "Hey, Doc? I just talked with Jorgenson, who
was down at the main entrance a while ago. He says not to
worry—Dr. Garcia made it out of the wheelchair and into the car
just fine. Those guys from paradise are really careful."

"Guys from paradise?"

"Paradise. The limo service."

WHEN I RETURNED TO THE CT scanner, Miranda was
just emerging from the side door of the trailer. She gave me a
thumbs-up sign of approval, though the grim expression on
her face—an expression I'd seen a lot lately—didn't match the
jaunty gesture. I suspected that the thumbs-up reflected her feelings about the scanner while the expression reflected her recent
feelings about me.

"You're never going to believe this," I said.

"Try me."

"Eddie Garcia checked out of UT Hospital a couple hours
ago."

"Yeah."

"He just— What do you mean, 'Yeah'?"

"I mean yeah, I know."

"You know? How the hell do you know?"

"He just called me. Right after he called Carmen."

"He called Carmen? He didn't go home when he checked out?"

"No. He called from the car. He was in Chattanooga."

"Chattanooga? What's he doing in Chattanooga?"

"Just passing through."

"Just passing through on the way to where?"

"Atlanta."

"Atlanta? Why the hell's he going to Atlanta? He's still recovering from surgery. And how come he's being all cloak-and-daggerish?"

"He's got an appointment at Emory. I guess he's nervous about it. Maybe he didn't want anybody to try to talk him out of it. Maybe he didn't want to raise people's hopes about it. Maybe he didn't want to raise his own hopes."

"What hopes?"

"His hopes for a total hand transplant. Emory has a new hand-transplant center, and they're looking for their first patient. They've agreed to evaluate Eddie as a candidate."

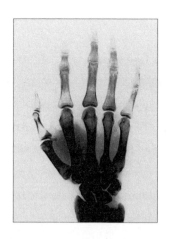

CHAPTER 31

FOR A BIRD OR A PLANE OR SUPERMAN, ASHEVILLE was seventy-five straight-line miles to the east of Knoxville. I was no Superman, unfortunately. I was an earthbound anthropologist with a truckload of amputated arms, and by road Asheville was forty miles farther than by air—forty twisting, turning, up-and-down miles across the backbone of the Appalachians. For much of the mountainous route, the interstate followed the gorge of the Pigeon River as it tumbled out of the mountains, and normally I enjoyed the rugged terrain and the demanding drive. Today, though, I might as well have been passing through blighted industrial wasteland, for all the attention I paid to the passing scenery. I'd glanced at the hydroelectric plant perched beside the Pigeon at the Tennessee-Carolina border, but everything since had passed unnoticed. Luckily, at daybreak on a Sunday morning, my truck was practically the only vehicle meandering this stretch of I-40.

My attention deficit had two causes: I was deeply distressed, and I was seriously sleep-deprived. But there were causes within causes. When I'd agreed to help the FBI, I hadn't anticipated how painful it would be to play the role of a greedy broker of body parts. I'd taken it on for worthy reasons, but inside the mask and the costume of corruptibility I'd donned, my soul's skin was itching and burning. Every interaction with Miranda now felt strained, and I deeply missed the easy collegiality and playful banter we'd shared for years.

I also grieved for the rift with Jeff. We'd not spoken since the night he walked out on me, the night I'd told him about Isabella and the likelihood that she was pregnant. I'd left several voice mails for him. I'd also spoken with Jenny, his wife, who—kindly but matter-of-factly—told me that this was a problem only Jeff and I could work out.

Isabella, too, was weighing heavily on me. Where was she? Was she indeed pregnant? What would it mean to father a child with a fugitive, a killer, a woman I'd totally misjudged? How had I been so blind? Would I be able to trust a woman fully—or trust myself—ever again? These worries swirled through my weary mind like dry leaves in some corner of a courtyard, seized by the hand of an unseen whirlwind that lifted them, spun them into a frenzy, and dropped them through its fingers into a lifeless heap.

My sleep deprivation was simpler: I'd just stayed up all night hauling bodies to the CT scanner and back, then amputating twenty arms. Over the past three weeks, I'd stockpiled ten bodies in the makeshift facility called the Annex, a corrugated metal building located a stone's throw from the stadium. The Annex contained a processing room for cleaning skeletal material, but we rarely used it anymore now that we had far better facilities in the Regional Forensic Center at the hospital. The Annex also contained a dozen chest-type freezers, most of which I'd filled as the ten bodies arrived. On Thursday I'd taken the bodies out to thaw, and I'd spent Saturday evening ferrying the still-chilly corpses across the river to the CT scanner, then back again. Except for the fact that I was hauling the bodies in a GMC pickup and delivering them to a high-tech scanner, I could have been Charon, the boatman from Greek mythology, ferrying the dead across the river Styx to the underworld.

I'd done the transporting myself, rather than have Miranda do it, because I didn't want to involve her in this—and because I didn't want to incur any more of her suspicion and disapproval than I already had. I'd also paid Eric, the scanning technician, the ruinous rate of three hundred dollars, from my own pocket, since I was taking six hours out of his Saturday night. It would have been far simpler to skip the scans of these ten and just begin the scanning project with all subsequent donated bodies, but I felt I owed it to the research project—to Glen Faust and OrthoMedica and to the dead donors themselves—to secure the scans before severing the arms. Finally, at 2:00 A.M.—an hour when I was sure I wouldn't have an audience in the Annex—I'd begun to cut.

Slicing into the first one, I'd felt slightly tentative. I didn't want to damage any bones, since they'd all end up in the skeletal collection, so I worked my way cautiously down through the muscles and tendons and ligaments linking the arms to the shoulders: the deltoid and teres major muscles, the four interwoven muscles of the rotator cuff, and the ligaments that helped secure the head of the humerus within the recesses of the scapula. I was grateful that I was removing arms, not legs; tucked deep within the acetabulum, the socket of the hip joint, was a ligament that was difficult to cut without gouging the bone.

By the third corpse, I'd found a rhythm, and by the fifth I was slicing as swiftly and ruthlessly as a butcher. Still, it had been a long, tense night, and by the time I'd finished packing the arms in five ice chests and wrestling the coolers into the truck, I was spent. After a quick shower at my office, I'd donned khakis and a button-down shirt, along with the digital recorder and a new video camera from Rankin, this one concealed in a fat fountain pen in my pocket—a pen whose gold clip was adorned with a small disk of "onyx," just like the tie clip I'd worn in Las Vegas. I merged onto I-40 East just as the Sunday sun was rising. Now—winding my way through the mountains toward Asheville—I felt fatigue replacing anxiety as my main problem.

I was startled out of my fog by the electronic whoop of a siren. Checking the side mirror, I was dismayed to see a North Carolina highway patrol cruiser close behind me. I put on my blinker and eased to the shoulder, hoping—though my hope didn't last long—that he would swing around me and accelerate away.

As the trooper approached, I rolled down the window. Above his left shirt pocket, he wore a brass nameplate that read OFFICER HARRINGTON. "Good morning, Officer Harrington. Did I do something wrong?"

"Sir, I need to see your license, registration, and proof of insurance, please."

"Certainly." I pulled my Tennessee driver's license from my wallet and removed the paperwork from a small leather notebook I kept in the glove box. I also unclipped my Tennessee Bureau of Investigation consultant's badge from my belt and handed it to him along with the other things. "Just so you know, I'm considered one of the good guys over on the other side of the mountains," I said.

He looked surprised when he saw the TBI shield. "Mr. Brockton, do you know why I stopped you?"

"I'm afraid I don't," I confessed.

"I've been following you for the last five miles," he said. "Were you aware of that?" I was embarrassed to admit I didn't know that either. "You've been driving very erratically. Slowing down, speeding up, drifting between the lanes. Have you been drinking, Mr. Brockton?"

"No. I don't drink. Ever."

"Are you sleepy?"

"Not really. I'm tired, but not particularly sleepy. I've got a lot on my mind right now. I guess I was just really distracted."

"This is a dangerous stretch of road for that."

"I know. I'm sorry. I'll pay better attention."

"That'd be a good idea. If you would sit tight for just a moment, Mr. Brockton, I need to call in a routine check on your license and registration. Do you have any recent citations that you know of?"

"None. I've never even gotten a speeding ticket."

"Never?"

I shook my head.

He smiled. "Congratulations. That's rare. Sit tight—I'll be right back." He turned and started back toward the cruiser, then stopped. He peered through the window of the shell covering the back of the truck, then turned to me. "Mr. Brockton?"

"Yes, Officer?"

"You've got a lot of coolers in your truck. What's in 'em?"

My heart caught in my throat. "Specimens," I said. "Biological specimens."

"Specimens of what?"

I SAT LOCKED IN THE back of the cruiser for what seemed an eternity while Harrington explored the possibility that I was a chain-saw-happy serial killer. He talked on the radio to his dispatcher, the dispatcher's supervisor, and the day-shift captain. Within seconds after Harrington had politely asked me to open one of the coolers, he'd drawn his gun and put me in the back of the car. Minutes later a second cruiser, lights strobing and siren screaming, screeched to a stop behind us, followed shortly by a third. The three troopers huddled at the back of my truck, chatting and shaking their heads in disbelief, raising the lid of the cooler repeatedly to confirm that yes, it really did contain four amputated human arms, nestled in the ice like fresh-caught fish, their tail fins replaced by fingers. The troopers' roadside huddle was periodically interrupted by radio consultations, not just with Harrington's supervisors but also with various officials of the state's hazardous-materials office and—last but not least—the Tennessee Bureau of Investigation.

I'd tried suggesting he call the TBI first, since I was pretty sure they'd vouch for my current standing (or at least my recent past) as a law-abiding, crime-solving consultant and professor. If I'd had the good fortune to be pulled over in Tennessee rather than North Carolina, I'd have been on my way within five minutes, I felt sure, but here in Carolina nobody knew me, so it was a thornier problem. I'd considered asking the trooper to call Ben Rankin at the FBI, but I quickly rejected that idea. Getting Rankin to rescue me from the North Carolina state police might save me some time and embarrassment in the short run, but it would compromise the secrecy of the sting. So instead I sat and chafed in the back of the police car while Harrington proved himself to be a thorough, dutiful cop, the sort who went by the book and worked things up the chain of command.

I'd noticed a pair of black Ford sedans cruise by, equipped with the radio antennas characteristic of law-enforcement vehicles. *How ironic,* I thought. *I'm wired for sound and video, but the surveillance van's fifty miles away in Asheville.*

I'd tried to phone Rankin while Harrington ran my tag and my license—"Is that you that just went past? Come back and get me out of here," I'd have said—but there was no cell-phone signal in this part of the mountains, so I had no choice but to let the drama play out however it played out.

Finally Harrington, his bosses, and the state's environmental-protection guardians seemed satisfied that I was neither a murderer nor a bioterrorist. The trooper opened the door of the cruiser, and I was a free man once more. "Okay, Dr. Brockton"—I gathered that someone at the TBI had vouched for me as "*Dr. Brockton*"—"we're gonna let you head on to Asheville now. I'm sorry this took so long. It's not the sort of situation we encounter every day."

"I understand," I said.

"Do you feel able to concentrate on your driving the rest of the way? Reason I ask is, if you had an accident and this stuff you're carrying got strewn all over I-40, we would have one hell of a mess to deal with, and I'm not just talking about picking up the arms off the pavement."

I winced, picturing the media circus and the scandal that would surely follow an arm-slinging crash. "I will pay total attention to the road," I said. "Scout's honor. I apologize for taking up so much of your morning."

"No problem," he said with a slight smile, handing me my license and registration. "Beats writing speeding tickets."

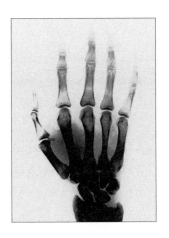

CHAPTER 32

I'D BUILT AN HOUR OF CUSHION INTO MY SCHEDULE, in case the logistics of parking and unloading at the Grove Park proved complicated. My unscheduled stop on the shoulder of I-40 had used every minute of that. I might have been tempted to make up the lost time by speeding, but that impulse was held firmly in check by my frequent glances in the rearview mirror. There behind me, a respectful but vigilant hundred yards back, hung Officer Harrington. He followed me all the way to downtown Asheville, then parted company with me when I took the exit ramp. I rolled down my window and waved. He answered with a brief whoop of his siren.

Rankin had phoned as soon as I'd emerged from the mountains and gotten back into the land of cell-phone signal. "Jesus, Doc, what was that about? You had us shitting bricks." When I told him, his reaction—half amusement at my predicament, half anger at my meandering driving, which had nearly derailed the operation—wasn't quite the dose of sympathy I'd hoped for, but Rankin wasn't inclined to listen to my woes. "I gotta go, Doc. We've got to finish setting up. Get here as soon as you can. Break a leg."

The Grove Park Inn was set on a hillside a couple of miles north of downtown Asheville, amid historic mansions and towering hemlocks. The original stone lodge was rustic and charming. The lobby was flanked by a pair of fireplaces large enough to roast entire oxen, and a broad veranda overlooked the floor of the valley. In recent decades, though, the lodge had been virtually swallowed up by a series of additions: two wings of guest rooms and meeting facilities, a golf course and country club, a sports complex, and a luxury spa.

For the training, Sinclair had booked a large room on the tenth floor of one of the new wings. I threaded my way to the underground parking garage, scanning for a truck or van that might contain half a dozen FBI agents and a raft of electronic gear. I didn't spot anything promising between the service entrance and the loading dock. I backed up to the dock and parked, feeling alone and uneasy. I pressed the "Deliveries" button on an intercom box, and a voice crackled through the speaker: "*ssszzztttsss* help you?"

"I'm here for the medical seminar that's up in the Heritage Ballroom," I said. "I've got some cases of material that need to go up the freight elevator. It would help if you've got a flatbed cart."

"*ssszzztttsss* there." A minute later, as I fumbled with the tiny switches on the audio and video recorders—I'd almost forgotten to turn them on—I heard the hum of an electric motor. In the wall beside me, a metal shutter door began to rise and the hotel's basement opened like a massive rolltop desk. A slight young

Hispanic man emerged, pushing a cart to the edge of the plat-
form. He helped me wrestle the five coolers out of the truck and
up onto the dock, which was a foot higher than the tailgate. Then
we stacked them on the cart, and he bent low over the handle,
putting his weight behind it. "It's very heavy," he said once it began to move. "What is it?"

I wished people would quit asking me that. "Refreshments," I
said.

I'd phoned Sinclair when I reached the hotel, and he was waiting for me as the elevator door opened on the tenth floor. "Glad
you're here," he said. "I was getting worried. We're cutting it a
little close on the schedule."

"Sorry. I'd meant to be here an hour ago, but I hit a little snag."
Without going into all the personal reasons for my erratic driving, I told him how I'd been pulled over in the mountains.

"Hang on, I want to hear the rest of the story," he interrupted,
"but let's take care of this first." He laid a hand on the shoulder
of the hotel worker, saying, "This is fine. We'll take it from here."
He pulled a twenty from his pocket and handed it to the young
man, who thanked him politely and left.

We'd stopped in front of a pair of double doors marked HERI-
TAGE A. Sinclair delivered a staccato series of raps, and the doors
swung outward, pushed by two clean-cut young men in scrubs,
followed by a third, who wheeled the cart into a cavernous ballroom, its floor dotted with tables draped in blue. We'd entered at
one end of the room, near a raised stage and an enormous projec-
tion screen. A podium stood at one side of the stage; center stage
was occupied by a waist-high table draped with blue sheets. A
video camera stood at one side of the table; perched on the other
side was a surgical microscope. As I studied the setup, a techni-

cian somewhere in the room flipped a switch, projecting a video image onto the screen. There, magnified to five times its actual size, was the image of the table's surface. A tray of larger-than-life surgical instruments was neatly arranged at one end. At its center lay a human arm, amputated as neatly at the shoulder as were the twenty specimens in the coolers beside me.

The ballroom's floor contained thirty tables, each outfitted with surgical implements and operating microscopes. And ten of the thirty already held arms. As I marveled at the ballroom's transformation into a surgical classroom, I heard the clatter of metal latches snapping open. Working wordlessly, Sinclair's three assistants rolled the cart down the center aisle between the tables, laying arms on the remaining tables, positioning each limb as methodically and swiftly as decorators setting out floral centerpieces for a banquet.

AFTER THE TRAINING—A TUTORIAL in microsurgical repair of blood vessels and nerves—Sinclair's assistants wordlessly collected my twenty arms—now crisscrossed with incisions and sutures—and loaded them into my coolers. Sinclair rode down the freight elevator with me and the hotel employee—this one a stocky African-American male—who'd been sent to help handle the coolers. After loading them into the truck, he latched the tailgate and hatch, accepted his tip from Sinclair, and disappeared into the basement of the hotel.

Sinclair turned to me. "Got a minute before you hit the road?"

"Sure." I unlocked the truck and nodded at the passenger door. "Step into my office."

We got in and closed the doors. "What'd you think of the training?"

"Fascinating," I said. "I had no idea it was possible to put on something like that in a hotel ballroom. And the microsurgery was remarkable. I don't see how they make such tiny stitches by hand, even with the image magnified by the scope." A question occurred to me. "What'd you tell the surgeons about where the arms came from?"

"Nothing," he said. "We have a 'don't ask, don't tell' policy. They'd rather not know. They realize that material's hard to come by, so they're grateful to pony up the cost of the training and keep their consciences clear."

Lucky them, I thought.

"Couldn't've done it without you, Bill. Here you go." He handed me a thick manila envelope, which he'd brought down in the elevator with him. I'd been dreading this moment ever since I saw him take the envelope from a briefcase. "There's a five-hundred-dollar honorarium check in there, in case you need something legit to show the accountants. And twenty grand in cash." He grinned. "Don't blow it all on booze and strippers."

"Thanks for the advice." I laid the envelope on the console between us, hoping the recorder and the video camera were successfully capturing the transaction. "And thanks for the opportunity."

"Let's hope it's the first of many. So now it's out to the Body Farm with these arms?"

I nodded.

"Man, I hate to picture all that perfectly good tissue rotting on the ground. Sure you don't want to leave it with me?"

"Can't," I said. "Any skeleton we add to the collection needs to be complete, unless the donor lost a limb during life. The skeleton needs to match the donor's medical-history file."

"Sure, I get it," he answered. "Sort of an all-or-nothing deal—none of the bones or all of the bones?"

"Right."

"Speaking of that," he said, "I wanted to ask you about something you mentioned that morning in Vegas. You said you're long on bodies, short on space. You ever turn down donations?"

"Haven't yet," I answered. "Well, except in cases where the donor had HIV or hepatitis—we can't risk exposing students to that. Otherwise we take all comers." I paused for half a beat. "But frankly, that could be about to change. If the university doesn't come up with some more land for us, we might have to start turning people away soon."

"Hey, we'd be glad to help. Any bodies you can't accommodate, we'd be glad to take 'em off your hands."

I shook my head. "Not that simple," I said. "When bodies are donated to UT, they become state property. The bean counters wouldn't want us giving away state property."

He drummed his fingers on the dash, then looked me in the eye. "What if the bean counters didn't know?"

Make him spell out what he wants you to do, Rankin had stressed. I returned Sinclair's gaze. "How do you mean? What do you suggest?"

"What if a body was never logged in, or whatever you call it, in the first place?"

I rubbed my chin; the simple roughness of the stubble felt comforting against my hand.

"Or what if you wrote it off as a loss somehow? You do all sorts of experiments, right?"

I nodded.

"So come up with some creative research, some destructive testing. Put a note in the inventory database or the files or wherever—'body destroyed' or some such."

"So what good does the body do you if I destroy it?"

"Jesus, Bill, you've got a Ph.D., don't be a dumb-ass. You

don't actually destroy the body, you just *say* you did. Creative accounting."

"And then what?"

"You send it to Tissue Sciences. It helps train surgeons, repair tendons, rebuild spines, all sorts of good things."

"Sounds great," I said, "but unless I misunderstand you, you're asking me to falsify records and steal state property. Tell me why I should take those risks. To borrow a phrase from your Las Vegas presentation, let's talk financial incentives."

"How about ten thousand a body? Would that be sufficient incentive?"

"I'll need to think about it," I said. "I feel a little like a peasant selling a kidney. If things go wrong, they can go really wrong. What's the fair-market rate for kidneys in Pakistan?"

"Twenty grand and some change." He said it quickly and matter-of-factly, like a man who had firsthand knowledge of the subject. "But you don't look like you've got starving kids. And I'm not asking you to sell part of your own body."

"No. You're asking me to sell part of my soul."

He tapped the manila envelope. "You already did." He smiled slightly, then got out of the truck, closed the door, and walked away.

SUNDOWN FOUND ME HEADING WEST on I-40, driving into the sun for the second time that day. The ice in the coolers had begun to melt. As I entered the serpentine stretch through the mountains, I could hear the ice and water and arms—the laid-open, tinkered-on, stitched-up arms—sloshing with each sway of the truck. And every slosh seemed the hiss of a serpent.

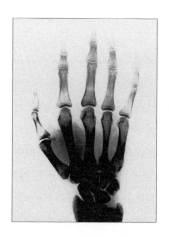

CHAPTER 33

I WAS STILL WAY BEHIND ON MY SLEEP AND WAY ahead on my stress Monday morning as I prepared to teach my ten o'clock Intro to Forensic Anthropology class. The topic of the day was forensic odontology: making positive identifications on the basis of unique features in teeth. The *CSI*-viewing public tended to regard DNA testing as far superior to any other method of identification, but I still considered dental records a powerful and often far faster means of identification.

I'd chosen three cases to illustrate the point. The first involved a missing toddler, a two-year-old girl who disappeared one night while her uncle was babysitting. Eight months after she vanished, a pair of hunters found a small skull in a nearby stream beside a cow pasture. The skull was missing most of its teeth, but when I went to the scene and sifted the sands of the streambed, like a prospector panning for gold, I managed to find most of the teeth that had fallen from the skull. The missing two-year-old had never been to the dentist, so there were no dental records for comparison. There was, however, a photograph: a snapshot showing the girl grinning at the camera. And in her grin I glimpsed distinctive notches at the corners of her four upper incisors—unique, identifying notches that matched the teeth I'd found.

The second case was the murder of a state police officer, gunned down in his driveway late one night after he finished his shift on duty. Investigators suspected he'd been shot by his brother-in-law, but the only evidence linking the suspect to the crime was a wooden cigar tip, found in the grass near the death scene. The tip bore deep indentations—bite marks—which meshed perfectly, it turned out, with the teeth of the suspect.

The third case gave me a pang as I reviewed it. The murder victim was a sixteen-year-old Japanese-American girl—a smart, pretty girl—who was abducted, raped, and bludgeoned to death with a baseball bat. I identified her by comparing the teeth of the skeletonized remains with the dental records of the missing teenager. The first hint that the records would match the teeth came when I inspected an incisor found in the woods at the death scene. The tooth had the scooped-out, shovel-shaped cross section that typified Asian incisors, just as I imagined Isabella's had.

I was flashing through the slides of this third case when Miranda rapped on the open door and strode into my office, demanding, "What in the world are you doing?"

"I'm looking at the slides I'm about to show to my ten o'clock class," I said, startled by her vehemence.

"I am not talking about those slides," she snapped. "I'm talking about what happened to those ten bodies over the weekend."

One thing I'd wrestled with on the drive back from Asheville was how I'd explain the ten mangled bodies and twenty stitched-up arms I'd parked in the cooler at the forensic center. "I told you I was doing a research project," I began.

"Research? That's not research. That's butchery. *Butchery.* What the hell, Dr. B.?"

The likelihood of this very conversation had filled me with dread, but the dread had motivated me to prepare for it, as best I could. "We've never studied differential decay in dismemberment cases," I said. "If a killer cuts up a body, does that body decay at the same rate as an intact body? I don't know. Nobody knows, because nobody's done a controlled experiment to compare the decomp rates."

"So now—on a whim—you've begun a large-scale study?" Her eyes bored into me. "If you're doing a controlled experiment, where are the control subjects, the ten intact bodies?"

I had a halfway-plausible answer to this, too. "We've got years of decomp data from intact bodies," I said. "We've got mathematical models that can calculate, at any range of temperatures, how long each stage lasts—fresh, bloat, decay, and dry. I've studied my ten control subjects, plus a whole lot more, over the past twenty years. The dismemberment study will be new data."

She glared. "But just arms? Why not arms and legs?"

"One variable," I responded. "Keep it simpler."

"Then why the surgeries—all the incisions and sutures in those twenty arms? You're studying differential decay in bodies that have been dismembered by murderous orthopedic surgeons? Is that it?"

I was angry—not with Miranda; angry with myself, and Ray Sinclair, and the FBI—but I vented the anger in her direction. "Miranda, it's my research project, and it's not your concern."

"Not my concern?" She looked furious and deeply hurt. "I

don't know whether it's what you're saying or what you're *not* saying that bothers me more, but I feel very concerned."

"Drop it, Miranda. The subject's closed."

She stared at me, and then her expressive, angry, hurt face became a lifeless mask. "Yes, massa," she said. She gave me a sarcastic version of a military salute, then left as suddenly as she'd appeared.

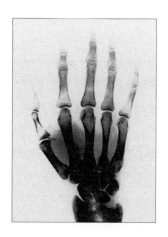

CHAPTER 34

IT WAS A PLAIN #10 ENVELOPE, ADDRESSED TO ME BY hand, in blocky letters, with no return address.

The envelope was distorted and lumpy. Most of it felt empty, but clearly its center contained *something:* something oddly shaped and perhaps a quarter inch thick. I wiggled a finger under one end of the flap and tore open the top of the envelope, then turned it upside down and shook it above my kitchen counter.

The envelope's contents—an angular, spiky piece of red paper—tumbled out. The bright red shape seemed to blaze on the speckled black granite, like a flame against a starry night sky. The paper was folded into an origami crane, the Japanese symbol of peace. The wing tips were blunted, I noticed; looking closer, I saw why: A tiny bit of each one appeared charred.

I plucked the crane from the counter by the long, slender tail jutting up from the body. The bird had been pressed flat by its flight through the U.S. postal system—a flight that had begun in

San Francisco, according to the postmark on the envelope. Taking care not to touch the scorched tips, I raised the wings partly to horizontal, then pulled them gently outward, slightly away from the body. As the wings spread and the bird took flight in my hands, a second snippet of paper fluttered from a fold in the bird's body. It was a second crane—a tiny replica of the first, so small it might have required tweezers and a magnifying glass to create—made of delicate white rice paper.

In her own way, Isabella was letting me know that she was alive and at liberty, and she was letting me know that she was pregnant.

It was with powerfully conflicting emotions that I phoned Oak Ridge detective Jim Emert. "I just got something in the mail from Isabella," I said.

Telling him felt like the right thing to do by the simple, objective rules of law and order, but it felt miserably traitorous by a more complex inner calculus of loyalty or human compassion.

"What'd she say?" Beneath the surface calm, his voice was taut with suspense.

"Nothing. And everything."

"Come again?"

"She didn't say anything. But it was a very clear message."

"Doc, any chance you could talk in plain English? I'm not so good at the riddles."

I told him about the two cranes in the envelope and explained why I was so sure of their meaning.

When Isabella had fled two months ago, her disappearance had been marked by a flock of origami cranes—a thousand paper cranes—swirling in an eddy of wind at the base of the Oak Ridge Peace Bell. The Peace Bell itself had been a key part of that earlier message. The bell had been cast in Hiroshima, Japan, as a step toward healing and reconciliation between two cities linked by a terrible destiny: one city that was created by the Bomb, another that was destroyed by it. The cranes at the bell had been Isabella's public gesture of atonement, I'd sensed at the time, for purposely killing an atomic scientist, and also for unintentionally inflicting such grievous harm on Eddie Garcia. The pair of cranes sent to my home, which I saw as a mother bird and her baby, was a very private message. It was a confidence, one I'd just betrayed out of a sense of duty.

"Doc? Are you still there?"

"Huh? Oh, sorry." I realized that my attention had drifted far from Emert. "What were you saying?"

"I was asking if you were careful not to contaminate the evidence."

"Of course I wasn't careful not to contaminate the evidence. Hell, Jim, the envelope wasn't exactly labeled 'Evidence.' It wasn't until I looked at the birds that I had any idea the letter was from Isabella." Just to make sure he got my point, I added, "I'm guessing twenty or thirty postal-service employees handled the evidence, too."

"I know, I know." He sighed. "In a TV-show world, you would have had a hunch about the handwriting or something and we could've opened it in a lab and gotten your buddy Bohanan to lift prints off the birds."

"You probably still can," I pointed out reluctantly. "I only touched the wings and the tail. I didn't unfold any of the creases, so most of the surface area's untouched, at least by me."

"Good point," he said. "We might also be able to get DNA off the flap and match it to samples we got at her house. Though by the time DNA results come back, everybody connected to the case is likely to be dead of old age."

"What's the waiting time for DNA results these days?"

"Long and longer," he said. "Six months in high-priority cases. A year or more otherwise. Most of the DNA headlines these days come from cold-hit murder cases, where a prisoner's DNA sample triggers a match with blood or semen collected and analyzed years ago."

"What's the point of it, Jim? We know Isabella sent it, apparently from San Francisco. What we don't know is whether she's still there. I'd bet not. I don't know how she might've gotten there, but I'd bet she's in Japan by now."

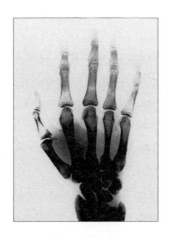

CHAPTER 35

A DAY AFTER EDDIE GARCIA'S SURPRISE DEPARTURE
for Atlanta in the Paradise limo, Carmen drove down—not to
retrieve him but to join him, to support him—during his evaluation by the Emory transplant team. Her mother had flown up
from Bogotá to care for Tomás while Carmen and Eddie stayed
in guest housing provided by the Transplant Center.

The evaluation was a detailed process. In addition to evaluating Garcia's medical past and present, the team had to consider
his likely future—his chances for a life that was productive and
healthy.

Hand transplantation was a huge investment in high-tech
hope—a giant gamble on the fortunate few selected to receive
transplants. As Miranda had pointed out to me weeks before,
saying yes to Garcia meant saying no to a host of other appli-
cants, other people who'd lost hands to disease or trauma. The
transplant team needed to feel confident that the investment and

the gamble could pay off, not just for Garcia but also for society. That meant they needed to assess a host of factors: Apart from the injury to his hands, was Garcia's health good? Did he fully understand the potential risks? Could he faithfully follow the postoperative protocols for physical therapy, infection control, and the lifelong medications required to suppress his immune system and prevent rejection? Was he psychologically prepared for the daunting endeavor—and robust enough to deal with failure, if the transplant didn't succeed? What would be lost, to Garcia and the world, if he didn't receive a transplant? What might be gained if he did?

I gained a better perspective on the complex considerations of transplant evaluations when I called J. T. McLaughlin, a former undergraduate student of mine who'd gone on to become a nephrologist—a kidney specialist—in Montgomery, Alabama. J.T. hadn't performed any kidney transplants himself, but several of his patients had received transplants at the University of Alabama's medical center in Birmingham.

After I'd described Garcia's injuries—which J.T. found personally horrifying but medically fascinating—he peppered me with questions. "Is he a smoker?"

"Heavens no." I couldn't imagine Garcia, who was immaculate almost to the point of fastidiousness, smoking a cigarette. "Does that strengthen his case much?"

"Sure. Smokers have lousy circulatory systems. Lousy blood supply everywhere in the body, and that jeopardizes anything that gets transplanted to them. That lowers the odds of a successful outcome. Has he ever had a transfusion—either because of the trauma to his hands or because of some prior injury or illness?"

"I don't know," I confessed. "Why does that matter?"

"If he has, his immune system's been sensitized; that means he'd be more likely to reject the transplant. But the Emory people are on top of that—they're among the nation's leaders in transplant compatibility. They've developed something called the Emory algorithm, which is used all over the country, to help predict rejection. And I think they're about to start clinical trials on a new immunosuppressant drug—supposedly the biggest advance in fighting transplant rejection in thirty years."

"Sounds like he's in the right place."

J.T. wasn't through with his questions. "How old is he?"

"Forty. Ish."

"That's good. He's fairly young, which helps in a couple of ways. For one thing, he's likely to rebound more quickly; his blood vessels and nerves would regenerate faster than some geezer's would. He'd potentially get a lot more benefit from a transplant than a geezer, too, and could contribute more to society. Helps that he's a doc, too."

"Doctors helping doctors? He's already a member of the club?"

"Well, that doesn't hurt," he hedged, "though nobody would ever put it that crassly. What I really meant was, as a physician he's highly educated and he already knows medicine. That means he understands the risks, he knows he'll have to take immunosuppressants for the rest of his life, and he realizes that the immunosuppressants have side effects and complications of their own—they can cause diabetes, and they make him more vulnerable to diseases. In a way it's like signing up for HIV or AIDS, for the sake of the transplant. The procedure's very risky, and the risk never fully goes away."

"That's discouraging," I said. "On the surface a hand transplant sounds like it would be a miracle for him."

"It might well be," he responded. "But there's no free lunch. Some medical miracles cost a hell of a lot." He paused, then added, "Speaking of that, can he even afford it? His health insurance would probably cover the cost of prostheses, but it isn't going to cover a dime of an elective, experimental procedure like this."

"I hadn't even thought of that," I confessed.

"Emory will sure think of it," he said. "I imagine this is a million-dollar procedure. But maybe they've got some research funding that would help underwrite the costs. Money aside, what's your friend's support network like? You think the wife would help him through the ups and the downs?"

"Absolutely. She's smart and strong. She'd be great—supportive, but I'm sure she could get tough with him if she needed to."

"Anything about him that might raise a red flag to a psychiatrist?"

"What does a psychiatrist have to do with it?"

"It's experimental surgery. Incredibly rare, very risky. They're gonna want a shrink's opinion. Can he handle the stress, follow the rules, do his physical therapy, take the meds religiously, handle the disappointment if the surgery fails? What's your take on his overall mental health?"

I thought about the fleeting suspicion I'd had—the possibility that Eddie had deliberately infected his right hand during Clarissa Lowe's autopsy, in order to qualify as a double amputee. I also took a quick look at myself in the mental-health mirror. "I'm sure he's every bit as well adjusted as I am," I said, and made a mental note to schedule another therapy session with Dr. Hoover.

While I was on the line with J.T., I got a voice mail from Helen Taylor, at East Tennessee Cremation. "I just talked to a friend of mine who's a funeral director in Memphis now. She was working here ten years ago, and she remembered meeting the guy that was talking about buying Ivy Mortuary. She thought it was weird that he spent more time hanging out in the embalming room than going over the financials. He wasn't with SCI or any of the other funeral-home chains—I remembered that wrong. He was talking about buying the place with his brother, some muckety-muck at a big pharmaceutical company with deep pockets."

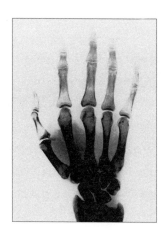

CHAPTER 36

I WINCED WHEN I LOOKED AT MY CELL PHONE'S DISPLAY
and saw the number of the incoming caller. It was Raymond Sinclair, the last person on earth I wanted to talk with. *Man up,* I
told myself, and answered the call.

"Bill Brockton."

"Bill, it's Ray Sinclair. Long time no talk."

"I know—sorry, Ray. I've been pretty swamped."

"Swamped with work or swamped with bodies?"

"Both," I answered.

"Well, I can't help you with the work," he said, "but I can sure
help you with the bodies. You've got supply, I've got demand—
lots of demand. You follow what I'm saying?"

I did follow what he was saying. Rankin had dropped by the
day before to tell me about a conversation they'd monitored with
the wiretap they'd finally put on all of Sinclair's phones. Sinclair
was slated to provide six torsos for a thoracic-surgery training

at a hospital in Dallas a week from now, and he was two torsos short. He'd been calling around to funeral homes and crematories that were also on his list of suppliers, Rankin had added,
but had come up empty-handed so far. "He's getting desperate,"
Rankin had said. "Play hard to get. Make him squirm. Make him
beg. Maybe that'll make him a little careless."

I'd chafed at the idea. "Why are we still doing this? Don't you
have enough to nail him yet?"

"One more nail," Rankin had said. "We want to make sure
the coffin's good and tight. The Newark office is drafting the
complaint right now. As soon as we get one more piece of evidence, we'll arrest him, then take the case to a grand jury up
there for indictment. Two, three days from now, we'll put the
cuffs on this guy. Promise."

Play hard to get, I reminded myself. *Make him beg.* So I left
Sinclair hanging on the phone for a moment. "You know, Ray,
I've been thinking about this, and the more I think, the more potential downside I see. The risk-benefit ratio is higher than I'm
comfortable with, if you catch my drift."

Now it was *his* turn to leave *me* hanging. "Are you saying
you're backing out on me, Bill? Because if you are, that would be
very distressing to me."

"I'm just saying the risks are really high, so the benefits should
be equally high. You're right, Ray, I'm not a Pakistani peasant
with a spare kidney and a pack of starving kids to feed. I'm a
middle-aged professor who's putting his job and reputation and
pension on the line for you. If you're asking me to commit fraud
and steal bodies for you, I want more than ten thousand a body."

"Cut to the chase," he snapped. "What do you want?"

"Twenty thousand apiece," I heard myself saying. I decided to try a shot in the dark, or at least in semidarkness: "Same thing you pay the Pakistani peasants for their kidneys."

"I get a hell of a lot higher return for a fresh kidney than for a decaying body," he shot back. "Twenty grand's robbery for what you're selling."

"So is what you're asking me to do, Ray."

He breathed a heavy, angry breath into the phone. "This disappoints me, Bill. I thought we were on the same page. I thought we had mutual interests. I thought we were building a partnership." I was glad he couldn't see the grimace of distaste I made when he said that. "You're putting me in a very difficult spot here, Bill. Do you hear what I'm saying?"

"I hear it," I answered. "You're putting me in a difficult spot, too."

"That's true, Bill. I am." He paused. "I'll call you tomorrow," he said, and hung up.

Ten minutes later Rankin called me, exultant. "Oh, yeah!" he crowed. "*Nail* that coffin shut. You're great at this."

"I don't want to be great at this," I replied. "I want to be done with this."

CHAPTER 37

the need for a more wholesome and pleasant experience, so I drove across the river to the Body Farm to check on Maurie Gershwin's decomposition. As the weather had begun to warm, day by day, the pace of the anchorwoman's decay had gradually accelerated. By now, some three weeks after her arrival, her eye orbits stared emptily at the camera and her cheekbones and chin jutted through the remnants of her face. Her blond hair had been stained a greasy gray by the volatile fatty acids leaching from her body, and her finger bones bore the fine tooth marks of small carnivores. I squatted beside her, studying her with interest and an odd sense of fondness—kinship, even. "It's been a hard month," I said to the vacant face. "For both of us."

A few minutes later, somewhat restored, I headed to the UT Hospital cafeteria for a sandwich. In the lobby I passed a gray-haired, scrub-suited doctor who looked like he'd been on his feet for the past twenty years. He looked up as our paths crossed, and his face brightened, taking a decade off his age. When he smiled, I recognized him as Jim Yates, a cardiologist. "Bill Brockton," he said, "your ears must be burning. I was just talking about you."

"Uh-oh. Am I in trouble again?"

"Nothing we can't fix with a new heart or a pig valve." He laughed. "Actually, I have a patient who's interested in taking up residence at the Body Farm. He's in the cardiac-care unit, and he's probably not long for this world. Have you got a minute?" I nodded, and he led me to an elevator and pushed the button for the floor that housed the CCU. "He's got myocarditis—inflammation of the heart muscle—and his right ventricle's failing."

"Can't you get him a new heart?"

Yates shook his head. "There's no time. He could have an arrhythmia and go into cardiac arrest at any moment. What would he need to sign to donate his body, and how could I get a hold of it for him?"

"Simple," I said. "There's a consent form he'd need to sign and have witnessed. I think it's all of two or three sentences long. I can send it over in a campus-mail envelope if you want, or I can tell you how to find it on the Internet and print it out for him."

The elevator stopped, and the doors opened on the cardiac floor. "You willing to step off long enough to show me?"

"Don't you think that would make me look a little vulturish?"

Yates held the door and motioned me down the hall toward the nurses' station. When we stepped behind the counter, a nurse—a heavyset African-American woman who looked to be in her late forties—glanced up. "Lord, Lord," she said, "the vultures are circling." I winced, but she and the cardiologist both guffawed.

Yates leaned over a computer and called up the hospital's Web-access page. I sat down in the armless chair and rolled up to the keyboard. I'd never managed to remember all the slashes and periods in our Web site's address, but I knew that if I searched for "tennessee forensic anthropology center body donation," I'd be rewarded with a link to the donor form. Three mouse clicks later, I saw the words I'd seen thousands of times before: "I do hereby dispose of and give my body, after my death, to The University of Tennessee, Knoxville, for use by the Department of Anthropology or its designee, for educational and research purposes. I request, authorize, and instruct my surviving spouse, next-of-kin, executor or the physician who certifies my death to notify The University of Tennessee, Department of Anthropology, immediately after my death of the availability of my body." In a room under the stadium, a file drawer contained nearly two thousand of these forms, each signed and witnessed and awaiting the death and delivery of the donor's body. In another, larger room, row upon row of metal shelves held almost a thousand boxed skeletons, the bones of donors who had already delivered on their promise.

I hit "print" and asked for three copies, and I was rewarded by the whir of the printer. "Done," I announced over my shoulder to Dr. Yates, but he didn't answer, and when I glanced around, he was gone. Puzzled, I looked at the nurse, who nodded wordlessly over the counter and down the hall. The cardiologist was emerging from a patient's room. He caught my eye and beckoned to me.

"Bring that form, please, Bill," he called, and I obliged, but when I realized what he had in mind, I flushed with self-consciousness and stopped halfway down the hall. He practically jogged toward me, this physician who'd looked dead on his feet just minutes before. "Don't be shy," he said. "When I told him you were out here, he was so pleased. He actually smiled, this dying man. It would mean a lot to him to meet you."

Slumping, I allowed him to steer me into the room.

"Mr. Miller, this Dr. Brockton. Dr. Brockton, Ernest Miller."

The man in the bed frowned at me. "Doesn't take the vultures long to gather, does it?"

Aghast, I opened my mouth to apologize, when he gave me a weak smile.

"He told me to say that," he said, glancing at Yates. "He was right—he said it would make you jump."

I looked at Yates, prepared to squawk, but he was exchanging smiles with his patient, and I realized I didn't mind being the butt of the prank.

"Good one," I said. "Y'all got me." I thought about adding, *My truck is parked downstairs by the morgue, if you want me to haul you on over there tonight,* but I decided that might be pushing the joke too far. "It's nice to meet you, Mr. Miller. Do you have any questions I could answer?"

Dr. Yates excused himself and left us alone.

"I'm pretty clear on the concept," he said. "That cute news gal—Maurie—she did some stories on the Body Farm a while back. I meant to sign up then, but I got sidetracked and forgot. If I'm gonna do it, I reckon it's now or never." He held out his hand for the donor form. It didn't take him long to read it. "Seems pretty straightforward. Can I borrow your pen?" He scrawled his signature, then glanced at the form again. "Could you witness it for me?"

"I'd be honored," I said, "if you're sure this is what you want to do. I wouldn't want you to feel any pressure, though." A thought occurred to me. Miller appeared to be in his early fifties—somewhere around my age. *Young fellow,* I joked to myself. I guessed his height to be somewhere around five-nine, give or take an inch: roughly the same stature and build as Eddie Garcia. I cast a quick glance at his hands. "If you don't mind my asking, Mr. Miller, do you plan to donate your organs?"

"Does that affect whether I can go to the Body Farm?"

"Not at all," I said. "If your organs have been harvested, we can't use you for a research project, but we can still add you to our skeletal collection. Measurements of your bones will help keep our forensic data bank up to date. And we want as many teaching specimens as we can get. Donating your organs wouldn't interfere with either of those things, and it might help some people who need corneas or kidneys. Or hands." I hesitated, choosing my words more carefully than I wished, but probably not as carefully as I should have. "Oddly enough, I know a man who needs hands. Dr. Edelberto Garcia. Maybe you've heard about him; he's the medical examiner here, and he lost his hands in a terrible accident a few months ago."

Miller was listening, so I plunged ahead.

"Dr. Garcia's a few years younger than you," I went on. "He grew up in Mexico City, but he came to this country for his medical residency. He's soft-spoken, a bit quiet. When I first met him, I thought he was standoffish, but once I got to know him, I realized he was just shy. That surprised me, that a man as smart and handsome and successful as Dr. Garcia—a man with a fine education and a prestigious job and a beautiful wife and a lovely child—felt any need to be shy." I stopped, knowing that if I kept talking, my next sentence would be a direct request that Miller donate his hands. The request would be only natural and thoroughly unethical.

As if seeing the unspoken request in my eyes, Miller shook his head. "I don't mind being eaten by the bugs," he said, "but I don't want to be chopped up for spare parts."

I fought the urge to speak—to plead on Eddie's behalf—and managed to stop myself. Miller was watching me closely. He shook his head again, more slowly this time, and I wondered if he was shaking it about organ donation or about me. "You can have me if you want me," he said, "but if you take me, I want you to take all of me." He handed me back the form.

We talked a bit more—mostly about his daughter in Kentucky, who was coming to see him soon—and then I thanked him and took my leave. As I stepped into the hallway, I glanced down at the Body Farm form he'd signed. I found myself thinking how easy it would be to forge a similar signature on an organ-donor form. After all, I was falsifying documents for the FBI and for Ray Sinclair. Wasn't Eddie Garcia equally worthy of my duplicity?

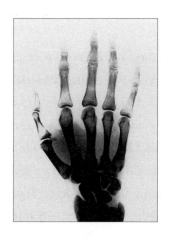

CHAPTER 38

PEGGY GAVE ME A SIDELONG, INQUISITIVE LOOK AS SHE handed me the manila envelope. "This just arrived by courier for you," she said. "Must be important."

The envelope bore a label printed with the words DR. BILL BROCKTON, PH.D., DABFA, in inch-high letters on the first line. Underneath, in equally large type, were the words PERSONAL AND CONFIDENTIAL. The third line, in slightly smaller type, read, TO BE OPENED BY ADDRESSEE ONLY.

There was no return address on the label. I flipped the envelope to see if the other side provided any clue about the sender or the contents, but all I found there was another label, identical to the first, and a strip of mailing tape sealing the flap. Could it be something else from Isabella? I exited the departmental office without opening the envelope, leaving both Peggy and myself in a state of suspense.

When I got to my private office at the other end of the stadium, I closed the door and locked it—something I could never remember having done before. I took a letter opener from the desk drawer and slit the top of the envelope, bypassing the tightly taped flap altogether. Just as I was about to reach inside, I remembered Jim Emert's disappointment when he learned that I'd handled the origami crane Isabella had mailed me. I laid the envelope down long enough to don a pair of latex gloves, then picked it up again and carefully slid the thin sheaf of pages onto the desk.

The top page was a two-line note, printed in the same font as the envelope's label. *"Let's talk risks and benefits,"* read the top line, and it told me that the envelope had come not from Isabella but from Raymond Sinclair. I was puzzled by the second line—*"You look like a man with a stiff overdue fine"*—but only until I flipped to the next page in the stack. Then I was overcome by a wave of dizziness and nausea. The rest of the pages were photographs, and they showed a young woman stripping off her clothes—a white blouse and a tight gray skirt—and dancing naked in front of a middle-aged professor sitting on a sofa. The professor's face changed from photo to photo, moving from shock and dismay through a series of more complicated and conflicted expressions, ones it disturbed me to see. As I studied the sequence, I remembered the night not that long ago when I'd studied my face in the mirror, the night after I placed Maurie Gershwin on the ground at the Body Farm and began photographing the sequence of changes in her face.

Maurie's steady decline, documented in hundreds of pictures by now, was inevitable and irreversible. I wondered if mine was, too.

Locking the photos in my desk drawer, I locked the office and went outside, into the bracing breeze of the early-April afternoon.

THIRTY MINUTES LATER I FOUND myself striding into the Duncan Federal Building, demanding that the startled lobby guard send me up to the sixth floor. "Who are you going to see?"

"Special Agent Ben Rankin," I snapped.

"Just a moment, sir," the guard said warily. "I'll need to call and make sure he's expecting you. What's your name?"

"Bill Brockton," I snarled, "and I'm sure he's not expecting me."

He picked up a phone from the counter and dialed, then murmured into it, keeping his eyes on me as he talked and covering his mouth with his hand so I couldn't hear what he said. "I'm sorry, sir, he's not in."

"Damn it. What about Angela Price?"

He murmured into the phone again, then paused to listen. He looked me up and down, then murmured some more. He hung up, eyeing me doubtfully, but motioned me through the metal detector, then escorted me to the elevator and pushed the sixth-floor button.

When the elevator door slid open, Price was standing in front of me. She held out a hand. "Dr. Brockton, good to see you. What can I do for you?"

"You can give me back my reputation," I said.

"Here, step into my office." She led me through the lobby, past its reception window of bulletproof glass and down a hall to an office whose windows offered a view of the Knoxville Convention Center and the eastern edge of the UT campus. Ben Rankin was sitting in one of the two chairs facing Price's desk.

"I thought you weren't in," I said accusingly.

"I wasn't. Just got back."

"Have a seat, Dr. Brockton," urged Price, "and tell us what's bothering you."

I told them about the envelope I'd just received, blushing as I described the photographs.

Price asked, "Did you bring it with you?"

"No. I locked it in my desk drawer. I started walking to clear my head. I didn't realize I was going to end up here."

She nodded slightly, then looked at Rankin. He glanced at me, then looked back at Price. A slow smile spread across his face.

She smiled slightly, too.

"Please clue me in," I said. "What do you see here that's worth a smile?"

"Blackmail," responded Rankin happily.

"Or extortion," added Price. "Maybe. If we're lucky."

"Lucky? I nearly passed out when I opened that envelope."

"Don't you see?" said Rankin. "We're looking at a whole new count against him now. We were already looking at theft, fraud, conspiracy to commit fraud, and interstate racketeering, but if we can add extortion to the indictment, that's potentially another twenty years." He grinned. "Man, I never really believed he would be so dumb." Price shot him a warning look, and the smile left his face.

For the second time in the past hour, I felt a churning wave of shock and sickness. I stared at Price, then at Rankin. "My God," I breathed. "You knew this would happen. You wanted me to end up in this position all along."

He frowned. "Not you, Doc—him. We wanted him to end up in this position. There's a difference."

I shook my head in disbelief. "You knew all along, didn't you? You knew the minute I agreed to go into that strip club that he'd do something like this, didn't you?"

"We didn't know," Price answered for him, "but yes, we thought it was possible. The FBI would be doing a pretty sloppy job if we failed to anticipate this sort of thing. It's a time-honored trap."

I felt betrayed, humiliated, and furious. "Do the words 'informed consent' mean anything to you? You didn't tell me the whole truth about what you expected when you pulled me into this. You got my consent under false pretenses. I deserved better than that."

"Fair enough. Yes, you deserved better," Price said, in a tone that sounded more like a challenge than a concession, "but we couldn't afford to risk giving you better. We knew you'd hate the strip club, and we knew Sinclair might try to compromise you. But what Ben said when you called him that night was dead-on: If you were too much of a goody-goody to set foot in a strip club, why on earth would Sinclair believe you'd lie and steal?"

The words stung like a slap—not just "lie" and "steal" but "goody-goody" as well. Was that what Price thought of me? Was that what Rankin thought of me? Was that, in fact, what I was?

"I'm sorry," Price added, her tone softening. "It was my call, not Ben's, and I had to hold my nose as I made it. An undercover sting requires imperfect choices and tough decisions. But I stand by this one, and I hope you can understand why. We've got great audio and video evidence on multiple counts—wire fraud, conspiracy, and interfering with interstate commerce, for sure. If you'll hang in there with us just one more step, we'll nail this guy for extortion, too. And then we'll let you get back to your normal life."

"Normal life? I have no idea what that means anymore."

I looked out the window for a long time. The sun was dropping toward the horizon. A few hundred yards down the hill from where I stood, a sliver of sunlight glanced off the bronze glass of the Sunsphere, one of the few remaining relics of Knoxville's 1982 World's Fair. A half mile or so beyond, just before the big bend where the Tennessee River first turns toward the Gulf of Mexico, Neyland Stadium glowed orange and white in the late-afternoon light. At this distance, at this moment, the massive stadium seemed small and unimportant, and my tiny office—my place beneath it—was an invisible, insignificant speck.

I looked back at Price. "I feel infected," I said miserably. "Diseased. Feels like toxic shock attacking every moral fiber I've got." I stared out the window at the river of cars flowing westward from downtown, taking normal people home to their neighborhoods and their families. "How do I get these toxins out of my system?"

A look of relief passed between the agents. They still had me. The bait was thrashing, but it was still on the hook, still twitching and writhing as the big fish opened its jaws.

RANKIN DROVE ME BACK TO my office, partly to save me the walk and partly to retrieve the envelope so the lab could fingerprint the photos. On the way he coached me about the call I needed to place to Sinclair. "You know the drill. Make him spell out the details, if you can. The more explicitly he threatens or pressures you, the stronger the extortion case is. So don't initiate anything. Get him to say what he wants you to do or what he'll do to you."

"Got it," I said impatiently. This was the third time he'd told me this, in slightly different words, since we'd ridden down in the elevator from Price's office, and I'd grasped the point the first two times.

We threaded the service road ringing the base of the stadium and parked by the stairwell at the north end zone. Rankin followed me up to my office and took a seat as I unlocked the desk drawer where I'd hidden the envelope.

For the second time that day, I felt close to fainting. The envelope was gone.

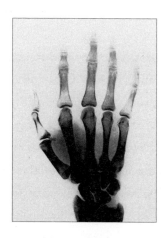

CHAPTER 39

"AND YOU'RE SURE IT WAS IN THE DRAWER?"

"Positive."

Rankin looked around the room. "What about the file cabinet? Couldn't you have put it in the file cabinet?" I shook my head. "How about checking it, just to humor me?" I unlocked the file cabinet and yanked open the balky top drawer, then each of the lower drawers. It was not in the filing cabinet, as I'd known all along.

I went back to the desk drawer. "Look," I said, removing a printout of an e-mail message that had been sent to me six hours before. "My secretary printed this out and handed it to me along with the packet from Sinclair. I put both things in the drawer."

"Maybe you put the e-mail in the drawer and the envelope in your briefcase," Rankin suggested. "You know, if you were upset, maybe you got the e-mail and the envelope mixed up."

I shook my head emphatically. "My briefcase is still in the

truck. I never even brought it in this afternoon. I'm telling you, somebody's come in and taken it."

"You're sure the drawer was locked? And you're sure the office door was locked?"

"Give me a break," I snapped. "I was mortified when I saw those pictures. If I could have bricked up the doorway and welded the damn drawer shut, I would have. Yes, I'm sure they were both locked."

He leaned down and inspected the edges of the drawer. "Doesn't look like it's been forced," he said. "So who else has keys?"

Before I could answer, the phone rang. The display announced the caller as Peggy. "My secretary," I said, lifting the handset by reflex.

"Oh, I'm so glad you're there," she said. "A Dr. Raymond Sinclair's on the line for you. Something to do with funding for a research project he says he's sponsoring. This is the third time he's called this afternoon. He says it's urgent he speak with you today."

"*Dr.* Sinclair?" Given Ray Sinclair's apparent scorn of advanced degrees, I could only assume the "Dr." was designed to carry weight with Peggy. I looked to Rankin for guidance. He raised his left hand to his head—his thumb at his ear, his pinkie near his lips—as if the hand were a telephone. He nodded, spinning his right forefinger in a rolling, forward motion that meant *go.* "Oh, yes," I said to Peggy. "I do need to speak with Dr. Sinclair. Please put him through right away." I heard the line click. "Ray, are you there?"

"Hello, Bill," he said. "How the hell are you?"

I caught Rankin's eye and pointed toward the speakerphone button on the phone, raising my eyebrows in a question. He shook his head emphatically, so instead I angled the handset slightly away from my ear. The agent leaned close, his ear practically touching mine.

"How am I? How do you think I am, Ray? I'm a little off balance. I had an unpleasant surprise this afternoon."

"I'm surprised to hear you say that. I thought you'd thank me."

"Thank you? Why?"

"For sending you mementos of that swell evening we had in Las Vegas. You looked like you were having quite a time while I was out of the room."

"How did you get those pictures, Ray?"

"A sweet young thing gave them to me. I believe her name is Marian. Marian, Madame Librarian." He chuckled at the joke.

"And what do you plan to do with them?"

"Do with them? I don't plan to do anything with them, Bill." Rankin flashed a thumbs-down sign, which I took to mean he was unhappy to hear that. "I just thought you'd appreciate taking a walk down memory lane. A walk down lap-dance lane. Oh, but you don't mind if I share them with our friends at The Library, do you? Those would be a nice addition to their Web site."

"You must be joking," I said. "Those pictures on the Web?"

"What, you don't like that idea, Bill? You don't want your colleagues and students and family to see what a great time you were having?"

"You know I don't want those circulating on the Internet—or anyplace else. You know that would be very painful to me."

"So here's what's very painful to me," he shot back, the phony cheerfulness gone from his voice. "You said you'd provide me with bodies, and you haven't. You thought you had me by the balls, and you got greedy. But who's got the tighter grip, Bill? Tell me, how does it feel?"

"It feels like you've got me," I admitted.

"Damn right I've got you."

"So what do you want, Ray?"

"I want two bodies by Tuesday," he said. "On ice, in Newark."

"Tuesday? That's not much time," I protested. "What if I can't get them to you that fast?"

"Did I mention there's video, too? You know what I think, Bill? I think you're gonna be the next big hit on YouTube if I don't get those bodies Tuesday. By the way, Bill, how's your cardiovascular health? Any history of heart attacks in your family?"

Before I had a chance to respond—even before I remembered that the FBI's previous informant against Sinclair had died of a massive coronary—Sinclair hung up.

Rankin flashed me a thumbs-up. I did not share his sense of success.

He made a call from his cell phone. "Did you get all that?" He nodded as he listened. "And the audio quality's good?" He nodded again. "Great. You guys are the best."

He hung up smiling, but then he remembered, and he frowned. "So the photos," he said. "We really need those. Think hard. Where else might you have put them?"

"I'm telling you, they were locked in the drawer. I'd stake my life on it."

"And who else has keys to the drawer?"

"No one. Well, almost no one. My secretary, Peggy. Some old guy, years ago, in the maintenance department."

Then it hit me, the day's third tsunami. "And Miranda."

THAT NIGHT I HAD A dream, and in my dream I was walking a wide, sandy trail in a park—maybe in Florida—with lots of palmetto trees. Some slight movement at my feet caused me to look down. There, an inch-long worm of some sort thrashed wildly on the sand, in a series of violent movements—as if a tiny whip were somehow cracking itself. After a few seconds, the convulsions stopped and the worm slithered off into the grass. I was puzzled: What had triggered the spasms, and why had they suddenly stopped? Then, two feet farther up the trail, I saw a second worm thrashing. This one was covered, from end to end, with fire ants from a nearby anthill. It managed to fling off a few of the ants, but dozens more clung to it and still more flocked to it. As I watched in fascinated horror, the worm's thrashing ebbed. It trembled a few times and then lay still, except for the quivering swarm of insects feeding on its dying body.

I awoke before dawn, trembling and drenched with sweat.

I'D BEEN UP FOR THREE hours, but the sun had been up for only one, when my home phone rang. It was Eddie Garcia, calling to say that he'd just heard from the Emory hand surgeon. "They've approved me," he said. "I'm on their list—first on their list—when they find a matching donor for me."

"That's great news, Eddie."

"That's not all. She—Dr. Alvarez, the surgeon—just got a big research grant from the federal government. The grant will fund the cost of everything—the surgery, the postoperative care, the physical therapy. It even covers the immunotherapy meds I'll have to take for the rest of my life."

"That's wonderful. Congratulations. Does she have any guess when she might be able to do the surgery?"

"No. Maybe tomorrow, maybe next year, maybe five years from now. There's no way to know."

I knew that some wait-listed transplant recipients spent months or years in limbo, inching up the list and praying for a match. Some died waiting and praying. But Eddie's situation was different: He wouldn't die from the wait, unlike someone whose heart was failing. What's more, his time in limbo might be far briefer than a heart or a kidney patient's, he pointed out. "The surgery's still experimental," he explained, "so the wait list is short. *Very* short, in fact—I'm the only one on it so far." He laughed. "So as soon as Emory gets a donor whose hands are a good match, it can happen."

"And what now? You just wait for the word? The proverbial Phone Call?"

"Not exactly," he said. "Dr. Alvarez says the blood vessels in my right wrist have probably regrown and recovered by now. She wants me to come back to Atlanta so she can reverse the pedicle graft and tidy up the stump. That way I'll be ready whenever she finds a donor."

"How soon does she want you to come?"

"Today. Carmen will drive me down this afternoon, and Dr. Alvarez will detach the graft tomorrow morning."

Eddie also had an update on Clarissa Lowe's death. The CDC—the Centers for Disease Control—had done a genetic profile on the tissue sample Eddie had sent after the autopsy. The CDC lab had identified the bacterium in Lowe's bone graft as *Clostridium sordellii,* a particularly toxic species. "They plan to look for other cases of bone grafts linked to toxic shock recently," he added, "in case there's a wider problem with improperly sterilized cadaver tissue."

Eddie himself had pinned down the manufacturer of the bone graft Lowe had received. "The graft itself was made by Ortho-Medica," he said, "but OrthoMedica made it from bone they bought from a supplier—a tissue bank." He named the four tissue banks OrthoMedica regularly bought cadaver tissue from. I'd never heard of the first three he mentioned—Gift of Life, BioLogic, and Donor Medical Services. But I'd damn sure heard of the fourth one: Tissue Sciences and Services, Incorporated. Given the bad blood between Ray Sinclair and Glen Faust, I was surprised to hear that Tissue Sciences did business with Ortho-Medica. But just as blood was thicker than water, perhaps money was thicker than blood—even bad blood.

After Eddie hung up, I called the FBI to relay his findings to Rankin. If Tissue Sciences was the source of the bacteria-laden bone, it was possible that the company's penchant for playing fast and loose included other crimes besides black-market body buying. I didn't know what federal statutes—if any—governed how a tissue bank was required to process or sterilize cadaver tissue, but if anybody was in a position to find out quickly, it was surely Rankin. Rankin promised to look into it. "By the way," he added, "we arrested Sinclair. Last night. I thought you'd want to know." He was right. I began to see light at the end of the tunnel.

I'd just finished talking with Rankin when Peggy transferred another call to me. "Hello," came a hesitant female voice. "I'm trying to reach Dr. Brockton."

"This is Dr. Brockton. How can I help you?"

"My name is Laura Telford," she said. "I'm calling because my father recently signed a form to donate his body to the Body Farm, and I need to talk to you about it."

Occasionally—not often, but once every few years—I'd get a phone call or a visit from a donor's family member who was upset by the idea of Mom or Dad or a brother or sister rotting on the ground. Our one-paragraph donation form was legally valid—in a court battle over a body, we'd probably win, if the form was properly signed and witnessed—but at what price, in terms of a family member's peace of mind or goodwill? No, I'd long since decided I would never get into a tug-of-war about a donor's body. "I won't try to change your mind, Laura," I said, "but I'll be glad to answer any questions I can. I'd encourage you to talk with your father about it again. Let him know you feel uncomfortable about the idea. Maybe one of you will change the other one's mind."

"It's not that I'm uncomfortable or that we disagree," she answered. "He thinks it's important, and so do I. I took your intro anthropology class back when I was a UT student. I even went out to the Body Farm on the spring-cleanup day. I got ten points of extra credit for picking up bones and slimy body bags. I believe in the work you do."

I was puzzled about why she was calling. "Well, I appreciate that," I said. "I hope we won't be seeing your dad for a while yet."

"Actually, I'm afraid you'll be seeing him really soon," she replied. "He's dying of heart failure. His heart stopped yesterday, and they managed to get it going again, but they say it could stop again at any moment. If it stops again, that's probably the end for him."

"I'm so sorry, Laura."

She paused to blow her nose. "But it helps to think his body could do some good after death."

"If it comes to the Body Farm, it certainly will," I promised. "Did you say your last name's Telford? That's not ringing a bell. How long ago did he send in the donation form?"

"He handed it to you. Last week. My father's Ernest Miller. Sorry, I should have told you that sooner. I changed my name when I got married. You spoke to Daddy in his hospital room, and he signed the form right then."

"Of course," I said. "He mentioned you. He said you'd be here soon. I believe he said you live in Kentucky?"

"Yes, at Fort Campbell. I'd hoped to come right after Daddy was admitted, but my husband's stationed in Iraq and he can't get home until next week. My dad has really spiraled down fast, so I figured I should call you as soon as possible. I need to talk to you about a change to his donation paperwork."

"Of course," I said, "but I'm a little confused. I thought you said you were comfortable with the idea that he'd come to the Body Farm."

"I am."

"Then what's the change you'd like to discuss with me?"

"Organ donation," she said, and I felt my breath catch at the sound of the words. "He and I talked about it on the phone Saturday, the day before his heart stopped. He told me about your friend, Dr. Garcia. About how he needs a pair of hands."

The hairs on my arms and my neck were standing up. "Are you saying your dad changed his mind? That he signed the organ-donor consent form?"

"No, he didn't," she said, and I felt something in me collapse.

"Oh. I see. I mean, I don't see, really." I drew a deep breath. "I shouldn't have brought up Dr. Garcia. I was wrong to try to influence your father. It's his choice, after all."

"Actually, it's not," she said. "That's why I'm calling you. My dad has given me medical power of attorney, so it's my choice now, and my choice isn't the same as my dad's. My husband's mom died while waiting for a kidney transplant, Dr. Brockton. My children lost a grandmother, for the simple reason that there aren't enough organ donors out there. So if I can make a difference in someone's life by overruling my father's fear, I'm at peace with that decision. I won't tell him; I'll let him die in peace, and then I'll do what I think is best." She paused, and the pause created a space in which my hopes soared. "Do you think your friend could use my father's hands?"

I didn't know, but I hoped and prayed he could. "Let's find out," I said. "And thank you."

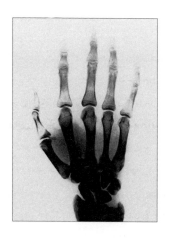

CHAPTER 40

I WAS STILL ELATED BY LAURA TELFORD'S OFFER AND Eddie's good news when I arrived on campus. But the moment I opened my office door, I knew that something was wrong.

At the center of my desk lay a large white envelope, precisely centered in a circle of light cast by the desk lamp. The lamp's long, hinged arm had been angled downward, close to the desk; the circular fluorescent tube spotlighted the envelope, and the round magnifying lens—through which I'd scrutinized thousands of bones—enlarged and distorted the hand-printed letters of my name.

My foreboding turned to horror as I tugged the contents from the tight confines of the envelope. It contained three things. One was a copy of the photos taken at the strip club in Las Vegas. Another was the folder where I'd filed a copy of the donor consent form from 37-09—a body I'd promised Sinclair—along with a copy of a letter I'd drafted to send to the donor's family, explaining that a hepatitis infection in the body had made it necessary to cremate his remains. I'd attached a copy of the donor form, on which I'd written *"biohazardous due to hepatitis C; incinerated and ashes disposed of 4/8."* It was a lie, of course, one I was supposedly spinning to cover my tracks. I'd sent a copy of the draft to Sinclair, asking for his experienced guidance on such matters.

The third item was a brief letter, printed on Anthropology Department stationery. It was dated the previous day and addressed to Dr. William Brockton, Head, Anthropology Department, University of Tennessee–Knoxville. The body of the letter was brief—as brief as a gunshot to the head. *"This letter is to inform you that I hereby resign my assistantship, effective immediately, and withdraw from the graduate program in Anthropology. Furthermore, be advised that I have contacted the Tennessee Bureau of Investigation to report what I believe to be theft, fraud, or embezzlement in your diversion of donated bodies for personal gain. Alas—how swift the tumble from greatness."* It was signed, in neat, careful blue script, *"Miranda S. Lovelady."*

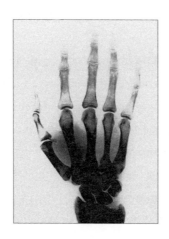

CHAPTER 41

CROSSING THE TENNESSEE RIVER ON ALCOA HIGHWAY, I stayed in the right-hand lane, the exit-only lane for Cherokee Trail and UT Hospital, and put on my turn signal as the exit ramp loomed. I'd tried to reach both Rankin and Price, but neither was available, and the receptionist at the FBI office had either not known or not been authorized to say when either would be available. I'd left urgent messages for both agents, everywhere I could think to leave them—with the receptionist, on their office voice mails, and on their cell phones. I'd also left a voice mail for Amanda Whiting, UT's general counsel, warning her that the TBI might be about to swoop down on me and complicate life for the university.

When I fled the stadium, I'd intended to swing by the Body Farm and distract myself by checking on Maurie Gershwin, who I expected was almost down to bare bones by now. But the Body Farm was part of what was weighing on me—for the first time ever, it seemed to fall under the heading of "problem" rather than "solution." On impulse I changed course. The sun was out and the April afternoon was shirtsleeve warm; winter finally seemed to be packing up for good, and I decided a dose of pure mountain air might clear my head or ease my heart. Flipping the turn signal from "right" to "left," I moved into the center lane, earning a loud honk from a Subaru station wagon, which had been rocketing along in that lane more swiftly than I'd realized. As the Subaru whipped around me, propelled by turbocharged rage, I glimpsed a protest rally's worth of bumper stickers on the rear hatch, including MAKE LOVE NOT WAR, MEAN PEOPLE SUCK, and BE THE CHANGE YOU WANT IN THE WORLD. Then the car hurtled out of sight around the curve, the driver extending his middle finger high into the air above the roofline of the peacemobile.

I took the highway south, past the airport, then angled east through Maryville and Townsend to Great Smoky Mountains National Park, which was forty-five minutes from Knoxville but a world away. A mile inside the park, I turned left at the road that led to the educational camp at Tremont, where virtually every kid in East Tennessee, including my now-grown son, spent a week of middle school learning about the flora and fauna of the Appalachians. The road to Tremont meandered up the Middle Prong of the Little Tennessee, a free-flowing river whose emerald pools were strung together with strands of white, tumbling rapids. At its low, the Middle Prong could be crossed in numerous places by the adventurous rock hopper; at its high-water mark, it could test the skill of serious kayakers, or drown those foolhardy enough to take to the torrent in inner tubes.

On this soft afternoon, the Middle Prong seemed to embody the idea of the Golden Mean: enough water to be lively—exuberant, even—but not so much as to seem menacing or ominous. Heartened by the river, I felt my own current moderating, settling into the mid-range of its spiritual channel. I slowed the truck, rolled down the windows, and took in the sounds and smells of the Smokies: the gurgling, seething water; the bracing tang of hemlock needles and, underneath their aroma, the rich dankness of mossy rocks and moldering leaves.

Two miles upriver from the turnoff, the asphalt gave way to gravel and the river tumbled more than it flowed. Then—after another three miles—the road ended at a looping turnaround area; beyond it a footbridge crossed the river to a trail that continued upstream. A dozen or so parking spaces were notched into the trees lining the loop's outer rim. On weekends the spaces would all be claimed, but today I had complete choice. I parked near the footbridge and walked to the midpoint of the steel span; twenty feet below me, the river churned swift and cold and clean. Ten miles downriver these waters would get dammed and dreary, but here they danced and sang.

On the far side of the footbridge, a wooden sign announced the mileage to various points up the Middle Prong Trail, the letters and numbers carved into the dark wood by a router and painted white: PANTHER CREEK, 2.3; JAKES CREEK, 4.6; APPALACHIAN TRAIL, 8; CUCUMBER GAP, 8.5. As I contemplated these destinations, none of which I had the time or the footwear to reach, I heard the crunch of tires on gravel, then the brief beep of a vehicle being locked by a remote key. The electronic beep startled and jarred me, so to dodge trailside small talk with the new arrival, I set out. A small, unmarked trail branched off to the right of the main trail, and I decided to follow that one, rather than the Middle Prong Trail, which was wide enough for a jeep and throngs of hikers. *The road less traveled,* I thought, ducking beneath hemlock branches and clambering over a pair of fallen trees.

A hundred yards up the path, I came to another footbridge, a makeshift one this time. Less than two feet wide, this bridge was made from a steel girder laid across the stream on its side; vertical posts had been welded to it, and steel cables threaded the posts to form flimsy hand railings. Gingerly I stepped onto the span. The girder flexed beneath my weight, bouncing slightly with each step. I paused near the center, gripping an upright with one hand and a cable with the other. Ten feet below, a small stream whose name I didn't know—the Left Prong? the South Prong? Frothy Creek?—hurled itself from boulder to boulder. Upstream it came rushing at me from a tunnel of dark, glossy rhododendron, leaping off a four-foot ledge before careening back and forth between the rocks.

I was just turning to look downriver when three things happened at the same instant: A brief flash lit the shadowy lacework of a hemlock sapling on the near bank; the air ripped and zinged beside my left ear; and a sharp crack reverberated within the narrow gorge of the stream. By the time my brain realized that I'd just been shot at, my body had already begun reacting instinctively, ducking and darting across the swaying I-beam toward the far side of the stream. The crack of another shot mingled with the clang of a bullet slamming into the steel bridge. As I reached the far bank, a third shot chipped the rocky embankment beside my head, sending shards of stone into my face and neck.

Jesus, I thought, *the TBI's shooting at me.* Then I thought, *No, that can't be. I'm a TBI consultant. I've worked with them for years. They might want to arrest me—they surely want to question me—but they can't possibly want to kill me.*

But someone obviously did. *Sinclair,* I thought, but then, *How can it be Sinclair? The FBI arrested him yesterday.* A fourth shot whanged into the rocks. *I guess he got out,* I decided. I ran, chased by a fifth shot.

I couldn't have said how far I ran; all I knew was that I ran, up and up the twisting trail, until I stopped to vomit from the exertion. My gasping breath was interrupted by the heaves of my stomach—heaves that left me gasping even harder for air. The edges of my vision began to go black, and I dropped to my hands and knees, fighting to control my panic and desperate breath. Once my heaves dried up and my breath slowed down, I took stock of my situation, and I didn't like what I saw. Somewhere below me was a person who had a gun and a wish to kill me, so heading back down the trail didn't seem to be the path of wisdom. I recalled two other trails in this section of the park—the West Prong Trail, which began at the point where Tremont Road turned from pavement to gravel, and Bote Mountain Trail, which the West Prong Trail hit at a T junction. It seemed possible, or even likely, that this trail would intersect one of those two trails and lead me safely to the road.

I stood and continued up the trail, shakily at first, then with more strength and confidence. Judging by the direction of the sun, I was heading southwest—the general direction of the Bote Mountain Trail, if my memory was correct. But judging by the angle of the sun, I didn't have much daylight left in which to find it. I checked my watch: It was four-thirty, and that meant I had an hour, maybe ninety minutes, before darkness would catch me in the mountains.

I hiked for half an hour, hoping to hit the intersection with the Bote Mountain Trail. As the trail continued to climb, the sun continued to drop; so did the temperature, and gradually my breath began to fog. Soon the trail snaked up a shaded slope through a patch of snow and ice—not a good sign. Off slightly to my right, perhaps ten miles away and thousands of feet below, I caught a glimpse of Cades Cove, a bowl in the mountains that had been settled and cleared in the early 1800s. Seeing Cades Cove gave me a better fix on my location, but the knowledge was unsettling. The trail, I realized with a sinking feeling, was taking me up to the crest of the mountains—probably up Thunderhead Mountain, the highest peak in the western part of the Smokies. The clothes I was wearing were fine for a warm afternoon in the sun, but not for a night on Thunderhead at five thousand feet.

Would anyone come looking for me—anyone besides Ray Sinclair? Nobody from the Anthropology Department, surely. Miranda had resigned. No one else would have given a thought to my early departure, and no one else would expect to see me before Monday. My one hope—the one silver lining to being suspected of committing fraud and theft—was that the TBI might somehow follow my trail to the mountains. But how? I'd told no one where I was heading, and I doubted that the TBI considered me worthy of an urgent manhunt.

I had two other options, as I saw it. One was to backtrack, hoping that whoever had been shooting at me had given up and gone away. The other was to bushwhack: to cut directly down the mountainside, then follow the small stream I could hear churning far below. I felt certain that the stream fed into the West Prong of the Little Tennessee River; I could even, in my mind's eye, picture the very bridge where the West Prong flowed beneath the highway. I decided to bushwhack. Veering off the trail, I began scrambling—half running, half falling—down the mountainside. But could I reach the highway by dark?

I could not. Twilight caught me at the confluence where the small stream joined the West Prong. The river gorge had darkened sooner and faster than the higher slopes, and the terrain was steeper and rockier along the water. My side of the river, the south bank, appeared rugged as far as I could see, with stone bluffs and thickets of rhododendron. The north bank looked more passable, but getting to it would require crossing the river. I scanned the stream for a narrows where I might be able to rock-hop across, but I didn't see one, and I was running out of time to search. Sitting down on a boulder at the water's edge, I shucked off my shoes, socks, pants, and underwear, then waded in, clutching my rolled-up clothes above my head and wearing my shoes draped around my neck by the laces, like a primitive tribal token of victory over some L.L. Bean–shod academic rival.

The water was cold—gaspingly, achingly cold, so cold that my feet felt as if they'd been clamped in a vise. Within seconds, though, the pain gave way to numbness, which was better but also worse, making it difficult to feel the slippery rocks underfoot. Twice I nearly fell, when my numbed feet stumbled; both times I nearly lost my grip on my precious bundle of clothes. The water was deeper than I'd expected, too. It knifed its way above my knees and up my thighs. "Ow, *crap*," I said as the cold stabbed at my crotch.

By the time I reached the other side—probably only a minute or so—I was shuddering. Sitting on a chilly rock, I used my hands to squeegee the water down my legs, then rubbed my feet briskly with my socks to dry them and to restore circulation and feeling.

I dressed as quickly as my shaking hands and quaking limbs allowed, then set off downstream.

As the darkness deepened, so did the growl of menace I heard rumbling in the water. Both sides of the gorge got steeper, the rocks became mossy, and the footing grew treacherous. The second time my feet slid out from under me, I decided to seek higher, drier ground. I could still follow the river's course by ear, I reasoned, but I'd be safer if I didn't need to negotiate every riverside boulder and ledge in the darkness. Overhead, in the wedge of night sky, I found the Big Dipper and the North Star, which confirmed that I was indeed headed westward, toward the highway. That knowledge was reassuring, but the absence of moonlight was disheartening.

Gradually the terrain I was crossing steepened, and soon I was reduced to side-crawling on all fours, scuttling blindly across the slope. Judging by the leaves beneath my hands, I was in deciduous forest of some sort—maybe tulip poplars, maybe oaks and maples. The leaves were dry; the winter snows that had fallen on this south-facing slope had long since melted.

The leafy soil under my hands and feet had just given way to bare rock when I took a step sideways and suddenly felt myself sliding off a ledge. Instinctively I flung out my arms, and as my legs and then my hips crossed the brink, I managed to catch hold of a small tree rooted in a crevice. Clinging to it, I prayed that it would hold, and I carefully hauled myself up onto the ledge. In the darkness I couldn't see the cliff that nearly claimed me, nor could I see the tree that saved me. Guided only by the sound of the river and the feel of the mountainside, I groped onward.

The feel changed abruptly in the space of one sideways step, and the mountainside grew loose and crumbly beneath my left hand and left foot. I stopped and swept my hand across the ground in an arc, from my foot up to shoulder height and above. I felt no trees, no twigs, not even dead leaves—nothing but crumbling soil and loose rocks. *My God,* I thought, *a landslide. How wide is this, and how unstable, and how in the world do I cross it?*

I crossed it by inches, feeling for handholds and footholds before committing to a move. After half a dozen such moves, I came to a rock the size of a watermelon, half buried in the loose slope to the left of my head. As I edged beneath it, the rock tore free in my hands. I ducked my head, shifted to the left, and dug my left toe and left hand into the loose soil, praying that they'd hold. Sparks sprang from the mountainside as the rock crashed down—fifty feet, eighty feet, a hundred or more. It clattered to a stop on the heap of earth and rock and trees that had recently sheared off and slid down the slope.

By the time I'd traversed the slide zone and reentered the forest, I was exhausted. I couldn't see my watch in the darkness—I couldn't even see my hand in the blackness—but I guessed it must be midnight or later, and my strength was gone. *I need to sleep for a little while,* I thought. Bracing my feet on a large tree, I lay down, though I was actually as near to standing as I was to reclining. Raking dead leaves from the dirt around me, I created a nest to retain whatever body heat I could.

Just as I began to doze, I was awakened by my body's shivering, mild at first, then violent. As long as I'd kept scrabbling across the slope, I'd felt tolerably warm in my thin shirt, except for the cold seeping into my hands. But with my internal engine now idling—and sputtering at that, given my lack of food and water—I couldn't withstand the cold. I had to keep moving.

But I was growing seriously dehydrated. There was water, and in abundance, only a few hundred feet below me. I was reminded of its presence, and its power, as I crept blindly past each roaring rapid. Reluctantly, fearfully, I began edging downward, relinquishing my buffer from the wet rocks and the churning water.

Soon the unseen stream filled my ears, only a few feet to my left. Now all I had to do was find a safe place to descend the bank and drink. Would it be safer—and sap less body heat—to scoop up handfuls of water or to lie on my belly and drink like a wild animal? My hands were already going numb, so I felt inclined to lie flat and put my face in the stream.

I was just beginning to anticipate the taste when I took a small step with my left foot and—for the second time that night— found nothing there. Odd: I'd been shuffling along, feeling my way with excruciating slowness, yet even so, the earth dropped away beneath me. I felt myself toppling, free-falling, and then landing in frigid water. Just below the surface, my left side hit a rock, and I felt a sharp pain in my ribs.

But it was the gasp-inducing frigidity of the water that imperiled me. If my head had been submerged, I would surely have inhaled a lethal lungful of water. As I struggled to gain my footing on the slippery rocks, I realized how little time I had. I was already on the edge of hypothermia; the frigid water would surely push me over the brink swiftly. And for the first time, as I began to shiver violently, I wondered if I should give in, simply surrender to the cold and the exhaustion and the pain. Hypothermia was said to be a relatively swift and pleasant way to go, after all. If I remained in the water, or even crawled onto a rock and lay still, perhaps I'd drift off painlessly after only a few moments of cold. Would that be so bad, really, given the turns my life had taken lately? Jeff wouldn't answer my phone calls, Miranda despised me, the TBI wanted to interrogate me, UT would surely fire me, Ray Sinclair wanted to ruin or kill me, and a federal fugitive was carrying my child. How much easier it might be to let go than to keep struggling and striving.

The river's current washed me onto a small, rocky beach, and I crawled out and lay on my back so I could see the sky before my eyes closed. The Big Dipper had shifted dramatically from its position at nightfall, rotating a quarter turn around the North Star. The great wheel of life and fate would continue to spin long after I was gone. I found that comforting and hoped that life would bring abundant happiness to those I cared about: to Jeff and Jenny and their boys, to Miranda and Art, to the struggling Garcias. I even wished some form of peace to Isabella, wherever she was.

But as I lay there, sending benevolent wishes to the universe on behalf of those people, a small realization forced its way into my slipping consciousness. My death would not bring abundant goodness to my family, friends, and colleagues; in fact, it would surely bring deep sadness. When I was three, my own father had killed himself, and although that act had ended his own inner pain, it had created untold pain in those he left behind. If I simply gave in to the cold right now, instead of fighting for life with everything I had, wouldn't that be a halfhearted, cowardly version of suicide? Did I want to let myself die instead of trying harder to live for the ones I loved?

I shook my head to clear it. I rolled onto my right side, then onto my stomach, and took a deep drink of the ice-cold water—the drink I'd come down to get, before my fall. Then I found a gnarled rhododendron branch snaking down the high, steep embankment, grabbed it with both hands, and pulled myself upward.

I found the pole star again, low above the opposite ridge. It was on my right as I turned downstream. That meant I was still heading west. Still heading for the highway. Still heading for life. I scrabbled uphill as quickly as I could, putting some distance between myself and the stream's treacherous gorge, and as I did, the effort gradually took away some of the chill.

Eventually I felt, rather than saw, an opening ahead of me. I still couldn't see my hand in front of my face unless I held it up to create a five-fingered silhouette against the starry sky. But the blackness ahead was suddenly less black than it had been. It seemed like open, empty blackness rather than forested blackness. Grasping a tree branch for safety, I used a foot to probe the ground ahead. It turned rocky, and then it turned to empty air. I was on the brink of another cliff, though I had no way of knowing if it was ten feet high or a hundred. If I turned slightly left, I could continue along what felt like the edge of the precipice—but that would be heading south, not west. Had I come to a sharp bend in the river gorge, or was this a side canyon, carved by a lesser tributary? If it was, then following it would take me back up into the mountains, and that would be disastrous. I had to stop until daylight. I hoped I could make it until daylight.

Once again I braced my feet on a tree and lay down on steeply sloping ground. As before, I began to shiver within a few minutes of lying down. This time, unable to press onward, I jumped in place to warm up. I shook my arms and hands—my fingers had remained numb ever since my tumble into the stream—to keep the blood circulating. After warming up, I lay back down until the shivering recommenced, and then I jumped and flapped my arms again madly.

The third time I lay down to rest, I must have slept briefly, because when I opened my eyes, the sky had gone from black to gray. I had survived the night—the near fall off a ledge, the near miss with the boulder in the landslide zone, the hard tumble into the frigid stream. As the terrain around me grew visible and the air began to warm, the odds began shifting in my favor for the first time since sundown. I took a deep breath and exhaled, smiling at the plume of fog in the cold, pale light.

I'd been wise to wait. I had indeed come to a side canyon, and the bluff here was fifty feet high, with only a few narrow notches that could be descended. A tall, thin tree slanted up through one of these. Leaning out, I grabbed the tree with both hands, braced against it, and chimneyed down the cleft. Once down, I stepped across the small stream that had carved the ravine and continued along the left bank of the West Prong.

A short distance after I'd crossed the tributary, the river curved to the left, and as I rounded the curve, I felt my breath catch: A hundred yards away was the bridge over Laurel Creek Road—the bridge I'd been aiming for all night. I was exhausted and hurt, but I was alive, and I'd made it.

As I approached the bridge, the left bank grew increasingly steep. There was no avoiding it: I'd have to ford the river one more time. *Damn,* I thought, but I half smiled. *I can do this. This is nothing.*

I stripped once more, rolled up my clothes, and hung my shoes around my neck again. The river was bigger and deeper here than at the spot I'd forded far upstream—this time the ice-cold water rose above my waist, nearly to my armpits. As before, I quickly lost feeling in my feet, but, mercifully, the river bottom was sandy and smooth, and I crossed without stumbling. As I emerged near the base of the bridge, steam swirled from my naked body into the golden light of morning. I dressed as best I could—this time there was no hope of tying my shoes—then ascended the bank and turned north onto Laurel Creek Road. I was miles from my truck—possibly farther than I'd been at any time since I made the fateful decision to bushwhack—but unless whoever had fired five shots at me happened to be cruising this stretch of road looking for me, I was in less peril now than at any time since I'd veered off the trail.

I heard a car winding up the road. Stepping into the center of the pavement, I waved both arms to flag it down. The driver, a middle-aged woman, rolled her window down half an inch, eyeing me with deep suspicion.

"I'm sorry to bother you," I said, "but I'm wondering if you have a cell phone and if you'd be willing to make an emergency call for me?"

"Yes, I have a cell phone." From the dubious tone of her voice, I suspected she might call to report that a sinister stranger was trying to abduct her.

"I was stranded in the mountains all night," I explained, "I think maybe I've got some bruised ribs, and I expect the park rangers are starting a search for me along about now."

She took a closer look at me, and I could see her eyes taking in the scratches on my face, the rips in my clothes, and the exhaustion in my posture. Her eyes softened. "Oh, my stars," she said, "get in the car." She unlocked the passenger door, and I eased myself down into the seat. "I'll take you to the ranger station at Cades Cove."

I hesitated. "I hate to impose, but my truck's parked at Tremont, and I'm guessing that's where they'll start the search. Would you be willing to backtrack and take me to Tremont?" Pulling onto the shoulder, she made a quick U-turn. A moment later I heard a loud, staccato clacking; when the woman glanced at me in alarm and cranked the heater up to full blast, I realized the clacking was coming from my chattering teeth.

"Thank you," I said. "You're very kind."

We reached the Tremont turnoff in five minutes or less, then made it to the end of the gravel road in another ten. *Amazing,* I thought. *In fifteen minutes we've covered the same distance it took me twelve hours to crawl last night.*

At the turnaround loop, two park-police SUVs were idling beside my truck. As I got out of the car and hobbled toward the truck, a ranger emerged from one of the SUVs. He glanced at me briefly, and then his eyes widened. "It's you," he said.

"Yes, it's me."

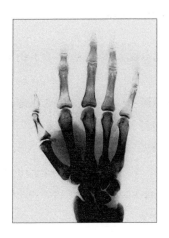

CHAPTER 42

"AND YOU THINK SOMEONE TOOK A SHOT AT YOU?"
The ranger, a bearded, middle-aged fellow named Stapleton, seemed skeptical, as if he suspected that my night in the mountains had played tricks on my mind. That wouldn't have been an unreasonable thing for him to suspect, I realized. Ranger Stapleton was sitting behind the wheel of a Jeep Cherokee that was painted pea green—a color so hideous that the park service could be certain no car thief would ever be tempted to steal the vehicle. I sat in the Jeep's passenger seat, the heater blasting blessedly hot.

"Five shots," I said, tipping aside the oxygen mask so as not to muffle the words. The mask had been handed to me by another ranger, a young paramedic named Nick, who was leaning through the Jeep's passenger window with a stethoscope and a blood-pressure cuff. Before offering me oxygen and checking my vital signs, Nick had draped my shoulders with his own jacket, a bright yellow fleece. I took another whiff of oxygen, then added, "Maybe the shell cases are still there. I can show you where he was."

"You stay put till the ambulance gets here," said Nick.

"What ambulance? I don't need an ambulance," I squawked.

"All ten of your fingers have frostnip," Nick began. "And technically—"

I interrupted him. "'Frostnip'? Is that really a word?"

"It is. A mild version of frostbite."

"That doesn't sound like it requires an ambulance," I protested.

"Not on its own," he responded, "but technically you're still in hypothermia. Your temperature's still below ninety-five degrees."

"Crank up the heat for another ten minutes and it'll be ninety-six," I argued.

"Nick's right," said Stapleton. "You sit tight. Tell me where you think this shooter was, and we'll take a look."

I pointed to the large footbridge that spanned the Middle Prong, then described taking the unmarked trail that led to the narrow, I-beam footbridge.

He frowned. "That's not actually a trail. Used to be, but not in years."

"It used to be a pretty nice one," I said, "judging by the view I had of Cades Cove just before I started bushwhacking."

He whistled. "Hell, you were way up Thunderhead Mountain. No wonder we couldn't find you last night. You got yourself good and lost, didn't you?"

I felt an absurd need to defend myself. "Actually, I had a pretty fair idea where I was," I said, and it was true, if you defined the term "pretty fair idea" rather broadly. "I came out on Laurel Creek Road right where I thought I would. It just took me a while to get there."

"That's some rough terrain you crossed in the dark. Cold night, too. You're lucky you made it down alive."

"When that guy was shooting at me, I felt lucky to make it *up* alive," I pointed out. "He was on this side of the stream, ten or twenty yards downstream from the I-beam bridge."

"Did you get a good look at him?"

"No. He was hidden by the trees."

"But you saw enough to know that it was a man?"

"Actually, no," I admitted. "I just assumed it was a man."

Stapleton frowned at me for assuming. "Any idea who might want to shoot at you, and why?"

I had a very clear idea about that, in fact, but I wasn't at liberty to mention Ray Sinclair or the FBI investigation. "I've helped put some people in prison over the years," I said. "Maybe one of them just got out. Or maybe it was that student I gave an F to yesterday."

Nick laughed, and that made me smile. But my smile evaporated when I saw a black Ford sedan pull in to the parking area and Steve Morgan get out.

Fifteen years before Steve had been an undergraduate student in my osteology class. Now he was a TBI agent. I'd kept in loose touch with him during the ten years or so since he'd joined the TBI; we'd even worked together briefly on the Cooke County corruption case. Now, though, I was a suspect, and that put a distinct damper on our relationship. As he approached the park-service vehicle and flashed his badge, his face looked grim and sad, and I was pretty sure mine didn't look any happier. Stapleton got out and exchanged a few words with him, and then the ranger spoke to Nick. Both rangers stepped away to give us privacy.

Steve leaned down and spoke through the open window. "Dr. Brockton, I hear you spent a long, cold night in the mountains."

"Hello, Steve. I did indeed. How'd you know I was here?"

He didn't answer the question. "I need to talk to you about something. Let's go sit in my car." He opened the door for me, and I followed him to the black TBI vehicle. I halfway expected him to put me in the back, but instead he held the front passenger door for me. The car's interior smelled of spilled coffee.

"The ranger also says you think someone tried to shoot you."

"I don't just think it, Steve. Someone did try to shoot me."

"Any idea who, and why?"

It was the same question Stapleton had just asked, but this time I couldn't deflect it with a joke. "I can't tell you, Steve."

"Because you don't have any idea?"

"Because I can't."

"Dr. Brockton, this is difficult. I need you to tell me what's going on here."

I was just flipping a mental coin—did the circumstances justify breaking my pledge of secrecy to the FBI?—when the hand of fate snatched the coin from midair: Another government-issue Ford pulled up alongside Morgan's, and out clambered Special Agent Ben Rankin. He showed Steve his badge, then asked for a word in private. They walked fifty yards down the gravel road, then turned around and walked back up to the vehicles.

Whatever Rankin said to Steve during that hundred-yard walk, it was enough to get me out of the TBI agent's car but not enough to remove the frown from his face. He opened the car door and informed me I could go, adding, "Take care. Good luck."

As Morgan's Ford fishtailed down the gravel road, Rankin motioned toward his own car. *Out of the frying pan, into the fire,* I thought. The FBI-issue vehicle at least didn't smell of spilled coffee. Rankin studied me. "You all right, Doc?"

I shrugged, then nodded.

"Sounds like you had a rough night of it. All things considered, you look pretty good."

I regarded him with a gimlet eye.

"Okay, that was a lie. Actually, you look like hell, but I'm glad you're alive."

"Thanks. Me, too. Twenty-four hours ago, I didn't realize what an iffy proposition that was."

"I've got an evidence team coming to search the area where you saw the shooter." He paused. "Sinclair was in Knoxville yesterday."

"No kidding. Even I was able to figure that one out. Where is he today?"

"Don't know. We're looking. He dropped off a rental car at the Knoxville airport last night and caught a flight back to Newark."

"Christ, Rooster. You guys arrested him three days ago. How is it he manages to fly to Knoxville, fire five shots at me, and then fly back to Newark without anybody at the FBI noticing?"

Now Rankin looked as unhappy as Morgan had—and as unhappy as I felt. "He's out on bail. That means he can go anywhere he wants to. Hell, he could flee the country if he took a mind to." He saw the expression of dismay and disbelief on my face. "Jesus, Doc, we don't have the resources to tail all the bad guys all the time," he said. "We hadn't picked up anything on the phone or computer taps that made us think he was heading to Knoxville to shoot at you. Sorry, Doc."

I stared out the window, then turned my weary gaze toward Rankin. "What'd you tell Morgan?"

"I told him we needed to have a meeting next week—my boss and his boss. I told him you were working with us on a sensitive investigation and we'd appreciate it if the TBI could give us a little room around you. Oh, I also told him we needed that file of photos your assistant gave him. We'll get them up to the lab in Quantico next week and see if we can still find Sinclair's prints underneath everybody else's."

The thought of the photos—and of their being seen by Miranda and Morgan and other people at the TBI—made me heartsick. "Did you tell him I hadn't done anything wrong?"

"I told him I expected we'd be able to answer all his questions very soon."

"So he still thinks I'm a sleazebag?"

"I don't know what he thinks."

"He thinks I'm a sleazebag. You saw the look on his face when he let me out of his car."

Rankin shrugged. "Maybe he just thinks I'm a jerk."

"And you're still not willing to tell the TBI or my assistant what's really going on?"

"We need to sit on this until after the grand jury hears it."

"And when is that?"

"Tuesday. Just three more days. Once he's been indicted, we'll take the lid off. It might not seem like much consolation at the moment, but if the evidence team recovers anything here that ties him to the shooting—prints on the brass, bullets we can match to a gun, tire impressions that match the tread on the rental car—we can add attempted murder to the list of charges."

"You're right," I said. "At the moment that doesn't seem like much consolation."

He made no move to offer anything more.

"So do you need me for something else here, or can I go home and sleep for a week or two while my life crumbles around me?"

"Go get some rest. But first show me where to send the evidence techs."

I took him to the fork in the trails and started up the path I'd taken. "Wait," he said. "Let's not disturb the area. Just show me." I pointed to the cluster of hemlocks where I'd seen the muzzle flash, and I described the various points on the footbridge and the opposite embankment where I thought the bullets had hit.

Then I got into my truck and headed back to Knoxville. By the time I turned in to my driveway and saw the garage door rising to receive me, I felt as if I were swimming underwater. I staggered through the living room and headed for the bedroom, but the blinking message light on the phone caught my eye. I debated briefly, then sighed and checked the voice mail. I had five new messages.

Two of them had been left by Steve Morgan and were long since irrelevant; the first one, which he'd left at midafternoon Friday, sounded casual and friendly, while the second one, which he'd left Friday evening—probably around the time I was wading across the West Prong for the first time—sounded official and ominous: "This is Steve Morgan with the TBI again. I need you to contact me immediately. This is an urgent, official matter. It's very serious, and it's important that you call me right away." Sandwiched between Morgan's two calls was an end-of-the-day call from Peggy, reminding me of my Monday-morning appeal to the dean for more land. The fourth message of the five was from Carmen Garcia. The surgery to reverse the pedicle graft had gone very well, she said. Her voice sounded teary, though, not at all like the voice of someone calling with good news. I was puzzled by that, but only for a moment, until Carmen dropped the other shoe. "The possible donor you found—that heart patient at

UT—his tissue does not match. Dr. Alvarez said Eddie would almost certainly reject those hands. So we are coming home again to wait. But we thank you so much for trying, Bill." Her voice broke as she said it, and her sadness, together with my exhaustion, brought me crashing down. I hung up the phone without even listening to the last message and turned off the ringer.

Shucking off my ragged, filthy clothes, I crawled straight into bed. By the time I'd tucked a pillow beneath my knees and arranged two more under my head, my eyes were rolling backward. I thought I heard the beginnings of a snore, but before I could listen for a second one, I was tunneling deep into sleep.

When I awoke, the house was dark and the digital clock on the nightstand read 4:17. I'd slept for eighteen hours. I took a long bath, in water that was seventy or eighty degrees hotter than the water I'd been in the previous night. My frostnipped fingertips still felt numb and still looked artificially white—like chicken that's been blanched in boiling water—and my left ribs felt bruised from my tumble into the stream, but the rest of me felt surprisingly rested and restored.

When I got out, I turned on the phones and checked for messages. I now had three.

The first one—the message I'd ignored before tumbling into bed—wasn't actually a message but a hang-up: a long silence followed by a dial tone. The call had been made shortly after midnight, from a restricted number, according to the caller ID log, but I suspected it had been dialed by Sinclair, checking to see if I'd managed to make it out of the mountains and make it home: checking to see if I was a sitting duck. Luckily, I'd been crawling and shivering in the mountains rather than sleeping in my bed when he'd called.

The second call came from Eric, the graduate student in bio-medical engineering who operated the mobile CT scanner. "I got your message, and I scanned that batch of femurs you were in such a hurry for," he said. "They're on the table behind the scanner. Did you want to pick them up over the weekend or just let Miranda get them for you Monday?" My first thought was, *Miranda won't be getting anything for me Monday. Miranda's gone.* My second thought was, *Huh? What message, and what batch of femurs, and what hurry?* I was on the verge of ending the voice-mail call so I could phone Eric and ask what he meant when the third and final message began to play.

This last message was from Culpepper, and the KPD detective's urgent tone stopped my finger just as I was reaching to disconnect. "Art got a match on the thumbprint from the bloody hammer," Culpepper had practically shouted into the phone. "It matches one entered into the FBI's database just yesterday. Somebody in New Jersey indicted for conspiracy. A guy named Raymond Sinclair."

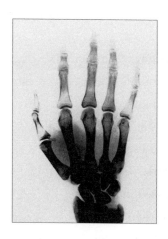

CHAPTER 43

it was not yet daylight, and it was Sunday morning, I realized—
but he snapped to alertness when I relayed Culpepper's news to
him. "Damn," he said. "Our man Sinclair's starting to look like
Public Enemy Number One. At this rate he'll be behind bars until
the Second Coming."

"Unless he's already skipped the country," I said. "Have y'all
found him yet?"

"Not yet," he admitted. "But we will. And this time we'll
make sure he's held without bail. Meanwhile, sit tight and rest
up. Don't open the door, and stay away from the windows."

"Now you tell me," I said. "I'll barricade myself in the house
again in a few minutes."

"Again? Where are you? Aren't you at home recuperating?"

"I was," I said, "but something's come up. I need to check on
something at the Body Farm. Some sort of mix-up at the CT
scanner."

"Can't it wait? Surely it's not an emergency."

"Hard to tell. I couldn't reach the CT tech who called me last night, so I figured I'd just go take a look."

"Where are you now?"

"Crossing the river on Alcoa Highway."

"Pull over and park. Wait for me. I'll be there in ten minutes."

I pulled off and tried, but I was too antsy to wait, so I took the Cherokee Trail exit, then turned onto the service road behind the hospital. When I did, I noticed a set of taillights crossing the upper staff parking lot. A car—a white minivan I didn't recognize—braked to a stop in the upper corner of the lot, directly in front of the Body Farm's gate. I stopped, switched off my headlights, and watched. A man got out and approached the chain-link fence, and a few moments later the gate swung open. Whoever it was had a key. I racked my brain, mentally running down the list of anthropology graduate students and their vehicles, and didn't hit a match. As I watched, the minivan drove through the open gate and into the Body Farm, and then the gate swung shut. It was six o'clock on a Sunday morning, and my alarm bells were going crazy.

Keeping my lights off, I eased into the parking lot and parked fifty yards downhill from the gate, hidden by the trailer of the CT scanner. When I reached the gate on foot, I found that it had been relocked, so I took out my own key to open the padlock. It didn't fit. Was I holding it upside down? I flipped the key and tried again, but again the lock refused it. Bending down, I cradled the padlock in my hands and studied it. It was a solid brass Master lock—as I'd expected—but the bright, unscratched surface of the brass made it clear that this lock had not been subjected to years of rough weather and rough handling at the gate of the Body Farm. Whoever had just driven inside had relocked the gate with a new lock, one meant to guard against interruptions. Higher up, dangling from one of the diamonds of fencing, hung the weathered lock that normally secured the gate.

For a moment I was puzzled. Then I was angry. Who the hell was inside, and who did he think he was, changing my lock? I felt invaded and violated, and as my anger spiked, I went back to the truck and grabbed a pair of leather work gloves. Then, furiously and recklessly, I began scaling the chain-link fence to break in to my own research facility. The concertina wire at the top of the gate clawed at the gloves, but the leather was thick and tough. At the top I teetered precariously, both hands gripping coils of wire as I swung one leg over, then the other. The metal points snagged at my pants—I heard fabric tearing and felt something sharp slicing down the calf of my right leg—but then I was over, dropping onto the grass in the main clearing.

The minivan was barely visible, tucked beneath the trees behind the mobile CT scanner. The morning was still dark enough to allow me to see a sliver of light through the gap at the base of the door. The knob was locked, but I had a key, and this one fit. As I turned the knob and eased the door open, it suddenly occurred to me to wonder what on earth I was doing.

Through the circular opening at the center of the scanner, I glimpsed a man bent over the table in the small room behind it. I edged toward him, using the scanner as a screen. As I got closer, my field of view widened to include a stack of boxes on the table—long rectangular boxes, one foot square by three feet long: the kind of boxes in which we stored the skeletons in our collection. The man, his back turned toward me, was opening one of the boxes. As I watched in astonishment, he removed a left femur from the box, wrapped it in bubble wrap, and tucked it into a black nylon duffel bag. Then, reaching into a red duffel bag, he removed a bundle and unrolled a layer of bubble wrap, revealing another left femur. He placed this second femur into the bone box, closed the lid, and set the box at the end of the table. Then he raised the lid on another box and repeated the process of swapping out bones.

I was stunned. He was taking bones from the skeletal collection, coolly and methodically, and replacing them with counterfeits. How many bones had he stolen, and over what period of time? I felt almost dizzy with shock, and I reached out a hand to steady myself on the scanner's table. My hand grazed something lying on the edge of the table, and out of the corner of my eye I saw a Bic pen roll and fall. I made a grab for it, but I was too slow, and the pen clattered to the steel floor.

The man at the table started. "Hello?" He stood and turned, and I could see his face for the first time. It was Glen Faust. He looked as stunned to see me as I was to see him. Suddenly it all seemed clear: Faust had been using us from the very beginning. The research collaboration had been a pretext, a smoke screen, a way to gain access to a reliable supply of material for Ortho-Medica's bone grafts and bone paste and product-development labs. How big was the annual revenue stream, as he liked to put it, from stolen bones?

"How long did you think it would be before we noticed?" My voice sounded foreign to me. It wasn't the voice of a man who'd made a triumphant discovery; it was the voice of a man who realized he'd been played for a fool. I crossed to the table and opened the box where he'd just planted the substitute bone. "The very first graduate student who looked at this femur would know it's a fake," I said, taking out the bone to underscore my point. I stared at it. It was stained, it was arthritic, it was labeled with the donation number—31-01—and it was gnarled from a badly healed fracture. The one thing it *wasn't* was fake. But how could that be? I'd just seen him take it from his bag, unwrap it, and put it in the box.

"I can explain this, Bill," he said.

"I seriously doubt that."

Laying down the femur, I reached into the black bag and snatched out the femur he'd just removed from our collection. I stared it at, wondering if I was seeing double. The bone was identical in every detail to the one I'd just removed from the box: it was stained, it was arthritic, it was labeled 31-01, and it was gnarled.

"What in bloody hell," I whispered.

My eyes darted from one bone to the other, seeking the differences between them. There were none—at least none that I could see. But as I grasped and shifted and rotated them in my hands, I perceived differences I could *feel*, though barely. One of the bones was a fraction of a percent heavier than the other—no more than the weight of a feather, I'd have sworn, but heavier. I rubbed each bone with a thumbnail. The lighter-weight bone felt slicker somehow, and as I bore down harder, the reddish brown stain on the shaft scraped off, revealing bright white bone underneath. Over the years I'd seen hundreds of thousands of stained bones, and the stain of time and decay and dirt did not, I knew, scrape off with a thumbnail.

"I'll be damned," I said. "A forgery. A counterfeit. Amazing."

"Let me explain," he repeated.

"You can explain it to the police." I laid down the femur I held in my left hand—the genuine one—and fished my cell phone from my hip pocket.

"Don't do that," he pleaded. "Listen to me." I flipped open the phone and dialed 911. In the split second that I glanced down to find the "send" button, he rushed me. Ramming his body into mine, he grabbed for the cell phone with both hands and tried to pry my fingers from it. I began flailing at him with the counterfeit femur. As we grappled, he pulled me off balance, and we toppled to the floor. His body slammed onto my rib cage, knocking the breath from me.

He straddled me then, pinning me to the floor and sending the phone skidding underneath the scanner. "Now, *listen* to me," he gasped. "We are on the verge of a huge breakthrough here. Synthetic bone, stronger and tougher than the real thing, created by combining CT images and composite materials and computer-controlled production equipment. Surely you, of all people, can understand the importance. We're so close, Bill. Almost close enough to fool even you."

"Why didn't you just tell me this was the point of the research, Glen? I would have done all I could to help."

"Because he was greedy," said another voice. Raymond Sinclair stepped from behind the scanner, just as I'd done moments earlier. But unlike me, Sinclair was holding a gun in one hand. "He didn't want to share the glory, and he didn't want to share the money. It's a billion-dollar revenue stream, isn't that right, Glen?"

"Get out of here, Ray," Faust snapped. "*Now.* Leave while you still can."

I stared at them, finally realizing that underneath the surface tension I'd witnessed between them there was a bond of complicity. "You supply tissue for his research," I said to Sinclair. "You sent him bodies and parts from a Knoxville funeral home you talked about buying." Neither of them denied it. "You bastards,"

I said. "You're like two sides of the same bad coin. Black-market bodies and stolen bones."

"You hear that, Glen? We're both bastards," said Sinclair. "Not just me. All our lives, you've rubbed my nose in the difference between us. You were the real son; I was the halfway version. But your precious Dr. Brockton's right: We're both bastards. Two sides of the same coin."

"Our circumstances were different," said Faust. "That wasn't your fault, but it wasn't mine either. It was our father's. Put down the gun, Ray. You don't have to shoot him. Just get out of here."

"It's too late for that," Sinclair said to Faust, and then—to me—he added, "He wasn't stealing the bones, Billy boy, he was putting them *back*."

I was struggling to keep up. "Putting them back? Why would he be putting them back?"

"Because he'd gotten everything he needed from them, right, Glen? Because he likes to think of himself as one of the good guys, right, Glen?" Sinclair waved the gun at Faust. "Get off him."

Faust released my arms and got to his feet. "Ray, listen," he said. "If you walk away now, you can get out of here and get a fresh start someplace else."

"It's so touching," said Sinclair, "all this brotherly love and brotherly wisdom. Do you have a big brother, Bill? A half brother? Doesn't that term, 'half brother,' sum up the genetics and the dynamics of it perfectly? It'd be wrong to con a full brother into robbing graves and committing crimes, but it's okay if he's only a half brother, right, Glen?"

"I didn't mean to hurt you," said Faust. "I thought that together we could do great things."

"No, you thought *you* could do great things, and you were willing to use me along the way. You were the beloved son, the golden boy, the stuff of medical school and engineering school. I was the bastard child, the dirty little secret your father never acknowledged. When I finally tried to join the family, you used me to do your dirty work. I got to get blood on my hands so you wouldn't have to."

"You didn't have to kill that embalmer, Ray. You panicked."

"Easy for you to say, Glen. You weren't the one who'd helped him dismember one body and steal another. You weren't the one about to take a fall."

"We could have worked something out with him."

"Bullshit, brother. That's twenty-twenty hindsight and hundred-percent bullshit. I had a split second to make a decision, and you weren't there to help me make it."

"But I'm here now," Faust said. "Let me help you make this decision. Dr. Brockton's a good man. He does good work."

"Helping the cops catch killers? Helping them catch scum like me?"

"Walk away, Ray. Give me the gun and get out of here. We'll wait an hour, and then I'll turn myself in. I'll confess to the Roswell murder."

Sinclair laughed bitterly. "Nice try, but you know it wouldn't work. You've got an airtight alibi, remember? You were off delivering some keynote speech at Johns Hopkins or the Mayo Clinic when I tried to call you that night."

"But you'd have a good head start."

"A good running start?" Sinclair gestured at me with the gun. "Not with him alive. You really think he'd keep quiet to give me a break? He already set me up. I have several powerful reasons to shoot him." He gave a bitter laugh. "If you really want to help me out, brother, you can confess to two deaths—the embalmer's and Brockton's." He aimed the gun at my chest, and I saw his finger tighten on the trigger.

I heard someone—maybe Faust, maybe myself—shouting "No!" as I closed my eyes to die. Something slammed into my chest as the crack of the pistol tore the air. The force of the impact knocked me backward, and my head hit the floor hard enough to daze me. Then I felt weight and warmth and wetness on my chest—groping with a hand, I touched the sticky wetness of blood—but I felt something else on my chest, too, and as my head cleared, I realized that the blood was not my own blood: It was the blood of Faust, who'd flung himself between me and Sinclair as a shield. Blood spurted from a bullet wound in his left temple. I managed to squirm out from under him, and I placed my hands over the hole and pressed. Blood oozed between my fingers.

I looked up at Sinclair. His eyes had a wild, crazed look, and his chest was heaving. He pointed the gun at me again, and again I closed my eyes to die, but again I heard a shot that I did not feel. Sinclair crumpled to the floor, and Special Agent Rooster Rankin—his weapon still smoking—sprang into the room, snatching the gun from Sinclair's slackening fingers.

Rankin's shot seemed to rouse Faust; he groaned, and his eyes fluttered open. He stared at me, his gaze gradually coming into focus, and then it flickered sidelong, to the place where Sinclair had fallen. His lids closed tightly, and tears seeped from beneath them.

He opened them again and looked up at me. "Oh, dear God," he said, "what have I done?"

"Don't talk," I said. "We're calling an ambulance." I checked the floor for my missing cell phone, but Rankin was already dialing 911 on his. "Just hang on," I urged Faust.

"Please," he said. "Let me die." I felt his hands clutching mine.

"No," I said. "I won't let you die."

Faust worked his fingers underneath my own, struggling to pry my hand off his head wound. I pressed harder, resisting his resistance, and I felt the strength ebbing from his hands and arms.

"Do something for me," he gasped. "Promise me." His voice was a whisper and fading fast. I leaned closer, my ear almost against his lips, to hear what he said.

I pulled my face away from Faust's and stared into his eyes, astonished.

"I promise," I said, redoubling the pressure on the wound as his eyes closed. "I promise."

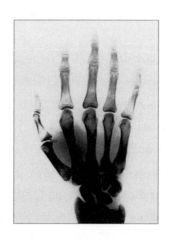

CHAPTER 44

I DID LET FAUST DIE, THOUGH NOT ON PURPOSE. BY THE time the ambulance transported him the quarter mile from the Body Farm to UT Hospital, his heart had stopped. The ER trauma team managed to restart it—but by then Faust was brain-dead.

Ironically, that half-living, half-dead state now made it possible, in theory, to grant Faust's second request, the one he'd whispered just before his heart had stopped. "Give my hands to your friend," Faust had breathed. "Give my hands to Garcia."

It was theoretically possible, but it was highly unlikely. For starters, Faust's tissue type would have to match Eddie's—UT was doing the needed tests now—and we'd already learned that having a potential donor wasn't the same as having a good match. Even if the match proved good, though, the hands might not be usable. Emory's hand-transplant protocol required a beating-heart donor, Dr. Alvarez had explained when I'd phoned her. If Faust's heart wasn't beating when he reached Emory, she couldn't accept the hands, couldn't transplant them to Eddie. And UT's trauma team gave Faust's weakened heart only fifty-fifty odds of surviving the trip to Atlanta.

In any case, Dr. Alvarez had explained, she shouldn't be talking with me about this. "UT Hospital needs to tell the Knoxville organ-procurement agency that there's a possible donor for a hand-transplant candidate in Atlanta. Then the Knoxville agency needs to call the agency here—LifeLink—and let them know. If it looks like a good match, LifeLink will call us. If, and only if, I decide to accept the hands, then I'll make the phone call to Dr. Garcia."

By the end of my brief phone call with the surgeon, my mood had swung from hope to despair once more, and I'd acquired at least a glimmer of insight into the emotional roller-coaster rides endured by countless organ-transplant candidates and their loved ones.

I didn't have long to dwell on my discouragement, though. Rooster Rankin phoned. "Can you be downtown in an hour," he asked, "looking professional but also dashing?"

"I don't think so," I said. "In fact, I don't think 'dashing' is an option no matter how much time you give me. Why?"

"We're holding a press conference on the steps of the Duncan Federal Building at two o'clock."

"What? Why? And why such short notice?"

"As Bogart said in *Casablanca,* 'Destiny has taken a hand.'"

"Huh?"

"The media's gotten wind of a fatal shooting at the Body Farm," he explained, "and somebody at KPD or UT Hospital indicated that the FBI was involved. So we're getting barraged by calls about that—but not just about that. We're also getting grilled about allegations of fraud and misconduct at the Body Farm. So the SAC—the special agent in charge —talked to headquarters, and they agreed that it's time to lay our cards on the table."

I felt my breath catch as the implications sank in. "So this means we can finally tell Miranda what's been going on? And the TBI?"

"We're working on that now. Let us handle it. Just get yourself spiffed up and downtown." He hung up without taking time to say good-bye.

THE FBI'S SKILL AT KEEPING things under wraps was matched—possibly even exceeded—by its knack for dramatically unveiling them, I decided shortly after the press conference began. The illegal trade in bodies and body parts was a nationwide criminal enterprise of titanic proportions, impenetrable secrets, and dire peril, according to the special agent in charge. Against all odds, he went on, the Bureau had managed to infiltrate this sinister plot and bring down its murderous mastermind, thanks to the brilliant strategy devised by one dedicated public servant. I glanced at Rankin, who'd masterminded the sting, glad that he was about to receive a pat on the back. But it wasn't Rankin the SAC credited as the brains behind the sting—it was me. This new spin on events—the suggestion that I'd approached the FBI and offered to help, rather than having been dragged kicking and screaming into a role I hated—astonished me. I stared at Rankin, who grinned at me and winked, then gave me a big thumbs-up. After two or three urgings by the SAC and a couple of gentle pushes by Angela Price, I stepped forward to accept a handshake and a medal expressing the FBI's gratitude for my service.

I stammered a few words of appreciation in return, but I demurred when asked to tell the story of the sting. Without missing a beat, Rankin stepped forward and gave a brief account, one that greatly magnified my foresight and courage in the face of deadly peril and that also—blessedly—omitted any mention of strippers, compromising photos, and amputated arms. Rankin's summary was followed, to my surprise, by glowing comments from TBI agent Steve Morgan and UT general counsel Amanda Whiting.

During their comments I scanned and rescanned the faces of the small crowd gathered below the steps, hoping that Miranda might be there to hear such kind words about me. But, alas, she was not, and when the SAC stepped forward to say a few closing words, Rankin took the opportunity to tell me he'd been unable to reach Miranda. "I left her a voice mail and sent her an e-mail, but she seems to be off the grid," he said.

I nodded and thanked him for trying, but the disappointment still stung.

As the event ended and the officials steered me toward the lobby of the Duncan Building, I heard a voice. "Dad. *Dad!*" The television and newspaper reporters parted, and Jeff dashed up the steps, followed closely by Jenny and their boys, Tyler and Walker. Jeff threw his arms around me, and Jenny threw her arms around me, and the boys hurled themselves against me, shouting, "Grandpa Bill! Grandpa Bill! You're a hero!"

We walked three blocks from the Duncan Building up to Gay Street, to the S&W Grand, an ornate art deco cafeteria from the 1930s. Shuttered and decaying for decades, the S&W had recently been lovingly and spectacularly restored to its former glory. We had a very late lunch—or a very early dinner, or a really big afternoon snack. The food was fine, but the ambience was better, and the company was the best part. Afterward, walking back to the parking garage beside Market Square, we ambled through Krutch Park, where dogwoods and redbuds and tulips were on the brink of blooming. As Jenny and the boys took turns jumping across the park's small stream, Jeff led me to a bench and beckoned me to sit. He took my hand—the same hand he'd let go of that night at Panera. "That was childish of me to walk out on you," he said, "and spiteful not to return your phone calls. I'm sorry. You raised me better than that. Please forgive me."

"I already have," I said. "I'm sorry for my shortcomings as a father. Please forgive me for those." I felt a sudden pang of very specific guilt. "Oh, and for not getting my tax records to you."

"I already have," he said with a laugh. "And I went ahead and filed for an extension. You've got until September fifteenth to bring me the rubble heap that passes for your financial records." He looked me square in the eye. "Dad, you did a good job of raising me, and if you end up raising another kid, you'll do a good job again. Tell me if there's anything we can do to help you. And please come out to the house for dinner next Sunday."

"Deal," I said. "On both counts."

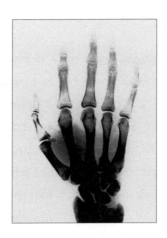

CHAPTER 45

THE WIND GUSTED AND SHIFTED, FLINGING RAINDROPS against the curved windshield of the helicopter. As the drops hit, they shattered into smaller droplets that rolled separately down the sleek glass like iridescent ball bearings. With each buffet I felt the helicopter shudder on the helipad. Through the headphones cupping my ears, I heard a faint click, then the voice of the pilot, a former army helicopter instructor named Mike Hawkins. "Y'all hold on back there," he said. "It's getting mighty lively outside." Beyond the headset's noise seals and above the rising whine of the turbine, the wind whistled and moaned.

Eddie had gotten The Phone Call from Dr. Alvarez an hour earlier. The good news was, Glen Faust's hands—and his tissue type—made him an excellent match for Eddie. The bad news was, Faust's heart was failing fast, and unless Eddie and Faust could be airlifted to Emory immediately, it was likely that Faust would finish dying and the hands would go to waste.

Faust's motionless form—the brain definitively dead but the heart tentatively, barely alive—lay on the narrow gurney beside me in the helicopter's patient bay. Taut nylon straps crossed his chest, hips, and legs, and another strap immobilized his head. An endotracheal tube snaked out of his mouth, and the bellows of a portable ventilator made his chest rise and fall in a steady rhythm. An IV tube led from one arm, and a bundle of wires ran from the gurney to a small monitor mounted behind the pilot's headrest. The monitor's pulse readout fluctuated between 77 and 83 as the beats traced a series of sharp little peaks across the screen. Perhaps it was only because I'd been told he was dying, but the peaks seemed provisional, as if even the monitor were already giving him up for dead.

I heard Hawkins press his transmit button. "LifeStar One to LifeStar Two." I looked out the window; a hundred feet to our right was a second air ambulance, where Eddie Garcia lay strapped to a second gurney. The neighboring helicopter twitched on its skids in time with our own. "I don't think we're going anywhere," said Hawkins glumly.

"Not for a while anyhow," answered the second helicopter's pilot.

"I don't think we have a while," said a female voice. It was the flight nurse, strapped into the rear-facing jump seat on the opposite side of the gurney from me. "His pulse is getting real thready. He's barely hanging on."

"Do we need to get him back to the ER?" It was the second pilot—Wimberly was his name, but his colleagues called him Wimby.

"I give this guy a couple hours, tops," the nurse said. "If we take him back inside, he'll be in the morgue by suppertime, and his hands will go to waste."

"I've got faith in you, Nancy," said Wimberly. "I've flown . . . what, fifty, sixty missions with you, and you've never lost a patient."

"I'm telling you, Wimby, this guy's close to coding."

"If he codes," asked Hawkins, "how much time do we have to get him to Emory?"

"None," she answered. "Their protocol requires a beating-heart donor. They won't take the hands if his heart's stopped."

From the helicopter base, the flight controller radioed with an update. "Radar's showing a solid line of storm cells to the west, Hawk, stretching all the way to Nashville. Won't blow through till tonight."

"Well, crap," said Hawkins. "This isn't looking like our day. Or Dr. Garcia's."

For what seemed a long time, there was no sound but the steady whine of the turbine and the fluctuating lash of the weather. Then, over the radio, came a soft voice. "Please," said Carmen Garcia, who was in the other helicopter alongside Eddie. "Please." There was no hysteria or panic in her voice, only sorrow. "If we go now, my husband still has a chance to use these hands. If we don't go, he loses them—he loses these hands."

Neither pilot answered, and the silence was excruciating. The flight nurse gave me an agonized look.

"Please," repeated Carmen. "I beseech you."

"Ma'am, I'm sorry," said Hawkins finally, "we can't take off in this. We'd be breaking federal regulations. And we'd be putting people at risk. You and your husband. Dr. Brockton. The flight crews. People on the ground, if we crashed. We can't take off in these conditions."

Through the background hiss on the radio came the sound of ragged breaths. "Of course. I understand. Forgive me. Forgive me for being selfish."

Across the gurney from me, the nurse removed her helmet and mask. Bending forward, she buried her face in her hands and wept.

I heard a long, shuddering breath, then Carmen's voice, practically a whisper, hypnotic and incantatory in its cadence. At first I couldn't make it out, but soon I realized she was speaking in Spanish. *"Ave María, llena eres de gracia . . ."* She was praying, I realized, and I recognized the prayer: "Hail Mary, full of grace . . ."

Suddenly the helicopter was buffeted by a ferocious gust of wind. The aircraft shuddered and rocked, and then I felt one skid lift off the pad as the wind swirled beneath the rotor from one side and flipped upward. "Jesus *Christ,*" said the pilot, "hold on," and with that we were in the air. It wasn't that the helicopter had lifted off; it was more that it had been ripped from the pad. The aircraft lurched and bucked, and the flight nurse and I grabbed for the handrails of the gurney and the vertical bars attached to the sides of the cabin. The outside world had vanished, as thoroughly as if the windows had been draped with white blankets. The helicopter slammed and lurched and whipped like a rat being shaken by a terrier. Finally the turbulence eased and the aircraft seemed to level off, or at least to find a reasonably stable zone of cloud. I heard a loud exhalation through the headset, and the pilot's voice—shaken but relieved—said, "Y'all okay back there?"

The nurse was tugging her helmet back onto her head. I was about to say that we were fine when an agitated voice cut in. "LifeStar One, LifeStar One, this is Flight Control, do you read?"

"Control, LifeStar One reading you loud and clear."

"What the hell, Hawk?" The agitation in the controller's voice had been replaced by a mixture of relief and anger—the mixture a parent's voice tended to have when a small son or daughter narrowly but successfully dodged danger. "Damn it, Hawk, what the bloody hell are you doing taking off in these conditions? This might cost you your job. Maybe your license, too."

"Look, here's what happened," began Hawkins.

"What happened," broke in Wimberly, "was the strangest damn thing. All of a sudden this hole opened up in the ceiling."

"Oh, bullshit," spat the controller. "You stay out of this, Wimby."

"No kidding, a hole," insisted Wimberly. "Four hundred, maybe five hundred feet high. Three, four miles visibility. I can't believe you didn't see it." The flight nurse and I looked at each other. She rolled her eyes and shook her head dramatically: *No way*. I began to catch on to what the second pilot was doing. "It was amazing," he said. "Hawk, how's the ride up there?"

"The ride's good," Hawkins said. "We're just coming out on top at seven thousand feet. Beautiful up here." He paused. "I don't suppose that hole's still open down there, is it, Wimby?"

"Say again?"

"Any chance that hole's still open?"

I held my breath.

"I'll be damned," said Wimberly slowly. "Sure enough, still is. LifeStar Two's departing." His voice ratcheted up half an octave and a dozen decibels as he said it. "*Whoa*," he added after a moment, "*that* was interesting."

The flight controller radioed again, and I pictured him scanning the rulebook to see how many regulations the pilots had violated. This time, though, his voice seemed to contain concern and a touch of admiration. "Wimby, did you make it up through that . . . uh, hole in the sky okay?" The nurse grinned at me.

"Sure did," he said. "Piece of cake. LifeStar Two's climbing to seven thousand." His voice had switched back to the polished smoothness of the professional pilot, though I thought I detected a big dose of relief and a slight hint of swagger underneath.

"Have a safe flight," said the controller. "You guys must have friends up there."

Let's hope, I thought, as the second helicopter emerged from the clouds below us and both aircraft banked toward Atlanta.

I glanced at the heart monitor above Faust's gurney. He was still with us. It was amazing he'd made it even this far. As an experimental procedure, hand transplantation wasn't covered by the standard organ-donor consent Faust had on file. Mercifully, the rules for organ donation allowed for verbal consent. I'd recounted Faust's last wish—"Give my hands to Garcia"— and Rankin had corroborated my story. I wasn't sure how Rankin had managed to hear the words, since Faust couldn't speak above a whisper, but he swore he had, and I chose to believe him. Within minutes after Faust's brain ceased to function, UT's organ-donation coordinator called Tennessee Donor Services, and a few hours after that, Dr. Alvarez had accepted the donation. Her original plan had been to bring Faust down by conventional ambulance, but when UT notified her that his condition was rapidly deteriorating, she'd arranged for the airlift—the airlift into the teeth of a gale.

We caught up with the storm front swiftly, just as the helicopter reached the crest of the Smoky Mountains. Pressing my head to the helicopter's window and looking down, I glimpsed the grass-lined bowl of Cades Cove and, looming above it, Thunderhead Mountain, where I'd been caught in the cold and the darkness.

I was still weary from the ordeal in the mountains and the maelstrom of events since, and I closed my eyes and let the aircraft's drone and vibration lull me to sleep. I was just drifting off when an urgent voice snapped me awake. "We're losing him." It was the flight nurse. "Guys, we're losing him." Her eyes were darting between the gurney and the monitor. "Pulse is irregular, blood pressure's dropping." The pulse line on the screen grew ragged, the peaks fluctuating in height, like a stock-market graph charting a volatile month. The heart-rate readout skittered rapidly: 88, 72, 79, 67, 59. The blood-pressure readout on the monitor edged downward: 140/80, 117/72, 88/60. Suddenly the blood-pressure numbers were replaced by dashes. The heart line went flat, and the pulse readout went blank. Even through the thick cushions of the headset, I could hear the monitor's shrill alarm. "He's coded; he's coded. I'm going to defib." She snatched a pair of defibrillator paddles from the rear wall of the compartment and pressed them to Faust's chest. She glanced to make sure I wasn't touching Faust or the gurney—"Clear"—and squeezed a switch in the handle of one of the paddles; as the electricity coursed through Faust's body, it jerked against the nylon straps. She glanced at the monitor, still flashing its dashes and shrieking its alarm. "Clear." The body jumped again, but that was the only response to the jolt of current.

"Damn it," said the nurse, "don't do this to me."

Flipping back the lid of a medical case, she removed a syringe and tore open a sterile wrapper, then depressed the plunger just far enough to spray a droplet out the end of the needle. "I'm giving him epinephrine," she said. Sliding the needle into Faust's arm, she slammed the plunger home and then yanked the empty syringe into a waste slot. She applied the defibrillator paddles again. "Clear." The body twitched, and the blinking dashes on the monitor were replaced by numbers. Fluctuating, frightening, beautiful numbers.

I took a deep breath and looked up. Out the front windshield, the approaching skyline of Atlanta glittered like the Emerald City of Oz. Minutes later we settled onto a small rooftop helipad. A metal door at one side opened, and a pair of nurses jogged a gurney toward the helicopter, ducking beneath the spinning rotor. I checked the monitor: Faust's heart was beating weakly and irregularly, but it was still beating, by damn. Within seconds the nurses had shifted him onto the gurney and hurried into the hospital with him. I unbuckled my harness, removed my headset, and followed.

Ten minutes later I found Carmen in an alcove outside a third-floor operating room. She hugged me and then wiped her eyes. I held my breath, bracing for disappointment again. "It looks good," she said. "The transplant surgeon says they're starting the procedure."

Over the next twelve hours, updates trickled from the operating room: The bones of Faust's left forearm had been grafted onto Garcia's radius and ulna by the left-hand team. The bones of the right forearm had been joined by the other team. Left-hand nerves. Right-hand nerves. Right-hand tendons. Left-hand tendons. Left-hand blood vessels. Right-hand blood vessels. By the thirteen-hour mark, I was exhausted, but Carmen seemed as focused and quietly intent as she had at the beginning. When the head of the transplant team, Dr. Alvarez, appeared, Carmen and I stood to receive the news, our eyes boring into the doctor's in an effort to see if she was bringing good news or bad. "We've had a setback," she said quietly, and for the first time I sensed fear in Carmen. "A damaged blood vessel on the left side."

Carmen's voice was quiet but hard as granite. "Does that mean the left hand will fail?"

Dr. Alvarez shook her head. "I hope not. We're taking a short section of vein from your husband's leg and splicing it in to repair the damaged section. It's not difficult to do, but we need to get the blood flowing to that hand as soon as possible. I'm going back to the OR, but I wanted to let you know."

Carmen nodded. "Thank you, Doctor. Thank you for everything you're doing for him."

The surgeon smiled through her mask of fatigue as she turned to go.

An hour later she returned. "We're finished. We got the bleeding stopped. Everything looks very good. There are no guarantees, of course. His body might reject the hands, the nerves might fail to regenerate, the immunosuppressants might cause complications. But if we're lucky, none of those things will happen. And if we're very lucky, within six months he'll be able to hold a scalpel again, and be able to hold hands with you and your son again."

Carmen's face quivered, and then she began to tremble from head to toe, and she allowed herself to cry. "I am . . . so very grateful. To you. To everyone here at Emory. To that man who gave his hands for my husband. To . . ." She raised her arms wide, then let them fall with a teary smile. "So grateful."

"So am I," said the doctor with a tired but warm smile.

I excused myself to make a phone call. Sixteen hours earlier, just after they'd begun the transplant procedure, I'd phoned Miranda. She hadn't answered, and the call had rolled to voice mail.

"I'm at Emory," I'd said. "They've just taken Eddie into surgery. They're going for the bilateral transplant. I know you don't want to talk to me or see me, but I'm sure Carmen and Eddie would appreciate it if you could come." Then I'd turned off the phone.

Now, when I switched it back on, it chirped at me. The display told me I had new voice-mail messages—twenty-three, in fact, a number that astonished me. Before I got a chance to listen to even one of the twenty-three, though, the phone buzzed in my hand. It was Miranda calling, and she sounded breathless. "Tell me what's happening."

"It's done," I said. "Both hands. The doctor sounds very hopeful."

The whoop of delight from my cell phone nearly split my ear. Then I heard a second whoop, this time in stereo: Miranda came sprinting around the corner, nearly careening into Carmen, the surgeon, and me.

"Ohmygodohmygodohmygod!" Miranda cried. "Oh, how wonderful. Oh, hallelujah!" She threw her arms around Carmen. "I was in Texas, in the middle of a job interview, when the FBI called me." The words tumbled out of her. "I ran out and jumped on a plane as soon as I heard the message. Oh, happy, happy day!"

Then she turned to me, her face wet with tears. "*Damn* you," she said, and I felt my heart begin to crack, but suddenly she hugged me, as unreservedly and joyously as she'd hugged Carmen. "Damn you," she repeated, this time through a mixture of tears and laughter. "Don't ever do that to me again." She pulled back and wiped her eyes. "I just saw your picture half a dozen times on the CNN monitors in the Atlanta airport. Black-market kidneys from Pakistan, butchered and stolen bodies, a murderous bone thief, and a daring professor who risked his life in an undercover sting. Hell of a story. If I weren't so mad at you for keeping me in the dark, I'd be really, really proud." She shook her head. "Damn you for playing your sleazy part so well"—she laughed—"and damn the FBI for being so secretive." She smiled and planted a big kiss on my cheek.

"Not so fast," I said. "You were in Texas for a job interview? Out at the Body Ranch—our new competition?"

She shrugged sheepishly. "They're just getting off the ground. They thought maybe I could be helpful." She smiled once again— her old, full-face, eye-contact smile. "It's nice to be wanted, but it didn't mean a thing. Really. If you'll take me back, I'll never stray again."

"Promise?"

She held up the three fingers of the Boy Scout salute. "Promise."

"Deal."

EPILOGUE

I AWOKE TO FIND A STRANGE HAND ON MY SHOULDER, shaking me gently. The hand was attached to a nurse, who'd found Miranda and me slumped and sleeping in chairs in the surgery waiting room. I checked the wall clock: Four hours had passed since the surgery ended. Before falling asleep, I'd spent a while checking my many voice-mail messages and returning a handful of the calls.

Steve Morgan had called; I hadn't gotten a chance to talk with him after the FBI press conference, so he'd phoned to relay his personal good wishes, as well as those of the TBI. "I should have known there was a good reason—a very good reason—for whatever you were doing," he said when I called him back. "I forgot some of the most important lessons you taught me in your class—lessons about character and integrity and trust. I'll try not to forget those again."

I also returned a call from Burt DeVriess. He'd dropped the

Willoughby paternity suit, he said—his client was not, the DNA reported, Willoughby's child—but he was suing for $20 million on behalf of Willoughby's legitimate daughter and the former students who'd paid for the burial of Miss Elizabeth Jenkins. Most of the voice mails turned out to be media calls—from WBIR-TV, CNN, the _Knoxville News Sentinel,_ the _National Enquirer,_ and a host of other news outlets I didn't know or didn't care about. Mercifully, my cell phone's battery died just as my brain and body began shutting down, so I had a good excuse for ignoring the majority of the messages clamoring for my attention.

At the moment, though, it was the scrub-clad nurse tugging at my sleepy sleeve. "He's awake, and he'd like to see you both." She smiled.

Miranda and I struggled to our feet. The nurse took us up an elevator and down a hall to an ICU room, which bristled with monitors. Through the large panel of glass that faced the nurses' station, I saw Carmen sitting beside the head of the bed, stroking her husband's cheek.

Eddie opened his eyes and smiled groggily when we came into the room. "My friends," he murmured. "My good, good friends." Then his eyes closed again.

His arms were fastened into an elaborate traction harness above the bed. Protruding from the ends of the arms were a pair of white oval bundles, roughly the size and shape of handmade loaves of bread. Five fingertips protruded from the end of each loaf. The swaddled hands looked awkward and out of place, strangely foreign, because just twenty-four hours before there had been nothing there. Nothing but emptiness and loss.

The hands—like the surgery's outcome, and like Eddie's future, and like all our hopes for it—hung in the air, suspended. And just for a moment, those bright white bundles of suspense and hope were transformed. In my mind they shone like a pair of binary stars at the center of the universe, and they were the most beautiful things I had ever seen, or ever would.

AUTHOR'S NOTE:
FACT AND FICTION

"THIS BOOK IS A WORK OF FICTION," READS THE disclaimer in the front of this novel. "Any resemblance to actual events or persons, living or dead, is entirely coincidental."

That very disclaimer itself is part fiction: Although many characters and most plot threads in *The Bone Thief* are woven entirely out of thin air, this book has many bases in scientific and biomedical fact. Within this subject area, truth rivals or surpasses fiction in ways that are mostly inspiring but occasionally horrifying.

The thriving trade in bodies and body parts—including illegal black-market sales of corpses and tissues—was recently the subject of a riveting nonfiction book, *Body Brokers,* by Annie Cheney. Published in 2006, Cheney's book documents—among other things—shocking postmortem "chop shops" (our term, not hers) operated by a California funeral-home owner and a Texas medical-school staff member. *Body Brokers* also describes multiple instances of bodies and body parts being sent to laboratories and even luxury hotels (including, Cheney reports, "forty-two heads and necks to the Marriott Marquis" in New York City's Times Square) for medical trainings. Cheney's book also documents the tragic case of a young man who died suddenly from toxic shock after receiving an improperly sterilized bone graft—one contaminated with *Clostridium sordellii* bacteria.

Crime fiction focuses, by definition, on the seamier side of life. The happier truth is that organ transplants and tissue grafts allow remarkable feats of medical repair and restoration. And as stem-cell technology advances—offering the potential to grow rejection-proof tissues and organs with the patient's own DNA and tissue type—the possibilities become almost miraculous. Indeed, near miracles are already being wrought: The surgery in Spain that was described by our character Glen Faust—in which a cadaver trachea was used as a scaffold to create a new windpipe from the recipient's own stem cells—is unvarnished fact. The one significant bit of artistic license we've taken with biomedical fact is the notion that by combining CT scans with advanced composite materials it's possible to synthesize bones that are virtually exact copies of their originals. That's not possible—not yet anyhow. But never say never.

A few footnotes about hands: Artificial hands are now very sophisticated and lifelike in their workings, as a glance at the i-LIMB Hand—with its individually controlled fingers—makes clear (www.touchbionics.com/i-LIMB). Soon bionic prostheses will become even more advanced, thanks to millions of dollars' worth of R&D sponsored by the Pentagon's Defense Advanced Research Projects Agency (DARPA). DARPA's Revolutionizing Prosthetics Program—motivated by the military's commitment to restoring function to soldiers whose arms or hands have been lost to trauma—is led by two premiere R&D laboratories: DEKA Research and Development (the birthplace of the portable insulin pump and the Segway scooter) and the Johns Hopkins University Applied Physics Laboratory (whose numerous other projects include interplanetary satellites and bomb-disposal robots). Within the next few years, Revolutionizing Prosthetics aims to create bionic arms that are virtually identical to natural limbs in performance and durability. For more information on this program, see www.darpa.mil/Docs/prosthetics_f_s3_200807180945042.pdf.

Hand surgery, too, has undergone remarkable advances. Toe-to-thumb transplantation, briefly discussed as a way to restore function to Dr. Garcia's right hand, is a well-established and highly successful way to replace a missing thumb, as Asheville, North Carolina, hand surgeon Bruce Minkin—a former student of Dr. Bill Bass—explained to us in detail over dinner and via many subsequent e-mails. After a teenage patient lost his thumb and two fingers to an explosion, Dr. Minkin grafted one of the boy's toes onto his mangled hand, creating a thumb that looks and functions almost like the original.

Total hand transplantation is, for now, an inspiring but experimental and very rare procedure. Worldwide, only about forty hand transplants have ever been performed; in the United States, just half a dozen patients have received transplanted hands—and only one has received a bilateral (double) transplant. Those numbers will rise, and the procedure will become more common, if Dr. Linda Cendales has her way. Dr. Cendales—the inspiration for the Emory surgeon we call Dr. Alvarez—is the only surgeon in the United States who has been formally trained in both hand surgery and transplant surgery.

Dr. Cendales helped perform two of the earliest U.S. transplants, including the 1999 transplant that—after more than a decade—remains the world's most enduringly successful hand transplant. Dr. Cendales is not just a gifted surgeon, she's also a pioneering researcher. She completed two research fellowships at the National Institutes for Health, focusing on ways to keep patients' immune systems from rejecting transplants. Now, through a joint appointment at Emory University School of Medicine and the Atlanta VA Medical Center, Dr. Cendales is building a visionary new hand-transplant program, one that combines surgical expertise with immunological research. During the research for this book, Dr. Cendales graciously invited Jon Jefferson into her operating room to observe hand surgery. Using a curved needle and strong sutures, she carefully stitched together a severed tendon in a man's hand, and then—peering through a microscope to guide an even more delicate part of the procedure—she snipped and spliced the ends of a damaged nerve together again. After the repairs were done, but before the hand was stitched shut, she flexed and straightened the sleeping patient's index finger repeatedly, nodding with satisfaction as the reattached tendon slid smoothly within the remarkable cable-and-pulley mechanism of the human hand.

As the first edition of this book goes to press, Dr. Cendales is evaluating transplant candidates—and preparing to test a powerful new antirejection drug that she hopes will revolutionize transplant medicine and bring hope and hands to more real-life patients like our fictional Eddie Garcia.

ACKNOWLEDGMENTS

MANY PEOPLE HELPED US MAKE THIS BOOK, AND HELPED us make it better.

At the Knoxville Police Department, Deputy Chief Gary Price was a helpful and gracious source of information about how KPD would investigate crimes involving dismemberment or mutilation of corpses. Art Bohanan, retired KPD criminalist extraordinaire, remains our favorite fingerprint adviser, patent holder, and real-life fictional character.

The Knoxville Division of the FBI has been remarkably cooperative throughout this series of books. Stacie Bohanan—the Bureau's media liaison—responded swiftly and kindly to our latest request for help, and Special Agent in Charge Richard Lambert shared generously of his time and expertise in advising us how Dr. Bill Brockton might play a pivotal role in a fictional undercover sting.

This book contains more medical detail than any of our prior books, and we're grateful to the medical professionals who helped us get things right. The autopsy scene in chapter 15 draws heavily on the advice of Dr. Dan Canale, a Nashville pathologist, whose knowledge is accompanied by equal doses of patience and good humor. Emergency physician Dan Cauble, M.D., graciously reviewed the air-ambulance scene; so did Dr. Jim McLaughlin, an old buddy from way back. At the University of Tennessee Medical Center, Dr. Leonard Hines, Dr. Victor Krylov (a pioneering Russian hand surgeon), and nurse Judy Roark—all of the Simulation Center—offered unique glimpses into the realms of hand surgery and microsurgery. So did Dr. Bruce Minkin, an Asheville hand surgeon who was once one of Bill Bass's best students . . . and who opened our eyes to the remarkable capabilities of reconstructive hand surgery, especially toe-to-thumb transplants. And at Emory University School of Medicine, Dr. Linda Cendales—a nationally prominent hand-transplant surgeon and a world-class human being—shared her inspiring vision of the promising future of hand transplantation.

We could never have embarked on the fictional journey of the Body Farm novels—nor continued it for an additional four books—without the unwavering enthusiasm and able assistance of our literary agent, Giles Anderson. We're grateful to Giles for getting us the chance to write these books.

We're also deeply grateful to HarperCollins/William Morrow for making us feel so welcome for six years now. We bid a poignant farewell to our longtime Morrow publisher and friend Lisa Gallagher, and a warm welcome to our new publisher, Liate Stehlik. Magic occurs at Morrow, where our electronic drafts are transformed into edited copy, and edited copy is transformed into printed books—and then, remarkably, those printed books are transformed, when the planets align for us, into bestsellers. We're delighted to be part of the HarperCollins/William Morrow family—and we're thrilled to have such a large and supportive extended family of readers. How amazing, that these stories and characters we invent take on a life of their own, finding believers and making friends across the United States and around the world.

A special thanks to Frank Murphy, Knoxville radio personality, comedian, and eagle-eyed reader. Frank joined us in proofreading *The Bone Thief*, and caught several errors that would otherwise have slipped through the cracks. *Gracias*, Frank.

Last but best, our families and friends remain wondrous sources of support, encouragement, and inspiration. To one and all, thanks evermore.

—Jon Jefferson and Dr. Bill Bass

THE SKULL

BONES OF

PARTS OF

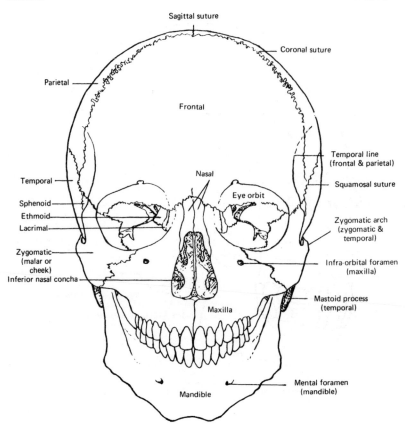

Sagittal suture

Coronal suture

Parietal

Frontal

Temporal line
(frontal & parietal)

Temporal

Nasal

Eye orbit

Squamosal suture

Sphenoid
Ethmoid
Lacrimal

Zygomatic arch
(zygomatic &
temporal)

Zygomatic
(malar or
cheek)
Inferior nasal concha

Infra-orbital foramen
(maxilla)

Maxilla

Mastoid process
(temporal)

Mandible

Mental foramen
(mandible)

THE SKULL

BONES OF

PARTS OF

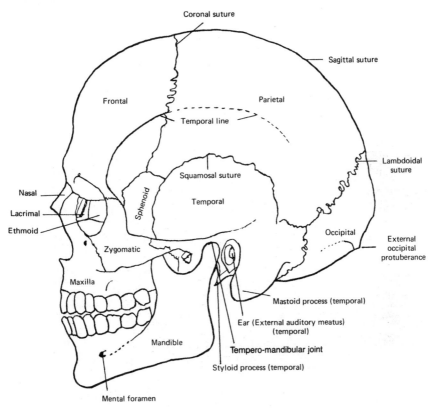

Coronal suture

Sagittal suture

Frontal

Parietal

Temporal line

Lambdoidal
suture

Nasal

Squamosal suture

Lacrimal

Sphenoid

Ethmoid

Temporal

Zygomatic

Occipital

External
occipital
protuberance

Maxilla

Mastoid process (temporal)

Ear (External auditory meatus)
(temporal)

Mandible

Tempero-mandibular joint

Styloid process (temporal)

Mental foramen

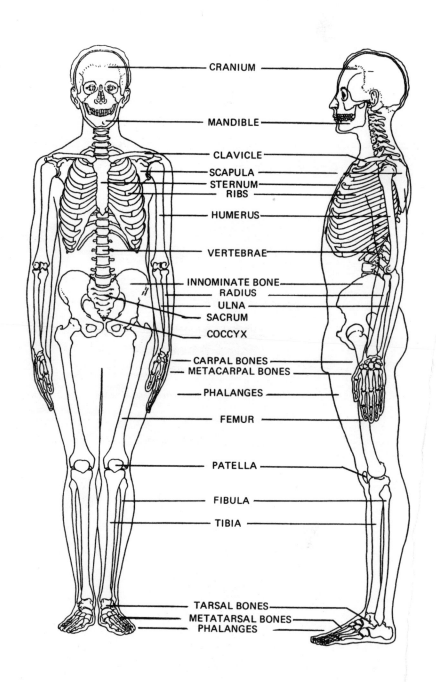

CRANIUM

MANDIBLE

CLAVICLE
SCAPULA
STERNUM
RIBS
HUMERUS

VERTEBRAE

INNOMINATE BONE
RADIUS
ULNA
SACRUM
COCCYX

CARPAL BONES
METACARPAL BONES

PHALANGES

FEMUR

PATELLA

FIBULA

TIBIA

TARSAL BONES
METATARSAL BONES
PHALANGES